KV-033-799

Those Measureless Fields

Those Measureless Fields

Caroline Scott

PEN & SWORD
FICTION

First published in Great Britain in 2014 by
PEN & SWORD FICTION
An imprint of
Pen & Sword Books Ltd
47 Church Street
Barnsley
South Yorkshire
S70 2AS

Copyright © Caroline Scott, 2014

ISBN 978 1 78346 396 1

The right of Caroline Scott to be identified as Author of this work has been asserted by her in accordance with the Copyright, Designs and Patents Act 1988.

A CIP catalogue record for this book is
available from the British Library

All rights reserved. No part of this book may be reproduced or transmitted in any form or by any means, electronic or mechanical including photocopying, recording or by any information storage a retrieval system, without permission from the Publisher in writing.

Printed and bound in England
By CPI Group (UK) Ltd, Croydon, CRO 4YY

Pen & Sword Books Ltd incorporates the Imprints of Pen & Sword Fiction, Pen & Sword Aviation Pen & Sword Family History, Pen & Sword Maritime, Pen & Sword Military, Wharncliffe Local History, Pen & Sword Select, Pen & Sword Military Classics, Leo Cooper, Remember When, Seafo Publishing and Frontline Publishing

For a complete list of Pen & Sword titles please contact
PEN & SWORD BOOKS LIMITED
47 Church Street, Barnsley, South Yorkshire, S70 2AS, England
E-mail: enquiries@pen-and-sword.co.uk
Website: www.pen-and-sword.co.uk

For Dottie and Kenneth

Chapter One

Lancashire, 1928

'It's from a poem,' said Laurie. His voice was just a whisper, then. It seemed to come from far inside him and Effie had to lean in close to catch his words. He asked her to bring a book.

'*A slumber did my spirit seal,*' she read.

'Please, will you carry on?'

'No motion has she now, no force;
She neither hears nor sees;
Rolled round in earth's diurnal course,
With rocks, and stones, and trees.'

Her eyes lifted from the page and met his.

'Can you hear the world turning?'

Effie listened. She looked down at the hands in her lap – at her hand in his – and tried to hear it all rolling round. There was just the difficult crackle of his breath.

'All I can hear is the clock.'

When she looked up again, he'd gone.

Effie chipped a saucer, tripped on the stairs and struggled with the telephone dial. The voice in the earpiece launched into civilities. A stream of words surged from the Bakelite and seemed to rush around her. She held her breath through the doctor's enquiries and then told him it was too late.

'The war wreaked havoc with Laurence's heart.' Dr Gill shook his head in the hallway an hour on. Light cut brightly through the stained-glass sunrise behind him. 'He suffered severe physical and psychological traumas. He was lucky to have lasted as long as he did.'

'Lucky?' Effie pressed her lips together. Laurie's hat was on the hall stand. It suddenly struck her that he would never again require it. 'Do you think that he considered himself to be lucky?'

'I do,' replied the doctor, with a certainty that implied he could measure it medically. 'I know he did. Every extra day was precious to Laurence – and he got ten years of extra days.'

'I hope you're right.'

'You'll let his loved ones know, Euphemia?'

'I will, Dr Gill. I will.'

He offered her a smile as she handed him his coat. 'Seems a shame to pass on just as the irises are coming out.'

'It does.' Laurie had liked her to cut a bunch of irises. The leaves reminded Effie of the blades of bayonets, but Laurie would have it that they were architectural. Having once visited Paris, he understood artistic arrangement. Effie watched as the doctor walked away, along the iris-lined front path.

She paused in the doorway of the parlour, where Laurie's parents were framed, she in ocelot and he in India. Who, then, were the loved ones? Effie could recall few living relatives. The Christmas card list was mostly old comrades and contracted each year. She would write letters later, though it would require the assistance of a measure of sherry. As Laurie's housekeeper, was she also permitted a measure of sadness? Standing amongst the family portraits and handed-down sherry glasses, amongst the relics of the loved and lost, Effie, for the first time, felt uncomfortable in the house she had kept. She felt the need to retreat to station, to role, to hide in her well-ordered kitchen.

As she closed her hands around a cup, she contemplated the room in which she had chosen to occupy herself for the past ten years, since Laurie had come back from Ypres gassed, and her Joe had not come back at all. The sprigged wallpaper buzzed at her in shadowed corners. Laurie's long johns loomed, ghostly from the clothes airer overhead. Two hours earlier he had gripped at her wrist. She could still feel the force of it. In that instant he was fiercely alive. He had quoted Wordsworth at her and told her he had always loved her. And then, with all of his rhyming schemes completed, with all of his secrets spilled out, he had lain back on the pillow and closed his eyes. Effie couldn't help but wonder: had Laurie managed to keep his secrets in, had he continued to silently contain those sentiments, would his heart have held out? Fat roses on the teapot bloomed obliviously. Effie's fingers touched Laurie's overblown roses. What would become of the teapot now, the kettle and the settle and the spoons? What would become of his hat on the hall stand? What would become of her?

Reginald scratched at the back door. She let him out and looked on as he cocked his leg on the lilac. The blossom was just breaking. Bees stirred.

'It's not a day for dying,' Effie mused in the direction of the dog. She gave him a peppermint for pity's sake. Her Joe had died in the rain, which seemed more appropriate, more considerate somehow. Laurie had ascended into cloudless skies, without a thought for his dog or his irises or the havoc unleashed from his heart.

It being Saturday, there were cutlets for tea and a Dundee cake in the tin. She had let Laurie arrange the almonds in decorative circles. Effie had watched him, smiling over his symmetry.

'Do I no longer warrant marzipan?' he had teased. 'Have my comestibles ceased to deserve your adornment? Is our ardour so cooled that I've no chance of icing?'

Would he have stayed for marzipan? Would a layer of almond paste have changed his fate? Could an effort with icing have lengthened his luck? Was he, at the end, still teasing?

Effie flung a teaspoon at the sink.

She walked into town, to the Café Monika. Along the edge of

the park there were arrangements of red, white and blue pansies. The sun shone on patriotic-coloured peace.

'No Laurence today?' asked Mrs Harwood.

Effie sat at their usual table by the window and took her gloves off tidily.

'Laurie is dead,' she said. 'His heart gave out this morning.'

Mrs Harwood made a sharp intake of breath and said, 'You poor love.'

Effie ate curd tart. The pastry disappointed. Laurie had always said he got better at home. She recalled him, gauchely nineteen, at the counter.

Effie had started out at the Café Monika, in the back at first, on parkin, tea loaf and coconut rocks. It was more ladylike than mill work, her mother had said. She had an aptitude for sugar paste and piping. Mr Schumann, the then owner, was of Austrian extraction (though sachertorte and strudel and the story of his grandmother's girlhood in Vienna had long since been deleted from the menu), and liked to think himself a cut above commonplace baked goods. Over the door the Monika declared itself *High-Class Confectioners and Continental Café*.

Laurie's mother had sent him in for macaroons, soon after they had moved from Leeds. He had nice vowels and a clean handkerchief.

'His father is in fuses and his mother is genteel,' Elsie Buckley had nodded after Laurie. 'He's at university, you know.'

They had cooed approval, Effie remembered.

'It's a shame about his eyes.' Mrs Harwood had smiled compassionately.

Laurie's green-grey eyes, even then, were framed in heavy horn-rimmed spectacles. The lenses magnified Laurie's eyes, so that he always seemed to stare. When Effie later imagined the gas, it was the colour of Laurie's lens-exaggerated eyes.

'Don't you go making eyes at what you can't afford,' Mrs Moorcroft had twinkled behind a cup of Ceylon.

Effie hadn't. Not like that. And besides, she was spoken for. Joe was well-scrubbed and had prospects and an upright piano. More to the point, he had asked. Joseph Young, they said, was steady. They offered it to Effie as a compliment, his steadiness. She had sometimes wished that he might be a little less steady. But he brought her soft fruit from his father's allotment and, in return, she made him palmiers – pastry hearts joined with raspberry jam.

They had been in the Pals together; Laurie, with his grammar school education, a captain and Joe, of course, a private. They were there together at Ypres. It was a comfort to Effie that they had been there for each other.

The shop bell brought her back and brought with it Lily Holt, who knew of Laurie's leave-taking from Dr Gill.

Mrs Holt hugged her tearily. 'Oh Effie, what will you do now?'

'I have no-one to cook for,' she replied.

She bought a box of macaroons, from habit, and a sugar mouse for Reginald and would walk home through the park.

'It was a horrible thing, the mustard gas,' said Mrs Holt, over the menu, as Effie put on her coat.

'It was,' she agreed.

There were daffodils still in the municipal gardens. He had been quoting Wordsworth at them too just a week earlier. Yellow trumpets now blared Laurie's absence. With that recalled image of him, reciting at the spring planting schemes, Effie had to take to a bench for a moment. She shut her eyes and tried to see Laurie spinning fearlessly and forever round with the rocks and stones and trees.

Effie sat in his chair in the front parlour. She had never done so before and wasn't quite sure why she felt the need now. The velvet had worn thin on the arms. She wondered if she should maybe have noticed this before, pondered whether reupholstering might somehow have helped sustain Laurie's flagging heart. Her own twin chair faced her. They took toasted teacakes here of an evening, while she read Hardy aloud. In return for *Tess of the D'Urbervilles*, Laurie would tell her about Joe dying heroically. Who would cry for poor Tess now?

The mantelpiece mirror reflected the polished facets of cut glass. Effie considered whether she had perhaps been over-attentive to polishing. Had she, when their twin-chaired companionship reflected in the mirror, not seen beyond the shine? Had she been more attentive to her seeing, had she actually *looked* in the looking glass, would she have divined signs in the violet creams, the literary quotes and his praise for her good hot dinners? A vase of tulips drooped. The carpets would need cleaning if there was to be a funeral tea. She fed Reginald a macaroon and decided to look at Laurie.

When her father died they had said his expression was peaceful, that he had the appearance of being asleep. Laurie did not look asleep. He looked vacated. Dr Gill had crossed Laurie's hands over his chest, as one must do with the dead. Effie didn't like to see Laurie in the pose of a dead man. She found herself wanting to un-cross his arms, to break him out of the pose that made him so definitely dead. She touched his hand. She did not like the texture of his vacated skin.

'I am not sure what to say to you,' she said. 'I do wish you'd said something sooner to me.'

On the dressing table were flints and fossils and himself, Laurie at twenty-two, in photographic pose with his mother, whole and healthy in uniform. Effie supposed that he might have been called handsome, only there was something shy about the way his fringe fell. Could he really have been so very shy?

'You are a fool, Euphemia,' she told her reflection. In the mirror Effie Shaw was thirty-one, red-eyed and had no role. She saw herself framed in portrait against wisteria-pattern wallpaper that wasn't her own. The portrait was a melancholy composition.

She angled Laurie-in-uniform next to Joe on her bedside table and looked at them, side-by-side in sepia. She transferred their soldierly poses to an imagined trench, with poetic mud and a percussion of guns. Was that really how it had been? Did Laurie have all of those secrets inside him even then? There suddenly seemed to have been so much going on behind Captain Laurence Greene's glasses. Could it truly have been the case that he and Joe had stood side-by-side in a trench? She took off her perpetual engagement ring – an eternity of patience in opal – and placed it in-between them.

'Why could you not have told me?' she'd asked Laurie that morning.

'I had my reasons. In time you'll realise why,' he had replied.

Effie curled in her patchwork quilt. She tried to picture Laurie being received by gentle Jesus, in a pastel-tinted afterlife, where there would always be kindness and irises and a marzipan layer. But something in Laurie's 'in time' was insistent. Something in the tone of his exiting tenderness cast a strange light over her happy hereafter imaginings. Effie turned to the wall. She concentrated on the tidy rhymes of prayers to cut out the discordant questions.

Chapter Two

Effie had hoped it would be raining by the morning, but the sun slanted callously through the parted curtains. As she examined the familiar ceiling from her bed, she realised that she regarded Everdene as her home, not her place of employment.

She pulled her dressing gown around her and decided to spy on Laurie one last time. The undertaker was due at nine. It seemed wrong somehow to take him away, to take him from home and from her, from the comforts of familiarity and family heirlooms, and put him in the cold unfriendly soil.

It was not a surprise that the gas had finally got the better of Laurie. He had once shown her the white ring that circled his arm, where his wristwatch had spared his skin. 'I am shackled to the gas,' he had smiled. Certainly no amount of camphor and eucalyptus had ever let him shake off that cough. It would overcome him, his eyes would stream and he would apologise into his handkerchief. There were always a lot of handkerchiefs to launder. Effie saw the gas as a green blur around Laurie, like the glow that signifies saints in old paintings. She wondered if she would have wanted Joe back, if he'd had to have Laurie's lungs, if it were just to have ten years of his dying. She thought that perhaps she might.

Effie willed Laurie's eyes to flick open again. She willed his chest to heave, his lips to gasp, his heart to re-start and splutter him back into life. But, looking at Laurie's face, she knew he had gone. There was nothing of Laurie left. No prayers, however nicely rhymed, however intently entreated, would open Laurie's eyes now. Effie heard her own lips gasp.

Laurie's face now was not his. He'd had a kind face, an amiable face; it might not be dashing or fashionable or finely sculpted, but it was a face that found a smile easily. Without animation, without a smile, Effie was no longer certain she knew him.

He hadn't smiled much at first, though. When he had first come staggering back they had whispered him a drunk. But it was his injuries. That was all. As she had placed buttered toast before him, Effie had told Laurie that she was glad to see him returned. He had taken to calling in the café with a book.

'I've read that one,' she had said, leaning in with tea, as she spied Sergeant Troy's swordplay over Captain Greene's shoulder. 'I think Bathsheba Everdene is rather fabulous.'

'My house is called Everdene.' Then Laurie had smiled. Thus they had taken to talking Thomas Hardy.

One day he had grasped her hand and, with a startling abruptness, said: 'Miss Shaw, I need help.'

She was accustomed, by then, to the strangeness of returning soldiers, and so, calmly, quietly, she had pulled out the opposite chair.

'Captain Greene?'

He seemed to be considering his face in the bowl of his teaspoon. His spectacles glinted.

'Miss Shaw – I… as you may know, my parents are dead and I now find myself in awkward circumstances.' He had fussed with his napkin as if to illustrate the awkwardness. 'Mrs Brown feels it is time to retire, and so I must, it seems, hire a new housekeeper. Your name was mentioned to me. And, well, epic poems have been inspired by lesser subjects than your Bakewell tart.'

Effie had blushed and flustered.

'Oh heavens, have I been inappropriate?' Laurie slopped lapsang souchong.

'No, not at all.' She sought a response from the table top. 'It's just most unexpected.'

'I'm not asking you to marry me,' said Laurie, and they had laughed. She had henceforth never considered him in those terms. There had been no complicated pull in their proximity, or at least not so that she'd noticed. They had shared a roof, a sweet tooth and a taste for pastoral romances, but propriety prescribed that their sharing end there. If there had been signs, Effie hadn't seen them.

After the undertaker had taken Laurie away, she seemed to spend a long time frozen in indecision with a duster in her hand. Effie watched her hand hesitate. It dithered between earthenware and ormolu. It wavered between porcelain and silver plate. She no longer knew what she must make it do. Eventually she sat in the front parlour and applied her hesitating hand to knitting, but realised that she was dropping stitches for dead soldiers and there was no longer any need. Effie stared at the unneeded hands in her lap.

Stuffed stoats blinked at her with glass eyes. Laurie had a weakness of anthropomorphic taxidermy dioramas. The house was full of marrying mice, stoats cheating at cards and cigar-smoking piebald rats. Effie had always worried that they could have mites, but she saw an amicable sadness in the glass eyes now. It wouldn't surprise her if Laurie's funereal arrangements stipulated that he himself must be stuffed. She wound the clockwork canary. It warbled through something by Strauss before seizing in a mechanical wheeze.

For lunch she ate the last of Laurie's potted shrimps and took a bottle of his stout. He had sat across the table from her, two days earlier, and helped with the shelling. They had talked about the café going up for sale and he had encouraged her with the cayenne.

'I do like a nice potted shrimp,' she said to Laurie's absence across the table. 'And I find I'm not averse to the stout. I may take to drink now.'

It was then that she had seen it. Her eye, through the open pantry door, fixed on the alien object. Quite certain that it hadn't been there earlier, Effie looked curiously down at Reginald and then, accusingly, at the bottle of stout. It wasn't, in fairness, a pot of gold or a unicorn, but it was sufficiently out-of-place that it might well have been the work of fairies. It was a brown Manila envelope and it was propped against the jar of glacé cherries. The chair scraped back loudly as Effie stood.

It was addressed in his handwriting, that much was familiar. The shapes that his letters formed, however, were strange.

Miss Euphemia Shaw
Hotel Univers
Ypres, Belgium

Having never visited, nor having any intention of visiting Belgium, Miss Euphemia Shaw stared at the cryptic envelope. Ought she to open it? Did he mean her to open it? Could Laurie possibly have been conducting a continental correspondence with another Miss Shaw? She shook her head at the possibility and took the envelope in her hands. A book slid onto the counter. It was bound in slightly battered green cardboard. *Laurence Greene's Green Diary*, he had inked, in a youthful, though identifiable hand.

Fortified with a mouthful of stout, Effie opened the cover. Inside she found Laurie being a sentimental shepherd. He had copied a poem onto the first page. *Come live with me and be my love*, curled Laurie's adolescent letters, *and we will all the pleasures prove.*

And I will make thee beds of roses
And a thousand fragrant posies,
A cap of flowers, and a kirtle
Embroidered all with leaves of myrtle.

She blushingly turned the page on his pastoral fantasies. The chapters beyond were crowded. His words seemed to be cramped within the page. Her flicking eye also noted the deleted words. He crossed through and re-selected sentences, as if it mattered to him to get it right, to be precise, to tell the truth. There were sketches too, swarmed around with script, and prints in spilled ink. Effie touched poor Laurie's long-ago fingerprints. It felt like stretching across a gulf.

A week earlier she had caught those same fingers dipping in the jar of glacé cherries. She had smacked the back of his hand and told him he'd spoil his supper.

'Oh, indulge me,' he had said, leaning back against the counter. 'I'm thinking about telling you a secret.' There had been an odd expression on his face as he said this last. For an instant he didn't quite seem like himself. She had chased him out of the pantry with a broom.

Was this, then, Laurie's book of secrets? On the first page of the diary it was March 1915. As she read the first line, she saw him put the pencil pensively to his tongue, as so inclined at the start of a sentence. *It begins with sportsmanship and rules*, his pencil commenced. *We are sent to the seaside to learn to be soldiers…*

Effie stared at her well-stocked shelves, at the orderly labelled lines of jams and pickles and chutneys. Had she made Laurie adequately happy with her bottling and baking? Had her curing and preserving been enough? She looked at the jars of crystallised fruit and thought them more beautiful than gemstones. She looked at her hands that had cooked and laundered and scoured and sewn and shooed him away. She looked out towards his unoccupied chair at the kitchen table.

Effie sank down onto the pantry tiles. She didn't quite recognise the sound that came from her own mouth.

Chapter Three

A cry came up from the bay. Laurence ran to the railings.

'Is it sinking?'

The wagon that was collecting up the firing targets appeared to have got stuck in the wet sand. Laurence could see the driver waving his arms. The men had abandoned their game of football and were heading down the beach to assist.

'Pull it from the front. Don't get behind it.' He shouted but the wind seemed to take his voice away.

After some commotion the wheels lurched forward and the driver's arms were now applauding. The men gave a cheer and began to walk back towards the scuffed-up area of sand that was presently serving as the field of play. Their feet made meandering patterns up the beach.

'They call it the Naples of the North, you know,' said Laurence. 'I saw it on a poster.' They continued their stroll along the promenade. An ice-cream cart was jangling out something appropriately Italianate. Three waitresses were sharing a bench and a bag of chips.

'The Neapolitan likenesses are slightly lost on me. They also call it Bradford-by-the-Sea, I believe. But this is agreeable, isn't it?' Alexander Allerton leaned on the balustrade and touched his hat to the girls on the bench. 'Somewhat bracing but certainly agreeable.'

Laurence watched as seagulls bent on the wind. He could hear the waitresses laughing behind. 'I recall that you used exactly those same terms to describe our Mrs Johnson.'

'I can put up with the Rupert Brooke recitations in return for the steamed puddings and the way that she spills out of that corset.' Allerton flicked his cigarette end down onto the sand. 'Definite bit of luck there, eh? A most fortuitous billeting. I may beguile my way to second helpings.'

Laurence couldn't recall Allerton being a beguiler at school. He remembered a boy who liked books about pirates and treasure maps. Allerton's future, even then, had been all mapped out in the family law firm. Laurence wondered at what stage the Turkish cigarettes, the moustache and the monocle had arrived. There was something rather deliberate, Laurence thought, about this collection of facial furnishings. It was as if Allerton had decided to take on a part. He recently looked rather like he had decided to take on the part of a blackguard in a play.

'I take it that you mean to beguile your way to somewhat more than just the odd extra bacon rasher?'

'The good woman is intent on keeping up morale. If she wishes to boost mine, I wouldn't be so cruel as to frustrate her patriotic efforts.'

'She makes excellent custard,' Laurence conceded.

Allerton rolled his eyes.

Fitton kicked the ball out and it bounced against the sea wall.

'What's the score?' Laurence shouted down.

'Seven-four. But they've got Arthur Midgely. He had a trial for Oldham.'

'They've rather more enthusiasm for football than they have for drill,' Allerton observed.

'Is that a scrum?' asked Laurence. They watched Fitton run back.

'No, it's a scrap.'

'See, the fighting spirit of the troops *is* excellent. Only I'm not sure that they really ought to be fighting each other.'

The men had spent the morning practising an attack with broomsticks. Major Bramhope, looking on as they pointed, jabbed and parried, had queried the vigour of their offensive spirit. He had given them a lecture about Agincourt in the afternoon, illustrated with photographs from his walking holidays through the Pas-de-Calais. '*Where are our uniforms? Far, far away,*' the men had sung as they were marched back to billets. '*When will our rifles come? P'haps, p'haps some day.*' School children skipped alongside.

'Fitton is Young's brother-in-law, isn't he?' Allerton asked. 'Have I got it right?'

'Almost. Imminently. Young is engaged to Euphemia Shaw. Fitton is married to her sister, Grace.'

'Of course.'

Allerton seemed to smirk. Laurence wasn't sure whether he had asked the question as a provocation.

'Goodness, isn't it complicated?' The provocative one went on. 'They really ought to have given us some sort of diagram. I feel conspicuously lacking in cousins-of-cousins and soon-to-be siblings.'

'My Uncle Herbert is being recalled. Mother says that Auntie Cissy is in a fluster about it.'

'*We few, we happy few, we band of brothers.*'

'Uncle Herbert has got gout. It makes him terribly short tempered. I think that, if I were Auntie Cissy, I might be glad to have him out of the house.'

'*And gentlemen in England now a-bed shall think themselves accursed they were not here.*' Allerton's fist made actorly emphases on the railings. He turned towards Laurence and laughed.

'Rushton is talking of organising a performance of *Henry V*. He wants to hire the Alhambra. Do I take it that you'll be auditioning?'

'What? God, no. There are amenable girls available for waltzing; why would I want to spend my evenings thee-ing and thou-ing?'

'Brooker has put his name down to play Katherine.'

'Quite.'

21

Laurence looked out across the bay. The far-off figures of the cocklers doubled in reflection. He was painting a series of wet-skied watercolours. Morecambe Bay was oyster grey, umbers and rose and a shifting liquid landscape.

'Full time.' Allerton nodded towards the sands. The men were coming back up the beach. Laurence waved towards them.

'Seven-five,' Fitton shouted.

The sea was taking back the trenches that they'd dug that morning. Laurence shut his eyes into the wind. He could hear the lines of bunting straining above. There was something about this saline wind that made him feel intensely alive.

'Alfie, you can't shoot me, you bugger. You're already dead.'

Laurence opened his eyes. A gang of children were playing Red Indians around the bathing machines. They whooped, sniped and gleefully scalped one another.

'Dancing,' said Allerton.

They walked up towards the Winter Gardens. Allerton was whistling *Wine, Women and Song*. He waltzed an invisible partner up the promenade.

'I've just signed up for French evening classes,' said Laurence. 'Did I tell you? I need to polish up my French verbs.'

Allerton held the door for a girl in sage-green satin and bowed with theatrical gallantry.

'As far as I'm concerned, French grammar can remain firmly in the past tense,' he said. 'I don't intend to be parted from Morecambe.'

Chapter Four

Lancashire, 1928

Effie handed her sister a tin of cake. 'Genoa cake, with glacé cherries,' she said. 'I have no-one to bake for now. I am a housekeeper with no-one to keep house for. I am as vacated as Laurie.'

Her sister gave her a humouring hug.

Grace still lived in the house in which they had grown up. Comparison with Everdene was not complimentary. Number 14 Jubilee Street was full of steam and the green sharpness of detergent; Grace took in washing and spewed out babies. Effie wondered how she could bear to with Frank, who drank most of his wages and offered no compensatory kindness. Frank Fitton had come back from the war, but he had come back a bastard. Sometimes Effie wished he had not come back at all. 'He needs to let off steam,' Grace repeated with measured patience. Effie thought that Frank looked like a boiler about to blow. She tried to imagine him as that young man in the diary, looking brightly up from a wind-blown beach. She found that she couldn't place Frank's face in the picture.

Effie was never sure that she liked Edward being here, in the midst of all of the steam and Frank's swearing and strangers' smalls. Edward remained on the sideboard, where he had been on the day that their mother was taken away – Edward in his sweet celluloid smile and Sunday tie, draped in mourning crepe. He was their younger brother, lost on the Somme. It had put an end to their mother's sanity. Margaret Shaw wore a curl of her son's mid-brown hair in her locket. It looked like a comma. 'It should have been a full stop,' Effie had once said to Grace. They called it a state of 'mental derangement'. Effie adjusted Edward's black ribbons. Either side of the framed photograph were a whalebone corset and a jar of fish paste. She vowed that she wouldn't let Laurie be so untidily memorialised.

Effie seated herself at the kitchen table while Grace shifted piles of folded whites away. The table top was stained with sauce bottle rings.

'Mind out.'

Grace straightened clean newspaper over the breakfast crumbs and they passed the teapot between them. A baby squalled in a bedroom above, children thundered on the stairs. Effie didn't understand why her sister stayed here, how she could make do with just making do, with frugality and Frank, with hands that smelled of carbolic, a stained table top and a teapot that poured so unsatisfactorily.

'It's too hot in here.'

They took chairs out into the back yard and sat between the lines of flapping bed sheets.

'Like sails,' said Effie. 'All at sea.'

Grace lit a cigarette. 'So what happens now?' She blew smoke at a forget-me-not blue sky.

'The funeral is set for Friday, at Saint James'. I'd started baking for a tea, but Laurie had pre-booked the Apollo – not knowing if the Monika would still be functioning for a function.'

'It was considerate of Laurence to spare you the effort,' said Grace, pulling a strand of tobacco from the corner of her mouth.

'If will be a finger buffet. I would rather have had the effort.'

Grace put her cup down on the flags. 'Have they told you when you'll have to be out of the house?'

'The solicitor told me not to fret about it until after the funeral. I'm not permitted to fret until Friday. He told me to keep my fretting on ice. Only I don't seem to be able to.'

She had spent the previous evening studying one of Laurie's family photographs. A collection of Greenes and Gatesgarths were arranged either side of an embarrassed-looking bride. Effie's finger had moved over maiden aunts and southern-counties cousins. Which one of them did her polished mirrors belong to now? Whose reflection would they next present? Who would inherit her stainless table top, her tidy range and her well-stocked pantry? Who now owned the stuffed stoats, Mrs Greene in ocelot and her narrow attic bed? Who had Laurie left *her* to?

'You do know that you might not be able to stay there, don't you? You know that you might have to move on, don't you, Effie?'

'Of course,' Effie nodded at her tea. She knew it, though she didn't enjoy the knowing. There were bluebells on the teacup that she gripped and contemplated. The teacups had once been her grandmother's. Her mother's mother had been in service and rather too generous with her own services. Effie knew very little about her maternal grandmother, other than her commitment to service and the pattern of her china. When she imagined the woman who had chosen the bluebell teacups she saw flashes of ankles on attic stairs and a smile that stepped back into alcoves. Perhaps, Effie considered, she had been a little too conservative in her own commitment. She thought about Alexander Allerton, the aforesaid solicitor, smirking in Morecambe at the mention of soon-to-be sisters-in-law. Did that smirk equate to some assumption of impropriety? She put down the too-hot tea.

'I do worry what will become of poor Reginald.'

'I worry what will become of poor bleeding me,' said Frank from the doorway. He wiped grease from his hands on a grey cloth.

'Frank,' acknowledged Effie.

'You can't come mopesing back here now that your fancy man is finally gone, you know.'

'Don't speak ill of the dead.' Grace flicked cigarette ash in the direction of her husband.

'I'd never consider seeking your charity,' said Effie, not

liking the 'fancy man' or the tapping toe of 'finally'. Frank believed Effie to be above her station. She had heard it said once, second hand. Effie wasn't really certain of her appointed station, which perhaps explained why she wasn't clear as to when she had over-shot it. She did know, though, that she could never come back to Jubilee Street.

'Well, you may take my *Gazette* with you for your studies,' said Frank. 'You'll find Situations Vacant on page sixteen.'

'Frank, don't be so ruddy rude,' said Grace. 'Effie brought us a cake.'

'And she'll keep on arriving with cakes when her wages stop? I have enough mouths to feed.'

Effie wanted to advise him that the mouths might be minimised if he could keep it in his trousers, but she finished her tea instead.

'Your husband is uncouth,' she whispered to Grace as she left.

'Your sister is unhinged,' pronounced Frank on the close of the door. 'And I'll not make houseroom for Laurence Greene's leftovers.'

Chapter Five

It was agreed that Reverend Brierley did a fine service. There were telegrammed testimonials from top-brass, a nicely-enunciated poem and a vigorous rendition of *Jerusalem*. It was as green and pleasant as a funeral could be and the goodly show of medals compensated for the small number of family members.

It had felt odd to hear her name listed amongst the bereaved; Effie wasn't certain it was entirely right. She tried to remember Joe's memorial service, at which she did have the right to mourn, at which it was correct that she should cry, but could recall only fragments and a confusion of feelings. There were white roses on Laurie's coffin. She thought of his tea service and blinked away tears.

Afterwards, they moved on to the Café Apollo. Effie had always considered the Apollo to be a second-best establishment, but she conceded the effort made in serviettes and table centrepieces. The trays of savouries were emptying rapidly. She worried whether sufficient effort had been applied to the provision of sandwiches. Albert McGrath told her, between potted-beef triangles, about his planned cycling tour of The Lakes. She asked him what it felt like to be gassed.

'There was a gas rattle,' he said, 'like at the football. Laurence spent four weeks under a propped-up sheet. He shouldn't have survived at all. He cheated ten years from death.'

There was a snow globe somewhere in the house – a long-ago Morecambe souvenir. Laurie had shaken it for her once and shown her how it flurried over the pier and promenade. Suddenly Effie wanted to put a glass dome over Laurie and keep him there in 1915 with his watercolours and amateur dramatics. She didn't want what had happened next to happen, for it all to turn to gas and ghastliness and him being under a propped-up sheet. The voice in the diary was unmistakably his; this faraway, ink-evoked voice was the one that twinned with her own across the table top. Hearing it again, having got him back, she didn't want to let him go. She stared at Albert McGrath's black armband.

'It made your brass buttons go all green, you know,' said Albert.

Mr Allerton, who had done the nice enunciation, and who would now execute the not-so-nice legalities, cornered her by the aspidistra. She was expecting it, but did not want it.

'Miss Shaw, would it be convenient if I were to escort you to my office afterwards?'

'Of course', said Effie, her hand extending towards a passing tray of sherry glasses.

They walked along the edge of the park together and made safe observations on the change of seasons. Effie looked sideways at Alexander Allerton. It was a curious sensation, she found, to be intimate with the foibles of a stranger, his boyhood reading matter and the lengths that he would go to for an extra bacon rasher. She wasn't certain, what with the smirk and all, that she liked the version of Alexander Allerton that she had found in the diary, but Laurie had always called him a 'good egg'.

He pulled out a seat for her and pushed his glasses up his nose. The office smelled of leather and liquorice.

'You are no doubt wondering, Miss Shaw,' he began with inscrutable expression, 'as to what is to become of you and Everdene.'

Though unable to determinate this question or statement, Effie offered an affirmative response. 'I have, indeed, wondered, Mr Allerton.'

He smiled with a shuffle of papers. The precision of his diction made her nervous. 'Well, you must wonder no more. Or, rather, you may be permitted to wonder but with the reassurance that your circumstances are secured.'

Accepting a proffered humbug from Mr Allerton's bonbonnière, Effie sucked on the meaning of this sentence. 'I am sorry. I'm not certain that I follow. Does that mean that I am to be retained?' She hesitated to hope.

'Exceedingly.' There was something mischievous now in Mr Allerton's demeanour. Effie felt excluded from a game. 'Your future employment is secure, on condition that you carry out certain instructions.'

'The carpets?' she queried over-keenly. 'I know that I'm behind with cleaning the carpets.'

'The carpets, dear girl, I suspect can wait.' Mr Allerton creaked back in his chair. For a second Effie's thoughts flicked to a storybook image of the Big Bad Wolf. 'Laurence left certain instructions for you. Specific instructions. If you carry them out to the letter – and I underline that word for you,' he waved a letter opener appropriately, 'you need not fret for your employment prospects.'

With a glint of an eye he flourished a key – and, from a desk drawer, presented a box. 'This, Miss Shaw, is your future.' Mr Allerton pushed the box across the desk. His fingernails, Effie noted, could have done with some attention.

It was a red satin box, and one that she recognised as having contained Christmas confectionary. She wasn't sure that she wanted to open it under Mr Allerton's lupine gaze, but, in the circumstances, she felt obliged to lift the lid.

She spied, in the white-lined interior, an envelope, bearing her name in Laurie's hand, and a jar of crystallised violets wrapped up in a five-pound note. *For the journey*, pronounced the attached luggage label.

'Like the Owl and the Pussy-Cat,' said Effie.

'They sailed away, for a year and a day...' Mr Allerton sang.

She took the letter back to the kitchen table and braced herself with a bottle of porter. Conjured with a waft of the pen, Laurie sat opposite her. He smiled.

I'm being a bother, aren't I? I really do hate to be a bother.

'If I didn't have you to bother about, I don't know what I'd do,' said Effie to the letter. She slid off her string of pearls as she read. Laurie had once told her that pearls were made of mermaids' tears. She turned the link through her fingers and felt a brief glimmering of sympathy for inconsolable fishfolk.

Everything is going to be fine, you know. It will all come up roses. But there's something that you have to do for me first, Effie. Something that you have to do for yourself.

She nodded and contemplated what the something might be.

You often asked me about Joseph. You said that you wanted to put flowers on his grave. I, for my reasons, discouraged you. You are probably too generous to have ever noticed. I didn't want you to look for Joseph. But now I think that perhaps you ought. I think that perhaps it is time. I have dithered over this. I have altogether been undone by dithering.

Effie took a swig of stout. 'Why now?'

There are things that you should know, things that it will hurt to learn. But, well, what use is dishonest experience? I'm with Mr Nietzsche on this one: I firmly believe that what doesn't kill us makes us stronger.

Effie imagined Laurie pausing after this nod to Mr Nietzsche, taking off his glasses and rubbing his eyes. Laurie looked exposed when not viewed through a lens. He didn't look as if experience had made him strong.

To that end, you will find tickets that will take you to Ypres in this envelope, and, from there, on to Paris. I mean to show you sights. I have made financial arrangement for you, Effie, so you must not skimp. A letter awaits you in the Hotel Univers in Ypres and I trust that you will have already discovered the reading material that I left you. It is my guide to Belgium, as it were. (Perhaps it might be best saved for Belgium?) Oh, and do have the Charlotte Russe. It is famed.

Effie gasped.

P.S. I loved you from the moment you first handed over my change.

Effie cried.

Chapter Six

They were there as Laurence rounded the corner onto Regent Road. He took a step back. It was their mirror images that he saw first; the Young cousins were standing in front of the windows of a gentleman's outfitters. They turned to take in their newly uniformed reflections.

'Well, I've seen some sights!'

'This season's colour is just so soldier.' Charlie Young made a mannequin pose.

'I could do with a few more pips on my shoulder.'

'Aye, I hear that they award them for running away. I'll refuse to take an order from you, you know.'

'Then I shall have you shot for mutiny. I mean to rise to general.' Joseph Young saluted flamboyantly at his own reflection.

'Balls to that.'

'Insubordinate illiterate, I've marked your card.'

Laurence cut through towards the Clarendon. Allerton appeared from behind a newspaper headline. The front page was full of the Dardanelles. It still felt like someone else's war. With the latest news from Gallipoli, Laurence was glad for it to remain so.

'I'm not sure that they're any smarter in khaki. We do look a bit of a motley lot.'

'Speak for yourself,' said Allerton and smiled at the star on his shoulder. 'The chappie on the door actually bowed at me. And I swear that I've been given a better measure.'

'It does somewhat crystallise it, though, doesn't it? I mean, it's going to happen now, isn't it? We're property of the War Office.'

'And all who sail in her.' Allerton raised his glass.

'But I keep looking down at my lapels and asking myself why. What qualifies me to wear them? How am I equipped for this? Aren't you asking yourself that? Why, just because I can decline a Latin noun and understand the rules of rugby better than football, am I assumed to know how to lead men into that?' Laurence nodded at the headlines.

'Fritz will be scarpering back to Berlin when he gets wind of our subjunctives and our pointy balls.'

'Really, though? Are you comfortable with it?'

Allerton shrugged. 'We have to make the best of it, don't we? You'll be fine.'

'I think that I'd rather be repeatedly kicked by a scrum-half whilst being made to recite Catullus.'

'I'd keep that peccadillo private if I were you, Lieutenant Greene.'

Laurence made sign language at the waiter. The bar piano was playing a song about the inconsistent ardour of a girl from Paris; the next-table clatter of dominoes detracted somewhat from the Gallic lamentations.

'Shall I go for heroic or haughty?' asked Allerton, exhibiting attitudes. He leaned across to see. Laurence had begun drawing him in caricature in his notebook.

'The haughty pose is less histrionic.'

Allerton had an amused mouth, Laurence thought, as he curled its line onto paper. He looked as if he was constantly savouring some private prank. There was something about his mouth that made Allerton look rather lewd. Possibly, Laurence considered, it was on account of the amount of blue jokes that issued from it.

'Can I ask you a question, Alex?'

'Oh dear. Not another peccadillo, is it?'

'Well…'

'Heavens.' Allerton folded the Dardanelles away. He tapped

the end of his cigarette on the table. 'Go on, then. Fire away, old man. Though don't necessarily expect to receive a useful answer.'

'Have you ever wished to dislike someone?'

'*Wished* to dislike someone? Doesn't disliking tend to be instinctive?' Allerton sat back with the cigarette as he considered. 'It's one of those things that comes from the gut, isn't it? Not normally something that requires mental application. Oh. Let me guess: would the someone perhaps be the fiancé of a certain purveyor of pastries?'

Laurence had confided in Allerton, some weeks earlier, on the matter of innocent eyes and peony lips – and had immediately realised that to have done so was an error. Elbows now made angles at him and every item of confectionary had become a matter of mirth. He was starting to develop a dread of teashops.

'The men call them Old Young and Younger Young, you know,' he offered as a diversion. 'For differentiation's sake.'

'I'm realising that it could be worse. My cousin has just been sent to a Welsh regiment. He's got a dozen Joneses, an octet of Evans and a score of utterly unpronounceables.' Allerton took a mouthful of his drink. 'It's Joseph, isn't it, the elder? Are you struggling with the disliking, then?'

'Of course. He's appallingly personable. How can you dislike someone who collects seashells and knows all of the words to *Ragtime Cowboy Joe*?'

'Quite easily, I would have thought. If you're collecting flaws, I have seen him sat outside the red light.'

'Exactly. He's always *outside*. It's Charlie Young that's inside. The elder doesn't appear to share the younger's penchant for ladies who sell their affections by the hour.'

'Would you have it otherwise?'

'I don't know. That's just it. I suppose that I'm glad for *her* sake, but, by the same motive, there's part of me that wishes him flawed.' Laurence nodded thanks to the waiter as he delivered his pink gin. 'I am a brute, aren't I?'

'I can think of another word for it,' said Allerton.

Chapter Seven

Lancashire, 1928

'I shall have to have a new hat,' Effie mused, whilst practising with a Frenchified assembly of flaky pastry. She dusted crumbs from the cover of the diary. She thought, as she did so, of their faces turning in the shop window. She also thought about Laurie, struggling to drum up dislike over his pink gin. 'I can't see Joe without a new hat,' she told Mrs Harwood.

Grace was late and Mrs Harwood was hovering. 'I hear that Captain Greene has left you well provided for. I am sure that you can stretch to a new hat.'

Effie licked icing from her fingers. 'I may venture an asymmetric brim.'

'But are you sure that it's safe?' frowned Mrs Harwood.

'An asymmetric brim?'

'No, travelling to the Continent on your own. It just sounds like a rather perilous venture.'

'I have never been beyond Bridlington,' said Effie. 'It's about time that I got brave. And besides, I'm with Joe and Laurie.'

'Exactly,' said Mrs Harwood.

Grace entered in a flurry of apology and warm air. 'I couldn't get anyone to mind the baby.'

'There are too many babies,' pronounced Effie. 'Does Frank mean to repopulate Lancashire singlehandedly?'

'There are too many old maids,' returned Grace.

Effie dismissed this with a flourish of her napkin. 'So, have you heard? I'm off to see Joe.'

'Have I heard? You're the talk of town. Why couldn't Laurence have had the nouse to put a ring on your finger?'

'It's not like that. It was never like that.'

'You two weren't carrying on, then?'

36

'No! Sometimes, Grace, you can be downright grace*less*.'

Mrs Harwood fussed in between with tea. They moved crockery aside to make space for the tray. Grace corrected her coiffeur in the gleam of the teapot. Effie corrected the alignment of cutlery.

'Shall I be mother?' Grace asked.

'You usually are.'

'Oh, heck. Have I put my foot in it?'

Effie stirred in sugar, sought steadiness in circles. 'Laurie wants me to visit Joe's grave. That's all.'

Grace sipped and sat back. 'And is that such a good idea?'

'I was thirty last year. I'm overdue an adventure.'

'It's not that,' Grace fidgeted with her teaspoon.

'I don't need your blessing, Grace. I am a grown-up and it's only a holiday.'

'I know.'

'Did Frank tell you to talk me out of it?'

'No, Effie. Will you just listen? I'm concerned about what you might find of Joe.'

'I will find Joe dead. I'm not a fool.'

'I do know that. I know you're not a fool. But I worry for how it will hit you.' Grace laid the teaspoon straight and looked earnest beneath her fringe. 'It's just that there were rumours at one time, that Joe wasn't possibly all that he should have been as a soldier.'

'It was gossip. It was malicious. Laurie told me the truth: Joe died beautifully. With heroics.'

'I do hope so,' said Grace. 'You must remember what his mother did.'

Alice Young had put her head in the gas oven. Effie could never quite decide which was worse: her own mother's madness or Joe's mother's suicide. Perhaps, there wasn't much to choose between them she supposed.

'Mrs Young was unsound. It tipped her.'

'Aye, well, just don't you go getting tipped.'

'I have no intention,' said Effie. But her reflection stretched to grotesque in the silver sugar bowl; she saw herself briefly as an electroplated mask of tragedy.

'Effie?'

They shall grow not old as we that are left grow old. They read that at Laurie's funeral. Oh, Grace. Joe is still twenty and I've got lines.'

'But Joe will never get chance to go to Paris, will he? Perhaps Laurence was right,' Grace conceded with a squeeze of Effie's hand. 'Say goodbye to Joe and hello to Paris.'

Effie realised that they were being watched from the counter.

'Nerves,' Mrs Harwood mouthed.

'Sherry,' replied Mrs Grimes.

'I look forward to this establishment being under new management,' said Effie over-loudly. 'The linen is tired and the silver somewhat tarnished. I expect that Paris will give me expectations.'

Grace laughed and ordered éclairs for show.

'Do they drink sherry in Paris?'

Grace shrugged. 'I suspect they drink anything in Paris. Is there a particular reason that Laurence is sending you there?'

'He means to show me a good time.'

'Shame he didn't get round to it while he was alive.'

'Laurie was aesthetic.' Effie had heard him voice the word. 'Or perhaps it was ascetic?' He had also told her about Paris – about little boats in the Luxembourg Gardens, peaches piled high on the Rue Mouffetard and a barrel organ that played *The Blue Danube.*

'And the dog?' Grace looked dubiously down at Reginald.

'He travels with me. Laurie stipulated that I have to buy him an ice-cream in Paris.'

'That's ridiculous.'

'No, it's not. It's nice.' Effie smiled benignly dog-wards. 'Though how I get him to Paris is proving to be a bit of a predicament. I'm not sure whether Laurie fully considered the complications.'

'The dog may be the least of your complications.'

'Can't you just be glad for me? Can't you just wish me a happy holiday?'

'With all my heart. To Paris!' said Grace and raised her teacup.

Chapter Eight

Stonehenge, January 1916

He could see the shape of the monolith against the sky. The bright-edged clouds made a sharp silhouette of it. Biplanes carved the sunset. They had spent the day marching along Roman roads, through a landscape that seemed poetic with mist-wreathed prehistory. The line of these roads took Laurence back to boyhood rambles across the moors, scrambling over the foundations of forts and blockhouses, where he had hoped to spy the ghosts of legionaries.

He walked away from the camp, away from the rows of white tents, the button polishing and the bugle call. He thought about Tess, sleeping in the circle of stones. It seemed momentous to step inside that strange, solemn circle, to enter beneath and between the shadowed columns. The darkness seemed to intensify within.

The wave of a hand glimmered towards him. His foot faltered. For an instant he might have believed it a ghost.

'Listen,' said Joseph Young, 'it hums like a harp.'

Laurence discerned the shape of two seated figures. 'It does,' he said. He walked towards them. 'Fancy that. It really does. He called it a Temple of the Winds.'

'He?' The second voice was Charlie Young's.

'It's a scene in a book,' explained Laurence. *'Tess of the D'Urbervilles*. She sleeps her last night on the altar, before she's taken away.'

'Is it a good book?' Joseph asked.

'Yes, the best. Only terribly tragic. They take her from here and execute her. You may borrow it, if you'd like.'

'I'm not much of a reader,' said Charlie. 'Mother says that people who read books have dirty houses.'

'Does she, indeed!'

Laurence saw the silver glint of a hip flask. 'You can borrow a bit of this if you like, Lieutenant. It keeps the cold off.'

'Thank you.' He sat with the cousins, their backs to the black heights of stone. They listened to the noise of the wind, the solitude seemed absolute. 'We could be the only people in the world,' he said, 'we three.'

Joseph nodded at his side. The last of the sun pierced red through the arch and then was gone. They watched silently as stars appeared.

The orders for France came in the next day. Laurence lost his hair to the regimental barber; the texture of his shorn scalp made him feel suddenly vulnerable.

'I think I'd rather have gone to war looking like a Mongol,' he said to Allerton, his fingers moving over the newly familiar curves of his skull.

'It's in case of a head wound. Apparently it makes life easier for the doctors.'

'Did you have to tell me that? I'm not feeling very Mongolian at all now.'

'You should send a ringlet to your shop girl for her locket.'

'You should send one to Mrs Johnson for her extra rashers.'

For once Allerton's ribbing brought back a memory that it didn't pain Laurence to re-play. He recalled a locket between the girl's fingers. She had just served his mother and they were standing in the doorway of the otherwise empty café, complaining collectively of the weather. There was rain on the window and grains of sugar glinting on the girl's fingers. Laurence had asked her what was in her locket. His mother had given him a look afterwards and he supposed that it was perhaps impertinent, but he had been reluctant to let her retreat back behind the counter. She had opened the locket and shown him a water-warped oval image that might once have been a face. 'My grandmother,' she had said and smiled. Laurence had felt her breath as her mouth made the words a chain's length away. He remembered the effort it had taken to step back. He told himself again that he needed to step back.

Chapter Nine

Lancashire, 1928

Effie said goodbye to the stuffed stoats, to poor Tess and Mrs Greene in ocelot. She locked the front door and looked down the iris path. Though she was walking towards Joe, with Laurie's on-paper voice as her travelling companion, it felt like she was walking away.

'I am a little frightened,' she confided in Reginald. He seemed more interested in the smell of her boots than her confided fear.

'Ypres, eh?' said the taxi driver, as he helped with her suitcase at the station. 'Why would a nice young lady want to go to Ypres?'

'My fiancé is there. Well, in the sense that he's buried there.'

'Too many were, flower. I was in the Pals myself. What was your feller's name?'

'Joseph Young,' supplied Effie brightly.

'Right,' replied the driver flatly.

'You didn't know him, did you?'

'No, love, but I know of the name.'

'He was a hero,' she asserted, feeling suddenly, strangely, that Joe's heroism was being critically assessed.

'It could be interpreted that way.'

'By which you mean?'

'Nothing, flower. It was a rotten show all round.'

'So I believe,' said Effie, without satisfaction.

Shrill children chased after the train. Effie watched the town accelerate past the window, and looked down on garrets, chimney pots and gutters, on hen runs, allotments, lean-tos and lines of laundry leaping at the wind. The familiar rows and yards and warehouses thinned to fields and farms.

She had brought *Jude* for the journey (she wasn't up to *Tess* yet), but the lines danced and she too couldn't quite make it to Christminster. Laurie's voice kept on replaying distractingly in her head. 'Who lives in your locket?' he had said. His diary had pulled the memory back into focus and suddenly it was as real again as the railway carriage around her. She – the shop girl – was everywhere in his account; it seemed that she, without realising, had gone to war with them. Effie closed her hand around the locket, which, for the last ten years, had held Joe's image. She stared at the green book. It seemed to want to spring open. What further surprises did it mean to spring at her?

There were lists, in between the diary entries, of intentions (*1. World travel; 2. Vegetable garden; 3. Dancing lessons; 4. Dog*), of novels that he meant to read on his return and meals that he intended to relish. Laurie's realised fourth intention looked up at Effie with laughing eyes. Her own eyes rolled in return. Did Reginald understand that Laurie wasn't coming back? He barely seemed to have noticed his master's absence. A little more moping wouldn't have gone amiss.

There were also drawings in the diary: boats in a harbour, a village well, a roadside calvary, faces. She recognised Alexander Allerton in caricature, with a juvenile moustache, and a girl behind a shop counter whom she chose not to look at for too long (though Laurie's eye had clearly lingered on her). She was accustomed to his drawing; that was what Laurie did. It was quite normal that her shopping lists were illuminated, that eyes and mouths ornamented the headlines of the evening paper and that curlicues sprang from the crossword. It filled the backs of envelopes, crammed the margins and spilled from the wrappings of his hill-walking sandwiches. Effie had sometimes wondered if it would burst out, all of this swarming illustration, but she'd never really considered what the eyes and the mouths meant.

Should she have looked a little closer at what expression they wore?

She turned onwards through January 1916. *We entrained for Folkestone,* Laurie wrote, *eight to a carriage and crushed in with packs and rifles. Carver and Horrocks insisted on singing and waving at every vaguely female form that passed the window. Dragging east, we traded whispers about illicit Christmas kick-abouts in no-man's land and deliberated the evacuation of Gallipoli, which is called a success. I felt the momentum of the train. I felt the distance pull. There was something about the motion of the train that gave me a feeling of absolute inevitability, of it all now being out of my hands. We sucked on pear drops and played cards to wear down the time.*

'Are you scared?' Alex asked me, between hands of whist. We haven't voiced the word before, as if it is bad luck, as if it were impolite. But the noise and the jostle of the train pushed us into hushed intimacy.

I wasn't certain what to answer. I wasn't sure what he wanted me to say. 'I was more scared of telling my mother.' It's true, really. I tried to read Alex's face. I watched his eyes calculate the splayed cards. 'Are you?'

He offered me the bag of boiled sweets. 'It's all a lark, isn't it?'

That's the language that we talk in now: it's all a laugh and larking. I leaned my cheek against the cool glass of the window. England smeared past in brown and green, my own soldierly reflection a ghost gliding over it. I felt a little light-headed with the motion. Am I scared? 'I am all anticipation,' I replied.

As Effie's train sliced south, England sped into that same indistinct strip of green and brown. She slept. In her dream Laurie was singing *Jerusalem* in his bathtub voice, but he gave her a warning look as the sword slept in his hand and the roses on the teapot sprouted sudden thorns.

London began with smart suburbs, turned to terraces and then to commerce and slums and grass-grown railway sidings. Effie observed its alien lines, the rooftops and tenement blocks, the domes and spires, the congestion and crush and on-and-on of it. The curve of the Thames brought back half-remembered childhood rhymes. London was an unending skyline. It was the colours of a pearl. It stretched, grey and glimmering.

Reginald yawned. Effie sat him on her knee.

'This, Reginald, is our capital city.'

He scratched himself and did not seem especially impressed. Reginald was a difficult dog to wow. Effie wished she had Laurie to share this journey with – not just his voice in a diary – and then wondered if she was disloyal to Joe for wishing it.

'The etiquette of this is not easy,' she whispered to her canine confidant.

Chapter Ten

The station was exuberantly gothic. Effie looked up at ornate engineering and busy brickwork. Steam romanticised an expanse of smutted glass. Pigeons cut arcs through vast vaults of airy iron.

Unsteadied with suitcase, soon-to-be-employed hat box and eyes full of architecture, she stumbled over Reginald's lead.

'Steady now,' a chap caught her arm.

'Thank you.'

'I'd offer to take your case, only I'm already doing my best packhorse impersonation.' He shrugged at suitcases and then attempted an unconvincing equine whinny. His eyes were kind at the corners. 'Can I get you a porter?'

'No, it's quite all right,' said Effie. 'I just must mind where I'm going. Only it's like a cathedral. Like a fairy palace.'

The implausible packhorse laughed. 'Maybe you ought to get out more?' He tipped his hat and smiled.

It was all push and bustle. Effie felt unbalanced by it.

'Don't dawdle, Reginald. We have to take a taxi.'

She made her way, with some difficulty, across the concourse. The smell of London seemed to wow Reginald, if its skyline did not, and animated him to a frenzy of sniffing. It took some persuasion to steer him to the taxi queue.

The hat-tipping horse and his lady were in front of Effie.

'Ah, Miss Fairy Palace. I'm sorry,' he nodded at her encumbrances. 'I do wish that I could have helped.'

'I made it. Little thanks to rotten Reginald. I have never seen him so vivacious.'

'Indeed.' They looked down at the small brown dog, who was now absorbed in olfactory examination of the gutter. 'Vivacious.'

The hat-tipper initiated introductions. 'I'm Henry. Henry Lyle. And this is Kate.' Kate had fine features and a collar trimmed with black felt flowers.

'Effie Shaw.'

She offered them one of Laurie's crystallised violets.

'So are you and your vivacious companion travelling far, Effie Shaw?'

'We are bound for the Continent,' said Effie, feeling like a girl who was getting out more, 'for Ypres and then on to Paris.'

'Splendid,' said Henry Lyle. 'The Boulogne boat?'

'Yes.'

'How fortuitous. We are fellow mariners. Perhaps we might share a taxi across town?'

Effie looked to the quiet but smiling Kate. 'Would you mind?'

'I insist,' said Henry.

'Do you always answer for your wife?' asked Effie, and then worried that her curiosity might sound like impertinence.

'My *wife*?' Henry laughed. 'What a notion! No, but I do sometimes answer for my *sister*, because she is shy.' He stroked the back of Kate's hand.

'Your sister struggles to get a word in edgeways,' said Kate, and took his hand in hers. 'It might be nice to hear a voice other than Henry's. It will be a pleasure to travel with you, Miss Shaw.'

'And vivacious Reginald,' added Henry, lighting a cigarette. The queue moved forwards.

'Did you know that the tower of your fairy palace is based on the Cloth Hall at Ypres?' He nodded back at the station. 'Only it's different now.' Something solemn momentarily rearranged Henry's features.

'Do you have an interest in architecture?' asked Effie.

'It's more that I collect frivolous facts, I'm afraid. Don't expect me to know anything useful.'

Effie wondered what she knew about. 'I collect old cookery

books. I've an *Experienced English Housekeeper* from 1769. I know a lot about baking,' she considered aloud. 'I am quite an authority on cake.'

'Now that *is* useful knowledge. There is nothing trivial about cake. I am partial to a well-constructed scone. Am I not, Katie?'

Kate's nod affirmed Henry's partialities.

'I am not sure how useful it is now. My usefulness might have lapsed. I am, shall we say, between positions.'

'Nonsense. The world needs decorative women who can bake. We have fought wars for lesser things. Be certain of your usefulness, Miss Shaw.'

They moved to the front of the queue. Henry insisted on loading their combined luggage into the cab.

'I am exhibiting chivalry,' he said. 'Please do feel free to observe and pass positive comment.'

Effie observed the lurch in Henry's movements. He pitched on his hinges like a toy soldier.

'Have you had a fall, Mr Lyle?' she enquired.

'Something of the sort.' Henry looked down and tapped his toes together. 'I'm somewhat askew, you see. Asymmetrical, as it were. Old leftie was last sighted in a casualty clearing station, approximately twelve years ago. I like to think that perhaps he hopped off somewhere and is happily-ever-aftering with a nice lady leg. Though, at our last convening, it has to be said that he wasn't looking too lively.'

Effie suddenly realised that her hands were over her mouth.

'Oh, heavens. I'm sorry,' said Henry. 'I default to flippancy. I haven't offended you, have I?'

'*You* offended *me*?' Effie stared at Henry's shoes. 'What an insensitive idiot I am.'

'And now I've embarrassed you.' He lowered his eyes to her level and wrinkled his nose. 'There are compensations, you know. I can play spoons on this new one. It's of a rather more musical disposition than my late lamented lower limb. I do the percussion part along to the radiogram. It drives poor Katie quite spare.'

'Clatter, clatter, clatter… It's insufferable. The word 'compensation' is a lie,' confirmed Kate.

It was rather cramped in the taxi cab. Effie wondered if this proximity was quite proper, given the newness of their acquaintance. Her leg somehow seemed to find itself pinned against Henry's. Should she say something? What was the polite convention? She tried to look out of the window, to see the shops and traffic and crowds, but could concentrate on little but the pressure of Henry's prosthetic leg. She stretched clumsily for distracting conversation.

'So were you there, then? In Ypres, I mean.'

'I was, but in 1915. I was there before the worst of it. It was still almost intact then. There were still bars and bun shops.' Henry looked away. He seemed to be studying the door panelling. 'Why are you travelling there, exactly?'

'My fiancé is there. He was there in 1917. I suppose that was the very worst of it. Joe is buried there,' she clarified.

'I am sorry.'

'Oh, don't be. There's just so much to be sorry for, isn't there?'

'There is.' Henry nodded.

Effie watched the meter roll.

They decided to take tea while they waited for the train.

'It's his nerves,' said Kate, as Henry went to find a waiter. 'He can't cope with silence. He has to fill the spaces.'

'He fills them very nicely,' offered Effie.

Kate smiled and Effie suspected that she was probably glad to let Henry fill the silences.

'I spent ten years as a housekeeper, as a companion, to a man that came back.' She hoped that that didn't sound indecent. 'It's Captain Greene who insisted that I take this journey, actually.' It seemed odd to explain the relationship to a stranger, especially now when she herself was no longer certain what their relationship had been.

'He died?' Kate asked hesitantly.

'Yes,' said Effie. 'Gas.'

'My husband didn't come back. That's why we make this journey. We go back every year. Henry is extremely patient with me. I want to see the cemetery finished.' There was a catch in Kate's voice. She was very small and blonde and slight; she looked like something that might break easily. But Effie also heard a determination in the tone of her last sentence.

'I am sorry.'

Kate shook her head. 'Now we have all apologised to each other and we are equal.' She laid her hands flat on the table top, as if to indicate the thing done.

Effie studied Kate from across the train carriage. She had fallen asleep hugging a crocodile-skin vanity case to her chest. There was something serene about her sleeping features.

'Your sister is very lovely,' said Effie, analysing at an angle. 'She's gauzy and fragile, like a butterfly, or a lady in a Pre-Raphaelite painting. Like Ophelia.'

'Isn't Ophelia usually dead?'

'Not always.'

'She's surprisingly strong. I sometimes think that I am the weak one.'

'You don't look weak.' She gave him a quick top-to-toe inspection. His shoes were well polished and the angle of his jawline gave him a dependable appearance. 'In fact, you look positively solid. You look like good soldierly stock.'

Henry smiled; he never seemed to be far from a smile. 'I

wanted to be a soldier, you know. I couldn't wait to sign up, to have a uniform and a purpose and be away from my humdrum life. And I'll confess that there were parts of it that I enjoyed. Not this, though.' He knocked a knuckle on his shin and gave her a sidelong look. 'Somme,' he said.

'My brother, Edward, is there. I probably ought to visit him too.'

'If you mean to look for his grave, I could help you.' There was a keen upwards curl at the end of this sentence that didn't quite suit the subject.

'That's very kind. It's curious, though: although Edward is there, bodily there, it's never felt as if he's far away from us. He doesn't feel distantly absent. Whereas Joe has always felt to be a long way away.'

Edward had been comical and kind. He collected cigarette cards and sentimental songs. Effie recalled his white-toothed grin, his smell of peppermints and the texture of his brotherly shoulder. Sometimes when she thought of Edward she still saw him as a ten-year-old boy walking down Jubilee Street, trying to catch a snowflake in his mouth, and then waving as he saw her at the upstairs window. Edward had never looked like soldierly stock.

'Kate wanted Patrick, her husband, brought back. She wrote letters at first. She held hopes, but, well, she contents herself with these pilgrimages now.'

'And you? Is it odd to go back there?'

'Patrick and I were in the same battalion. I have a lot of old friends in the same cemetery. It's not easy to go back, but I do like to pay my respects.'

At a loss to come up with an adequate reply, Effie watched the south coast be picturesque. There were pale lengths of beach, bleached dunes and white cliffs.

'So, given that my sister is Ophelia, I take it that you're

partial to art?'

She smiled at him for steering the conversation back to happier matters. 'Laurie liked to go to exhibitions. And I liked to go with him. He made up stories about the paintings.'

They had been to see the Millais and Holman Hunts in Manchester last summer. Laurie liked the sin and salvation; Effie liked the curves and the cobalt blue. A band was playing on the street outside, she remembered. Muffled brass had intruded with *Land of Hope and Glory* and Laurie objected. She hadn't understood why it was quite so objectionable, but Laurie explained that it detracted from the allegories and, because Laurie knew about such things, she nodded. She'd bought a souvenir postcard of *The Light of the World*. Effie recalled that Laurie's eyes were the same colour as Holman Hunt's supernatural sky.

'I suspect that you must miss him.'

'Yes,' she said. 'I suspect that I do.'

She missed his presiding with the teapot. She missed the beat of the gramophone from the floor above. She missed the smell of his shirts as she pressed them. She missed noticing the colour of his eyes as she looked up from a book. Did she still miss Joe? It had been eleven years since he had died and she was accustomed to his absence. Travelling towards him now, Effie realised that her memory of Joe had somehow become blurred. All of his details (his habits, his sound, his smell) seemed to have lost their definition. What precise colour were Joe's eyes? Effie turned her everlasting engagement ring.

'Are you married?' she asked Henry, and then found herself sounding over-familiar.

'Steady on! You're a quick worker,' he laughed. 'Oh, don't blush. I'm only teasing. I live with my sister. We live in Harrogate. I've probably given poor old Kate rather a lot to put up with.'

'Laurie used to go to an auction house in Harrogate,' she recalled. 'Perhaps you know it? He took me once and we had a very nice afternoon tea.'

Henry talked of Canton and Willow Ware, of engravings and etchings, of fondant icing, meringues and macaroons. She enjoyed the sing-song sound of his voice and his apparent appreciation of *petits fours*. He gesticulated as he talked and Effie watched his fingers flit. They were capable hands, she noticed – the sort of hands that might know what to do with broken clocks or crockery. His nails were very neat. He apologised, stopping suddenly, his hands stilling, and said that he had nothing of significance to say, that he could only converse in trivialities.

'I'm not at all averse to triviality,' she said. 'It's a relief, really. Life has been rather heavy recently.'

'I am sorry to hear that. My levity is at your disposal, you know. Is there any way in which I might assist?'

She looked down at her own fingers, which danced patterns around the brim of her hat. She looked up to the hat box on the luggage rack and then to Reginald who was asleep at her side. There was something that Henry could maybe help with.

'I have a concern about Reginald.'

'Reginald looks perfectly robust to me, though perhaps less vivacious now that he's parted from the gaiety of London.'

'It's how I get him across the channel. Quarantine, you see.'

'Ah, I had wondered. You don't intend to declare him, then, I take it?'

'He might pine,' proposed Effie uncertainly. Reginald hadn't yet shown much inclination to pine, but it remained a pressing possibility. 'It might kill him. I couldn't live with that.' She bit her lip. 'I have a plan.'

'And could I assist you in its execution?'

'I'd hate to implicate you, though I'm sure that you would

make a good accomplice.' Her gaze flicked appraisingly between Henry's dependable jaw and laughing eyes. 'It is a bit criminal.'

Henry seemed to brighten at criminal. In fact he positively sparkled. 'I do like a bit of mischief.'

'Yes, I imagine you do.' Effie imagined that Henry might like mischief rather too much. 'I could go to jail for this. You could go to jail for this. If we end up in the dock, I'll say that I lured you into it.'

'Luring, eh? Splendid. Lure away.'

She lured Henry to the lavatory compartment, along with Reginald and the hat box. Unlike Reginald, Henry didn't take very much luring.

Effie concentrated on the smell of bleach and suppressed an urge to laugh. She composed herself by contemplating the potential consequences. 'Reginald doesn't do much. He's not a do-er of a dog, but I do fear that, if this goes wrong, he'll un-do me.'

They had conducted a trial run in the back bedroom. Reginald had raised no ethical objections to his role as smuggled goods, but the box did issue a suspect snuffling.

'I wish I could sedate him.' The obliging Reginald blinked up at her with mildly inquisitive eyes and then continued to examine the lavatory.

'I have a hip flask,' offered Henry. 'Would he take a tot of brandy?'

'He's liverish,' said Effie. 'I try to keep him off spirits.'

'Well, how about one of my pills? They're nothing knockout, only herbal. I just have trouble sleeping sometimes.'

Henry fumbled in a pocket and produced a box. It was enamelled with the convincingly innocent motto: *A Keepsake from Salisbury Cathedral*. Effie examined the pills within. 'Happen just a half.'

Remembering the caramel that conveniently lingered at the

bottom of her handbag, she began working it to the required texture with her teeth. As she concentrated on chewing, Effie realised that Henry was staring at her. He smirked. Effie liked the lines that appeared around his mouth when he smirked.

'This is a bit odd,' he observed, 'isn't it?'

'Do you think?' It was difficult to smile with glued gums. 'I do this sort of thing all the time.'

They decided to proceed with caution and a quarter of pink pill was encased in caramel. Reginald, after an experimental sniff, swallowed cooperatively.

'I do hope it doesn't kill him,' said Effie. 'I am very fond of him, you know.'

Reginald, seemingly reckless in the face of risk, looked up in hope of another sugar-coated sedative. Henry's herbal medication appeared to have had little immediate impact.

'Do you think we could have risked a half?'

The train lurched and they staggered together. 'Golly,' said Effie, suddenly finding Henry's hands on her shoulders. 'Crikey,' he replied. They stepped apart with apologies.

Reginald, duly drugged, was placed in the hat box. He sniffed, shuffled and looked amenable to the idea of sleep.

Effie leaned back against the door and laughed. 'I am sedating dogs in lavatories with strange men.'

'Less of the strange,' Henry grinned. 'I thought you did this sort of thing all the time?'

Effie glanced guiltily up and down the corridor as they, and the now snoring hat box, vacated the lavatory.

'Is the stowaway sorted?' asked Kate.

Henry winked at his sister. 'Katie has contraband of her own.'

She nodded and Effie was admitted to the secret.

Henry took down the vanity case from the overhead rack and

showed Effie its contents. A sapling grew inside.

'From the garden,' said Kate. 'We have a bench under the plum tree. Patrick used to sit there with his pipe. I'd like a tree to grow by the side of his grave. This is the third time that I've brought one over. They weed them out, it being contrary to uniformity, it not conforming to the architect's plans. I know why it's wrong; I know why they don't want it. But I care more for him than I do for democracy or symmetry.'

'She takes a souvenir handful of soil home in return,' said Henry.

'You probably think I'm unsound,' smiled Kate.

'Not at all,' said Effie.

'So, you see, we are all miscreants.' Henry concluded in a stage whisper.

The train travelled up the pier, jutting out into the blue. They stood up at the window and remarked on the boarding houses and bathers and ice-cream carts. They agreed it appealing.

Effie flattened her hand against the cool of the glass.

'You're scared?' Kate asked.

'Yes,' said Effie. Joe had made the same crossing in February 1916. She'd just read Laurie's account of it and wondered if Joe had felt the same sensation. Did he too feel the fear that Laurie couldn't quite admit to? 'I'm scared of what I'm going to find,' she confessed.

The turbine steamer had white funnels and jolly flags. They looked back at retreating England with its fishing boats and Victoria Pier and pleasant seaside untidiness. A lot of the passengers wore black. Aside from a pleasure garden pedalo, Effie had never been on a boat before and her anxiety was compounded by the contents of the hat box, which occasionally shifted and groaned.

'I'd better sit on the deck.'

Henry back-and-forthed between her and Kate, who feared to catch a chill. Effie put her face into the sharp, saline wind. She squinted at the shimmer of the sea and felt acutely alive.

As Henry chattered, bright and positive and noisy, Effie started to think about Joe, who was silent and distant and dead. She tried to remember Joe's face, but all she could visualise was his photograph. She tried to remember Joe's voice, but realised that all she had was the shape of his words and not their sound. She couldn't remember the texture of his touch.

'It's a splendid day for it,' said Henry.

She searched the skyline for a hint of France. Laurie had given her a book of Cezanne landscapes, so she expected France to arrive in ochre and vermillion and vibrating greens. She wanted it to arrive and feared its arrival. She feared what France contained. Most immediately, though, she feared that France contained prying customs officials.

It was early evening by the time they docked in Boulogne. The lights were just coming on. It wasn't the colours of Cezanne, but Effie was pleased to find it quietly genteel. There were red-sailed fishing boats and a smart white boulevard. The cathedral was a sharp shape against the sky. Gulls cawed and curved.

'It's charming,' said Effie.

'All the king's horses and all the king's men shall not get me back to France again.'

Effie looked at Henry, unsmiling in profile, and suddenly wanted to take his hand.

'I know,' she said.

'Are you travelling on to Ypres tonight?'

'No, I have a reservation in Boulogne.'

'I shall be sorry to say goodbye to you, Fairy Palace.'

'Perhaps it might be *au revoir*?'

'Do you have an address in Paris?'

'Not as yet. Laurie is being cryptic. I may well know tomorrow. I could forward it on to your hotel?' offered Effie, and then wondered if she was being forward.

'I should like that,' said Henry. 'I've enjoyed being your criminal accomplice.'

She felt a flutter of fear as they walked past the customs officer. She suppressed the instinct to run by forcing herself to imagine what sensations Joe had faced as he disembarked here.

Henry had volunteered to carry the culpable hat box, but she would not have him that far implicated.

'Lured,' he hissed mischievously.

Effie made wide remonstrative eyes.

'You must get your sister to the station.'

'But I'm worried about you. I'm worried about Reginald. You'll have to hook another feller to drug him on the return trip.'

'Henry, go.'

'You will send me that address, won't you?'

'I will.' She smiled. 'Thank you.'

The Hotel Windsor smelled of simmered sauces undercut with the familiar yeastiness of baking. Effie was too tired to eat. Her room had nice linen but no view. She opened the window and listened to the sigh of the unseen sea.

Reginald staggered woozily from the box. Effie offered him a sausage, which she had earlier secreted in a napkin. Laurie and Joe, silver framed, looked out from the top of her suitcase. She arranged them on the bedside table.

With two wounded soldiers aligned at her side, Effie decided it might be excessive to encourage the attentions of a third. She resolved that she would contact Henry only in the event of requiring emergency frivolity. Looking at Laurie's photograph face made emergencies seem unlikely. But, then, Laurie was no longer there. She would never again look up and see his face by the fireside. That realisation, in itself, suddenly felt like an emergency. She slipped Henry's address inside the cover of *Jude* and wondered what rules applied in a world that no longer contained Laurie.

Chapter Eleven

February, 1916

'There's a Manet painting of the beach at Boulogne,' said Laurence, 'with bathing huts and donkeys and dainty-ankled mademoiselles carrying white parasols. The sea is a perfectly wet aquamarine and the sand is the colour of sunshine.'

'Do I take it that it's failing to match up to Manet?'

'I just somehow expected more from my first footsteps on foreign soil.'

The weather had closed in by the time that they had docked. The basilica split the mist. Boulogne was tones of grey and cold and they had called it a poor comparison to the gentility that was Morecambe. The quay was all shouting and heavy movement. Sacks of oats were swinging from cranes, a chain of Chinese labourers were passing crated provisions, barrels rumbled along the cobbles and great springs of barbed wire were rolling.

Allocated a few hours leisure, they walked away from the noisy dockside and now found themselves critically assessing an extent of sand.

'Not so much as a thick-ankled matron,' said Atherton.

Their running footsteps accelerated down the not quite sunshine-coloured beach. Allerton made his name in the sand, in ten-foot-high letters, and announced himself to France. The tide frothed it over.

'We're here,' Laurence said.

'Or not,' said Allerton, as a wave erased his name.

They travelled inland by train as far as St Omer and then marched for two days towards the war. Laurence's head filled with songs, worked to the beat of their marching feet. The tempo propelled them with some hypnotic compulsion, made a momentum and one soldierly being of them. Laurence was conscious, as he marched, that he was leaving something of himself behind.

'Are we downhearted? No!' they sang. *'Not while Britannia rules the waves. Not likely!'*

They progressed along poplar-lined roads. Farmers moved antique-looking agricultural implements through the either-side fields. There were ox carts, orchards, water wheels, rabbit hutches, shrines and roadside calvaries. The region seemed to be keen on gibbetting Christ on crossroads. Laurence didn't find it an encouraging thing to see. It did little for his officerly confidence. His passion in painted wood seemed too mortally immediate.

The roads became worse as they moved further east. The ruts broke their rhythm and sent them stumbling, broke the incantation and gave them suddenly sore feet and aching backs. Packs gathered weight with the lost momentum. They paused in a side lane and smoked. Some fools took off their boots. They stared at the ditch; there were primroses, celandines and a stack of brownly rusting hand grenades. Laurence was reminded of the unintelligible objects that he'd once seen pulled from an archaeological dig.

The people of the towns didn't acknowledge them. There were no garlands or crowds. It wasn't quite like it had been in the newsreels. There were just shifting curtains and sideways glances. They lamented a want of welcome from girls in white dresses.

'This is a rum deal,' said Frank Fitton. 'I have been short-changed for my heroics.'

'Happen they want the heroics up front,' suggested Edward Shaw.

'Aye, well, happen I'd like to glimpse the goods before I wager my heroic arse.'

Only the stray dogs paid them any heed.

Laurence bedded down with the men in a barn. The names and dates of other regiments were recorded on the walls. They made makeshift mattresses, encasing the sharp straw in ground sheets and rolled together for the warmth. An old woman, wearing wooden clogs and a moustache that could well have graced a general, set jugs of coffee down on an iron stove. The barn filled up with smoke and Laurence's eyes smarted. Week-old copies of the *Daily Mail* were passed around, telling them that the spirit of the troops was excellent.

Younger Young carved a note on his fiddle and a barn full of men was his. He weaved it up to a melody, his foot working the beat. They clapped on the rhythm and willed it familiar. They looped and larked to *The Dashing White Sergeant* – and the tune and the laughter were everything.

Frank Fitton collapsed, panting at the roof beams. 'I'm doing my bit for the *Daily Mail*,' he grinned.

The roof above Laurence was more sky than tile. Stars slid across the spaces.

They proceeded to trenches. They moved towards names that Laurence knew from the previous summer's newsprint. The road's curiosities sustained them for a while. They passed a mobile military bakery, belching steam and the sweetness of warm yeast, and a troop of Hindus crouched around braziers, bronze-faced like demigods. They wore beards and turbans and were smoking like their lives depended on it. The bronze warriors waved as they passed. There were abandoned automobiles by the sides of the road, cart wheels, handcarts, wheelbarrows, prams, split mattresses and a kitchen dresser. Laurence wondered who these things had belonged to, who had thought them precious enough to try to salvage, and then had thought again. Columns of men marched the other way, coming up out of the line. Laurence looked at the flow of faces.

'Trust you left the kettle on?' Jack Taylor shouted. They broke into welcome but uncertain laughter.

The sky flashed and quivered ahead. Occasionally there was a deep, heavy boom. They found themselves flinching and ducking and made a comedy of their shared anxieties. Then the whispered order came back: 'Single file. Absolute silence.' The comedy stopped. They advanced, all eyes, through communication trenches. Laurence was reminded of Morecambe Bay's exhibition trenches. It was not familiarity that jolted him into recall, but, rather, it was the gap between textbook and truth, the disparity between actuality and his expectations. It all looked rather more makeshift than he had expected; an amateur, improvised thing, with its wattle and hurdle where the corrugated iron ought to have been. It had a determinedly temporary air, a whimsical patchwork. In one stretch honeysuckle threatened to take over, tangling its claim. The walls of the trench became higher. A sign instructed them not to loiter.

'What a pity,' said Horrocks. 'And there was me in the mood for a nice loiter.'

Laurence's own innocence, his ignorance, his inexperience suddenly felt like a momentous thing that he must negotiate his way around. He tried to take it all in. He tried to maintain an assured tone. Was this why, then, they had started with *Henry V*? Light slammed in the sky ahead and again that resonant roar. Rockets shrieked and showered red and green. Laurence found his acting skills to be much tested.

It was dark by the time that they assumed their position. They were hidden in the black but for the congregated fairy lights of fag ends. Rations came up and they ate out of mess tins. It tasted of old campaigns, of proper soldiering. Laurence was ordered to a listening post and invited to peer forward into No Man's Land through a periscope. Magnesium flares lit a dainty picket fence of wire and corkscrew. It was El Greco's world of ghastly light.

The enemy line was three-hundred yards beyond. He felt heavy in his flesh and wet boots. He could feel his nerves vibrate. His nerves felt close to the surface. He wasn't sure how he would sleep.

Allerton sidled to his side. His face, in the trench-light, was bones and flashing whites of eyes. 'It's cushy enough,' he lied.

'Your acting is as lousy as mine,' whispered Laurence.

Chapter Twelve

Northern France, 1928

As her journey turned inland the landscape became flat and Flemish. There was something foreign in the pitch of the orange roofs, the gables and shutters, in the fold of the fields, in the pale light. There was a lot of cornflower blue, soft yellow, a shimmering grey and wide skies. Effie tried to imagine them marching across this same landscape.

She sat with Joe's letters on her lap. They were tied with a ribbon and, at the top of the pile, was a copy of the same photograph that she kept by her bedside. She brought Joe's photograph face close to her own. His image was the last thing that she saw each night. For the past ten years she had said a prayer for him before she switched off the light, her eye flitting over the shape of a soldier to whom she had once made promises. Her eyes opened onto him each morning but, she realised, she hadn't actually *looked* at him for a long time. In scrutinising his face thus, in dissecting its familiar whole into unfamiliar parts, she unmade and re-made him and saw him anew. Joe had a reliable face. Steady eyes. A sensible mouth. He looked like a breadwinner, like a safe bet.

He had said they should be married. That way she would have got twelve shillings per week for life. It didn't seem the right reason. She carved her initials in the window's condensation. Would she feel different now if the last letter was his? France sliced through her wet, bright letters and, refocusing, she saw her own misted face moving over it. Today she had dressed in black and with more care than she was accustomed to take. The woman reflected in the glass looked like a widow.

She pulled the ribbon on Joe's letters. She had kept them in chronological order. Holding the first envelope, she tried to recall the sentences contained within. His envelopes had always felt light, she remembered. He wrote on thin notepaper – the sort of paper that slips through fingers and inclines to flutter away. It was always the paper with the grey ruled lines. There had been a time when his words still managed to balance on the line. His handwriting shook apart over the course of 1917, which perhaps wasn't so surprising given the facts it communicated. He had been gassed three times and wounded twice over the course of the year. She counted it out on her fingers and then tried to remember how she had replied. In the September they had sent him to Étaples for re-inculcating with offensive spirit. He'd told her how, at the training ground, he'd had to practise being gassed. It had surprised Effie that being gassed required rehearsal and that Joe hadn't already had enough goes at it. There were only a couple more letters after that. She knew that he had gone back into the line after, north of Ypres, and then, in the November, was dead.

At first, back then, she had cried for the right to be able to stand at his graveside. Now, as she moved towards that marker, she wasn't sure how she would feel, what emotions his name in stone would incite. She wished that she had brought him some palmiers. She smiled at the sentimentality of an imagined gesture, at an image of herself smiling appropriately.

Effie tried to re-find Joe in his words, to conjure him up as she could Laurie, to see his lips speak his sentences, but he was too distant. He wasn't quite there in his letters. She couldn't find his voice. She felt guilt for it.

Chapter Thirteen

February, 1916

They were attached, for instruction, to the 14th Welsh. Laurence had been told that they were to learn the latest methods of making war. However, they were presently chiefly occupied with housekeeping. The trench was called Saville Row and it stank.

'Horrocks has composed a poem that rhymes 'excreta' with 'fleas-ier', Laurence told Rushton. 'He was giving a recitation. They all applauded.'

'Can you put a man on a charge for crimes against rhyme?'

'Alas, I suspect not – nor can I contend the verse's documentary content.'

This trench was full of other people's rubbish. Laurence wondered who the men had been that left so much of themselves behind. The duckboards, in stretches, had gone through. Water stagnated rattily beneath. They bailed out with biscuit tins, dyked, diverted and patched as best they could.

'I feel like a sailor on a sinking ship,' said Edward Shaw.

The earth didn't have the old smell of English earth, the black-sour smell of prehistory, but reeked of too new rotten things. They burned incense, liberated from a church behind the lines. It made them cough briefly and then was gone.

'The Holy Ghost might smell sweet, but the bugger doesn't seem inclined to linger,' said Fitton.

'Happen he's not daft,' theologised Billy Rigby.

There was something epic about these old trenches – something timeless and venerable and awful. It felt like camping out in a graveyard.

Morning rolled in. Laurence watched it arrive through a frame of barbed wire. Mist wreathed the in-between. He thought about ancient campaigning, about Charlemagne and Alexander, about antique battlefields that he'd read about in books. The wire ahead dripped. The trenches steamed. He stretched in the numbing cold, yawned and tried to stamp life into his legs. His fingers ached. Rushton said there would be snow within the week. Blue smoke rose from the enemy line, bleeding through the mist like watercolour.

'The bloody bastards were bloody wild last night,' said Sergeant Thorpe.

'It made more noise than damage,' replied Laurence, trying to exhibit more officerly pluck than he had felt at the time. Trench mortars, he had noted in his diary, arrived in slow crackling arcs. He had also noted that his heart beat so fast that he thought it might burst. He shrugged and offered Thorpe a cigarette.

Younger Young was at his shoulder. 'Is it true that their dug-outs have curtains and carpets – that they have electric light and wallpaper?' He sniffed. 'I know that the sods have sausages.'

'I'd kill for a sausage,' said Edward Shaw. He was practising his one-handed shuffle. The deck of cards tilted through his fingers. The cards slipped and spilled, falling to tell their fortune on the clay-slicked duckboards.

Fitton was watching a dog-fight above, making a romance of it with commentary. He twirled a matchstick at the corner of his mouth, his tongue flicking along his teeth. Volunteering a gypsy grandmother, he looked down and read the cards.

'A tall, dark, handsome stranger is coming your way,' he said. 'You'll be a bride by Christmas.'

'If he'll throw in a barrel of beer, I'm his.'

'Too bloody right. Have you seen this?' Horrocks was unwrapping a bottle from a parcel. 'Ruddy nerve tonic. *Provides the exceptional nerve force and vigour needed for hazardous duties in the battle zone,'* he quoted. 'I can think of other ways in which she might have gone about invigorating me. A bottle of whisky might not have been a bad start.'

Shaw, cards retrieved, walked away. His feet left prints in the clay. Laurence wondered, briefly, if it were all to fall in, whether they would be found one day, like seashells in split limestone.

Old Young was shaving. His eyes shifted in a strip of mirror. He meant to pose in gallant profile for Euphemia Shaw, and, via Laurence's hand, to send himself home.

'I will wed her, you know.' He nodded at the photograph face that was wedged in the frame of his shaving glass. 'I'll do it proper. I'll let her have daisies and lace.'

'You are engaged.' Laurence tried to take a superior-rank tone. 'It is the common courtesy.'

She was tinted in pretty pastels – pink cheeks and blue eyes and a sweetheart smile. Laurence felt her breath on his face, a locket's length away, saw her lips speak a silent sentence, and blinked in mud and metal.

'You wouldn't say 'No,' would you?' Younger Young's eyes, grinning in ignorance, were on Laurence's.

'No,' he replied.

Chapter Fourteen

Effie looked out at passing-by Pas-de-Calais and tried to picture it as a battlefield. Even in peacetime, it was not a soft landscape. Sharp verticals (belfries and windmills and lighthouses) surged upwards as if to compensate for the land's lack of gradient. The land itself was crosshatched with hedges and roads and waterways. The sea cut into the land and Effie tried to imagine it cut with trenches.

Joe's mother had kept his room ready in the hope that he would return. She continued to light the lamp every night, until she held the safety razor that had been sent back without its owner. Then, knowing him truly gone, feeling it in the flatness of this dispossessed possession, she had ended her own life. Even back then Effie couldn't comprehend the intensity of that emotion. Even then she couldn't imagine choosing to stop. She couldn't draw a line through hope.

The train passed through place names that she remembered from newsprint. She had imagined all of the places much bigger. They seemed very ordinary and very small, these headline towns. Rushing past in astonishing seconds, they seemed much less significant than they somehow ought to be. She didn't recognise the names of most of the locations in Laurie's diary, but then, he rarely seemed to have much idea of where he was or quite why. *I feel like flotsam*, he had written, *propelled by an unintelligible tide. But I do fear where that tide is taking us. And I am afraid of being afraid.*

She was all eyes for Poperinghe, which she knew from Joe's letters. It was after that she began to see the small clusters of crosses and then the great white expanses of stone slabs. Effie thought about flotsam and tides and fright. She shut her eyes.

In her girlhood, Ypres was to be found in the haberdashery

department: it was lace, ribbons and printed cottons. Edward had sent their mother a silk handkerchief edged with Flemish fancywork. But then, somewhere around the time of the silk handkerchief, it had changed and Ypres was suddenly synonymous with gas, mud and frightfulness. As the train pulled in, Effie struggled to stitch together her fragments of association. She surveyed the town from the station steps. Her imaginings had been many and various, but she had never pictured Ypres quite like this. It wasn't haberdashery or muddy battleground. Rather, Ypres appeared to be a building site. She saw cranes, stacked stone and a great deal of scaffolding. There were skips and immense iron girders. Laurie had told her that Ypres was all ruin at the end and they had proposed to leave it as such in eloquent memorial, as a symbol of sacrifice. She supposed they had subsequently decided otherwise. Ypres was busy being reborn.

A stall at the bottom of the steps was trimmed with flags and arrayed to catch the eye of tourists. Effie stared. Shell cases had been worked into ink wells, ash trays and napkin rings. They were engraved, embossed, given appliqué work and floridly lettered with the slogan *Souvenir of Ypres*. There were bowls of salvaged regimental buttons (fifty-centime keepsakes for the budget-conscious vacationer) and a tray of jewellery items that appeared to have been enterprisingly recycled from all manner of polished-up military metal. Effie wondered what face a sweetheart ought to assume was she to be gifted bullet earrings or a bully-beef bracelet. She decided that she would probably run rapidly in the opposite direction. There were crucifixes formed from cartridge cases and a monumental dinner gong that seemed to have been fabricated from a particularly nasty-looking lump of ammunition. What variety of person might wish to be summoned to table by such a monstrosity? The man behind the stall had no legs and a sign that said *No pension*.

'Day trip to Tyne Cot, Miss?'

She turned. A hand containing a flier was extending towards her, and then hands and voices were surrounding her, all selling their services. There was cheap but clean hotel accommodation, guided motor tours of the Salient and a circus performance with a high-wire act, two clowns and a tiger. Effie shook her head and pushed through the crowd.

'*Bonnes vacances!*' the cheery voice of the day-trip man called out.

As she walked towards the centre she tried to see Ypres as they might have seen it. She made it charred and ragged again, spilled stone and tile, blasted it back to ruin and jagged gothic spires. A horse and cart trundled past, selling ice-cream wafers. Ypres insisted its resurgence.

Despite the encumbrance of suitcase, hat box and dog, and the challenge of new-laid cobbles, Effie decided to make a detour.

'You must see the Menin Gate,' Henry had said.

She and Laurie had read about the unveiling in the newspapers last summer, how the structure had proved too small to contain the names of all those who had no graves, about the long procession of bereaved and the black flags. They'd listened to the service of dedication on the B.B.C. She'd watched Laurie's face as the Last Post crackled out.

Effie stood, as instructed, below the arching white. She looked up and the letters blurred, became just a pattern and then nothing. It was incomprehensible. It dizzied her.

'When they find them, they chisel away the name,' Henry had said. She wondered if one day they would all be found and chiselled out, but couldn't imagine how. There were an awful lot of names.

Chapter Fifteen

February, 1916

They came out of trenches in the early morning and marched eight miles into peace. The unfolding leaves of the overhead branches had a new beauty. Civilian sounds enchanted Laurence's ears: female laughter, a dog's bark, a blacksmith's hammer. There were painted railings and rows of cabbages. They passed orchards and curtained windows, garden gates and gooseberry bushes. It seemed abstractly colourful. Their apprenticeship was done.

They were billeted on a farm. The barns, which became their barracks, still had the ripe green stink of cow. The men were told they were to be given bombing practice. Laurence thought that this locale looked like it had had rather a lot of experience of explosives. In the village, beyond, all of the angles were strangely askew. The Bombing Officer showed them cross-section diagrams of Mills bombs and talked about bowling actions.

There were bodies in the wood behind the farm and violets. They were tasked with moving the old dead out. Laurence handed out rubber gloves and a rum ration. As his foot found the brittle parallels of a ribcage he wished that he'd taken a swig from the rum jar himself. He looked down to see shrunk-back lips that thrust a smile. The body shrugged into dust as he dragged it back. It was light and dead as kindling. It was only mud that had preserved the relativity of bones. *Take thy rest,* he pencilled onto a crude cross, at a loss to come up with anything weightier. They threw branches into the shallow graves and took their hats off. No tree was entirely whole in the wood. It needed no wolves or witches.

They bartered tinned rations with the few locals that clung on. In return, filthy children pestered them in pidgin English, selling lace handkerchiefs, fingered chocolate and their sisters. There was no pretence of welcome and it wasn't sought. There was rumour of collaborative signalling, of conspiracy spoken in plough patterns and smoke signals, in the hands of clocks and windmills, in white washing and white mares. The men were fitted out with fur coats and waterproof capes. They played mouth-organs and tin-whistles and sang *I Want to go Home*. The officers played cricket.

Laurence slunk away and sketched the orchard – the filigree of branches against a white sky, the tapering lines of trunks, the rooks and sharp shadows. It was perfectly silent. Autumn's apples rotted sweetly about his feet. He rubbed his hands. They were red with cold and raw where he had hotly gouged after lice. He watched the pencil tremble between his fingers. Concentration couldn't still it.

'The men call you Gertie Greene, you know,' Allerton said, suddenly scrutinizing at his side.

'Gertie?'

'Yes, dear. Short for Gertrude, I should imagine.'

'Why?'

'Probably because you're like a spinster on a watercolour holiday.'

'Oh.'

'Don't make that face. At least it's an affectionate insult.'

'I shan't be so indiscreet as to repeat what they call you.'

'Scandalous?'

'Slanderous.'

'Splendid.'

'It helps,' said Laurence. 'The drawing, I mean. It helps me to commit it to paper, to make a record. I feel lightened by it. I carry it here, not here.'

He pointed from the sketchpad to his head. The sketchpad recorded the smashed villages, the stuck-fast farmers, the card players and the busy horizon. It contained nightmares, imaginings and all of the images that he wished not to remember. There was already a lot that he meant to forget. Laurence used and re-used every scrap of paper and traded pencils for flattering portraits that were dispatched to wives, mothers and sweethearts. He imagined the enveloped progress of these smiles and smartness, saw them pass hand-to-hand across borders. Did the smiles alter with distance and passing, like a whispered lie? Did they brighten or fade? He could not picture their reception. The shavings from his pencil curled and fell.

'What you need, Lol, is a drink.'

Laurence shook his head. 'I think I need something more than a drink. I'm not sure I have the balls for this, Alex.' He gestured at the khaki crowd around the farmhouse. 'I'm not sure I have the mettle for it. I'm not convinced I can lead from the front. I don't know that I have it in me.'

The Corps Commander had addressed the men that morning. 'Each one of you, fighting men and fighting fit, is equal to three Germans,' he had said through a megaphone. Even with such assurances being shouted at him, Laurence feared he equated to three rather shoddy examples of German manhood.

'I don't suppose any of us know what we can do until it's tested.' Allerton patted Laurence's shoulder. 'My father named me after ruddy Alexander the Great. Do you know what it feels like to have that on your shoulders? I'm actually scared of horses.'

'Didn't you flunk Greek?'

'With some considerable enthusiasm.' Allerton laughed joylessly in recollection. 'Anyway, you'll be all right, I reckon.'

'Will I?'

Allerton nodded. He exhaled smoke and offered Laurence his hand. 'Come on. Allez up. Let us seek out the temptations of wine and women.'

The walls of the estaminet were papered with 1914's newsprint. *'Guerre!'* exclaimed a headline, as if it might otherwise have escaped their attention. Laurence deciphered diagrams of infantry movements over a plate of egg and chips. It looked like ancient history. The table top was sticky with spilled grenadine and grease.

'Is she not extraordinary?' Allerton's cutlery prodded at the proprietress. From the perspective of their table it looked as though Allerton might fork her, like a plump sausage.

From Laurence's angle this forked example of female form looked entirely ordinary. Furthermore, if subjected to Allerton's fork, he suspected that this particular sausage might spit. 'Suzanne?'

'There's something about grease-stained satin,' went on Allerton and smiled reflectively at the seemingly unfathomable something.

Suzanne, self-appointed Pride of Paree, presided over a cauldron of leaping fat. She had a fluent vocabulary of English obscenities and wilting wax flowers in her hair. They watched her from the far side of the room, in red-faced exchange over the chip pan. Suzanne advertised her daughter at fifty centimes.

'Have I given you my father's lecture about dirty foreign women? You've clearly been a soldier too long,' Laurence observed.

'And you a spinsterly watercolourist. Anyway, I thought shop girls were your thing. All of that winsome proletarian politeness and the titillating smell of small change?'

Laurence replied with a two-fingered salute.

'Here. Have you seen?' Allerton magicked a handful of postcards from his pocket. He fanned his hand of cards, revealing glimpses of *déshabillé demoiselles*. 'I swapped them with Harrison. They cost a large block of chocolate.'

'Not really attired for the climate, are they? What would I get for two bars of chocolate?'

'What you need requires more than two bars of chocolate.' Allerton shuffled his pack and produced a sepia view of Arras. 'Though I suspect that this might be more to Aunt Amelia's taste.' He carved a pencil to a point and set about slapdash salutations.

'What do you find to write?' asked Laurence, leaning to see.

'Heavens. Everything and nothing.' Allerton shrugged and dipped a chip in Laurence's egg. 'Assorted tawdry details of our soldierly domestication. And I ask for soap and cigarettes. An assiduous blend of suffering and well-wishing can be most conducive when applied to maiden aunts.' He licked the pencil and, eyes down, dashed off an aunt-enchanting sentence. Allerton's compositions – however conducive – never seemed to require much concentration. His handwriting, Laurence observed, was all loops. It was as unintelligible and beautiful as Islamic script. He wondered how Aunt Amelia might unravel it.

'I ought to send a letter. Only I struggle to know what to write home. There's only so many times I can say that I've got cold feet and the food is worse than Mrs Brown's.'

'You always seem to be writing. You forever seem to be in the middle of something.'

'Not letters, though. Not something to be sent. It's one thing to commit it to paper, but quite another to commit it to be read.'

'You are a queer bird,' said Allerton. He slipped the pencil behind his ear. There was a flamboyance to the movement that suggested he might have practised it in front of a mirror. 'You over-complicate everything. Just write it down: eating chips in France. Trying not to get shot. Still scared of girls. Love, Laurence.'

'I wish I had your gift for literature.'

Laurence watched the men flirting with the fast mademoiselles. He was thinking about sketching the transactions.

'Maybe I should buy you one.'

Allerton grinned his foxy grin. He looked the stuff of heroes, with his pomaded blond hair, blue eyes and the easy charm. There was a jay feather in his buttonhole, striped in the colour of June skies.

'I'll bet that your senior females all dote on you.'

'Don't start to pity the old girls. If I don't come home a general, they'll probably have me shot.'

'I shall just be glad to get home,' said Laurence.

'You should have joined a ballet troop, not the army.'

'My pirouettes weren't up to the mark.'

'No, there are advantages to this soldiering life,' reflected Allerton, dismissing pirouettes. He tried his best smile on the waitress and a *comment-allez-vous*. 'I find that I do enjoy the sightseeing opportunities it affords,' he said to her retreating backside. He stretched his legs and grinned ceiling-wards. 'I think I shall partake of some native hospitality. Will you join me in a diplomatic mission?'

'I might try to write that letter instead.' Laurence wiped bread around his plate.

'You have a bloody odd idea of a good time. It falls off if you don't use it, you know.'

Allerton whistled as they walked back from the village. Laurence sang along. He was just thinking how agreeable this was, to stroll along twilight lanes, sharing a bawdy melody with an old school chum, when their chorus gained an impromptu percussive accompaniment.

'Why the off-beat bastards!'

The farm where they were billeted was hit by a shell. Brick dust bloomed pinkly. They saw the shape of the barn crumple.

'Come on.'

There was a scuffle of men in the road. They pushed through

79

the crowd.

'Was anyone inside?' asked Laurence, in a voice that attempted to be authoritative.

'No, it's just this idiot that wants to be.'

The elder Young was holding back the struggling younger.

'I'm going in. I've got to get it.'

'Don't be a ruddy fool,' said Allerton. 'Unless 'it' is Mary Pickford in a bathing costume, you don't need to get it.'

'Charlie!'

Joseph lunged to stop his cousin, but he was gone. The blown-out doorframe swallowed him and suddenly flames were writhing at the rafters. Laurence followed Joseph as he ran towards the burning building, unsure of the extent of his officerly duty. He looked through the yellow flame, trying to discern a shape that might be Charlie. Heat now roared from within. His eyes were streaming as he stepped back. Laurence heard the roof slump, beams break and fire crack. And then Joseph was gone. Laurence looked to Allerton. It was a few seconds before he registered that the scream he could hear was coming from his own mouth.

Charlie plunged out, black faced and blaspheming, pursued by smoke and his cousin.

'You stupid bastard,' coughed Joseph. 'Of all of the fucking stupid things to get killed for.'

Charlie hugged his fiddle case. Joseph looked unsure whether to hit or hug him.

'It was grandad's.'

'Aye, and you nearly got to duet with him.' Joseph stared at Charlie. He held him square by the shoulders, suddenly earnest. 'I'm frightened for you. I'm frightened of losing you. Without you I'll be afraid.'

'Touching though this show of familial sentimentality is, you lost me when it wasn't Mary Pickford.' Allerton walked away shaking his head.

They watched the building burn, their packs and new fur coats and Euphemia's photograph smile within. The roof sighed as it sank. Smoke rolled. Laurence patted his pockets to find the reassuring rectangle of his watercolour box.

'We could put potatoes in the cinders,' said Charlie.

'Aye, and make treacle toffee.'

'It's not bleeding bonfire night,' said Billy Rigby.

Laurence tried to straighten out a crushed cigarette. He tried to look nonchalant as he offered Joseph the packet. He took one between black fingertips.

'Will you recommend him for a medal?' asked Charlie.

Laurence shook out the match and spluttered a laugh. 'You're bloody lucky I don't put you both on a charge.'

Chapter Sixteen

Ypres, 1928

The Hotel Univers was in a square that was architecturally as busy as Flemish lace. It was all fancywork, gables and spires. Grotesque gargoyles leered over the lintels of the hotel entrance. It was a relief to receive the straightforward smile of the receptionist within.

'We are newly equipped for dignitaries,' she advised Effie, in English that was evidently also newly polished, as she handed her the room key. 'And, Madame, there is a letter for you.'

Effie stared at the envelope. It was addressed in Laurie's handwriting. The postmark indicated that it had been sent six weeks previously. Effie thought about him in the estaminet, not knowing quite what to put in letters. Seemingly, six weeks ago, he had known rather more than she had. Could he really have been certain, as he addressed this envelope, that six weeks on he would be dead and she would be standing in a hotel reception in Ypres? She wondered how she had missed seeing it. But, then, there seemed to be rather a lot she had missed seeing.

She locked the door on Ypres. The hotel room was floral and smelled of new paint. She pushed back the shutters and let in the light. The leaves of a chestnut tree twisted away from the wind and there was the noise of a chisel striking stone. She left Reginald to examine their new quarters and opened Laurie's envelope.

So you made it, then? he said. *I knew you would, my resilient, resourceful Effie.*

She smiled at his familiar inflection.

This next bit is where it gets complicated, though. This next bit, I fear, you are not going to like.

She saw him turn the pen in discomfort. 'I know, Laurie. I know why I'm here.' She looked around at the complicatedly rosy walls and nodded at fear.

The next bit is going to hurt you, and I so don't want to hurt you. I have agonised over this decision. But, ultimately, truth is the only way, isn't it? On the attached paper you'll find directions to the cemetery. As to what you'll make of what you find there, well...

She saw Laurie shake his head. She didn't know what she was going to make of it.

I want you to read the diary that I left you. You need to understand what happened here. Though, you may well hate me by the end of it.

She frowned at the word 'hate' formed in Laurie's letters. She couldn't imagine circumstances in which she might ever hate him. She could not conceive of how she might align that emotion with Laurie's image. It did not fit.

You have to understand this. You have to understand why. Trust me, Effie. Stick with me. We've only just begun.

Chapter Seventeen

Pas-de-Calais, June, 1916

There were brigade sports in Béthune, before they were to move south as striking forces. There were races and wrestling and tug-of-war. At a concert party on the last night, Pierrots told them, through painted smiles, that they were winning.

They were in billets in Annezin when it began, in a room with chintz wallpaper and a girl's perfume bottles still on the dressing table. Laurence was sitting in the window seat, turning his new tin hat between his hands. He looked down on a brick-walled cottage garden, on lines of carrots and lettuces. Allerton was directing experimental brim angles at the cheval-glass. The dressing-table bottles began to rattle. It was a low booming resonance, a deep bass, which seemed to be vibrating the very fabric of the building. Their eyes connected in the mirror.

'Is that the sound of winning?' Laurence said.

Captain Clayton called it a 'hurricane' over the dinner table – an 'apocalypse' and a 'holocaust'. The enemy trenches would just be obliterated, he said. There would be havoc in the German lines. This was the beginning of the end. Laurence watched the wine in his glass tremble. Beyond the dining-room window, beyond the shuddering sash and the rooftops, a yellow haze hung in the sky. Laurence remembered that it was midsummer's day.

They entrained south into benignly rolling chalk downlands that put Laurence in mind of the landscape around Salisbury Plain. From the train he saw camps, supply depots, piles of spent shells and a valley filled with white hospital tents. They talked of advances, break-throughs and captures. The guns boomed and groaned. The horizon shimmered, like summer lightning. They were billeted in Neuvillette on the 1st July. In another girl's rosy bedroom, Allerton suddenly turned to Laurence. The landing clock struck the half hour. The artillery barrage had stopped.

'Is that it?'

They spent the day in a field, practising taking Ovillers-la-Boiselle in facsimile. They advanced as a line, past flagged markers and taped lines of attack, and swept towards the to-scale enemy trenches. A drummer beat a rhythm to replicate the bursting of shells.

'Steady walking pace.' Sergeant Thorpe instructed from the sidelines. 'Don't bunch! They'll pick you off like rabbits.'

An old woman moved between them, selling chocolate from a basket, as they lay down to give covering fire. She clapped politely as they rushed, overran and routed the Hun. They cheered as they stormed into the empty enemy line. They sang along to the drum-beat barrage.

It was evening before they got word of it. They were camped out on the trampled, well-won grass, opening letters that had just come up with the rations – envelopes full of larder hardships and cousins' marriages – and sharpening their bayonets. Strange colours bled skywards on the horizon. The edges of their ready blades glinted in the gathering dusk.

'A hundred-thousand Germans captured,' said Carver, arriving in a rush. 'A thousand guns taken. They've broken through along forty miles of the line.'

'You are about to play your part in the mightiest battle ever waged in the history of the world,' speechified Captain Clayton. His fingers plucked at buttercups.

'Steady on,' said Allerton.

'Whizz-bang!' said Shaw.

Laurence walked away from the speech making, towards the shadowed borders of the field. There were scabious and cornflowers in the margins and a smell of sweet cut grass. He could hear a blackbird singing and the voices of the haymakers on the hillside beyond. He smoked a cigarette and considered what playing his part might involve.

Motor lorries moved them up as far as Bouzincourt. Marching east, with orders for assembly trenches in Aveluy Wood, they heard and they smelled and they felt war. They were told about the splendid work of the Manchester battalions at Montauban and then told what that splendid work had cost. The chalk road glared. It dazzled Laurence's eyes when he looked down. A white cloud rose from the line of men ahead. Ammunition wagons and ambulances reverberated past. They passed casualty clearing stations and a field of freshly dug graves.

They sang, the rhythm and cheap sentiments propelling them in a direction that logic resisted.

'I'd rather stay in England, in merry, merry England, and fornicate this bleeding life away.'

A shell rushed overhead and crashed thirty yards to the left. It tore into a terrace of houses, hurling brick and beams. Laurence thought, for a second, that the blast might suck his insides out. He clung to the convulsing ground. The air fragmented and shook. Debris scattered slowly about. He watched the sinews of Edward Shaw's hand clench and flex. He held a triangle of glazed tile out towards Laurence. 'A souvenir,' he said.

Laurence found himself in a bombed-out church. It was blown back to bare bones, its rafters like a dinosaur's ribcage. Bright light broke in too crudely. There were fragments of angels on the floor. A yellow cat curled amongst the stacked chairs and lightly-dusted saints. Laurence ran his hand along its back, not altogether sure whether it was dead or alive. It twitched its ears in confirmation of the latter. He prayed quickly, then, conscious that the creaking roof could fall. He wasn't accustomed to praying, but fear suddenly reignited his faith. It felt like a hot thing inside him. Laurence prayed vehemently that he might live. Christ, in ebony effigy, gasped.

The roads became a stream of retreating wounded. They passed bloodied and bandaged men. They passed men who shook and men who raved, men who convulsed and clawed at their mouths. Instinct told Laurence to turn and run. He looked at the men to his left, at their feet's rhythmic forward fall. He looked at the horizon. It was his duty to lead them forward. It was his duty to resist his own instincts.

In Aveluy Wood they were told that their orders had been changed and that they must move on to bivouac camp in a place called Happy Valley.

'You see?' smiled Allerton.

Laurence wasn't altogether sure what it was that Allerton saw.

There were enemy prisoners moving up the road. They stared at them – the white dust on their boots and the shadows on their faces. They looked more meek than monstrous. They looked slouched and haggard. They weren't at all the spike-helmeted ogres that they had expected. Their ordinariness, their lack of otherness, struck Laurence.

'Smartly, now,' Captain Clayton said.

They slowed, at first, to stare at the roadside corpses, but then they began to avert their eyes. It wasn't, though, always easy to avert their eyes. There were embankments by the sides of the road as they came closer to the area of recent fighting. The banks were made of mules and horses, spent shells, broken waggons and broken men, all tangled together with telegraph wire.

Younger Young cried at the sight of all the dead horses. Edward Shaw vomited.

'Jesus Christ, that smells evil.'

'Is that winning?' said Old Young. 'Is that the great advance?'

Happy Valley was full of lively horses and guns, men sleeping on groundsheets and under greatcoats, those coming out of the line and those going in. The howitzers boomed and heaved amongst the crowds and the camping. The horses reared and screamed.

They went up towards the front line in the evening, over land that was cratered and gouged and turning to mud. There were stacked shell cases and everywhere a litter of abandoned kit. Guns were being moved up and casualties carried back. The wet hem of Laurence's greatcoat flapped heavily against his shins. He focused on the man ahead of him, on Carver's narrow shoulders and the clattering clumsy weight of his pack. The swinging mess tin reflected sky and earth and shifting khaki colours that Laurence recognised to be himself. Light leapt on the horizon.

They passed through the old German front line and paused to look at a trench full of Bavarians. The guide, who was leading them into the line, showed the scene as if it were a tourist curiosity. The Germans had been packed in and were standing still where they had died. They had been standing there since the 1st July. Their faces were shiny and swollen and grotesque.

'Crammed in like sardines,' said Hindle.

'But the colour of kippers,' suggested Horrocks.

'Concussion wave,' said the guide. He nodded at the phrase as if he was proud of it. 'In new boots too.'

They moved up a sunken lane and then into the line. There was a lot of wire and a lot of dead. It was difficult to avoid stepping on the dead. They went into a forward position with the French on their right.

'We are pretty much the absolute end of the British line,' observed Allerton. 'Rather odd thought that, isn't it? We're the cul-de-sac of English civilization. Does that make us very good or very bad?'

'I suppose we'll find out in the morning. I'm not sure that I wish to think of myself as a dead-end, though.'

Ahead was a pile of rubble that might once perhaps have been a farm. On the other side of it was the enemy line. They were told that, the next morning, they would take it.

It must once have been a gentle bucolic landscape, Laurence considered. He wondered if it would one day be again. He saw, in years to come, the rows of beets and the bright tides of wheat. He imagined the corrupt earth grassed over, saw where the hamlets and holm oaks and hayricks would be, saw the sun reflect off pastoral peace. But now it was all mud and the skeleton trees. Black air billowed and rushed, with heat and sound and surging shock.

They crouched down in their ditch while artillery roared overhead. It crashed and slammed. The sandbag walls convulsed. Laurence thought of quiet classroom cross-sections of volcanoes and earthquakes, of magnitudes of violence that he hadn't really comprehended at all. It sounded like the sky was being ripped apart. It felt like a cataclysm. A twelve-inch howitzer fired in Trafalgar Square would, they were informed, take out Woodford Green. Laurence had never been to Woodford Green. He wondered if he ever would now. The glowing hours moved slowly around his luminous wristwatch. The surface of his tea pulsed concentric circles.

He was tasked with giving a talk about duty, but he was no longer certain what that word precisely meant. He told them, with a strained voice, to have stout hearts, to think of their families, to fight for their friends. His words, however loud, sounded weak and a long way from promenade recitals of *Henry V*. He repeated positive artillery statistics and the promise of no resistance. Nobody could live through this, he said, as instructed. Just to be sure, the names of the court-martialled, condemned men, were to be recited and no mystery left as to their fate. He'd been told that the odds in their favour were three to one, but decided, on balance, that this wasn't a sufficiently reassuring ratio to share.

'Make yourselves proud today,' he said.

He prayed that he might do the same.

The first light was in the sky. Allerton was in the next bay along. Laurence had given him a short, cheery, final note for his mother, folded with a forget-me-not, and to be passed on in the event of his demise. He had found that he could not be earnest, at what might be the end. He had hesitated to find the right words, the right tone, the right way to write goodbye and, failing to find it, had scribbled out a flippant last sentence. The notion of there being no tomorrow was beyond earnest comprehension. There weren't adequate words and so he exited with an untidy toodle-oo.

Billy Rigby, standing next to him, pissed in his boots.

'Fuck's sake,' said Fitton.

Laurence attempted sounds of reassurance but they were lost to the barrage. It was like a thousand church bells madly ringing, like a hundred cathedrals full of organ crescendos. He felt minuscule, puny, nothing, yet that huge dissonant energy was pumping into him. It thundered into him. He was full of the almighty crash and boom and clamour. He looked, from Rigby's trembling profile, along the bristling line, all bayonets fixed for the expectant hour. The sky quivered ahead and then seemed to still. Captain Clayton told them that they had five minutes. And, with that, with the measure of it, they were silent. Laurence was suddenly aware of the action of breathing, felt the blood push through his veins, felt powerfully, vulnerably alive.

It is time to do or dare, Dolly Gray.

'Oh, God,' said Old Young.

Laurence blew the whistle. He stared at his hand on the ladder. He had to think how to climb, to engage mind and muscle. His body resisted. It was a conscious thing, a difficult thing. And then they spilled over the top with a howl of adrenaline. Suddenly, from the silence, was a roar of men and metal.

'Forward!' shouted Laurence, but then he was falling backwards.

Billy Rigby was in his arms, a deadweight, gushing red. Laurence felt the bullets' thrust, like fists into a pillow. The shock of it took his breath. He stumbled as the ground convulsed. Men pushed past and ahead of him. He heard the cry from the left 'Don't bunch!' and, throwing off Billy's embrace, he lurched forwards.

Laurence ran. He ran on, though he could no longer see the men that had pushed past him. He ran, faltering over the uneven terrain, floundering through splintering, shrieking sharpness, stumbling through the all-around falling down, diving at duty, responsibility and right.

'Amo, amas, amat,' Laurence spat.

A shell hit ahead. It threw him wheeling upwards, and then he was gasping at the ground. His opened eyes looked sideways along the line. He looked around for his men. Through the smoke and the dust he saw Edward Shaw. He was in a shell hole, waving and then dying.

'Whizz bang,' said Laurence.

He lay face down, doggo, in the mud. Small things crept in the busy earth. It was all that he could bear to comprehend. His red hands clung to the ground. But the blood on his hands was not his own and, therefore, he must move on. Latin grammar and Union rules said that he must go on. Laurence tried to slide forwards on his belly. He tried to move without movement. His fearful limbs felt large.

Allerton slammed down at his side. 'This is fucking impossible. This is fucking suicide.'

Jack Taylor lurched across, holding his split stomach together with wet fingers.

Allerton's lips trembled. He swore in wide-eyed seizure. Laurence saw it flash in Allerton's dilated pupils. He stared. He watched Allerton's eyes move. Laurence daren't move. He looked, hoping to find some courage in Allerton's eyes, but all there was was the flash and fear.

Younger Young was past then. Laurence watched him leap and tumble and turn. As he turned Laurence saw that Younger Young suddenly had no face. What, seconds earlier, had been a familiar profile, had been the boy whose grinning reflection Laurence had watched turn in a shop window, was now a shock of red and bone and dead. He fell over slowly, bubbling blood. He spilled teeth. It was garish, his blood. It was fraudulently vibrant. Horrocks bellowed from behind.

'Come on,' screamed Laurence. He grabbed Allerton's hand and dragged him forwards. 'Come on!' Allerton's fingers slipped through his.

Something animal pushed Laurence on now. It was no longer rational. There was no longer responsibility and right. He was now just a fast pulse, fear and forward momentum. Terror tore through him. And anger. And hatred. And love. He was all emotions and none. He was instinct and ignition and screaming into the guns.

He ran and reeled and fell. His hearing went. He saw the metal's slow spiral. He knew that it was his. It picked him up and laid him silently down.

Then it was back. Reality returned with a rush of sound and pain. He slid into a shell hole. He started at the blood, a startling slash of vermillion in a sepia landscape. He watched its progress, marbling in the mud. Dirt fell in fragile showers that fizzed like fireworks. The mud was in his eyes, in his ears, in his mouth. The dirt ground against his teeth. His teeth chattered. The mud dragged him under. Laurence let it.

Chapter Eighteen

Ypres, 1928

I have to tell you bad news, Joe had written. *I am so very sorry to be having to write to you with this. I wish that I could take your hand in mine before I speak these words. But I can't – and I can't seem to find a way to arrange the next sentence that makes it sound any better. Edward is dead. He died yesterday in an attack on enemy trenches near Guillemont. Know that he died quickly and didn't suffer. I hope that you can take some comfort from that, but know that you will feel his loss keenly. I have lost Charlie too. There have been an awful lot of losses. It seems but luck to be alive.*

Effie thought about Edward's portrait on the sideboard in Jubilee Street, between the corset and the fish paste. She pictured his photograph face in a shell hole. She watched her brother die. Joe's letter fell to her lap. Reginald looked up at her. He blinked at Effie with eyes that were a melancholy cast of brown. She pushed the diary away.

'I had no idea,' she told him. 'I never knew. How can I not have known what they went through?'

But it seemed to be no revelation to Reginald. She supposed that Laurie might perhaps have required someone to confide in.

'I wish that he could have shared it with me,' she said.

She looked at Joe under the bedside light. She had forgotten that Charlie (inseparable, as ever) was next to him when the photograph was taken. There had been another portrait, a step further back, of the two of them together. Effie had a copy in a drawer somewhere. She remembered them side-by-side, looking louche in caps and collars, with cigarettes and swagger. Charlie was perched on a faux-stone plinth, laughing at the camera. Joe leaned on him, a hand in his pocket. His jacket concealed a bottle of rum, which they had passed between them, because they were now soldiers. A minute earlier they had been playing with the theatrical props – the peacock feathers and the Japanese fan, the wooden sword and red cavalry coat. Effie and Edward had stood behind the camera while the photographer arranged a backdrop. Charlie had winked at her and she had looked away. There were potted palms and ornamental birdcages in the corners and swags of decorative drapes. Effie had turned and taken in that room, all faux and show and fantasy, and her brother standing there smiling. She remembered, in that instant, she had felt an impulse to grip Edward's hand. But holding hands with sisters really wasn't on. Edward was already apart; he was already part of an adventure into which she was not admitted. He had glanced towards her briefly and grinned – rum on his breath and his eyes elsewhere. She remembered a fleeting feeling of jealousy.

'The world is ours for the taking,' Charlie had laughed into the white magnesium light of the photographer's flash.

Effie had quite forgotten about Charlie. How could she have done? What else had she forgotten, misunderstood and not seen? She recalled the burst of flash-powder blindness. How could she have been blind to what had happened to them? Had *her* eyes been elsewhere?

Chapter Nineteen

Somme, July 1916

Dear Effie,

Edward was buried today. He is in the same spot as Charlie. Major Bramhope said a blessing and we paid our respects. We buried forty-nine men this morning, so know that Edward is amongst friends. I understand that his effects will be forwarded to you.

I am grateful to you for going to see my mother – and sorry if she wasn't more civil. I expect it is just the shock. I know that the telegram will have hit her hard. I am appreciative of your kindness, even if she isn't yet up to visitors.

Thank you for the cigarettes and the home-made cake. I know that I shall never want for home comforts. So many parcels are arriving for men that are gone.

I shall write you a better letter as soon as I can.

Yours,

Joe

The plot was dug out already. They had passed down the same road just over a week earlier and made ghoulish jokes about the grave digging. They had had no idea that they were marching past their own graves.

Major Bramhope spoke about supreme sacrifice, about Christ giving up his life for others. He rushed the service, Joe thought. He hurried through the words as if even he didn't quite believe them. The ditch seemed to gape. Major Bramhope called them the worthy, the glorious and the blessed.

Joe had had to take Charlie's equipment off and empty his pockets that morning. A sandbag had been put over his head. It was black and clotted with blood. He had had to unwind the identification tag from around Charlie's neck, untangling the twine away from that stiff black canvas. He could still feel the texture of it. He couldn't fathom how Charlie was blessed.

His name was spoken and a blanket-wrapped shape fell stiffly into the earth. There were twenty-four of them sharing that shallow plot. They threw the first handfuls of earth in gently, but then took up shovels and covered them over. It felt very light, at first, that earth, and then very heavy. It began to stick to their shovels. They had to scrape it away. It seemed to take an awfully long time to fill the void. Joe leaned on his shovel. His arms ached. The crosses were all at slightly different angles. The turned-over chalk made the grave seem to glare. They were allowed a tot of rum in their tea.

'They make you pay for those bleeding blankets, you know,' said Carver. 'They deduct it from what you're owed.'

'What's the price of a bleeding blanket?' asked Frank, his hand on Joe's shoulder.

'It's the principle that's not right.'

'Bugger principle.'

They were assigned to provide working parties in support of an attack on the village.

'Donkey work, in other words,' said Hindle.

'I prefer donkey work to walking into guns.'

But to get to the village they must pass through the wood. They had been told tales of the wood back in Happy Valley – the wood that refused to be taken. The wood ate men, they said. It had been consuming companies since the start of July.

They moved back up on the evening before. Trones Wood was a jagged shape against the sky. Joe swore at the bluebottles.

'You're going to need to go in in single-file. You could easily lose your sense of direction in there, so it's best you go in linked.' Behind Lieutenant Rushton there were stacked crates of grenades. He wafted at them with a swagger stick. 'Box of bombs in your right hand; left hand on the equipment of the man in front. Linked, you see.'

'Wouldn't it be nicer to go in hand-in-hand?' joshed Horrocks with a girlish flurry of eyelashes. 'More romantic, like?'

'Like Hansel and Gretel?' suggested Baxter.

'Romance – incestuous or otherwise – and gingerbread house unlikely,' considered the lieutenant, 'but cannibalistic witches aren't utterly beyond probability.'

'Hansel and Gretel, Baxter? Aye, and if we're lucky we'll get to breakfast with the three bears.'

'And then we'll all live happily ever after.'

They gave a collective sham-sentimental sigh.

'I wouldn't object if some woman wanted to put me in a cage and fatten me up,' mused Frank.

An observation plane droned overhead.

'You might get your chance, Fitton. Now she knows you're coming.'

It was still dark when they started moving into the wood. Mist obscured the approach. Joe could just make out the ragged tops of trees. He held onto Frank in front and Daniel Briggs linked behind. They moved forward in small steps, picking cautiously through smashed branches. It was all the colour of shadows in the wood. It was all twisted, tattered, gnarled and inter-tangled. It was all brittle and sharp. Joe found himself listening to every crack of twig. He realised he was holding his breath. It was then that the line of men in front began to swear.

'I don't like this,' said Frank. 'There's something not right about this.'

The undergrowth seemed to want to wind around their ankles. It was difficult to keep upright, moving at the chain's pace and with the boxes' weight, over the undulations of the forest floor and with the sharpness of the blasted trees all around.

'Christ!'

The line halted and bunched up ahead. In the gloom Joe could just make out that there were piles of rags all over the forest floor. He wondered at the stench – and then understood why the men ahead were swearing. Moonlight showed that the forest floor was solid with dead. Bayonets and tin hats glinted. There were black gashes and blue-white flesh. They sprawled and crumpled and spilled limbs. It was impossible not to stand on the dead.

'This witch is some evil bitch,' said Briggs.

The mist clung to the trees making it somehow unreal. They stumbled, like sleepwalkers, through brambles and bodies and tree roots. It was sweet and sticky and reeking in the wood. Joe retched. Suddenly a hand rose up from the undergrowth and grabbed at his leg. Instinct made him kick it away and then instantly regret the reaction. The forest floor clamoured. The bluebottles droned. It was hot in the wood but Joe found himself shivering.

With the mist and the moaning and the tangling awfulness underfoot, they were soon disorientated. Frank glanced back towards him. Joe could see the whites of his eyes. He had never seen Frank Fitton look frightened before. At a sudden beat of black wings they both cursed and slid.

Up ahead there was a shout and then the wood was full of screaming. Shells crashed in. A tree roared as it tore apart. It was all splinters and explosions and the undergrowth convulsed. Joe was on his knees. His hands pulled through sharpness and stickiness. Barbed wire and brambles tangled together. He didn't know if the wetness on his hands was his own blood. Frank's arm was through his elbow and they were up and running. Joe didn't care what he ran through now. He only knew that he wanted to be out of the wood.

With a cry of 'Gas!' they stopped and fumbled into helmets.

Joe could see very little with his misted mica eyes, but what he could see was a nightmare. It was a double effort to breathe. As he grabbed Frank's strapping, he realised that he'd lost the link behind. He looked back. There were shapes and frenzy and shouting, but no shape that he recognised to be Briggs. Frank tugged him forwards. Frank's mask-muffled voice was an imploring bellow. They stumbled on together through the shrieking wood.

They ran, as best they could, bomb-linked, mica-eyed, through shrapnel, shards and splinters, and fell into the assembly trenches on the far side of the wood. The link broke. Joe pulled off his mask and gasped.

'Sweet Jesus!'

Frank kicked at the walls of the shallow ditch. 'What the fuck was that?'

Other men fell out of the wood. Far fewer fell out than had gone in. Joe lay on his back and tried to remember how to breathe. Daniel Briggs didn't fall out of the wood. He had let go of Briggs. Just like he had let go of Charlie.

Frank looked out into the whiteness beyond. He slid down again as bullets sprayed across the lip of the trench.

'Shit.'

Beyond here was mist and machine guns. Joe recalled another white-grey morning, when he had looked through the smoking remains of a bonfire. They had danced around the fire the night before and he had pledged that if Charlie joined up, well, he would too. They had called it the start of an adventure. Today felt like an end.

They waited on orders. The mist cleared. The road ahead was full of dead.

Sergeant Thorpe fell into the trench. 'It's like a shooting gallery up there. They've got machine guns posted in the quarry. We'd be picked off like a row of ruddy ducks.'

They crouched down as an explosion tore into the wood behind.

'I hate this village,' mouthed Horrocks.

'Is this the same one that we were meant to have taken last week?'

'Aye, and the same one that we'll be trying again to take next week.'

Joe leapt back as a runner dived over the edge of the trench.

'Jesus, I almost shot you,' lied Thorpe.

'Shut up, Thorpe,' said Frank.

They watched the runner gasp. His eyes were huge. He didn't seem to be able to catch on to his breath. His eyes looked about.

'Take your time.'

The runner spluttered. His chest heaved. 'The 18th have managed to get a position in the village. Lieutenant Fairford wants to get this lot in.' His foot indicated the boxes of bombs. 'They're going to try to knock that machine gun out first.'

Frank spluttered then. 'I should bloody well hope so.'

'Orders are to sit tight for the moment.'

They watched the runner move on.

'Do you think we'll have to go back through there?' asked Joe.

'I suppose it depends on whether they take this village.'

There was screaming in the wood behind and a groan of toppling trees. Joe put his hands over his ears.

Chapter Twenty

Ypres, 1928

'Tour of the Death Trench, Miss?' said the man by the charabanc. 'Perfectly preserved. Just as it was in the war. Shrapnel Corner? Hill 60? All the circuits and comfortable seating. Do you want to see the cemeteries, Miss?'

'No, thank you,' said Effie.

'English-speaking guide! Careful driver! Bruges is two pounds, but we do a buffet lunch *en route...*' The voice followed her across the square.

Did she want to see the cemeteries? Did she really want to see Joe's name on a gravestone? She recalled the first time she had seen his name on the memorial. Seeing it there, in the garden of remembrance, with its ring of rose bushes and its sorry-looking bronze soldier, for the first time she had known him definitely dead. How would she feel, then, to stand in that place where his body was? Imagining herself standing there, she felt a strange sort of vertigo. It made her knees want to buckle. The thought of standing at Joe's graveside seemed like teetering on the edge of a cliff. Effie supposed that she was afraid. She knew, though, that she had to see the cemetery. She knew that was why she was here.

The square was full of motor cars and tour buses. A tourist guide was waving arms at the scaffolded ruins of the Cloth Hall. Gazing up at the jagged stonework, she understood why the recollection of it had cast something solemn over Henry's face. Fragments of medieval colour glimmered here and there beyond the barbed wire. A stern notice warned her to resist the temptation to steal a piece of it for a souvenir. *This is holy ground*, said the sign. *It is a heritage for all civilized peoples.* Effie thought that it looked more grisly than holy. With its charred timbers and shored-up fragments of gothic, it could well have been a besieged feudal castle. A jackdaw flapped from the top of the scaffolding. It didn't look like a railway station at all and it certainly wasn't a fairy palace. It also wasn't something that she would pick a piece off for a dressing-table keepsake. It looked gnarled and stern and sorry. She walked away from the square.

Re-reading Joe's letters now, she remembered how she had felt when she first knew him dead. Imagining them moving forwards towards the front, advancing along the white road when logic told them to run, she had felt a great rush of protectiveness for the boy who had brought her raspberries from his father's allotment. And he was still just a boy. Reading back, observing them through Laurie's eyes, it had also struck her how important Charlie had been to Joe. They had always been together. Whatever they had done, they had done it together. She pictured Joe standing by his cousin's grave. Had his knees wanted to give way too? How un-whole, how unstable must he have felt without Charlie? Suddenly Effie wanted to take back all of her letters to Joe and re-write them. She wanted to tell him how sorry she was, to say that she would be there for him, to put her arms around him. Only it was twelve years too late. She needed to see Joe's grave. She also didn't want to see it.

A staircase took her up onto the ramparts. She looked across the still water of the moat. A figure was fishing on the opposite bank, the line glittering as it arced. Laurie said that Ypres was all fallen stone, feral cats and ghosts. Sitting here, listening to a gardener whistling a tune in the allotment below and watching the light on the water, Effie wondered momentarily if she was in the wrong place – or him inclined to exaggeration. But great chasms were gouged out of the brickwork below. The town walls looked like something left by an ancient civilization. She wished she could believe that Laurie had been inclined to exaggeration. She threw a stone at the water and walked on. The ramparts rippled away.

Laurie had remained in his shell hole while she read Joe's letters. Laurie's diary had stopped on the 20th of July. There was a gap in the dates. Effie knew that a bullet wound to his leg accounted for his temporary silence. She also knew that he had felt guilt that he hadn't been with his platoon as they pushed on towards Guillemont. Retrieving the diary from her pocket, she found him in a monastery garden. It was the 2nd of August 1916 and Laurie was contemplating what luck was.

My hobbling explorations advance outward, he wrote. *There is a row of beehives on the far side of the walled garden. They appear to have been long since abandoned. I took a cigarette with one of the doctors today. We perched together on the edge of a raised bed in which medicinal herbs have multiplied with a merry delinquency. We discussed the tonic properties of wormwood and debated how one goes about the distillation of absinthe. He revealed to me that, alongside a seized cider press, there is a still in one of the barns. I got the impression that a pet project may shortly see the magicking of green fairies hereabouts.*

There is something rather magical about this neglected garden. It is a somehow profoundly calm place (perhaps it is the everywhere incursion of the wormwood?) There is, at times, an intense quiet here. It is utterly still. In these moments it is not difficult to put myself back there, to imagine the lives that have been played out in this place. I can half hear the chant of long-ago prayer and the hum of honey bees. A monastic life seems not unappealing, particularly one that is equipped with a cider press and still.

I found a dog yesterday. It was in the road and dead. A motor vehicle must have hit it. Suddenly I was on all fours and crying over the body of the dog. I couldn't stop. I couldn't seem to force it back in. It felt as if something inside me was tearing. I sat in the middle of the road and screamed over a dead sheepdog. They got me a spade and I buried it then. Philips, the aforesaid medical chap, patted me on the arm this morning and gave me a look. I'm afraid that I have made rather a fool of myself.

Philips tells me that a nice clean bullet counts as luck these days. Sitting in the old kitchen garden now, the wall warm behind me, with just the noise of insects and smell of the fruit ripening on the pleached pear trees, I can't rightly refute my allocation of luck. I must remember that. I must force it back in. I must keep it in. I mustn't make a fool of myself again.

Swallows dipped and left circles stretching over the silent water. The lights were flickering on in the cafés and the Saturday night traffic was coming in along the Menin Road. Effie watched the beams of traffic lights moving across the arch. She tried to imagine what those fifty-five thousand misplaced men might look like. She tried to imagine how long a column they might form were they to march through the Menin Gate. She tried to feel the vibration of it, to put herself back then, to feel the roar and the flash and the tramp of marching misplaced feet through the gate, those men all moving on to the places that logic resisted, but all there was was the revving of a motorcycle and the chant of a playground game in the streets below. At least, she supposed, she had a grave to go to.

Suddenly a sharp note cut through it. Effie found herself crouching with her hands around her knees. The bugle call blared across the town and seized it into stillness. The last note trailed away and the silence and the stillness were absolute. The silence was intense. It was so intense that it roared. She put her hands over her ears. The roaring silence stretched and in it, images from the diary flickered back at her. She saw Joe at his cousin's graveside. She saw her brother in a shell hole waving and dying. She saw Charlie turning and horribly falling. She saw Laurie's face, in the front room last summer, as the Last Post had crackled to a close on the radiogram. Their eyes had connected in the long silence. His gaze was perfectly steady and she had held it. Only she had had no idea what his eyes had seen. She had no understanding of what he was holding in. She looked down to see his diary trembling in her hand.

Chapter Twenty-One

Picardie, August 1916

It all ran ragged beyond the terrace. Bindweed bound the roses.
Poppies were papery bright. There was red clover and the scent
of unseen elderflower. Laurence stood at the end of the garden.
He looked to the fields beyond.

He had been moving through a different landscape. As he lay
unconscious on a stretcher, he had walked over Blackstone Edge.
His imagined steps had taken him up the old packhorse way, to
the boundary marker. He had felt the pull in his legs as he
ascended towards the standing stone, the wet wind soft and
stinging on his face, with the smell of peat and the cries of
lapwings all around. He walked down the Roman road and found
himself in a casualty clearing station. There had been a paper
label tied to him when he had come round – the sort of label that
might be attached to a suitcase. Laurence had worried, his logic
fevered, that he would mislay it, and so be misdirected and sent
back. He remembered seeing dandelions then, somewhere,
yellow in a ditch, and the motor ambulance doors closing behind.
He had no recollection of how he'd got from the shell hole to the
dressing station.

The hospital had been set up in a requisitioned monastery.
Painted saints loomed over their bedsteads and plasterwork
blessings blistered above. Laurence had contemplated the
architecture to cut out the noise. Leonard Sutcliffe, in the next
bed, had a face that was a melted mask. Only his red eyes had
animation. Laurence tried to sleep but couldn't. The all-around
agonies had been loud in the dark and the images convulsed
when he closed his eyes. The flexed fingers of a severed hand
flashed in recall. Then it was Edward Shaw's hand foolishly
waving goodbye and always, ultimately, Charlie Young in that
slow-frame turn of slicing shrapnel. Laurence had spent a

fortnight in that bed, trying to keep his focus on the vaulted ceiling and the flaking angels.

He pushed through the hedge now. Beyond fields rolled in friendly undulation. Hay bales waited to be collected. There was a five-bar gate and antique hedgerows. A hawthorn was jagged against the skyline. It smelled of innocent agriculture. Laurence breathed it in.

The sketchpad was bound in yellow card. He ran his fingers over its smoothness. It was good paper, heavy paper. He had bought it in Béthune and had been saving it. The pencil slid, soap-soft, under his control. The lead line glinted starkly on the receptive white. His hand moved unhurriedly.

'Is this an escape bid?'

Laurence turned to see Joseph Young emerging from the hedge.

'Something like that.'

They shook hands.

'How is it?' Joseph nodded at Laurence's leg.

'Better than it looked. They told me I was lucky.' He thought about Charlie Young, who hadn't been fortunate enough to get a nice clean bullet and a tidy scar to show his grandchildren. 'I wanted to say sorry to you. About Charlie.'

Joseph's face offered no animating emotions. Only the lines around his eyes indicated a reaction.

'I owe you a cigarette,' said Laurence. 'And somewhat more.'

He patted the rock next to him and Joseph sat down. The stretcher bearers had told him, afterwards, that it was Young who had brought him back, had dragged him unconscious from the shell hole and back to the line. Joseph had dragged his cousin back too, they had said, but there were limits to what medicine could mend.

'There was a miscommunication,' said Laurence. He

somehow felt obliged to say it. 'Other companies were meant to arrive. There was meant to be a Lewis gun detachment. There was meant to be a second supporting wave to fill the gaps.'

'Fill the gaps? Wasn't it all gaps?'

Billy Rigby's spectacles had still been in Laurence's pocket when he woke up in the hospital. He had stared at them, wondering at their fragility. He had salvaged them from the mud. He wasn't sure why. Billy's blood was down his fingernails. He had worked it out with a matchstick, until determined working made his own blood run. His heart hadn't felt right. He'd wondered if he was over-strung. He made himself write it down. Red fingerprints illustrated his account. He was all too aware of the gaps.

'Major Clayton and Captain MacDonald are dead. Three other officers. Twenty-eight other ranks. Ninety-eight wounded. Nine shell-shocked. Thirteen missing.' Laurence had made an effort to remember the numbers. It seemed right to do so. Allerton had been in to see him and had given him the statistics. He'd apologised for his funk. Laurence had said that the statistics justified the funk.

'We had double rations – that night, I mean, when we got back,' said Joseph with eyes cast down. 'We ate what they couldn't. Frank said: 'We're eating dead men's dinners here.' We knew it. We did. I ate Charlie's rations and the worst is that I then threw it up.'

'Sitting in a dugout suddenly seems like an attractive option, doesn't it? Perhaps we could just sit it out in a contest of endurance, like a party game.'

'We buried forty-nine men yesterday.'

Laurence decided that it was perhaps inappropriate to tell Joseph he had buried a dog yesterday. He certainly shouldn't tell Joseph how he had cried over the dead dog.

'We're on burial party again tomorrow. It's like the rules of the game have changed, isn't it?'

Something had changed in Joseph's face, Laurence saw. It wasn't just that he looked tired. Laurence saw something in Joseph's face that he wasn't quite sure how to negotiate his way around. He flicked the end of the cigarette away and buried his hands in his sleeves.

'I could recommend you for that medal now.'

'What would be the point?' said Joseph.

Laurence shrugged. 'It might make your mother proud?'

Joseph stared at him. Laurence wasn't sure where to look.

'He was my brother, you know.'

'I'm sorry?'

'Charlie, that is. He was my brother. Or, at least, he was my mother's son. I wasn't meant to know, but I always did. Mother came home one day and said that she'd found God. She went off on a pilgrimage to somewhere in the south and then, suddenly, Aunt Florrie was taking in a foundling. Mother told me to look after him. She said that I had to take care of him. But I didn't, did I? I haven't done her proud and now I don't know what to write to her.'

'Christ,' said Laurence inadequately. He rocked forwards. 'My responsibility was to get you all out of there. I am sorry, Joseph. I am so sorry. Would you like me to try to write to your mother?'

Joseph nodded. Laurence watched his hands clench and unclench.

'I do owe you. I do know that.'

'You owe me nothing.'

'I owe you everything. I wasn't ready for it to end.'

'Is anybody – ever?'

Laurence supposed not. 'Well, say that you'll let me return the courtesy.' He took the pencil, wrote across his just-begun landscape, dated it and signed.

Caroline Scott

'*I.O.U. 1 life,*' read Joseph.

'A gentlemen's agreement,' said Laurence. 'An *entente cordiale*, if you will. Shall we shake on it?'

'I'd rather scrounge another cigarette,' said Joseph.

Chapter Twenty-Two

Flanders, 1928

Joe was buried in a place called *Les Deux Arbres*. At first they had not told her where he was, as if they wanted to keep it a secret, but she needed to have a name for it. Effie needed to be able to place and picture him. When Laurie had finally spoken about *Deux Arbres* it had pleased her. She had thanked him for giving that place a name. And it was a name she liked. She had pictured a graveyard with two yew trees and weeping angels in stone.

'Is that what it's like?' she had once asked Laurie, in between chapters. 'Are there trees and angels?'

'There are,' he'd said and smiled. So with that she had known that Joe would be all right.

They had read about the new cemeteries in the newspapers, the whiteness of the English stone and the exactness of the symmetry.

'I should like to visit one day,' she had said.

'And you shall. One day I shall take you.' And so, finally, he had.

The name of the village was an unlikely congregation of consonants. Despite a decade of practising, Effie still wasn't certain that she could pronounce it correctly. It sounded sharp and unfriendly in her mouth, but she supposed that was on account of association. The road from the unpronounceable village was all rut, but sun shone on the straight lines of vegetable gardens. There were dahlias, then rows of beet and the rippling whisper of a field of wheat.

She thought about them sitting in a field together, looking out into Laurie's landscape scene. She had read as far as the point where the I.O.U. passed between their hands. Joe's tragic secret had left her reeling. Had he always known that they were brothers? How had she never seen it? Why couldn't he have shared that knowledge with her? She wondered if that was why Laurie expected her to hate him – because he was privy to secrets that she was excluded from? Or was it that he felt responsible for not having been able to honour the bargain that he had offered? Joe's luck had held out for another fifteen months. This, though, this unpronounceable place, was where Joe's luck had run out. This was the place where Laurie's I.O.U. had lapsed.

The cemetery, they had told her in the village, was on the left. But Effie knew that already. In the early days she had spent a lot of time looking at it on the map, mindful of the significance of the symbol, knowing what that little cross contained. It seemed enormous then to be here, to stand now in front of that cross, which wasn't a cross at all, but a wall and a gate. She feared now what the place beyond the gate contained.

Effie put her hand to the latch. It was warm with the sun. It seemed such an unassuming gate – a pretty thing of plaited ironwork. It was a gate that should have opened onto a country churchyard, a gate to pass through to christenings and weddings, to swing on on a summer evening, a gate to walk through in faith and hope. She stared at her hand on the latch. It suddenly felt as though her faith was being tested. She raised her eyes, with an effort, to a green avenue lined with white stones. It tapered to a crucifix in parentheses of yew trees. She thought of the iris-lined path down which she had watched Laurie's coffin carried and considered whether to run. But Laurie said *Trust me* and she did have faith in him. The gate closed silently behind her.

Effie looked down to the black shine of her newly-polished boots and up to the mute white glow of the crucifix. There were no people in this place. There was no noise. The only sound was the ragged rush of her breath. There were no angels.

She walked the path between the stones. The sun cut slanting shadows, drew shadows the height of men. The shadows swung together as she looked along the line. The shadows stretched on and on.

Effie knew the statistics. She knew the awful largeness of the numbers. But, until this point, until she stood amongst the stretching shadows, she somehow hadn't comprehended the scale of it, hadn't fully understood what the largeness of those numbers meant. Effie thought of Kate and of the smuggled sapling, of wanting to break the symmetry with a tangle of nature that was imperfect and personal. Suddenly she understood.

She looked at Laurie's directions – though it was hardly necessary to do so. The coordinates of Joe's location had been in her head for the best part of a decade. Laurie's steadily-shaped letters read *12M*. It was the end of a row, he had said – a semi-detached, which was nicer than a terrace. Plot two, row twelve, grave M. The piece of paper wouldn't keep quite still in her hands. She walked the numbered rows, navigated through algebra and epitaphs. There was something about the numbers that didn't seem quite nice, but there were carnations and orderly care.

Effie stood at the end of row twelve. Her stomach lurched. What with the mathematics and enormity and proximity, she felt slightly light-headed. She steadied herself on *A Soldier of The Great War*. It wasn't possible to walk the row without reading the names. The names made her cry. 12J was a nineteen-year-old Harry from the Cheshire Regiment (*Missed by Mother, Bessie and Ethel*). 12K, she saw at the grass line, was a grandfather. 12L was *Buried Elsewhere in this Cemetery*. 12M was elsewhere.

Effie rechecked her compass. She stared at Laurie's so familiar but suddenly so confusing co-ordinates.

'Laurie!' The paper crumpled in her hot hand. 'How could you have got this wrong?'

Joe's place was a space, was innocent grass and absence. Joe was not there. She looked around, as if he might be hiding or idling absentmindedly aside. Effie walked back along the row – and then the next line and the next. She looked for Joe's name. She looked for him amongst the boy soldiers and grandfathers, the men *Within These Walls*, the gassed, the missed and the men with no names. The names spiralled around her. There were too many names. There were too many dead. This was a tidy, silent city of the dead. She found herself back where Joe's name should be. Her knees crumpled.

'I don't understand.' Effie told it to the grass, to the end-of-row rose and 12L who too was elsewhere. How could a man be mislaid? Joe wasn't the sort of man who got mislaid. He was an on-time man. Joe was dependable. He was solid and safe. She had occasionally wished him a little less safe. Joe was now not solid and he was not here. Effie put her head in her hands.

The shadows slid. The shadows of stones circumnavigated the bones that they signified. Morning turned to afternoon. Effie sat where Joe should be, but wasn't, and watched the shadows turn.

Was it a clerical error? She scrutinised Laurie's characters. The figures were neat, definite, beyond doubt. The '1' had a straightforward downward stroke. The '2' curled confidently. The 'M' was constructed of strong, direct, deliberate lines. She saw no uncertainty there, no tremble of hesitation or messy misunderstanding. Could it have been a mistake in translation, a mathematical miscalculation, or, worse, a lie? She couldn't imagine, looking at Laurie's lettering, that he could have lied about so important a coordinate. And why would he have lied? Laurie didn't lie.

Effie looked down at her hands, which were green-flecked with grass. She looked down at the empty earth. How could it be empty and him gone? Her fingers felt through the coarse grass and touched the cool ground below. The earth pushed behind her fingernails. Some alien momentum, then, was pushing her on.

The tendons in her hands tightened and suddenly she must dig to him. Her frenzied fingers pulled at grass, scraped at soil, tore hotly through root and stone and sharpness. She cried as she clawed. Her blood beat fast. It became an animal scramble. The earth scratched and stung and yielded nothing. Her hands were black and green and bled. She looked at the mess that she had made, rocked back and wept. Where was Laurie to hold her hand?

Effie staggered down the row of tidy dead. Were any of them really there? Were they any more real than the names on the arch? Were the white stones all lies? She was running down the row then, every muscle pulling fast and fearful, pushing through the all-around white lies, and away from the place where she had trusted Joe to be, with two trees and weeping angels. The unassuming gate banged behind her. She stood in the road and gasped.

Chapter Twenty-Three

Picardie, February 1917

Dear Effie,

Thank you for your letter – for the soap and the smokes. I can't smell Pears soap without thinking of you.

I am sorry to hear that your mother is unwell and that you had such an upset. I hope she will make a full recovery. My mother still does not return my letters. I am grateful of any news of her that you are able to send me. Just one word from her would put my mind at rest. Her silence feels like a great responsibility.

New drafts have been coming in over the last few weeks. We find ourselves trying to sound like old timers. 'We have filled one cemetery,' I overheard Bob Carver boasting, 'and are well advanced with a second.' That is the sort of thing that passes for humour here now.

There is much training in consequence of the new drafts – much drill and inspection. A medical officer poked and pinched us and looked in our mouths. Some men, found to be faulty, have been sent to a tunnelling company. I am declared fit to be a soldier. I am not sure that I have ever been quite so envious of wheezing chests or rotten teeth.

It is extremely cold here. At nights we put newspaper down our tunics for the extra warmth, but the cold still bites through. It is only tea and smokes that keep us going.

Rumour is that we're moving to another sector shortly. Percy Wilson was shot through the wrist this week, and us seven miles behind the lines. They are calling it an S.I.W. – a Self-Inflicted Wound. It is the first time that we have heard of such a thing.

Know that I think of you.

Yours,

Joe

'Your grandad kept pigeons, didn't he, Young?'

'Aye.' Joe looked up from the letter. He was hesitating over whether to cross out Percy Wilson – the censor would probably put a line through him anyway. 'Short-distance racers,' he said.

'There you are, then, bird man. Racers in the blood. There's the candidate for your vacancy. This chap's lost his oppo,' Frank explained to Joe, 'and needs a man what knows his way around birds.'

'Does Joey know what to do with a bird?' Horrocks was shaving and amused by his own insinuations. His smirk glinted in the mirror.

'Aviary qualifications aren't compulsory,' clarified the bird man, who seemed to be called Skinner and who looked to be about the same age as Joe's grandad. 'Bradbury bred champion fantails, but that didn't help him dodge a bullet.'

'This Bradbury copped it on the way in,' put in Frank informatively. 'Gone to the great roost yonder.' His eyes rose piously skywards.

'Sniper,' said Skinner. 'He had a lovely manner, did Bradbury. Quiet. Calm. Steady hand. Fell with great consideration for his birds. Had to bring this lot up myself.' He nodded at the two wicker cages. 'Strictly against regulations that.'

'Getting shot?'

'Carrying two baskets,' corrected Skinner. 'Four birds per man. That's the rule. Precious cargo, see.'

'Four birds per man?' repeated Pollard. 'How do I get myself a transfer to this bird fancying battalion?'

'Anyway, if you're up for it, you'd better get a wriggle on, lad.' Skinner bent, put his arms through the strapping and hoisted a basket onto his back. 'Like this, see. Got to have these up to H.Q. by three and the next lot back before dark.'

Joe knelt and lifted the basket's canvas cover. Feathers ruffled within and a smell that put him back in his grandad's yard.

'Hello birdy. Who's a pretty boy?' Horrocks crouched next to him, still with half a face of shaving soap. He stretched an explorative finger into the basket.

'They're not bleeding budgies,' said Frank.

'If you molest a pigeon you can get six months in prison,' advised Skinner. 'Defence of the Realm Act, that.'

'Times might be hard, but I wasn't going to molest his bloody budgie,' Joe heard Horrocks protesting as they headed away.

The road towards Albert was straight and lined with poplars. There were sheepfolds and turnip stacks, glimmering with frost. Mist shifted around cattle in a valley, their solid stillness taking Joe's thoughts back to circles of standing stones. They leant against a fence and watched a farmer struggling to pull a plough through the frozen earth. Big clods fell stiffly to either side and the broken earth smelled sweet. The blade jammed again and the farmer looked up to the sky.

'Don't say much, do you, lad?' said Skinner after they had been walking for some time.

Joe shrugged.

'Not that I'm complaining, mind. Can't be done with gobby beggars. And the birds like a quiet type. Easily ruffled, they are, pigeons. Sensitive, see.'

Joe remembered his grandad placing a pigeon in his hand. He was ten years old. It seemed like a great honour that he was being handed, a great responsibility. He wasn't an especially gentle man, Joe's grandad, wasn't a one for fancy words or soft sentiments, but he was different around his pigeons. You had to be careful with the birds, George Young said. 'Cossetted,' Joe's nan had called it. He remembered the shock of the bird's lightness, as it was transferred to his hand. He also remembered the pulse that he felt through his fingers, the insistent vibration of life within that fragile frame. Charlie was there, then, at his shoulder.

'Can I?' Charlie's finger had stroked along the bird's back.

'You're not old enough.' Joe had replied before his grandad had opportunity to answer. Charlie was nine.

'My grandad said that birds are the souls of the dead.' Joe told Skinner how most of George's pigeons had been named after departed relatives. There was an Auntie Evie and a Great-Uncle Alf. Joe's nan said it was morbid and threatened to put poor Evie and Alf in a pie.

'Don't mean to challenge your old man's philosophies, but the sky hereabouts would be solid with them if that were the case.' Skinner looked up.

They stood together for a moment in silence and surveyed the overhead blue. There was nothing above but high cirrus cloud and the droning of an aeroplane.

The battalion H.Q. was in a school house. The *'Garcons'* side of the building seemed to be faring rather better than the *'Filles'* which had lost most of its roof. The signal officer leaned in the doorway. He was wearing a fur coat and eating sardines out of a can.

'You get held up, Skinner?'

'I lost Bradbury on the way up.'

'Lost him? That was careless. Trust he's got homing instinct?'

'Not this time. Sniper got him just as we'd started heading back.'

'Christ, I am sorry,' said the signaller. 'Good chap, Bradbury. You were great mates, you two, weren't you?'

'Aye, we were that.'

'Come in. Will you have a drink?'

'Go on. A quick one, mind. This chap's called Young. And this is Guardsman Yates.' Skinner nodded introductions.

Guardsman Yates saluted and smiled.

119

There was a makeshift cosiness inside the school house. A woodstove burned brightly and there were camp beds, armchairs and a sleeping cat. Joe spied a gramophone and a harmonium. A child's alphabet blocks had been arranged over the fireplace to spell the word, *CRIKEY*. There was a kettle steaming on the stove.

'Come in, Young,' directed Yates. 'Take a pew.'

Skinner went off to change over the birds, while Yates arranged a tea tray. Joe moved papers and playing cards aside and settled himself in an armchair. He stretched his fingers towards the fire.

'Fortnum and Mason's finest Ceylon,' said Yates. 'Food parcel from my mother.'

They raised tea cups in a toast to motherly comforts. Joe tried to remember the last time he had drunk from a china cup and saucer. The cup had a picture of Windsor Castle on it. He tried to recall the last words that his mother had written to him.

'So you sticking to your theory that they're about to move back, Yates?' Skinner wiped his feet on the doormat. The gesture seemed slightly superfluous, Joe thought, when, beyond the fireside congregation of comforts, the floor was littered with plaster, lath and broken glass. There were stacked bibles and candle ends in the cobwebbed corners.

'Sure of it. Surveillance expects that they'll start pulling back any day.'

'Pulling back?' repeated Joe. 'They're withdrawing?'

'They're consolidating.' Yates shook his head, nearly spilling his tea with the emphasis of the gesture. 'Knuckling down. Reinforcing behind their lines – all fortified with iron and concrete. They mean to hold fast.'

'Long haul this,' said Skinner. 'I'll still be back and forth with the birds when I'm eighty-five. Might as well get cosy. Not that we can, lad.' He gulped his tea in one go. 'No knuckling down for us. At least not yet. Come on, young Young.'

'Old Young,' corrected Joe.

Skinner looked him up and down doubtfully. 'From this side of sixty you're young.'

'I am sorry about Bradbury,' said Yates.

'Me too,' said Skinner.

As they were reaching the outskirts of the village a shell tore through the barn just behind. Tiles clattered and Joe found himself staring at the packed-earth road. Suddenly the cage on his back was full of thrashing. The basket was full of feathered frenzy. Panic flailed in the box and then in his own chest. The wings seemed to be beating inside his rib cage and Joe couldn't breathe.

'Get it off me!'

Skinner helped him shrug the basket off.

'Jesus!' Joe staggered backwards. He knelt on the roadside banking, hugged his knees to him and rocked the shock away.

'Easy, son. You're all right.'

Skinner laid the basket gently on the ground.

'I'm sorry,' said Joe. 'I *am* sorry. Are they hurt?'

Skinner looked inside. 'Nothing broken. No harm done. Just a bit of a shock. That's all.'

Joe felt the flutter subside. 'I thought the wings would break. I thought that they were going to break themselves.' There was something primitive and awful about that confined frenzy – the directness and desperation of it. He hoped very much that his grandad had been wrong and that he hadn't just subjected the souls of the departed to claustrophobic terrors in a wicker basket.

'They'll be fine. These birds fly over the front. Just think what they look down on. They'll have their share of shocks.' Skinner handed Joe a cigarette. 'Take a minute. We'll get another mile back and then we can let them go.'

They smoked together quietly for a while. They watched the

roof of the barn crumple.

'Your feller said that you had a hot stint in Arras?'

Joe deduced that 'your feller' must be Frank. 'We threw a lot of trench mortars at each other.'

'Heavy stuff too, your man said.'

'Says a lot, doesn't he?'

For someone that professed not to like gobby beggars, Skinner seemed to do a lot of talking.

'Come on.'

They took the road back west. When they'd walked for half an hour or so Skinner turned off and opened a gate. 'This'll do.'

A new-ploughed field rolled down towards a valley. The poplar trees cast long shadows across it. Joe watched Skinner reach inside his basket. A sleek bird emerged in his hand. He held it to his chest.

'Pigeons are immune to tear gas, you know,' he began, in informative voice. 'Faster than a runner, not daft like a dog, more wily than a telegraph wire. This bonny lad is a veteran of the 1st July.' The bird blinked impassive eyes.

Following Skinner's example, Joe reached a bird from the basket. He held it in his hand. It weighed nothing, but trembled emphatically with life. He ran his finger along its back.

'Let him go,' said Skinner.

Joe hurled the bird into the air, watched it flap and find its wings. 'How do they know which way to go?'

'Internal compass? Something to do with magnetics? Beauty is in the mystery. I honestly couldn't tell you, son. All I know is that they do.'

Joe watched the pigeons angle away towards the valley. 'And where are they going now?'

'Only home. Just exercise flights these. We have to keep taking them out and drawing them home again. They have to keep on remembering where home is.'

'They never want to go somewhere else?'

'Why would they? The loft is safety, see. And food and rest, a bath, a drink and grit. They're just the same as us. Save for the grit bit.'

Joe smiled.

'German birds are very inferior. Don't have the pluck or nouse of your English pigeon. Or the training, if I can be so bold.'

Joe laughed.

They cut across a field of cabbages, finally stepping out onto a road that was more pothole than *pavé*. The field at the far side was planted with crosses. These graves looked like they had been here for a long time. Grass had grown over them. Joe wondered if Charlie's grave would be the same.

'Field ambulances came in here,' said Skinner. 'Bit busy round these parts back in July.'

The road inclined downwards towards red rooftops. They walked along the side of a high brick wall.

'What is this place?'

'Want to see? Fancy a trespass?'

The wall turned a perpendicular, away from the road, and there, hidden in brambles and shadow, was a gate. Skinner winked back towards Joe as he put his shoulder to the wood. They crouched under rhododendrons and emerged onto a lawn. The land rose towards the ruin of a house.

'It was a hospital last summer. Busy one, too. Lots of men and munitions passing this way and so they shelled it. Went up with incendiaries.'

The roof had gone in, leaving only the chimney stacks and gables pointing raggedly into the sky. The plasterwork was blackened. It looked like a gothic horror.

'And before?'

'Home to some double-barrelled family. Crust-less cucumber

sandwiches and croquet on the lawn...'

They walked through the pleasure garden as Skinner conjectured the details of once-upon-a-time parties and picnics. Marble deities were assuming haughty poses, in between the fir trees and specimen shrubs, as if in defiance of the obscenities with which they had been tattooed. A stone satyr grinned beneath a Pickelhaube helmet. Willows dipped towards an ornamental lake and an accumulation of mangled ironwork. Shattered greenhouses glittered beyond.

Joe found himself looking up into the branches of an apple tree. It glowed white with blossom. There was something shocking about this ancient tree, full of white scented life. Is seemed out-of-place amongst the ruins. Miraculous, almost. They leaned against the gnarled trunk and didn't speak for some time.

'My old man was from Herefordshire,' said Skinner, eventually. 'End of December every year, he'd have a skin full of cider and then go out and fire his shotgun up into the apple tree. Wonder he never shot himself. It was meant to scare the evil spirits out, you see. Proper old pagan, he was. A right one who'd crawled out of the woods. I reckon that, with the knock this place has had, there can't be many evil spirits hereabouts.'

'I fell out of an apple tree once,' recalled Joe.

'Some drunken old sod shoot you out?'

'No,' said Joe.

He was eleven and Charlie was ten. Bunking off from school, they had skulked in another forgotten garden, where everything was wild and height and tangled. They had pulled through forbidding brambles. Joe remembered feeling in an element over which he had no control. He had felt that sensation again in Trones Wood.

'I'm the king of the castle.' Charlie had sing-songed.

It wasn't that they had wanted the apples. It was a dare. Charlie had been up the tree ahead of him, lithe limbed and goading. Joe recalled the texture of the trunk, his fingers trying to find a hold. Charlie's challenging voice pushed him higher and then he was the one at the top of the tree.

'You're the dirty rascal.'

He'd looked down on Charlie and laughed at him, drunk on daring and teetering and falling. His hands had grasped for branches, floundered for solid but found only fast-falling sharpness. He slammed to the ground. It had reverberated through him. Everything had stopped for a second before the blood came. Then his split lip gushed red. He remembered staring at his red hands. Joe, nine years on, looked down at his grey, grimed fingers.

'It knocked the wind out of me. I cried like a girl. It fucking hurt. But the worst of it was that he wouldn't stop taking the piss.'

'Your mate?'

Joe nodded. He blew smoke at the memory.

But Charlie had scrambled down the tree, linked his arm through Joe's and walked him home.

'I bled all over him. I bled like a bastard.' Charlie had held Joe's red hand.

'How does a bastard bleed?' asked Skinner.

'A lot.'

Joe thought about the clotted canvas bag. Why hadn't he held Charlie's hand?

'They say that heaven is an apple orchard.'

'Who says?'

Skinner shrugged. 'Pagans? Romans? Greeks? Pissed-up old prats who shoot apple trees?'

They walked along the balustrade, crunching through glass. Smoke-coloured curtains still shifted at some of the windows. They saw blistered panelling inside, blackened bedsteads and a carbonised grand piano.

'Here, this is worth seeing.'

To the far side of the house was a tower, standing quite removed. It was round and squat, like a pepper pot.

'Incendiaries didn't get this,' said Skinner, as if there was something crafty about this pepper pot tower.

'What was it?'

'*Colombier*, the French call them. Luxury lofting. Only not quite what it once was. Come on.'

Skinner dragged a door open and they stepped inside. Joe looked up to a circle of sky. Built into the walls of the tower were apertures where doves would once have roosted.

'A beehive made for birds.'

'Or the ghosts of birds.'

A web of ivy held the walls together. It smelled of damp, of minerals and earth. They stepped over fallen beams and slate tiles. The tower made an echo of the wind.

'Like a seashell,' Joe said. 'I can't hear the war at all. All I can hear is the wind.'

'Built in 1317, this.' Skinner indicated numerals above the door. 'I'll bet you a guinea that it won't be standing by the end of 1917.'

'I don't like the odds of that bet.'

'You know that until the revolution, only the toffs were allowed to own pigeons in France. *Vive la revolution*, eh?'

They squeezed back through the gate and made their way along the village street. It was a straggling, rather downtrodden-looking village. It seemed for the most part to be composed of granaries, barns and sheds. Joe wondered whether the populace had danced when the cucumber sandwiches and croquet mallets went up in smoke. A troop of children danced around them now and made amicable cooing and flapping mimicry at Skinner. This was evidently something of a ritual. Skinner looked to Joe with a grin. He tried to return a smile.

There was still that ripple of wings. They turned off into a field at the far end of the village.

'Is that a bus?'

'It was a bus. It's now a mobile pigeon loft.'

'It says *Trafalgar Square*.'

'It's running a bit behind timetable.'

A couple of the birds were waiting, perched on the bonnet. With a rattle of a grain can the rest swooped down.

'All present and correct,' said Skinner.

He shook Joe's hand on parting. 'Good lad. Good job. Keep your chin up now.'

'I'm sorry about your mate – about Bradbury.'

'And I'm sorry about yours. All this will pass, though.' Skinner waved goodbye.

Joe forced the gate again. He walked back through the grounds of the ruined house. The blasted building was just a silhouette now. The blown-out windows showed bright slivers of light. A rook croaked from a black chimney stack.

He stood in the tower, looking up to a circle of twilight sky. The walls closed in with the flare of his struck match. Broken bottles and brown leaves flickered. He remembered sitting in the stone circle back in Salisbury. It seemed like ancient history. He sat down with his back to the stone. 'Whatever happens, we're in this together,' Charlie had said that night on Salisbury Plain. They had made a promise and shaken on it: they wouldn't be parted. Joe knew now that there was no such thing as ghosts or hereafters. There was no next room, no other worlds or under worlds. There was no happy-ever-after land of apples. He knew that this wouldn't pass. Charlie's absence felt absolute and endless.

Chapter Twenty-Four

Flanders, 1928

She knew it had all changed. Laurie had told her that. He had explained about the ribbons of crosses that had threaded across the landscape. He had told her once how, seen from a hill, those scattered crosses had stretched like a constellation of stars. And she understood what had happened at the end. He had told her that too. Effie knew how it had all had to be cleaned up and cleared. She knew that all the names had started changing then. Edward had gone from a spot called *Neuf Moulins* to the cemetery at Guillemont. The dead had risen up and been reshuffled. Was it, then, much the same for Joe? Could that account for his absence? Had Joe never actually been in *Deux Arbres* or had he once been there and then moved on? Had she been looking at the wrong map reference all along? She thought of Laurie's finger directing her to the place on the page. He had seemed so certain that this was the right place. Had Laurie's certainty been misplaced?

Effie swallowed the last of the brandy. She looked at her hands on the glass. Her nails were black. There was blood and scratches. Her opal ring was caked with earth, with the earth that should have contained her fiancé. She counted out her coins on the bar and walked on. A woman in mink and service medals jostled against her.

If it *wasn't* the case that his grave was elsewhere, could it be that Joe was nowhere? She began to consider whether Laurie's pointing figure had been a misdirecting act of kindness. That could explain why he hadn't encouraged her to come here before. It could also explain why he now seemed to think that she might have cause to hate him. Had he mislead her? Could it be that Laurie knew that Joe's grave had gone? There was another year of war after Joe had been buried. Effie had watched the line start to move in the newspaper. In the April of 1918 it had seemed like it was all being undone. The ridge that they had fought for, six months earlier, had been lost. For another five months, the place where Joe had died was on the wrong side of that line. It wasn't until the September that it was re-taken. Could it be that Joe's grave had been destroyed in that back and forth? She knew that it had been all swamp and explosions north-east of Ypres. Had Joe's grave disappeared in all of that disorder? Had she lost Joe again in those last months of the war?

A gramophone in one of the cafés was playing *Crazy Rhythm*. Effie stood in the centre of the square and looked around at the shops and hotels and bars. Tourist parties were reminiscing and raising toasts. Moroccan carpet sellers were touting their wares. A drum was beating for the start of the circus performance, while a girl in well-patched tights and a paste tiara offered last-minute reductions on the ticket price. The drum beat took her back to their practise assault before the Somme. The beat was insistent. It pushed her out of the square.

Effie stood below the Menin Gate and looked up. She re-read the legend carved above. Suddenly now, with Joe's absence, the words had an altered resonance.

Here are recorded names of officers and men who fell in Ypres salient but to whom the fortune of war denied the known and honoured burial given to their comrades in death.

It struck her, as she read the words on the gate, that there was a third possibility. Had there ever actually been a grave? Had there ever been anything left of Joe to bury? She understood that it was sometimes the case that there wasn't enough of a man left to gather together and stick a name to. Men were obliterated. They were blasted into fragments. She looked up at the fifty-five thousand missing men. Was it the case that Joe was one of them? Had he simply disappeared into dust? Was that why Laurie had taken so long to name a cemetery and then had seen fit to create a fiction? Had he tried to spare her that truth?

She walked back to the hotel, through the bright, busy, early-evening streets. There was laughter and songs and, with her green-black hands and head full of questions, she wanted to hide from it.

Reginald had scratched at the door. There were claw marks in the new paintwork.

'We have both been clawing,' she told him.

She held him to her – warm, silky, slightly off-smelling, reliable Reginald. He wriggled from her arms and made meaningful eyes at the door.

'I know,' said Effie.

For all of Grace's doubts, she was glad of him then. She thanked Laurie for the chaperoning of a toothless Yorkshire Terrier who needed, and now pleaded, to pee. She put Reginald on the lead and the diary on the bed.

It had all started with sportsmanship and rules. But Joe's absence without leave felt like not playing by the rules. This hide and seek didn't feel terribly sporting. Had the rules broken within the two years that Laurie's diary documented? Was this, then, what the fortunes of war meant?

Chapter Twenty-Five

Belgium, October 1917

Dear Effie,

I am back with the battalion and back in the north. Most of the past fortnight has been travelling. There has been a great deal of marching and not much sleep. I seem to have seen a lot of northern France over the last month. I have seen some sights that I am glad you will never see. We are now in billets in a village in Belgium. All of the places hereabouts are unpronounceable combinations of z's and q's and there is an awful lot of mud. We are not so far now from where we were first in trenches back in February of last year. It feels like much has been lost in that past year and not much gained.

'What we need is an away day,' said Frank.

'Charabanc to Blackpool?'

'I'm not Thomas bleeding Cook.'

They hitched a lift on a lorry that was going towards Poperinghe. It might not be Blackpool, but there was Bass beer and obliging mademoiselles to be had for two francs. Sam Hindle tagged along on a promise of girls and gravy.

The lorry made halting progress. All of the army seemed to have taken to the road. Joe lit a cigarette and watched it all pull past. There were horse-drawn limbers, London buses painted War Office green, signallers ringing the bells of their bicycles and columns of marching men. Because they were on a day out, feet dangling from the back of the van, they called out to the trudging columns. There were ambulances, top-brass in shiny cars and weaving dispatch riders.

'Like musical chairs,' said Sam, 'before the music stops.'

'What happens when the music stops?' Frank asked.

'That's when we all go home, I suppose.'

'I can't imagine going home any longer,' said Joe.

Though he had rejected the Thomas-bleeding-Cook role, Frank did seem intent on acting tour guide for the day. He pointed out camps, workshops, stores and supply depots. His finger identified bake houses, bath houses and grand civilian residences that were no longer quite so grand. French soldiers were fishing in a ditch with a makeshift net. A field kitchen steamed. Women waved between long lines of khaki laundry. They passed munitions dumps, white hospital tents and newly dug cemeteries.

'Chicken and egg,' philosophised Frank.

They walked the last few miles and made faster progress. A line of ammunition waggons rolled weightily past. Joe felt the might of them through his feet. They paused to pick blackberries in the verge while they showed off their skill in artillery identification.

'It makes me think about cancelling my contract,' said Sam.

'Chance asking for a pay rise before you write your letter of resignation.'

'Gartside saw Allerton writing his will.'

'Is he sure it was a will?' Joe asked.

'And to mater I leave my extensive collection of vintage Parisian smut.' Frank did Allerton's vowel sounds.

'Gartside reckons it'll be real nasty stuff this time.'

'Allerton's mucky postcards?'

Sam rolled his eyes.

'Well, it's about time we did some shooting, instead of getting shot.'

'With that command of military strategy they ought to make you a general.'

'Or perhaps not.'

Joe's first sight of Poperinghe wasn't encouraging. It looked like a shanty town, all lean-tos, patched sheds and irregular shacks. It seemed, for the most part, to have been constructed from packing cases, discarded doors and corrugated iron. It looked like an afterthought of a place.

'Have we arrived too late for the party?'

It improved with perseverance. They followed the crowds. They crowded into the square. It opened colourfully and noisily about them. The shops boasted their wares to the street: folding toothbrushes, propelling pencils, razorblades, rosaries, souvenir pincushions and pastel-tinted postcards of Ypres in ruin. Any currency would seemingly do. There were theatres and concert shows, and even a picture palace showing Charlie Chaplin. There were barrel organs and gramophones, bands and pianos.

A group of Service Corps were playing dominoes outside one of the cafés.

'Frank Fitton?'

Joe recognised Cecil Greenall from the Rochdale Road greengrocers.

'Bloody hell. You know Joe, don't you? Effie's intended? And Sam Hindle from off Morley Road?'

They shook hands and amicably mocked each other's uniforms and scarcity of stripes.

'All the world is in Pop,' said Frank.

'It would seem so.'

'*Tout le monde*,' added Sam, displaying new-found French.

'I was sorry to hear about your Charlie,' said Cecil to Joe. 'Our Alice saw your mother. She said she hardly recognised her. Alice reckoned she'd taken it badly.'

Joe nodded.

'Maybe the odd letter wouldn't go amiss?'

'A letter?' said Joe. 'You're telling me that I ought to write her a letter? I write to her all the time. Only she doesn't write back to me. She hasn't written to me for the best part of a year.

A letter wouldn't go amiss at this end either.'

'All right, son.' Frank put his hand on Joe's shoulder.

'Anyway, how's that grand Gracie?'

'Expecting.'

'Good lad!'

Joe observed that Frank seemed somewhat less than delighted to receive Cecil's slap on the back. With his turn at the dominoes, the table howled for Cecil.

'Will you join us?' he said. 'We're playing for money, only you have to watch Redmond because he cheats.'

'We're looking for Charlie Chaplin,' lied Frank.

They shook hands again.

'Take care, eh?'

They crossed the square.

'Pillock,' said Frank.

'Oh, he's all right.'

'I'll give him grand Gracie.'

They sat outside a café in the weak sunshine, ate fried potatoes and passed a running commentary on the khaki crowds. A gang of London-Scottish had knocked over a table and were scuffling over the rules of gin rummy. There were drinking games and singing games and arm wrestling and a sergeant-major snoring under a newspaper hat. They pointed out the insignia of other regiments and mimicked a crowd of officers who were debating the comparative merits of various restaurants' cellars. The café phonograph crackled out *If You Were the Only Girl in the World.* Joe thought about his mother taking things badly.

'Shall we go and look for a gaff with a piano? There's places that will pay in kind for a tune.'

'Was I brought along just for barter?' asked Joe.

They settled in an estaminet off the square, where Frank seemed set on working a deal with the waitress. Joe watched Frank's hand on her hip. He wasn't entirely certain what the terms of this deal were.

'Come on,' said Sam and pulled out the piano stool. 'Something sentimental. Something about lost love and roses. That's what the ladies like.'

There were a lot of Australians, just out of the line, packed into the estaminet, loud, intense and intent on drinking. Bets were being taken on a game of billiards and the height of a house of cards. Joe thought that love and roses might be lost on them. The keys of the piano were sticky and not best in tune, but he played irreverent soldierly favourites and it soon turned to a sing-along. Joe's notes crashed, though, as a blast made the room quake. He watched the water level list in the vase of piano-top chrysanthemums. The bottles behind the bar clinked a crescendo. A glass smashed. Balls rolled on the billiard table. The house of cards fell. A waitress' scream broke into a laugh.

'Christ! What was that?'

'Don't tell me that you've never been shelled before?' asked one of the Anzacs at Joe's elbow.

'Long-range guns. Only practising their aim.'

'Doesn't appear that they need to practise.'

'It's all right. It's a way off.'

Glasses were refilled. Cards were reshuffled. The pictures on the wall above the piano were suddenly all askew. Joe himself felt slightly askew. Plaster dust was still falling from the ceiling, but the lightly-dusted Anzacs appeared entirely untroubled and clapped for the music to continue.

'Is our instrumentalist an invertebrate?' shouted a wit.

'Is the pianist a pansy?'

'Is our performer in a funk?'

Joe looked to Sam, but he was laughing too.

'Tune! Tune! Tune!' came the chant. And then 'Funk! Funk! Funk!' when the tune didn't follow.

Joe put his hands back on the piano keys. He leaned his

forehead against the lacquer. A dissonant reverberation seemed to be coming from somewhere inside the piano. Somehow his fingers made a string of notes.

It hit again. He felt the keys lurch under his fingers and suddenly the vase of flowers was sliding.

Joe was out in the street then and running. He didn't know where he was running to, or exactly what he was running from, but an instinct propelled him out and across the square. Poperinghe streaked past. He ran through courtyards and under archways, stumbled over cobbles and plunged through a crowd. He ran past the drinking games and dominoes and the officers' menus, past the shops, the musical side-shows and the picture palace. He left behind the crowds and the conviviality, the drinking and the singing and the strolling soldiers and the shouts of 'Funk! Funk! Funk!' He ran until he couldn't run any further.

Joe hugged his knees to him. His breath was hot and damp against his hands. He parted his fingers and saw segments of old stone and plaster saints. There were ancient agonies carved in oak and stained-glass sinners. The walls, he saw, were painted with blue angels. There were cherubim and seraphim, angels and archangels, wheels and zeal and wings. He heard the texture of the feathers first, a stirring and flexing and a brittle bristling. He felt it then. The air shifted against his skin. It began with a whisper that formed into a pulse and grew into a beat. The angels beat their wings. Joe's shoulders slammed back into the corner. All around was feathered frenzy. All around and within. He felt the writhing rise within him – that scrambling, scrabbling, flailing fear. His chest was full of feathered terror and from his mouth came a silent scream.

Chapter Twenty-Six

Ypres, 1928

Effie stood in the square and Ypres writhed and flickered around her. It jostled and shouted and shoved. Where must she begin? How could she start to look for a grave that had possibly never even existed?

'*Attention!*' A man grabbed her by the shoulders as a block of stone swung upwards on a crane. '*Regardez où vous allez, hein?*' the workman jabbed his fingers towards his eyes. He had oiled-back hair and bar breath. She watched the carved block sway weightily behind, with its new-cut trills and trefoils. '*Tête dans les nuages,*' the oily one said, before giving Effie an impertinent push along the pavement.

The block disappeared up through a plank walkway and into the screened scaffolding above. A row of new-made angels peered down. Effie stepped back, suddenly struck by how it was all being put back and patched and reproduced. Ypres was all a copy and covered-over and pretend. It was all being tidied up and prettied up because the alternative was just too awful. She thought about the at-the-end constellations of graves, those crude crosses blinking like little stars across the blackened landscape. Had Joe been tidied up too? Or had there been nothing left of him to tidy up?

She replayed sentences from his letters. It struck her now that there was a lot of pretend in them too. Had it always been awful underneath? Was it always ghastly behind the camaraderie and courtesies? Reading his letters again, alongside Laurie's diary, Effie was left with a sense that Joe couldn't quite tell it like it was. There was an awkwardness to them, an embarrassment almost. There seemed to be a great, and growing, distance between the writer and the reader. Hadn't she seen that before? Could she have done anything to narrow that distance? Why couldn't he have talked to her about Charlie? She continued along the street. Rubble heaps and crumpled hollows were cordoned off. Did she have the right to pry into the cordoned-off places in Joe's past? Was it wrong of her to want to look between the lines?

She considered whether Laurie had cordoned-off corners too. Apart from the confectionary confessions, she still recognised his voice. When she read his words she could hear the scratch of the pencil, see his eyes flick along the line, could smell his shaving soap and his liquorice lozenges. How could he have expected her to hate him? Was it because he wasn't there to help Joe out of corners? Because he came through it, but Joe didn't? Did he really believe that it was his fault? She thought about Laurie with the blood down his fingernails and his heart not feeling quite right. They had felt the same fears. All that she could feel for him was pity.

A stall was selling lemonade. Crowded-round old comrades joshed in shirtsleeves and took snaps with cameras. A lorry rumbled through, loaded with salvaged wire. The old soldiers cheered and raised glasses. A young man tripped over Reginald's lead and glanced back with an apology. Effie caught a fleeting glimpse of profile. She stood and stared as he jogged along the pavement and pushed into the crowd.

'Joe?'

He was wearing a white shirt and a waistcoat and a flat tweed cap. His hair was newly trimmed at the back and his neck looked slightly sunburnt.

'Wait!'

She ran after him, cursing the lead and apologising through the crowd. Male faces turned towards her. She span in a circle of faces, but none of them was his. Then he was there again, the white sleeves were crossing the square. He was heading towards the cafés, looking at his watch and raising a hand in recognition to a friend. Effie's fingers stretched towards the distant figure as she pulled through and out of the crowd. He was weaving through the café chairs and tables. She was stumbling on the cobbles and scrambling to her feet. Three men at a table stood to greet him.

'Joe!'

Effie pushed chairs aside. There seemed to be a great stockade of café furniture to break through. She could hear the blood pumping in her ears. She stretched and grabbed towards his arm.

He turned. He stared at her. His mouth stretched into a smile.

'Miss?'

The friends at the table were staring too.

'Can I help you, Miss?'

He had pale blue eyes. He didn't even really look like Joe. Effie felt his blue gaze moving over her face.

'Are you quite well, Miss? Can I get you a glass of water? You look like you've seen a ghost.'

She let go of his arm. He was only about twenty, not even old enough to have been here back then. She stepped away, staggered and caught her balance on a chair.

'I'm sorry. I'm so sorry.' It came out as a stammer. 'I thought you were someone else.'

She ran back across the square, dragging Reginald behind. She ducked down a side street, wanting to be away from the eyes and the noise. There were courtyards and archways and the echo of her own quick footsteps. Corner girls with kohl-ed eyes called out and laughed at her. Effie didn't know where she was going, but she wanted to be away from it. She wanted to be away from the drinking and the singing, from the crowds and the conviviality. She wanted to hide away from it all.

She leaned against a railing. The metal felt cool against her forehead. She wiped the hot tears from her cheeks. On the other side of the railings there was a civilian cemetery. Effie stared at the gaudy graves. It wasn't so much the strings of tinsel or the blowsy silk flowers that struck her, but what was pasted in between: the headstones were stuck with photographs and letters and fragments of ephemera. There was something unsettling about this for-all-to-see reliquary, something ghoulish and garish and too loud in these statements of loss. Effie sat down on the wall and tried to steady her breath. Reginald pawed at her knee.

'I'm such a fool,' she told him. 'I'm such an utter bloody fool. How could I even have thought it?'

Where, though, was the grave that she ought to stick Joe's letters to? She needed to know what had really happened. She needed to go back to Laurie's diary.

Chapter Twenty-Seven

Flanders, October 1917

Laurence watched the child peer around the door. Female faces had been peering out for much of the morning. He had observed a certain amount of consternation behind the lace curtains as the old man had set up the camera. The child made a run for a row of lettuces now. Screened behind the hollyhocks, she studied the khaki-coloured strangers.

Laurence looked around with her. The garden was full of soldiers. They leaned against the fence, lolled back on her mother's chairs (teetering on two legs, as she was probably told not to) and were being untidy around the outhouse. There were a lot of cigarettes and alien-accented hilarity.

The old man had set up the camera between the poultry pen and the orchard wall, so his subjects were contained within a corridor of chicken wire. A foreground framing of honeysuckle softened the composition. He issued instructions, in broken English and articulate hand gestures, as if they were in a Parisian studio. Laurence suspected that today's queuing customers were perhaps somewhat less smartly attired than the photographer's typical clientele. What was lacking in elegance was made up for in enthusiasm, though. They assumed poses with bicycles and canes and the family pet dog. They were photographed in paired pals and groups with linked arms and grins. Two brothers swaggered for the camera now, woodbines between their lips and new stripes strategically angled.

'Since you are loitering, you may bring me a coffee.' The photographer emerged from under the black cloth. 'If you do mean to be a spy, you will need more practice, Manou.'

The girl skipped back to the kitchen door, shook the lettuce on the step and stuck out her tongue towards her grandfather's back.

Laurence watched the woodbine brothers fix their expressions for the shutter and then laughingly step back. The photographer gave them a thumbs-up gesture, which they dually returned.

A woman walked across the scene carrying a coffee pot and cups on a tray.

'*Merci, ma poule*,' said the man with the camera. The *poule* straightened his hair, smiled and took away a stack of photographic plates.

Beyond the photographer's impromptu studio Carver and Horrocks were walking through the orchard. Laurence watched them practising poses with a pitchfork and a scythe.

'*Monsieur?*'

He had been observing from under the cherry tree for some time, surveying the line of faces and the attitudes that they chose to express for the lens. But the hand extending towards him with a coffee cup suddenly turned Laurence from spectator into participant.

'Yes, thank you. That's kind. Our coffee always tastes slightly of petrol. Coffee that tastes uncomplicatedly of coffee is something of a rare treat.'

The child examined him from behind her mother's skirt.

'She likes the ones who make the comic poses,' said the woman, *la poule*, nodding towards the photographer. 'The ones who wear skirts, the ones who make faces and the ones who are foolish with Solange's dog.'

'The dog doesn't mind?'

'He probably thinks it's his birthday.'

'And you don't mind?'

'I'm enjoying it nearly as much as the dog.'

'You speak excellent English,' remarked Laurence, as the woman offered him the sugar bowl.

'I was in London when I was younger. I was a waitress at the Savoy hotel. It was very grand and quite – extraordinary.' She paused to select the apposite adjective and took the proffered seat next to Laurence. 'I served at receptions where everyone was in costumes – Greeks and pirates and Venetians. I watched Anna Pavlov dance, heard Caruso sing and once I saw an elephant. That was before I met my husband.'

'My mother took me for afternoon tea at the Savoy once, when my father was on business in London. We had smoked salmon sandwiches and scones with clotted cream and the pianist played an Argentinian tango. There was no elephant, though.'

They smiled together at recalled tangos and elephants.

'I am sorry. I forget my manners. My name is Elodie Roland.' She offered Laurence her hand.

'Laurence Greene. And I'm the one forgetting my manners. We seem to have rather taken over your garden.'

Elodie Roland shrugged and smiled. The child stood at her side, waiting to be presented.

'And this is Manou, who is finding it rather exciting that her *papy* has just emerged from retirement.'

Laurence bowed formally to the child and then straightened with a wink. '*Enchanté, mademoiselle.*'

Manou took a seat on her mother's lap and stared at Laurence as if she found him exotic. Her staring eyes were a glittering mineral green. Laurence recalled that his mother had a cocktail ring that was the same colour.

'El-i-fant? *C'est quoi, maman?*'

'*Éléphante,*' said Elodie and made her arm into an enthusiastically trumpeting trunk.

'El-i-fant,' repeated the child, seemingly finding the anglicised sound of the word highly amusing.

'And the ones who wear skirts are Scottish. I have friends who would flog me if I didn't correct you on that.'

'And the ones who wear ladies' hats?' A subaltern was now grinning under a flower-embellished brim.

'Just silly?'

The subaltern stood, smoothed his hair, shook the hand of the photographer and passed the hat to the next man in line.

'He's a professional photographer?'

Elodie nodded. 'Lucien had a studio in Ypres. He only got this small camera out. Most of his equipment is still there. Or perhaps not now.'

'It's very generous of him, all of this.' Laurence gestured at the garden. It was looking rather trampled. A lance-corporal was helping himself to the grapes that grew against the house wall.

'It is important to him. It is important that the families have photographs. We have too few of Emile and now it is too late. It is a regret to Lucien that he did not take more photographs of his son. How can you be the son of a photographer and so rarely have had your photograph taken?' She addressed the question to the bottom of her coffee cup. 'Solange is making lunch, but he won't stop for it.'

'Emile was your brother?'

'My husband. Verdun.'

'I am sorry,' said Laurence.

'So am I,' said Elodie.

Two Lancashire Fusiliers in sheepskins bah-ed and beckoned to Manou. In exchange for a cube of chocolate she was persuaded to sit on a fleecy knee and smile for the camera.

'You queue very politely,' observed Elodie, looking at the line of men leaning against the fence. 'I remember that the English queue very politely.'

Carver and Horrocks had now set about scrumping in the orchard. Laurence could see them, over Elodie's shoulder, filling their tunics with fallen apples. He thought it best not to bring this lapse in English politeness to Elodie's attention. 'We're not always polite, you know. If you were German I'd be obliged to be beastly to you.'

'I'm afraid that my sister-in-law may think that you are all slightly beastly.' She pointed to the front of the queuing line. 'It's her gardening hat they've all been taking turns to wear.'

Manou returned to her mother's knee having negotiated the remainder of the bar of chocolate from departing sheepskinned soldiers. They waved back as they went out through the gate.

'They look like ancient Greeks,' said Laurence.

'They look like sheep,' laughed Elodie.

'I'm sure their mothers will be delighted.'

'Perhaps they will. Lucien means to perpetuate them – that's his purpose – to give their families something to remember them by.'

Two young officers had requisitioned a potted fern and a plant stand and were now debating the arrangement of these props within the photographer's frame. A woman followed, making protesting gestures, but was then petitioned to join the officers in the image. They linked her protesting arms through their own. Laurence watched her face soften into a smile.

'To *perpetuate* us?'

'Is that not the right word?'

'No, it probably is the right word. It's just an alarming thought.'

He thought about the pose that he had chosen to perpetuate for his mother. He was swaggering by the henhouse with a walking stick and a hat full of silk roses. He wasn't convinced that his mother would be altogether proud of the attitude he had chosen to put in aspic.

'Would I want to be remembered as a sheep?'

'There are worse things.'

'*Maman*?' The girl curled fingers through her mother's hair and dipped down behind her shoulder.

'There are some that she is frightened of,' said Elodie.

They turned towards the camera. Joseph Young was standing in front of the photographer now. He made no poses and conveyed no concern for props. There was no show or smile for the camera. There was no expression on Joseph Young's face at all. He looked emptily at the lens.

'She is frightened of the ones with blank faces.'

'There are some faces that frighten me too,' said Laurence.

Chapter Twenty-Eight

Ypres, 1928

Effie sat on the floor of her hotel room, his letters fanned out around her. She held the last one in her hand. It was postmarked the 21st October 1917. Joe's handwriting looked like knitting unravelling. The words leapt and lunged about the line. The last two letters had been sent from a locality called Cabaret Camp. Laurie called it a 'gloomy and insalubrious spot'. *It appears that we have arrived too late for the song-and-dance show*, his diary recorded. *Alas, I can find no can-can girls, no jugglers or comics or clowns. There are no follies. There is a lot of mud and guns*. It was from here that Laurie had walked into the village and found the garden full of posing soldiers and Joe staring blank-faced at the lens.

Effie looked up at the rosy walls. She had never seen that photograph of Joe. She wondered whether he had ever collected it from the photographer. Was Joe's empty face in an attic somewhere north of Ypres? Was he hidden away in a biscuit tin somewhere with a stack of other lost soldiers? Would she have wanted to see that face? Effie turned towards the steady-looking soldier by her bedside and tried to imagine him with an expression that might scare small children. It frightened her too to think of that photograph face.

Effie had bookmarked her place in the diary with Joe's last letter. She leaned back against the bedstead and opened the pages. It was the 20th of October. Laurie had had orders that they were going back into the line.

We hear frightful stories, he wrote. *They say that it is all bog and gas and concrete block-houses east of Boesinghe. They say that the countryside is black, all landmarks quite obliterated, but seemingly there are objectives that we are required to acquire. We are to be part of an attack north-east of Langemarck. Pollard shot a hare today. I'm afraid that I railed at him. Mother always said that it was good luck to see a hare. I fear that killing one may be the contrary. We need all the luck that we can muster.*

Luck seemed to be needed in some quarters more than others. *I am concerned about Joseph Young*, said Laurence's next paragraph. *I am worried that he perhaps shouldn't have been sent back here. There is something not right about his eyes. I fear that his string has snapped. I am worried how he will fare when we go back into the line. I fear how we all will fare.*

Effie stared at the envelope in her hand. She couldn't remember the moment when it was delivered. There had been no ominous roll of her stomach. She couldn't recall which room she was standing in or what the weather was doing. It had not arrived with any aura of significance. She realised that it was a very long time since she had last read this letter. She felt guilt suddenly for that. Joe's notepaper had discoloured in the creases. It was only three lines. Sandwiched in between thanks for a tin of insecticide powder and a request that Effie call on his mother, Joe had written, *I don't know if I can do it again. I feel all in. I feel like I've had my chips.*

Effie felt the force of those few words anew. Did he know, then? Did he feel that his luck had run out? She had heard stories about soldiers having premonitions that their time was up. Soldiers in stories always seemed to be seeing signs or dreaming of their deaths. Or did he just no longer have the energy for it? She thought about her brother being put in his grave and remembered all of the prayers she had said to keep Joe out of his. But then everyone was praying, weren't they? How many thousand whispered petitions had bent shrapnel this way and that? She had willed him to keep dodging away from it, but perhaps he had lost the resources to keep out of death's way. Was that what Laurie saw in his eyes? Was that what Laurie meant when he speculated about snapped strings?

Effie tried to remember how she had replied to this last letter. Could she have said something in reply that might have made things different – some magic formula of words that could have made him blink, refocus and hold on? She pictured the sky over Ypres swarming with prayers, four years of pleas and bargains and promises seething and tumbling over the broken town. She looked to the window. There was nothing above but swallows.

Chapter Twenty-Nine

Houthulst Forest, October 1917

'Are you all right, Joseph? You look like your own ghost.'

'Aye, sir. Fine, sir.'

'Good man.'

Rain glinted from the brim of Laurence Greene's tin hat. In the dawn half-light, Joe could only make out the whites of his eyes.

'If I can be so bold,' the boldness was Frank's, 'you're hardly giving off a peachy glow yourself this morning, lieutenant.'

'No, I don't suppose so.' Joe saw the flicker of Laurence Greene's smile and then heard him resume his officer tone. 'The target position is one thousand yards north-east. It's the road junction just beyond the crest, bearing up towards the right... though it's distinguishability as a junction might now be as doubtful as my peachy glow. It's like a bog ahead. That I do know. Taking the terrain into account, the barrage is going to go forwards very slowly – a hundred yards every eight minutes. So let's have no sprinting for the finish, no swearing at the referee and no getting shot. You understand?'

'So, what, we follow the barrage forwards and in eighty minutes it will all be over?'

'That's the game plan. Kick-off in fifteen minutes.'

In fifteen minutes I shall die, thought Joe.

He watched Greene splash on to the next crater. He stumbled and slipped and looked back. His eyes connected with Joe's. Joe looked away. Their forward position wasn't so much a trench as a line of shell holes. There were no trenches here. A trench would have been luxury, Carver said. A trench would have been a treat. But, then, you can't dig a trench in a bog, can you?

'I can't even light a ruddy smoke,' said Frank, his fingers

working again through matches that were too damp to strike. 'I wouldn't care if I could only light a gasper.' Matches fell through Frank's fingers and scattered on the surface of the water.

They'd come up the night previously, through a region of crumpled brickwork. Where it was solid, there were ammunition dumps and dead men, halved horses and guns up to their axles in mud. They'd progressed then between the great black lakes, slithering in single file over wooden tracks. The heavy shells sent columns of water roaring a hundred feet into the sky. They'd been instructed to keep a hand on the shoulder of the man in front, warned that it wouldn't be possible to stop for anyone that fell off the tracks. It made the Somme look like a picnic, Horrocks had shouted ahead. Allerton said it was like Dante's Inferno. But wasn't an inferno a fiery place? Pollard had asked from behind. Frank said he meant to do something bad today, so as to make sure that his future in the fiery down-below place was secured. At least down there it was warm. Maybe, Sam had said, this was the place that you got sent to when you'd been very bad. Joe considered what act of absolute badness he had committed to warrant the leaping black waters.

They'd been formed up on a tape line which had been laid by the engineers. There seemed an out-of-place precision to this measure, here in this place of mud and eruption and ruin. They crouched down together in their waterlogged holes. White flares arced ahead. The water in the shell hole stank of sulphur.

In ten minutes I shall die, he thought.

Joe hugged his saturated greatcoat to him. Rainbows split on the oily sheen of the water. He leaned back his head. There was still little light in the sky. The rain ran down his face.

'I'm fucking freezing. I can't feel my feet,' said Frank, arranging his limbs for the umpteenth time. His boots surfaced from the shell hole and made short-tempered splashes. 'When I get out of here my feet won't work. I shan't know how to run.'

'Oh, I think you'll remember all right.'

They had seen boots in the water as they picked their way along the track. There were legs and arms and bloated faces in the water. There had been a hand, severed at the wrist, that gripped onto the walkway. They had laughed at it, with ghoulish soldier's humour, but there was something about its round white knuckles, something in the tension of its tendons, that had spoken to Joe of struggle and a striving to cling onto life. He clenched his jaw to stop his teeth from chattering.

In five minutes I shall die.

'Fix bayonets,' shouted Captain Hughes from a hole further along.

Joe disconnected the blade but couldn't get it to clip on. It vibrated about and wouldn't catch. It jittered against the muzzle and then jumped from his hands and into the mud.

'Jesus wept,' said Frank.

They fished about together in the water. Joe's fingers fleetingly skimmed against Frank's. He had an urge, for an instant, to grasp Frank's hand, but could imagine what Frank might have to say if he thought that Joe wanted to sit holding hands in a shell hole.

'Here,' Frank held the dripping knife up. 'Excalibur. Will you let me help?'

'Thanks.'

Frank fixed the blade on and handed the rifle back to Joe. 'Ruddy useless things.' He smiled.

In three minutes I shall die.

The barrage started up. It roared in. A shell hit just ahead, spouting fizzing splinters. 'Fucking hell!' said Frank. 'Are they actually aiming at us?'

Joe put his arms around his knees. The water in the shell hole quaked. 'Funk! Funk! Funk!' said the guns.

'It's all right,' said Frank. 'I'll watch your back. We'll get out of this.'

'Will we?'

'What was it? Eighty minutes by Gertie Greene's reckoning? By ten-past-seven we'll be feet up in Jerry's dug out, dry socks and a pan of bacon on.'

'Do you believe that?'

'Nah.'

Joe watched it flash on the surface of the water. He felt the ground lurch and rumble. His fingers dug into the mud.

'No, I reckon the bacon's off today, but what say we liberate a few kraut bangers?' Frank nudged him with a grin. 'Joe?'

He looked at Frank. He looked to him in terror. Joe felt the flutter of fear rising from his guts, the wings of panic beating upwards within him and his chest then full of feathered terror. He pushed his knuckles into his mouth to stop himself from screaming.

'Joseph?'

In one minute I shall die.

He heard a whistle blow. He ran.

Laurence blew the whistle and beckoned them on. Beyond the line of craters was black water, barbed wire and shrapnel explosions.

On the higher ground, to the left, he could see the jagged verticals of what was meant to be Houthulst Forest. The sky wavered behind it. He knew from the memorised map that the target, Six Roads Junction, was over towards the right. There was also meant to be another battalion to the right.

'Where the fuck are the Scots?' He shouted to Thorpe. 'Our right flank is going to be completely in the air. We're going to be totally exposed.'

'Perhaps they've a more pressing engagement?'

Laurence stumbled into a shell hole and swore. It was difficult to get a foothold in the mud. The mud sucked at his legs and seemed to want to pull him down. It was all slipperiness and explosions.

'Keep them back.' He shouted across to Allerton who was getting further forwards. The barrage threw up fountains of earth ahead.

'Lots of this stuff is falling short,' said Thorpe.

'Keep back,' Laurence screamed again along the line.

'Would Boulogne do?' he heard Horrocks say behind.

100 yards.

'Jesus Christ!'

A Focker swooped low, strafing machine gun fire along the line. 'Fucker!' yelled Carver. They dived down. Horrocks fell forwards.

Laurence crouched in a shell hole with Edwin Pollard. They watched the aeroplane turn and track back.

'What's this they say in the papers about British air superiority?'

'They're doing sterling work at superior altitudes, don't you know? They're invisible to the naked eye.'

'You can say that again.'

200 yards.

Wire entangled around Laurence's ankles and sent him pitching to the ground. His hands clung on to the edge of a crater. It must have been twenty feet deep. Mud-coloured limbs writhed down below. Laurence slid away from the edge.

He rolled onto his back. The sky was full of flying metal. He thought about the arrows, turning the sky black over Agincourt. Three days earlier he had looked up to a sky full of swallows. The autumn sun was on his face and then Elodie Roland was passing him a slice of apple tart. Laurence thought about another woman's face. Had he seen Joseph Young running backwards? He didn't suppose that it mattered any longer.

400 yards.

Laurence's binoculars scanned along the line. The Lancashire Fusiliers, to their left, were moving forwards, but were moving far out to the left. To the right it was all gap.

'Where are the fucking Scots?' shouted Thorpe.

'Scotland?'

A blast, just ahead, ripped through Sam Hindle's chest. He staggered a couple of paces back and dropped his rifle. He looked towards Laurence, his mouth round with shock, and fell over quite gently.

600 yards.

A group was pushing forwards to his left, making a run for the higher ground. He recognised Pollard and Carver amongst them. All that Laurence could do was look on as a machine gun mowed them down. It was coming in from the right then and suddenly also from the pillboxes towards the railway lines at the rear.

Allerton slid into the shell hole next to him. He was holding his shoulder with a red hand.

'*Thus we went,*' said Allerton, '*circling round the filthy fen.*'

'Here. I've got some morphine pills somewhere.'

'*Son, thou now beholdest the souls of those whom anger overcame.*'

'Although, frankly, you sound as if you're already medicated. Is that Dante? Should I attempt a dressing?' He unbuttoned Allerton's tunic. The wet shirt stuck to his chest. 'I think it's a bullet wound.'

'It suddenly seems annoyingly apt. It's the wrathful. Fifth circle. Seems a bit unwarranted, really. I'm not certain that I've ever felt wrathful. Apart from about Latin grammar, maybe.'

'How can you quote Dante? How can you be quoting Dante at a time like this?' Laurence struggled to get hold of one of the white pills. He didn't seem to be able to quite control his finger ends. 'Let it dissolve on your tongue.'

Caroline Scott

'I'm better with Italians than Greeks.'

'Clearly. Should I try to get you back?'

'Would you mind awfully if I didn't, Lol?' Allerton asked. 'Would you mind terribly if I just stayed here? Only I'm feeling a bit winded. I'm not feeling very bright. And, well, you ought to press on.'

The red bloom on Allerton's tunic was spreading.

'Jesus,' said Laurence. 'How did it come to this?'

'*And now we are sullen in our sable mire.*'

'Alex, stop it. You going hellfire and brimstone is the last thing that I need. It really is the last straw. I shall be generous and put it down to drugs.'

'Better move on, old man. *Tempus fugit* and all that. I'll get picked up by the stretcher bearers when you've secured the position.'

'*When?*'

He shook Allerton's red hand. '*When.* Take care, old stick. First drink in Berlin is on me.'

'Not too much mixer. Go easy on the ice,' Laurence shouted back as he plunged forwards.

Machine gun fire was rattling in from the left now and from up front towards the crossroads. The all-around rattle of it sounded like madness. He could smell the heat of the guns. He managed to scuttle a few yards forwards before he was knocked backwards by Thorpe. He pinned Laurence down and loomed over him. He gripped his wrists. Blood was coming from a head wound and dripped from Thorpe's face onto Laurence's. His wet red face was fierce. All the sinews in Thorpe's face seemed to be straining. He looked all sinew and nerve and fury. His lips trembled. He showed his teeth. Blood bubbled in his nostrils. He stared at Laurence intently before mouthing the word 'Will' and running, yelling, towards the enemy line. The machine guns came at him from every side. His arms lifted, in a gesture that looked beseeching.

650 yards.

Laurence slid down into the water. Thorpe had shared a theory with him the night before. He had told Laurence, in a quiet but firm voice, that he had developed an invisible armour, that he had, by force of will, made himself immune to shellfire. It was all about mind over matter. He would come through this unscathed, he had said, because his will was strong enough to repel bullets and shells. Laurence had wondered, the night before, listening to his whispered certainties, if Thorpe was perhaps mad. He watched his body convulse and finally still. Suddenly Laurence wasn't quite certain what sanity was.

He looked back. There was just mud and ruin behind, just the flooded low places and the shattered trees and the stretching, empty wreckage. Light pitched and rolled in the sky. Laurence shut his eyes.

Chapter Thirty

Less than sixty of us made it back, Effie read. *Thorpe is dead, and Horrocks, Hindle, Pollard, Carver. Eight officers killed. Five wounded. 20 other ranks dead. 115 wounded. 55 missing. I don't know yet whether Young will be counted amongst the missing. I can only hope that it is so. We have been withdrawn from the line. We will be in billets for some days.*

There were terrible pictures on the next page. They looked like the Old Testament agonies that she had once seen on the walls of a church. Effie turned quickly through them. She turned until she saw his name again. The page was dated the 1st November.

Training. Inspection. Ribbons handed around by Divisional Commander. Young has been arrested north of Poperinghe. He was hidden in a barn. There is talk that he is to be brought back and tried by Field General Court Martial. He told the military police that he wanted to walk away from the war. I don't know where he meant to walk to. I do sincerely hope that it doesn't come to a court martial. There is too much death. This is too much. I do not have the heart for this. Poor Euphemia.

Poor Euphemia stumbled down the steps of the hotel.

'This is too much.' She told it to the diners in the cafés, to the evening promenaders, to the gargoyles and the gothic gables and the blue-black sky.

To be tried by court martial: what did it mean? Had Joe, then, not been everything that he should have been as a soldier? Had he really run away? Did running away from the certainty of his death make him a coward?

In the bars and the cafés they raised glasses. They dined and smiled because, after all, it was picturesque and Ypres was rising.

There were candles, sounds of cutlery and Josephine Baker singing *I Want to Go Where You Go*. Effie looked at the diners. They, in turn, looked at her. She wasn't sure where she wanted to go, but she wanted to be away from the eyes. She crossed the square, her ankles threatening to betray her on the cobbles.

What happened to court-martialled men? Were soldiers condemned to break rocks? Did they get cookhouse duty? Were they flogged? Was it worse? There had been talk.

She remembered, then, the blur of Market Street from the taxi window and a front-seat voice that had questioned Joe's heroism – that heroism of which she had been so sure. 'It was a rotten show all round,' the driver had said. Did he know? Did they all know? Had Joe's mother known when she had drawn a line through hope, closed the curtains and turned on the gas?

She found herself before the gate. It was floodlit, up-lighting swags of acanthus and the stone-cut words *No Known Grave*. She stepped through the arch and looked up at the well-lit missing.

'There is too much death,' echoed Effie.

I feel all in, he had said. *I feel like I've had my chips*. Had she not realised how entirely all-in he was? How could she not have heard it? She opened the locket and stared at his likeness. She scrutinised his miniaturised features for cowardice, for instability, for a tendency to run away and a tell-tale signifier of soon-to-be-snapped strings. But it was just Joe, who was steady and sensible, who was gentle and likeable and who had asked.

She walked through the gate and across the bridge. The still water darkly reflected the arch of unplaced dead. Bullfrogs croaked below. She walked on, down streets of boarded shops, through the night-shuttered daytime places. There were no longer any candlelit diners. There was a lot of corrugated iron. It became more ragged at the outskirts. There was more improvisation and impermanence. It was slumped shanty and makeshift making-do, but on she walked. The streets became dark.

Would she have rather had Joe one of the eighty ordinary ranks decently dead? She wondered if she was ashamed. Those other men had not walked away. They had walked into it. Would they have walked away if they could? Had Joe felt brave or had it felt an act of betrayal? He had, after all, hidden in a barn.

Effie found herself on a country road. She turned and looked back at Ypres, which was just lights. There was not much light here. The road tapered palely away. The moon gave the clouds bright threading edges. She felt the blood rise through her veins and it pushed her on.

Why hadn't Laurie told her? Why had this act of un-telling kindness been necessary? She knew Joe officially 'Died of Wounds' on the 6th November. Could it still be that Joe had died heroically? Could this just have been an unsavoury incident that his subsequent act of heroism had supplanted? What had happened between the 1st and the 5th November? She needed to go on with Laurie's words but, just now, she did not have the heart for it either.

Trees were sharp twists of blackness against the ink-blue sky. There were tumbledown shapes of once-habitations and a smell of waterlogged decay. The road had turned from cobble to compressed earth. Puddles at Effie's feet shivered with reflected night. The moon-hinted landscape was scarred and foul and unfriendly. She heard an owl's screech and the scrabble and scratch of nature. There was the noise of unseen water running and the creek and sigh of trees. The wind bellowed the tarpaulin of a fallen-in barn and then there was the whisper of something else. She heard her heart bang.

Effie spun and stumbled. Her cheek slammed into mud and grit, into cold and then heat. She gasped and blinked at a vertical horizon that was suddenly hostile. She too felt the will to run. She pushed her hands into the road's hostile sharpness and scrambled to her feet.

Ypres was a faraway blinking of lights. She ran to Laurie and the light.

Chapter Thirty-One

'Could you please give me directions to Cabaret Camp?'

The receptionist looked at Effie blankly. This clearly wasn't a question that she'd been briefed to receive from dignitaries. Effie flicked through November 1917 looking for same-period place names.

'Elverdinge? Boesinghe? Wippe?'

Having little faith in her Flemish, Effie turned the diary for the woman across the desk to read. Blonde curls nodded and, in turn, a map was inverted for Effie's attention.

'Your husband is there?' A manicured hand moved from Elverdinge to Effie's arm.

'No. That is... I'm not sure.'

She managed to find a taxi to take her north. But, as Effie travelled, as she watched the Flemish fields pass the window, she realised that she didn't know exactly where she meant to go. All that she had been able to glean from Laurie's diary was that they had brought him back under arrest to a farm west of that place where there were no dancers or clowns. It wasn't much to go on. And, even if she could find the place, she didn't know what she meant to do there. She didn't know what she ought to feel there.

The taxi left her in a proximate village. Effie walked through seemingly abandoned streets. All of the angles were awry. Shutters were aslant and beams plunged. Walls showed wattle beneath. Nothing was quite aligned as it ought to be.

In one of the wrecked houses – the doorframe remained intact, but the front wall of the building was otherwise gone, opening it up like a doll's house – she saw a piano. Effie stared at the shook-apart domesticities. She stepped across blown leaves and broken crockery. Pictures still clung to the striped wallpaper: polite bourgeois prints of pastoral scenes and portraits, his and hers. Could it really be, she wondered, as she walked through the inside-out house and acquainted herself with the photographic poses of its owners, that the war had been over for the best part of a decade? With its consequences made so physically real here and the circumstances of Joe's death suddenly in doubt, it seemed like the war hadn't ended at all.

She lifted the lid of the piano. Her fingers found the optimistic first line of an old song. Joe had liked a piano. He had liked a song with a sing-along chorus. He wasn't one for melancholy or maudlin, for sailors lost at sea or misused maidens. How had a lad who liked a chorus ended up trembling in shell holes and hiding in barns? Effie's slightly out-of-tune notes cut bluntly through this place of silenced violence. She wrote the date in the dust-dulled piano top, forming the numbers in black lacquer. It was eleven years since Joe had let go. How could so much time have passed and she never have known?

Effie walked on through the forgotten village. The church had evidently taken a heavy shelling. The empty windows were edged black. Pigeons roosted in what was left of the roof. Christ was rusting on a cross in the churchyard, his arms broken away. There was a smashed sewing machine and a fire-cracked stove by his feet, and a posy of sweet peas. The sunlight shone in this jam jar of flowers. It seemed to glow. Ought she to be seeking Joe with flowers? She pictured herself as a flower-bearing widow. Could she summon the courage to put flowers at his feet, knowing now how he had run away? The broken bell tower called noon.

She looked at the angle of the shadows and walked on along a road that seemed to head west. The road west was a mess. She had read that afterwards, after the war, the ground had spontaneously erupted colour. Poppies, cow parsley and cornflowers had sprung from the worked-over earth, a tricolour of red, white and blue for the freedom of France. There were no patriotic floral displays here, though, just the sharp insistent fists of thistles and brambles of barbed wire. The trees were black and branchless. Here and there concrete erupted and crumbled. The roadside accumulations looked like a rag and bone yard.

Effie felt exposed out on the road. Her footsteps along it were the only sound. All around her was silence and stillness and oddly contoured landscape that required explanation. She found herself thinking about those instants in the pictures when the film reel jams; there was something similarly straining and pressured in the atmosphere of this place. Effie felt it press in on her chest and found herself holding her breath. Was it just that she knew what had happened here? But then, did she really understand what had happened here?

A whistled tune stopped her steps. Had the jammed reel restarted? There was a newly constructed wall by the side of the road. Beyond it Effie saw a row of chaotic crosses, earthworks and waiting stone. There was also a man in a trilby. He kicked a roll of turf and, straightening, raised his hat to Effie. She raised her hand in uncertain acknowledgment and stepped over the low wall. They were evidently working from the back, progressing towards the road. The new-laid turf curled at the edges. The symmetrical stones glared white. Was she any closer to the place where it ended? Could this be where Joe was? She stared at her foolish raised hand and wondered whether she could now acknowledge him.

'It will be an English garden. It'll be a thing of beauty when it's done; a fit resting place for Albion's heroes.' A figure leant against a tree, camouflaged in greatcoat and silence.

Effie swore, startled.

'Didn't mean to give you a turn, young lady. Alan Welch.' He bowed flamboyantly and shook Effie's still hesitating hand in his. 'Earth-shifter, gravedigger, shit-shoveller and purveyor of pretty petals.'

The dirt was engrained in his skin. He looked as if he himself had been disinterred from the earth. Alan Welch had ragged hair, a sing-song accent that she couldn't place and a slightly deranged smile. He wore his yellow medal in his waistcoat. With his eccentric attire and theatrical manners, he reminded Effie of the Shakespearian fairy folk that had once mischiefed for her amusement on the stage of a Huddersfield repertory theatre. She wondered whether he was a trickster or a wise knave – and whether his trousers hid hairy haunches.

'It's to be a graveyard?' She looked about.

'Not much gets past you, eh?' Alan Welch's smile curled upwards. 'But, no, it will be no mere graveyard, mademoiselle. That is too small, too civilian, a word. This is a fitting commemoration of England's fallen, of her best.' He doffed his cap in mock solemnity. 'If you'll pardon me for picking at your noun.'

'Forgiven.' She eyed the fastidious linguist. He leaned on a shovel and spat.

'So, you work here?' Effie wasn't altogether certain that she wanted Joe's bones bequeathed to a man who must tease and spit and pick at nouns. But, then, she wasn't sure what she wanted for Joe's bones and Alan Welch might at least call him England's Best.

'Aye, here and hereabouts. Five in all, of varying size, mind. There are six of us together, myself and young Wellesley here included.' He gestured at the elderly man in the trilby. 'And Foch, who is a cur of a dog. A rare travelling circus, indeed. I was a head gardener before.' He added, frowning at the afterthought. 'With rhododendrons and rhubarb and an orangery.'

'And I an innocent,' said Effie, the details of dog and rhubarb inclining her more to trust.

'Will you have some tea, Miss? 'Tis army tea and fresh brewed.'

'Thank you,' she said.

165

As Alan Welch pushed up his sleeves to attend to the primus, Effie saw that his arms were circled with tattooed spirals of vine. Effie wondered (but did not wish to see) how far the ink tendrils wound. She watched him administer the domesticities, nodding for a shot of rum and giving scant regard to the tarnish of his teaspoon. He clinked his tin mug against hers.

'I thought that it was all done. I thought that it was all finished – the cemeteries, I mean.'

'Done? It's years off done. They come in every day, the dead, like home harvest. Farmers get ten francs if they find a body – and so they find plenty of them. They come in by the cartload. The official term is Concentration. It's a very long way off done.'

She joined Alan Welch against the tree. He gave off a foxy stink. They sat side-by-side on a crate that was stamped with the word *Explosive*.

'The slabs will file in line, thirty by twelve.' The gardener gestured the ranks. 'Like a battalion on parade, see? Ten pounds per man. And clipped lawns and polite remembrance, and a cross that is also a sword, for these chivalric times. It will be a thing, when it is done.'

'So many?'

He looked at Effie as if in wonder. 'But of course.'

She leaned forward to read an inscription on the waiting stones. Alfred was much missed by Mother and Kitty.

'Three pence ha'penny for each letter and the same for the space in between,' Alan Welch nudged her and laughed. 'Thruppence ha'penny for a space, eh? It inspires brevity.'

'And the old graves are being replaced?'

'The old graves are just the tip of it. It was all smashed to shit at the end. We know who is here, we have a list, but fuck knows where. Pardon my French.' He smiled crookedly. 'This place is more bones than earth.'

'And the men on the list will have a grave?'

'As such. *Known to be Buried Within these Walls*: that's the formula. *Within these Walls* it will say.' He garlanded the phrase with a flourish of fingers. 'Took 'em months to come up with that.'

Was Joe within these walls? Dare she ask whether Joe was on the list? The tea scalded Effie's tongue.

'Pleasant though this parlaying is, and you are certainly pleasanter and prettier to parlay with than Wellesley, are you looking for someone in particular, mademoiselle?'

She wanted to say 'Yes.' She wanted to tell him about Joe. She wanted to ask him whether men who had been arrested got concentrated, and, if so, where Joe would be. But Effie found that she couldn't. She found that she couldn't name him. She couldn't tell him what Joe had done. Was this emotion shame?

'Miss?'

Effie shook her head. 'No,' she said. 'I'm not looking for anyone.'

'So, did you just stay at the end?' She was now sharing Alan Welch's hipflask.

'Nah, I went back for a while, but it was no good. I'd just as well be here with my bones and my flowerbeds to tend. I mean to bring on nasturtiums for next spring.'

He offered her a cigarette. She took one and blew smoke at the overhead blue. Alan Welch pared black crescents from under his fingernails with the used match.

'I'm a wonder with roses, you know. There'll be polyanthus and hybrid teas. Roses shining in Picardy, eh? In the hush of the silvery dew.'

Effie gave a measured smile of acknowledgment. She didn't mean to encourage him to sing.

'And pinks and alyssum and columns of hornbeam. It will be

a garden of hope, you know, a garden to end wars, where Lewis guns failed. Look on my works, ye mighty.'

'You sound contented.'

'I am. I am proud of this. You should have seen this place before.'

She nodded. To some degree – through Laurie's diary – she felt that she had seen this place before. She understood some of it. Though she still didn't understand what had happened here in that first week of November, how it had got from Joe being under arrest to being dead of wounds.

'You can tell me, you know, mademoiselle.' Alan Welch leaned his head back against the tree trunk and smiled at her with a kindly incline of nicotined teeth. 'I get told all manner of secrets. I know about the illicit loves, the illegitimate sons, the kissing cousins. And I don't spill secrets. I'm the veritable model of discretion. If you'll tell me his name, I'll whisper you where he is – and won't earwig what you whisper to him.'

Effie couldn't think what she might whisper to Joe. She had no idea what she might say to him. She certainly had no idea how she might explain it to Alan Welch. 'There's nothing to tell.' She flicked her cigarette away and turned from the gardener's too-seeing eyes.

'As you see fit.'

He gave her a lift back to Ypres on the back of his truck. Effie held on amongst the shovels and stakes and rolls of canvas and looked out at the secret-keeping curves of the landscape. Alan Welch helped her down in the square and, with an ostentatious sweep of arms, magicked a rose from behind his back.

'*Félicité et Perpétué*. It's the name of the rose,' he clarified. He held it for her to smell.

Effie shut her eyes. She was back in the garden at Everdene, dead heading after a week of rain and Laurie just coming out onto the lawn with the tea tray.

'Such a pity, eh? *Soft voices had they that with tender plea whispered of peace, and truth, and friendliness unquelled,*' Laurie quoted at the rotting roses.

Effie opened her eyes and saw the gardener's grin.

'You can't hold your breath forever,' he said.

He bowed, turned away with a wink and left her standing in the square.

Effie had never liked heights. But, then, she was doing a lot at present that she didn't altogether like. Somehow she found herself at the top of the tower of the Cloth Hall. There had been staircases and ladders and scaffolding. She had watched her hands and feet climb. She had watched them as if they weren't her own. It didn't seem to be her own will that propelled them upwards.

Effie looked at her boots on the ledge and thought that they could perhaps do with polishing. The square, beyond her insufficiently shiny shoes, was a far-below blur. Her stomach lurched as she refocused. Her hands gripped the scaffolding.

The wind billowed and whipped her skirt sharply about her legs. Swifts streaked around the tower. Effie felt that she might soar like a kite. She shut her eyes and saw herself spin over the sharp rooftops of Ypres. She thought about Jude on the frozen pond, the jagged crack with his forward footsteps on the ice. She thought about Tess, the rope in her hand, preparing to hang herself under the mistletoe. Effie's fingers slowly let go. She spread her arms, released her held breath and welcomed the decision of the wind.

Chapter Thirty-Two

Effie dreamed about the gardener that night. The land had fissured. While the world above was green, below, in the split earth, they writhed red, like maggots in a wound. Alan Welch stood astride the chasm, part-man, part-tree. His arms were twisted trunks, roses flowered from his fingers and his head sprouted the branches and boughs. Meandering behind him, binding together the torn earth, were stitches that were white crosses. The gardener's chasm-spanning legs tapered to hairy hooves.

She wasn't certain that he had been any more than a dream, but the rose that was soundlessly dropping petals onto the dressing table indicated otherwise. When she had climbed down from the tower it had still been there, waiting, on the cobbles. Embarrassment had obliged her to pick it up. There was a somehow accusatory quality to the scent with which it had now filled the room.

She stared at her hands. Her stretched fingertips had convulsed and re-found stone. Unlike Jude, she couldn't jump. Even now, her fingers had gripped. Unlike Joe, unlike his mother, even now she couldn't let go. Effie had gripped onto life.

Her knees had shaken as she climbed back off the ledge. She had crouched with her back to the scaffolding, buried her face between her knees and not been able to move for some time. She had felt acutely aware of every fibre, every pulse, of her precious, treacherous, trembling body.

With the door of her hotel room locked behind her, she had vomited in the bathroom basin. 'What am I reserved for?' Effie had asked her reflection. Her reflection didn't seem at all sure.

'I might get a little drunk,' she said to Reginald. She ordered the celebrated Charlotte Russe and a bugger-it bottle of champagne. Reginald offered neither caution nor objection.

She had left the diary on the dressing table. Laurie had started talking about casting away arms, mitigating circumstances and the legal implications of changing into civilian clothing. She knew that she had to read this. She knew that this was the most important part, but Laurie's words had ceased to shape themselves into arrangements that made sense. Effie had pushed the book away and put her head in her hands.

She sat at a table in the square and looked out at sharp-pointed Ypres. She was scheduled to move onto Paris tomorrow, job here done and sights to see. How could Laurie imagine, after he had taken her through all of this, that she would want to see sights? Was she now meant to raise a dismissive glass, forgive and forget and look forwards? How could he ever have thought that? Did Laurie really know everything but not know her at all?

Effie thought about Laurie in Paris. She tried to picture him there. She planted him, with his glasses and his gaucheness, between an Eiffel Tower and a strawberry tart. She animated him with a whistle and a Maurice Chevalier walk. It didn't work. He'd gone to Paris when the war was finished, she knew. He'd told her that he couldn't yet bring himself to come back home. Now, recalling the page that she had just pushed away, Effie perhaps understood why.

The waiter smiled at her professionally as he presented her cold pudding. It was prettied with angelica and glacé cherries and propped within a palisade of finger biscuits. It made Effie sad to recall her pantry, her candied peel and careful provisions. She had cured and jammed and bottled under mistaken assumptions. Would she be happier had her mistaken assumptions been left undisturbed, if her ignorance too had been preserved? Truth might be the best policy, but Effie wasn't presently sure that she liked the taste of it.

She took a mouthful of champagne. It prickled pleasantly on her tongue. She raised the glass to her canine dining companion.

Reginald looked at her doubtfully.

'It's all very well giving me looks, but I know that you've been keeping secrets.'

She wondered why Laurie had to tell her his secrets. Did he need, in death, to purge himself of this unvoiced history? Or did he think it right for Effie to know – to go forward informed? But where was forward? She wasn't at all sure of its direction.

'Couldn't you perhaps have said something? Couldn't you *say* something?'

Reginald cocked his head to one side.

'I'm frightened,' she said to him. She put down her spoon. 'I'm frightened of what I'm going to find next. And I need someone to tell that to.'

She thought of Henry, then, who had lots to say, who had opinions on culinary constructions and umpteen other matters. Was it so wrong to want someone to tell it to? Would it really be so very improper if she were to write to Henry? Effie turned her glass and wondered if her understanding of properness had perhaps been misplaced.

She pushed the Charlotte Russe towards Reginald and began to rummage through handbag clutter. Henry's particulars emerged from amongst the handkerchiefs, toffee papers and the co-ordinates of a fictional grave.

'Should I?'

Reginald looked up from the plate. His only concern seemed to be for the Charlotte Russe. Perhaps he held herbal medication against Henry?

'It was my fault, really. I brought up sedation.'

The vigorously-licked plate banged a rhythm against the bottle. Pudding was clearly a higher priority than the assigning of blame.

Effie's hand hesitated over the blank page. She hardly knew the man that she was about to write to. Did she have any right to tell Joe's secrets to a stranger? She wasn't even sure how she ought to address him. Could she call him Henry? Or should he be Mr Lyle? Seeing as they had shared tea, opinions on patisserie and a conspiracy in a lavatory compartment, Effie decided, on reflection, that she was permitted a degree of informality.

Dear Henry, Effie wrote.
I'm afraid that I have been rather otherwise occupied. In truth, I've been having the most utterly rotten time of it. I have, however, not forgotten that I promised to send you my address. I will, from the 8th, be at the Hotel Lutèce, Paris. It would be awfully nice to see you again.
With kind regards to Kate.
Effie Shaw
P.S. I do hope that the sapling stays. X

From inside the restaurant came the noise of scraped chairs and china. At the next table a couple were planning excursions over a battlefield atlas. The green book was waiting for her upstairs. Effie poured out the last of the champagne and shut her eyes. She thought about looking down on the town last night. The prospect of what might be waiting on Laurie's next page made the recalled rooftops spin.

Chapter Thirty-Three

Flanders, November 1917

His mother had sent him Dundee cake and Hardy's *The Breaking of Nations*, copied out in her curlicued hand.

> *I*
> *Only a man harrowing clods*
> *In a slow silent walk*
> *With an old horse that stumbles and nods*
> *Half asleep as they stalk.*
>
> *II*
> *Only a thin smoke without flame*
> *From the heaps of couch-grass;*
> *Yet this will go onward the same*
> *Though Dynasties pass.*
>
> *III*
> *Yonder a maid and her wight*
> *Come whispering by:*
> *War's annals will cloud into night*
> *Ere their story die.*

Laurence thought about the maid who maybe baked the cake. Could their story die? The candle guttered and hissed. He took a mouthful of rum and looked up at the dugout. Gibson, who had been seconded from the Cheshires, was bent over a letter. The pen tilted a pattern through his fingers.

'I before E, except after C,' said Laurence.

'I am thinking of proposing', said Gibson. He bit on the pen then and stared at the page.

'A motion to the House, or marriage to a maiden?'

'A girl,' said Gibson. 'I think I might marry a girl.'

'It is the conventional choice.'

'What with all of this,' went on Gibson, nodding to the mud walls, 'I might as well. You know?'

'I know,' said Laurence.

Gibson passed a photograph. An agreeable-enough brunette smiled in a high-necked blouse.

'Millicent,' said Gibson. 'She means well.'

'Does she mean enough?'

Gibson took a drink. 'I think so.'

Laurence thought of a girl behind a shop counter, of whom his mother would never have approved and of whom he might have made a choice. He cut a slice of fruit cake.

'Take your chance,' he advised.

But the fruit cake did not taste as it should. The girl had made a choice: she had chosen that boy who now looked like his own ghost. Laurence swallowed the last of the rum. It hit the back of his throat. He felt for a second that he might throw up. He was still reeling from the order that he had just received. A firing squad was about to take away Effie Shaw's choice.

The car growled and jerked and Laurence looked out on a mess of muddied agriculture. It should have been autumn – russet hillsides and the sweet blue smoke of first fires – but it was just turned earth and brown ruin. The sky was white. The light was flat. Laurence felt flat.

The car pulled up before a symmetrical-fronted farmhouse. The prisoner was in the barn, he'd been told. A female face glanced out behind a brief shift of lace curtains. Laurence thought about Elodie Roland and her garden full of soldiers. He was sorry that this place was still a home and not yet just stone – that what was about to happen here would become part of this home's history.

The priest leant against the wall of the barn. He saluted with a cigarette.

Laurence put out his hand. 'Father.'

'Michael Bladen.'

'Laurence Greene.'

Michael Bladen offered Laurence the packet of cigarettes. They leant against the wall together and looked at the damp and darkening farmyard.

'How is he?' asked Laurence.

Bladen shivered. It was cold in this place. 'As lucid as any man I've ever met. He's just had enough.'

'Haven't we all?'

'I guess that that's the point of this,' said Bladen.

'I'm not sure that it's a point that needs to be made by such heavy-handed means.'

'No.'

The priest smelled of stale alcohol. Laurence noticed that his hand shook as it went to his lips.

'We must make this insanity as sane as we can.'

'Agreed.'

A dog barked inside the house. Laurence felt himself watched.

'Come on, then.'

It was warmer in the barn. They had lit a fire and it smouldered cheerfully. There ought to have been comradeship and a thermos flask to pass. A dining table had been dragged in from somewhere. On it was a half-drunken bottle, glasses and the laid flat hands of Joseph Young. Laurence thought it an eloquent still life. Joseph looked up as Laurence entered and smiled. Laurence wondered how he could.

They let the red caps go. Bladen lit a candle and Laurence filled glasses. He patted Joseph on the back, unsure how to begin to form an appropriate sentence. It was a relief when Joseph's voice broke the silence.

'I seem to have become a person who hides in barns.'

'Perhaps you should have been a shepherd.'

'I'd never considered that,' said Joseph and looked as if he might. 'Still, my vocation isn't a worry now.' He raised a glass.

'You look well.' Laurence observed with some surprise.

'I am, Laurence. It's over.'

Bladen took a chair at the table and distributed cigarettes.

'Why did you do it?' Laurence turned the matchbox between his fingers.

'Do you need to know? Don't you know?'

'You're right.' They leaned together to share a match. 'It's a bloody silly question.'

Joseph rocked back in his chair, wide-eyed and expansive, teetering back as if at post-lunch leisure. 'No, you've every right to ask it. I just couldn't face it. I'd rather die like this. I suppose that I am a coward, but so be it.'

'Joseph has made his peace,' précised the priest.

'So it would seem,' said Laurence.

Candlelight made the barn bigger, but gave it pressing shadows.

'Did you not care what they'd think back home?'

Joseph shook his head then, as if this was beyond contemplation. His chair rocked forward. 'I can't think about that. There is only this.' He gestured at the glass, the table and the barn. 'There is only here and only now and I don't want to carry on with it. I *can't* carry on with it.'

'Have you written?'

Joseph looked blankly at the polished table top.

'You should write. It's only fair to give them your explanation. It's only right to tell them your side.'

Joseph turned his glass. Its shadow shivered. 'And what do I write to them, Laurence? My apologies?'

'They will be informed.'

'Of everything?'

'I don't know. I'll do what I can.'

Joseph clinked his glass against Laurence's.

'There's paper if you want it.'

Joseph nodded. 'I know. And I don't.'

'Have you really thought all of this through?'

'Why? If I say sorry very nicely will it all be forgiven and forgotten?'

Laurence refilled the glasses. They had told him to get the prisoner drunk if he could. They had said that it was the humane thing. He stared at the still surface of his own drink. There was no vibration of war here. Beyond the barn there seemed to be no noise at all. It might well all be over. The rosary, winding slowly between Bladen's fingers, was the only thing that stirred. Christ, silver-plated, spun.

'Would you like to pray?' asked the priest.

'No,' said Joseph. 'God is dead.'

Laurence felt the shock then, felt the reverberation of Joseph's desolation. He wanted to take his hand. He looked to Bladen, expecting him to counter, to deny, to give Joseph hope, but he shook his head and pocketed the prayer beads. Laurence wanted him to say something about a forgiving God. He wanted him to say *something*. Did he too think that God was dead?

'I want to die, Laurence. I want this all to go away, even if there is nothing more. It needs to stop.'

'It does. But not like this.'

'I need some air,' said Bladen.

They watched him walk to the door of the barn. Laurence looked down at the table top. Ash fell silently from the end of his un-smoked cigarette. He turned towards Joseph.

'You shouldn't be here,' he said. 'I shouldn't have let this happen. I shouldn't have let it come to this.'

'It's not your fault.'

'I could have done something. I could have got you out of the line. I should have insisted that you be sent to the Medical Officer.'

'I'm not mad, Laurence. I've not lost my senses. I've quite possibly found them.' Joseph put his hand to Laurence's shoulder, as if he were the condemned man, the one to be pitied. 'You remember the bargain that we made? The *entente cordiale*, as you called it.'

'Of course I do,' said Laurence. 'I'm just about to break it.'

'No, you're not. You're not going to break it. I'm about to change the terms.'

Joseph slept somehow. Laurence drank and listened to the calm rhythm of Joseph's breathing. He had envied him before. Perhaps he did so again now?

At first light they were to take the prisoner down to the field below the farm. Laurence followed the minute hand's too-fast rotations and willed his watch to stop. The firing squad came at six. He heard the scuff of their boots in the farmyard. He passed a bottle. They took it without thanks.

'I knew his father,' said Victor Jones. 'I've known him since he was a lad. He's not a bad lad.'

Laurence wasn't sure what to reply to that. Samuel Butler cried.

Captain Hughes arrived by car. He read instructions in a voice that wasn't altogether unsympathetic. 'If it comes to it, you must finish him off,' he told Laurence.

Laurence's head felt fragile. He felt like he too had had enough.

'And that is an order,' said the Captain.

The red caps brought Joseph out of the barn. The morning light made him older. His eyes were darkly shadowed.

A lane descended before the house, lined with sloes and

brambles. Laurence could smell wood smoke and the brown tobacco scent of autumn. A cobweb pulsed with white caught light. The morning grass licked wetly at his boots. Bladen walked ahead with a chair over his shoulder. It was an entirely ordinary and unremarkable chair, but, as Laurence followed it, it assumed extraordinary significance.

They placed the chair under an ash tree. Laurence wondered why there was the need to surround this act in ceremony; but he supposed that the ceremony, of which they must later speak, was what this was all about.

Joseph was brought down, then. They flanked him, though his movements didn't look like those of a man who might run. He didn't mean to fight against this thing. Laurence stared at the prints left by Joseph's boots. They put him in the chair and began tying his hands behind. Laurence stepped forward and shook his head at the man tightening rope around Joseph's wrists.

'Do you want the blindfold?'

Joseph raised his chin slowly. It was an answer. Laurence wished it otherwise.

He had been instructed to attach a marker to the prisoner's chest, to highlight his heart. Laurence took the handkerchief from his pocket. It was one of his father's, he noticed, best Irish linen and embroidered initials. He had been given a safety pin. He regarded it between finger and thumb. It seemed a ludicrous object, an absurdly domestic and awful thing.

He crouched before Joseph, acutely aware of the textures of him – the feel of the cloth of his uniform and the grain of his skin. He saw his own hands shake and fumbled with the safety pin. Joseph's breath was warm and sour. Laurence tried not to look at his face, but was conscious of the flick of his eyes, following his own.

'You will finish it, won't you?'

Their eyes connected. Joseph's up-close eyes were brown, long-lashed and dilated with fear.

'Yes.' He stepped back. He felt an urge to retch. His father's handkerchief glared whitely in this clay-coloured place.

The squad were lined up. They seemed not to know where to look and so opted to examine the grass. They looked unsteady. Bladen shifted on the sidelines.

The red caps returned the rifles, one supposedly loaded with a blank round. It seemed a silly charade for troubled consciences. Laurence felt that his own conscience was somewhat taken for granted.

He recited the instructions that he had been given: 'Take care of your aim. Fire straight. It's the humane thing.'

'Humane?' Frank Fitton was shouting now. 'This is murder. I volunteered for this army. I don't have to do this. I won't do this.'

'Don't make me a murderer,' Jack Roberts pleaded.

Laurence shook his head. 'That's an order.'

'Fuck you,' said Fitton.

Laurence stood to the left. He didn't want to see it, never mind to speak the word. This silent instant was an agony and an eternity.

'Fire.'

The volley cracked and reverberated through the valley. It stretched and shook and afterwards a stillness, as if it had all stopped. A flap of wings came from the copse behind, a caw of crow and the firing squad ran. Laurence vomited. Joseph slumped.

He was driven back with Bladen in a Ford. The priest talked about God and testing and design. Laurence knew that he meant it to be a comfort, that he meant it well, but these words seemed just sentiment and too late. He had stared at the dead man's footprints on the grass. He had completed his half of the bargain. He felt broken by it.

Gibson was polishing his boots. Millicent, who also meant well, was propped against the bottle. Laurence looked at her sepia smile.

'Beastly?' said Gibson. The brush beat a rhythm over his boots.

'Barbaric,' said Laurence. He shut his eyes and swallowed whisky.

'I sent the letter. It seemed for the best.'

'Yes,' said Laurence. 'I too have a letter to write.' Only he didn't know where to start.

Chapter Thirty-Four

Northern France, 1928

Effie stared at the green book in her hand. She had read as far as the beastly and the barbaric. Neither adjective was adequate. The man who had said he loved her had killed the man that she was meant to love. Effie wondered who she loved. At this moment love seemed like an entirely alien emotion.

She shut her eyes to the slipping-past scenery. An instant earlier she had felt an impulse to fling the book from the train window, to lose it again into that scenery. The voice that had been so familiar was now showing her scenes from their shared past that were entirely removed from what she had believed to be the truth. In giving a different version of that week in November 1917, Laurie had altered the whole of the past ten years. Did he realise that? In the space of ten pages he had re-written their history. Everything had suddenly changed. She couldn't throw the book away but she also couldn't turn another page.

He had said it himself: *You shouldn't be here. I shouldn't have let this happen. I shouldn't have let it come to this.* Effie's eye kept returning to this statement. He clearly believed that it was his responsibility. How could he, then, have let it happen? How could Laurie have let it come to that? How could she have had no clue?

She leaned her head against the glass and looked out at the slowing city. Paris was similar shapes, but a different palette to London. There was a different quality to the light. It was paler and more iridescent somehow, as if its surfaces were smoother. Had she the heart, she might have found it beautiful. The train juddered with a steel-screech of brakes. Her reflection wiped tears away.

The Gare du Nord was all populous and push. It surged and pulled around her. She stood and waited to find the will to move

Caroline Scott

forwards.

'Madame?'

The red-jacketed porter extended a hand towards her suitcase. Effie nodded dumbly.

A motorbike weaved within inches of her as she took her first tread out onto the pavement. Effie stepped back, her shoulders slamming against the station wall. Braced against that wall, and measuring her breaths, she looked out at the city. It seemed, at first, an ordered and symmetrical place; there were cafés on both facing corners and parallel lines of plane trees. But with movement it became turmoil. There were motor cars, omnibuses, trams and traps, all wrapped in unintelligible lettering. Paris capitalised, honked its horn, revved its engine and shouted. Above it all, though, she could hear his footsteps on the grass. She heard his breathing as Laurie leaned in with the safety pin. She heard the word 'Fire' and the volley. Their rifles ricocheted across the city. Joe's last gasp silenced Paris. Her fingers gripped onto the station stonework.

Effie took it all in from the backseat of a taxi. Beyond the glass there were smart shops and bustling boulevards, bohemian strollers, flouncers and hawkers. She observed that there was a penchant for flamboyant fashions and a proclivity for daytime drinking. Paris seemed to be an anything-goes sort of place – and everything seemed to be going rather fast. She tried to see Laurie here. What had he (who had never been fast or fashionable) done here, she wondered, apart from ogle strawberry tarts, listen to barrel organs and know that he had killed Joe? Did he drown it in drink? Did he succumb to sin and gin and jazz? Did he too keep on hearing his own admission of responsibility? She looked out at the Seine, which reflected the colours of old stone and sky. There were saints and scholars in the speeding-past architecture.

The hotel was on a corner and had a tidy green frontage. It was newly re-painted and smart in the afternoon sun. Virginia creeper hung in architectural swags and the heads of Grecian-looking gentlemen were displayed in niches. Inside she could see white tablecloths set for dinner. Had Laurie, in his last weeks, secreted Paris guide books? Had he clandestinely crouched over street maps seeking dog-friendly hotels? Had he thought through what she would be feeling in this instant?

A gramophone was playing polite piano inside. The reception was elegantly polished and upholstered. Having already made a spectacle of herself in front of one receptionist, Effie took a deep breath and attempted a smile for the young woman with the Peter Pan collar. Effie imagined herself a confident client, a lady of independent means who was accustomed to travel on the Continent, who had never been in service or on the Somme. She introduced herself in unhesitating English. Peter Pan produced a room key and passed letters across the desk. This was becoming an unfortunate pattern.

Effie looked at Laurie's distinctive E's. Hadn't he had his say? What more could there be to say? Had he not finished with her? Had he not already said and done enough? She wasn't sure that she could stand one more word of Laurie and his revelatory recollections. She forgot to look confident.

The room was less rosy than the last. It had lots of acute angles, monochrome zigzags, mirrored surfaces and a chaise longue. Effie supposed that it was *à la mode*. The mirrors reflected a dowdy and flowery girl amongst the geometric black and whites. She applied her backside to the bedroom door.

Effie sat on the fashionable bedspread and looked at the two envelopes. Though her instinct was to open Henry's first (because the jaunty script was surely his), she considered what more Laurie might have to confess? Which rug must he pull next? She tore his envelope open cautiously and read.

Caroline Scott

My dearest Effie,

You made it this far, then. It'll have been a rough ride, I'll warrant. I dread to think what you might be feeling right now.

I'm not going to start to attempt to defend myself. You have the right to make your own judgement of the facts. I have to say, though, that I never for one moment meant you – or him – any harm. For your sake I could never have hurt him. For his own sake I would never have hurt him. Only, sometimes life can be horribly complicated. In November 1917 it was suddenly all desperately complicated.

It isn't quite over yet. There is something else. There is a reason why you're in Paris. You will find an address enclosed. If you feel up to it (and I understand that you might already have had enough), you should go there. You should have gone there a long time ago.

You mustn't blame Joseph or think him a coward. It is I that am the coward.

I am sorry. Please believe me, Effie, how entirely and unendingly sorry I am.

Laurence

Effie stared at the enclosed address. It meant nothing to her. She wasn't aware of having obligations in Paris, any visits that she was owing and neglecting. She wondered, after all of Laurie's awful secrets, whether this address would lead her to some appeasing offering. Something in the tone of the brackets, however, told her otherwise.

'Have we not had enough?' she asked Reginald.

She opened the window. Paris rushed in with a push of loud vitality and car horns. She looked across the rooftops. The city was twinkling into blue twilight below. Effie shivered. She wondered where, amongst the silver rooftops and pink-tinted chimney pots, the Impasse Charal was and what this impasse constituted.

She shut the window and turned to the envelope with the sprightly F's.

'You won't thrust any revelations at me, will you? Tell me that you won't spring any horrible secrets.'

Effie unfolded Henry's notepaper and smiled at his straightforwardness.

Bonjour Fairy Palace,

I'd given you up as a fling. What can be so occupying that it's kept you from me? I'll look you up in Paris on the 10th. Do you like oysters? I hope so.

Henry x

Effie wasn't sure whether she did like oysters, but what she wanted more than anything now was to see Henry's straightforward face looking over them.

Chapter Thirty-Five

There weren't many people in the downstairs brasserie. Effie had sat aside Reginald on a leather banquette and pointed a finger recklessly at the menu. Finger pointing produced an onion soup, a broiler in a well-reduced sauce and a confection of whipped egg whites and caramel. It was all really very decent, but Laurie's voice kept saying the word 'Fire' in her head and it didn't do much for her digestion. She apologised as the waitress took her plate away.

From her table she could see into an alley, where the restaurant staff took turns to smoke fast, furtive cigarettes. Tin soldiers manoeuvred amongst the windowsill's potted geraniums. Soon the light in the alley had faded and the brasserie lights bled.

Were the toy soldiers on the staircase really there? Was she imagining herself stalked by miniature fusiliers and grenadiers? It was with some relief that Effie closed the door of her hotel room, but then her own image was spinning round in the bedroom mirrors. She hid her face in the black-and-white bed.

Champagne, on this occasion, failed to drive the dreams from Effie's sleep. Her sleeping eyes looked down on Joe. His nightmare eyes flashed open.

The window of the hotel room was a rectangle of blue-white light. His bare feet – which were her feet – hit the floor one, two, three times. He was running out of the wood. He ran from terror and tree roots. He dived into the blue-white night.

Glass slammed and splintered. Sharp fragments of moonlight spiralled and fragments of his mirrored splintering self. He was diving through it, leaping with it and gasping at the black, bright sky. His legs wheeled and for an instant he flew. For an instant he had the perspective of angels. Only the cats that cried across the rooftops saw Joe fly.

He tilted. His eyes, full of sky, saw height before he plunged.

Five floors flashed past; he fell past balconies and gargoyled Grecians, past sleeping caged canaries and the midnight-grey geraniums. He fell in a glitter of glass. The gutter was a strip of liquid sky and a soldier falling from it. The street rushed up.

Effie ran to the window when she awoke and passed her hand over the glass to test the truth of it. There were café tables down below. Circles of zinc glinted. They made a geometric pattern from above. There was no fallen soldier. She flopped back down on the bed and stared at the ceiling. She found it difficult to breathe.

'So, do I go there today?' she asked the ceiling mouldings. The pomegranates in the plasterwork didn't offer a reply. But tomorrow was the day that Henry arrived. She needed a reprieve of levity. She needed to catch her breath. Parisian mysteries would have to wait. She nodded at the non-committal pomegranates.

Effie put on airs and too much make-up. She wondered, as she looked at herself in vamp-red lipstick, whether she should crave the hand-holding of someone with whom she had only shared tea and conspiracy. For some reason she trusted Henry, whereas she was no longer certain that she could trust the people she actually knew – or had thought that she knew.

Effie and Reginald strolled through the streets of Paris. It was brash, fast and busy. She listened to barrel organs (though she didn't hear the *Blue Danube*), to a street corner chanteuse and swing and jazz that leaked from bars. Paris was doing the *Low Down*, the *Mooch* and *Makin' Whoopie*. There was a lot of brass section and bright young things. A clown was juggling champagne bottles on the street corner, while goats walked on two legs around a miniature circus ring. A cross-legged Indian fluted strange music as a serpent swayed from a straw basket. Images spun on postcard stands. Paris flickered in snapshot circles.

Effie looked in shop windows. Scent bottles twinkled prettily in a parfumerie, conjuring lilac, lavender and violets through the glass. A department store displayed a fanciful fan of leather gloves, a pyramid formed from cloche hats and coloured umbrellas arranged in a rainbow. Effie stared at the strawberry tarts in the window of a patisserie, the Charlottes, the millefeuilles and the bavarois, constructions of choux and chocolate and hearts shaped in spun sugar. She saw her own reflection in the window. She saw a woman who ought to look like a widow, but didn't. What right had she to consider confectionary when Joe was casting his arms away in the face of the enemy and her brother was in a shell hole waving and dying, when they were all so atrociously, terribly dead? Effie saw an awful woman in smeared lipstick.

She walked through a market, past fish stalls and flower stalls, past stacked rows of pigs' trotters and June's first peaches piled high. A confusion of smells came at her. It pushed loudly around her. She blinked at its brightness, at the pink of the peaches and the glistening knuckles of the pigs' feet. Effie was suddenly horribly reminded of all of the lost limbs that had spilled out of Laurie's diary. And, with that, it suddenly seemed so wrong that she was standing in the middle of a Parisian market. How could she stand here smelling peaches when there was such sadness and she had been so appallingly inadequate? How could she be looking at sides of bacon when she was meant to be quietly, sadly tending gravesides? It was suddenly all so very wrong. A woman collided with her and grunted an insult. Effie stared as the market jostled obliviously about her.

But wasn't it the case that peach trees still flowered? They had flowered eleven times since the November of 1917. Was it so very wrong, then, to appreciate the smell of peaches, when the world still turned and spring still came and she had been so awfully lied to and left? Joe had let go of her hand too. He had made that choice. Hadn't he?

Effie looked up at the ceiling girders. Her sister's voice seemed to be echoing around them; Grace's voice was telling her not to get tipped. Had she inadvertently been tipped? Did teetering on a high ledge constitute being tipped? Effie decided to spend some of Laurie's money.

'Don't skimp,' she said to Reginald. There was a note of something nasty in her own voice.

She walked into a bar that was all bright chrome, dark wood and cigarette smoke. Effie decided to have a go at smoking. It seemed the thing to do, to make an exhibition of oneself in Paris. She meant to dive at her own dereliction. Effie decided to sample being a care-not, cigar-smoking woman who unashamedly smelled peaches.

She ordered a cigar and a brandy while she contemplated the menu. It didn't trouble her terribly that this might be back-to-front behaviour. But, when the cigar came, she was not quite sure what to do with it. She had smoked cigarettes as a girl, as everyone did, but had given them up for the sake of Laurie's lungs. She had given a lot up for Laurie and his lungs. The barman smiled at her sympathetically. He cut the end from the cigar, put it in Effie's mouth and winked as he moved in with the lighter. She could smell the aniseed on his breath and tried to keep her eyes on his flame-bearing finger ends.

'*Et voila*,' said the waiter.

'Indeed,' said Effie.

The cigar tasted bosky and naughty and wasn't at all objectionable. She thought about trying a smoke ring, but decided not to push her luck.

'I have had a very sheltered life,' she told the barman, who seemed to be called Lolo or Lulu or some such. 'I really have absolutely no idea how the world works.'

He shrugged uncomprehendingly. His incomprehension was

perhaps for the best, Effie considered; she preferred Lulo to think of her as louche.

'Are there oysters?' She circled her cigar indicatively over the menu, trying to look like a woman to whom oysters were an everyday occurrence. Receiving Lulo's persistent incomprehension in reply, she made a cupping gesture with her hands.

'*Fruits de mer?*'

Effie attempted a shrug and consented casually to Lulo's indecipherable suggestion.

A table set for two was remade for one. Beyond Reginald, who took the opposite chair but who did not require cutlery or crockery, Effie looked out at the colour and movement of Saint-Germain.

Lulo had pointed at a white wine. Though Effie was reluctant to be diverted from her customary champagne, she decided to concede to Lulo, who knew one end of a cigar from the other. She was just about to take out her notebook and add Muscadet to her list of new vices, when the waiter arrived with implements. Various steel apparatus were aligned side-by-side with Effie's plate. There were pins and prongs and very literal vices. Effie had not anticipated that oysters might require such extensive surgery.

And then it arrived. The waiter wobbled with a precarious pyramid of crustacea, a three-tier tower of claw, shell and seaweed. It needed only a mermaid to complete the tableau. Reginald disappeared behind the top-heavy triangle of *fruits de mer*. Effie wondered what she had gotten herself into, but Lulo nodded encouragement and so she contemplated where to begin.

It was all rather more than Effie had expected – but that seemed to be becoming a theme. She chewed on a bread crust while she formulated a strategy as to how to tackle the crustacean cornucopia. Effie knew her whelks from her winkles and had perfected, to some acclaim, an embellished variation on Mrs Beeton's Prawns in Savoury Jelly. But this three-tier array of shell overwhelmed rather than enticed.

She began with the familiar *fruits*– the whelks and cockles and shrimps. But the shrimps should have been potted and eaten with Laurie, who often spoke of his liking for a shrimp. She wondered why he was brave enough to declare his liking for a shrimp, but not for her? Was she more fearsome than a shrimp? Was it Laurie who was really a coward? Effie swallowed the agreeable wine.

She wished for a bottle of malt vinegar for her cockles, but knew, from reading, that the Continentals had yet to embrace these subtleties. As she compromised with mayonnaise, she recalled a garnished lobster she had once prepared for a supper party of officers. Preparing mayonnaise had made her wrist ache. She found it tasted pleasanter when the product of another's wrist, but the thought of what that room full of lobster-eating officers had known about Joe detracted somewhat from the pleasantness.

Though Effie worked manfully through crustaceans, the pile did not seem to diminish. She also worked through wine. Thus far she had worked her way around the oysters, but decided that it was time. She sniffed cautiously; they smelled of the sea. She poked exploratively and was not wholly allured. Effie put the shell to her lips. She recalled getting an accidental gulp of the North Sea in Bridlington. Effie concluded that oysters were just seawater served with disagreeable texture.

Effie finished the bottle and looked up from the chaos of untenanted shell and claw. The room juddered slightly and took a second to catch up. She peered through tiers of seaweed and dripping ice to check on Reginald, but his seat was also untenanted. She spied beneath the tablecloth to see if he was scavenging around her feet, but all there was was prawn shells and her pink-smeared napkin. Her legs felt slightly unsteady as she walked between the tables, seeking Reginald among the shopping bags and shoes. She called his name above the clink of glasses, clatter of voices and hiss of the coffee machine.

Lulo took her elbow. '*Madame*?'

'It's Reginald. Reginald has gone.' She felt the panic rise, felt herself slightly ridiculous and saw it confirmed in the barman's eyes. She looked ludicrous rather than louche now. She grabbed her coat and threw notes at the empties and oysters.

It was dark outside and, as the cool air hit her, Effie swung, stumbling, on the door.

'Bloody dog!'

How could she lose Reginald? How could she have been so careless? How could she have been so distracted that she didn't see him go?

Effie ran through the street, eyes everywhere, dodging the evening promenaders. Zigzagging through the crowds, she felt her pulse race. Paris loomed and blurred around her - the painted-faced strollers, the neon signs, the flash and flounce and lurid flesh. She reeled through it, bounced off it, faltered, shouted his name and fell.

Effie found herself on all fours looking at a gutter. There were dog ends and glittering unpleasantness. There was no dog. She sank despairingly.

'Steady on, old girl.'

There were also shining brogues in the gutter. Effie looked up. Henry Lyle tipped his hat.

'Fairy Palace.'

It was not how she had hoped to remake his acquaintance. But in compensation, he did have Reginald under his arm.

Henry helped her to her feet, licked his handkerchief and wiped something frightful from Effie's forehead. He looked at her with up-close concern.

Effie resisted the urge to cry. 'I have had a bad oyster,' she said.

'So it would seem.' Henry smiled.

Chapter Thirty-Six

Effie woke up in the geometric bed. As the ceiling mouldings slid into focus, she registered that her head felt unusual. Her hand reached out for Reginald and found him warmly present at her side. Recalling hazily that he briefly hadn't been there, a rush of panic rose and then subsided as her fingers curled through his hair. In her experimental exhibitionism Effie had neglected him. She gave him a contrite tickle behind the ears. He grinned at her with ghastly breath.

'I should feel ashamed of myself, shouldn't I?'

'I wouldn't go that far,' replied Henry's entirely unexpected voice. He reared up from the chaise longue.

'Good God!' Effie pulled the bedspread around her shoulders.

'After all, it was only a bad oyster, wasn't it?' He laughed. 'Oh, don't worry. I won't bite. Though, it has to be said that you were hardly bashful last night.'

Effie rubbed at her eyes and groaned. Had she really let go? 'Was I horrendous?'

'Horrific.' He smoothed his disarrayed hair. 'You were smashed.'

Though she had taken to exploring alcohol, Effie had never been smashed before. She wasn't sure that she meant to go there again.

'I feel a bit sick.'

'I'm not surprised.'

'You didn't medicate me?'

'You medicated yourself.'

Effie was relieved to find that she was still in her sensible skirt. She wasn't keen on the idea that Henry might have undressed her in her drunkenness – or that, in her hardly bashful state, she might herself have seen fit to exit her sensible attire.

'I smoked a cigar.'

'I'm sure you did.'

She could still taste it. She could taste a curious cocktail of mistakes. Reginald panted. He too looked a little worse for wear.

'Where was he?'

'Being vivacious with a poodle.'

'Heavens,' said Effie. She wasn't quite certain that was what Laurie had intended for Reginald's Parisian holiday. 'I was meant to buy him an ice-cream.'

'I think that he prefers canoodling with poodles.'

'He does look rather pleased with himself.'

'Poodle pleasuring,' said Henry and shook his head with feigned affront. 'Can I not leave you two alone for five minutes? What on earth have the pair of you been up to? How did it get to oysters and poodles and being blotto in a Parisian gutter?'

'Could the poodle be a cry for help?' Effie asked, although there was something rather rakish about Reginald's face today. If he needed help, he was keeping those sensibilities well suppressed this morning. 'Poor Reginald has been through so much.'

'Come on.' Henry got up and began to fold the blanket he'd used. He stood at the end of her bed, the blanket to his chest, and gave her a sympathetic look. 'I'll run you a bath and then we shall find some lunch and you will tell me all about what *you've* been through.'

All of this flapping about with blankets was presently slightly trying, but she was glad to have someone other than Reginald to share it with.

'Oh Henry, I have had a time of it.'

'It's all right,' he said. 'I'm here now and I shall make it all right.'

They went to a café. Effie sipped cautiously at too-weak tea, while Henry ordered wine and oysters.

'Are you doing that just to provoke me?'

'I would never be so cruel to you, Fairy Palace. I just happen to like the things.'

'I don't think that they like me.'

He looked at her meaningfully. She looked down at her teacup.

A girl delivered bread and wine to the table. Henry filled his glass and rolled up his shirtsleeves. Behind him, the bar was loud; they stood three-deep at the counter and shouted. The brasserie was peopled by gangs of labourers, market traders, shop workers, clerks and a butcher in whites. The chef leaned on the kitchen door and surveyed the reception of the oysters. Effie wished there wasn't quite so much shouting.

'So must I prize it from you?' Henry dabbled expertly in a shell with a fork. He sprinkled copious pepper and sneezed into an oversized handkerchief. 'What has kept you so thoroughly otherwise occupied and reduced you to grovelling in gutters?'

Effie wondered where to begin; how could she shape it into something that might be shared across a table? She re-wound to her arrival in Ypres and proceeded to tell Henry all of the intervening events. She watched him sniff and season and slurp as she told. He didn't say anything. He seemed occupied in oysters. Henry gulped at the wine as if he wished to be rid of it and then refilled his glass. Effie wished that he would say something. Finally he emptied the last shell, wiped his hands on the napkin, took a swig of wine and spoke.

'I am sorry, Effie. I truly am so sorry.' He took her hand then.

'It's not *you* that should say sorry. I'm sorry, Henry. I'm sorry for them. I'm sorry for you. I'm sorry for all of you. How could I not have realised what it was like? How could he have got so low that he wanted to let go? How can it all have got so awful that he needed to draw that line?'

'It's a clean one. There isn't a sneeze in it.' He offered her a handkerchief and a solemn look. 'I had a good friend who was in that sector in the winter of 1917. He told me once how he had seen a man put the muzzle of his own rifle in his mouth. I'll never forget him telling me that.'

She shook her head.

'I possibly shouldn't share that with you, but, well, perhaps better what Joseph did than that. Men were tested terribly. It pushed them to their absolute limits.'

'But, really, he just got someone else to pull the trigger for him, didn't he? Laurie was the person that pulled that trigger.'

'Don't think like that.'

'I had absolutely no idea, you know. It's like they were always wearing masks. How can I have lived with Laurie for so long and not have known any of this?'

I am doing things that intelligence and instinct tell me that I shouldn't. She recalled the passage from Laurie's diary. He was writing in the September of 1916. *I do things that are unlike me. It is teaching me things that I did not know about myself.* Effie wondered if she had ever known Laurie at all.

'You hardly know the man whose hand and handkerchief you're holding.' Henry squeezed her hand. 'You did know them. You knew them all along. This is just two men that you knew forced into exceptional circumstances, *really* exceptional circumstances.'

She looked at the man across the table and wondered what exceptional circumstances he might have had to cope with. 'Did you ever want to run away from it?'

'Of course. I'm pretty confident that everyone had those moments.' He took his hand from hers and put it through his hair. 'There were times when every atom of my body told me to run. And there are times when it might have been better had I listened to those instincts.' He rat-a-tatted on his knee with a teaspoon.

Effie sometimes forgot that Henry was un-whole. But he was wholly serious now. She wanted to take his hand back in hers but took the teaspoon instead. 'I just wish that I'd realised. How can Joe have felt like that and I not have realised? Should I have seen it in his letters? When I read them again I can see the clues there now. But I'm seeing them a decade too late.'

'Are you sure it's not just hindsight that's picking out a pattern?' Henry replenished his glass. 'I had to vet letters. Laurence would have done the same. There were things that you just couldn't put in a letter. He couldn't have told you. And, even if he had, what could you have done? Not everything can be cured with kind intentions. With all of the best will in the world, you probably wouldn't have been able to make this right.'

'I don't know what to think, Henry. I don't know what I'm meant to feel. Am I meant to be ashamed? Am I meant to be angry? I'm not a silly girl: I know that there has to be discipline – that serving men can't be permitted to run away in wartime. And the other men with him, they didn't run away, did they? But, at the same time, I can't help but feel desperately sorry for Joe and angry at the people that did this to him. Then I'm ashamed of feeling ashamed. I lived with the man that did this to him. Should I feel ashamed?'

'Absolutely not. Apart from about your gutter antics,' he digressed with an encouraging smile.

'Laurie said that he shouldn't have let it happen, that Joe shouldn't have been sent back into the line. How could he have let it happen?'

'From what you say, he evidently spoke out in Joseph's defence. He couldn't have done much more, you know. I mean that. It sounds as if he probably did everything he could. Think what it must have been like for him to live with this secret. I'm sorry for Joseph, but I also feel extremely sorry for your Laurence.'

'He was a kind man, Henry. He was a gentle man. He liked poetry and painting and butterfly buns. He had a sweet tooth and sensibilities. He couldn't shoot someone. He couldn't shoot Joe. But he did, didn't he?'

'We all saw horrible things. We all did horrible things. War is like that unfortunately. It throws unavoidable horridness at you. I'd like to think, though, that it didn't make us all irredeemably horrible people. This is one part of Laurence's past, a part that he clearly keenly regretted. It doesn't mean that he wasn't a kind man. I'm quite sure that he genuinely was the man that you thought he was.'

She watched Henry turning the box of matches between his fingers. It rattled emphases through his sentences. He never seemed to be entirely still. There was always some surplus energy that must tap or beat or make a percussion of a match box. What horrible secrets did Henry have to live with? What regrets made him need to tap and rattle?

'You're a fidget,' she observed.

'I know. I'm sorry. Kate threatens to put me in mittens.' He sat, contritely, on his hands. In the background Maurice Chevalier was rolling his R's through *La Leçon de Charleston*. Effie found that it was hard to concentrate on horridness when there was Maurice Chevalier and talk of mittens.

'I can see why you took to the spoons.'

'It's a calling.' He stilled and then was staring at her. 'You have to look forwards now.'

'Joe said that in his last letter. It's the last thing that he signed off with: '*Go forwards. Be happy.*''

'And he was right.'

'It feels like he ran away from me too, you know. That he let go of my hand too. That probably sounds terrifically selfish.'

'No. Not at all. It just sounds perfectly human.' Henry sighed. He reached across and took her hand again. 'Shall we order

Reginald that ice-cream and try a hair of the dog?'

'At least Reginald never lied to me.'

'Well then, you must reward him for his integrity. And afterwards we shall go and fidget on a dance floor.'

Effie was pleased to discover that Henry was also familiar with the pleasures of champagne. They dipped biscuits in it and called themselves decadent. Reginald had *glace au vanille* and seemingly that was pleasurable too.

'This is the life, eh, Miss Shaw? This is what we fought wars for.'

'For the right to dunk finger biscuits?'

'Absolutely. Can you think of anything more deserving of defending?'

At that moment she could not.

Reginald belched vanilla. 'I concede. He might have liked that more than the poodle.'

'Was it a terribly vulgar poodle?'

'An utter gutter slut.'

It was a relief, after the shocks and the revelations, this amicable insulting.

'There was something else.' The saturated end of Effie's biscuit fell into the champagne coupe and she retrieved it with Reginald's unused sundae spoon. 'There was another letter from Laurie when I got here. He's given me an address. I have to visit it, but I have no idea why.'

'A Parisian mystery, eh? How exciting. Perhaps he has left you a present.'

'That's what I thought at first. That would be very like him. But there's something in his tone that implies otherwise.'

'Do you have any connections to Paris?'

She shook her head.

'Did he?'

'He was here after the war. I suspect he might have gone slightly wild here.'

Henry's brow creased. 'How wild?'

She considered. 'I don't think Laurie was capable of being terribly wild. He probably listened to bad jazz and read some rude poetry.'

'Could he have, erm, left a Parisian souvenir?' He made a rocking motion with his arms and looked amused by the possibility.

'No!' Effie dropped the sundae spoon. 'Or, at least, I really don't think so. Could he?'

'It happens.'

'It doesn't happen to Laurie.' She really couldn't imagine it. 'Laurie was ascetic.'

'That's what they all say.'

She wondered. 'What does ascetic really mean?'

Henry smiled. 'That he probably secretly liked looking at Victorian nudes.'

Effie walked through the rooms of Everdene trying to recall evidence of Victorian nudity. 'He did have a Rossetti in his bathroom.'

'Did he, by Jove?' Henry gave her an up-and-down look.

'And what do you mean to imply?'

'Rossettis in his bathroom? All of that big hair and pouting diaphanous sensuality? I don't think I need to imply a thing.'

'He liked the sin and salvation,' said Effie.

'Of course he did.'

Effie tried to make an affronted face, but the mischievous look that Henry returned made disapproval difficult to sustain.

He drained his glass and stood up. 'So, about this dancing, then.'

'Dancing? I assumed you were joking.'

'I can, you know. The old peg manoeuvres a mean tango. In

fact my doctor says that it's the very best treatment,' Henry elucidated. 'With enough tango it might even grow back.'

He swivelled his hips illustratively. Effie wasn't quite sure where to look. He hooked his arm and waited for her to take it.

'But Reginald?'

'From what I witnessed last night, there's nothing wrong with Reginald's tango either.'

'But is it *right*?' italicised Effie.

'It would be downright dangerous not to. I don't have to be a doctor to see that your morale is in dire need of dancing.'

Effie took his arm. 'If you insist,' she assented.

'Insist? My darling guttersnipe, I command it.'

Chapter Thirty-Seven

They went dancing at the Kitty Kat Club. Effie looked up to the sign above the door. As a neon cat lifted a top hat, its feline features split into a toothy leer.

'While the cat's away, the mice dance,' said Henry.

Seemingly the cat had been gone for some time and the mice liked their music loud. Noise leapt out as the doors of the club opened.

The dance floor writhed with swinging limbs and shimmy. It was all energy and giddy letting go. The room moved with the beat of the music. Effie felt the beat move right through her.

They seated themselves at a table and ordered more champagne. Henry had to shout above the hoofing of feet, the blare of the brass section and the busy up and down of glasses. Effie looked up to a ceiling that was a grotto of gaudy mosaic daisies, mirrors and whimsy. She looked down, following the reflected lights that skittered, like bright sprites, between the painted faces and the dancing feet.

The house band played a raucous *Black Bottom* while a woman in ostrich feathers, and very little else, demonstrated the moves from a spot-lit podium.

'It's demented. It's indecent,' said Effie.

'Are you terribly scandalised?'

'Horrifically,' she laughed.

There were Charlestons and Foxtrots and the Varsity Drag and everybody seemed to know the steps. It was all kinetic kick, a syncopated, sequinned, in-time anarchy. Hands swung, hips synchronised and feet slammed the beat.

The white-liveried waiter filled their glasses and they mimed foreign thanks.

'Bottoms up,' said Henry in her ear as they touched glasses.

Effie surveyed the haircuts and hemlines and the dapper man in hound's-tooth who had whispered in her ear. The number finished and it broke into applause. They leaned apart and clapped. Effie wasn't sure whether she wanted to lean apart or not. The band struck up *Let's Misbehave*, then. Effie averted her eyes from Henry's face. She smiled at the bubbles in her glass instead. The crooner was crisply English.

'What the heck do we care?' sang along Henry and gave her a care-not wink.

Effie wondered. She thought of Laurie, the fall of his feet on the floor above, as he circled the gramophone to the Piccadilly Players. She had practised her travelling steps in the kitchen below, checking the Charleston hands of her windowed reflection. 'You're the cream in my coffee,' Laurie had chorused when she took the tea tray upstairs. They had never danced together.

'Come on,' she stood up and offered Henry her hand. 'Let's see these mean tango manoeuvres, then.'

He didn't need asking twice.

They dipped and rose and circled. Henry, true to his word, managed a surprisingly smooth shuffle. They camped it up and sang along, eyes raised to the decadently daisied ceiling. They collided with other dancers and laughed. They collided with each other and grinned.

It turned, then, to *Crazy Rhythm* and they bounced like bright young things. They made theatrical eyes, exaggerated hands and straight-faced through the sod-it spins. They spun and it all blurred together, the lights and the colours and the laughter. The room full of dancers spun around and spun away. There was nothing but the beat of the music. The room continued to move when Effie's spinning circles stopped.

'I think that the old peg has just about had it,' said Henry as they clapped the band. 'You don't mind, do you?'

She shook her head, took his proffered arm and they wound back to the table.

He refilled her glass. 'Sorry to wimp out, Effs. I am a bit out of practise.'

'I was feeling a bit upsydaisy, anyway.'

'You are awfully sweet.'

He put his arm around her. It had been a very long time since a man had put his arm around her. For an instant fifteen years reeled back and she was leaning into Joe at the pictures – Joe who was dead, condemned and elsewhere. Suddenly Henry's arm around her was a betrayal. His arm around her wasn't right. She shouldn't be here, dancing and drinking and smiling; she should be looking for a grave to cry besides.

'Forgive me, Henry.'

Then the dancers were a barrier and a trap. She tried to part the crowd with apologies, but they jolted into her and off her and laughed. Did they laugh at her? They sang and grinned and couldn't care. The flickering lights spun and they were nymphs and satyrs. It was grotesque and obscene and she was the worst of it. She had spun in drunken circles knowing full well that it was wrong.

Effie ran for the doorway and gasped at the evening air.

'This is not me,' she told the strolling strangers. 'I am not like this.'

But, then, who was she, when everything she had thought to be truth suddenly wasn't?

She walked through the too-glittering streets. Henry swore at his knee joint as he approached from behind.

'Effie, wait.'

He caught her arm.

'Effie, I'm sorry. I didn't mean to push you.'

She stopped then and looked at Henry, who was dashing and danced and who had put his arm around her. Part of her wanted his arm around her again. Paris glimmered busily about him.

'It's not what you did, Henry.' She looked down at their

facing feet. She wondered if she was being quite fair to him. 'It's me. I don't know who I am.'

'Crikey, that's quite a predicament.' She heard a smile in his voice. 'You're a girl who's getting out more. You're a girl who, for a second, was looking forwards. And you should, you know. It's not wrong. It's really not.'

He put his hand to her face and lifted her chin. She wanted to believe that he was right.

'It's just all been a bit too much.'

'I know, Fairy Palace. I do know.' He curled his arm through hers. 'Come on. Let's get you home. Let's get you back to dependable Reginald.'

'He's the only one I can trust.'

'You can trust me. You trusted me with the smuggling of Reginald, after all.'

'I did, didn't I?'

'Lured me, no less.'

She turned back to face him. 'Promise me you wouldn't lie to me. Promise me that you are who you say you are.'

'My track record might have the odd pothole, but I am fundamentally an honest soul. I do want to be honest with you, Effie. I do want to tell you the truth. I'm actually presently suffering from an uncommon compulsion to tell you all of my truths.'

He looked sincere. She couldn't help wondering, though, if there was a gap between the wanting and the telling.

'I'm sorry. I am being a bit intense, aren't I?'

'Ardent,' said Henry, 'veering towards the frontier into fervent, even. It's really rather exciting. I may have to have a cold shower when I get back to my room.'

She gave him a Seine-wards shove.

Chapter Thirty-Eight

Effie was sorry not to spy Henry on the chaise longue that morning, but she had made her mind up that today she must tackle the Parisian mystery and, for all of his friendly declarations and talk of trust, it was perhaps excessive to expect him to accomplice her a second time.

She ate breakfast over a street map. The Impasse Charal, she discerned between croissant crumbs, wasn't so very far away. Perhaps, then, that was why Laurie had chosen to place her in this hotel. And why, in turn, Henry Lyle now entered this particular breakfast room. What linked them to this alien address?

'Morning, mademoiselle.' Henry looked jaunty in striped sports casual. He looked like he was going to play polite lawn sports. 'So it's mystery day, eh?' He sat down opposite her and made coffee-confirming gestures at the waitress.

'Well, I should, shouldn't I?'

He nodded. 'So shall I reserve a table for three for dinner tonight – you, me and Laurie's frog sprog?'

'Don't be vile.' She threw a sugar lump at him. 'You honestly don't think it is, do you?'

'Only one way to find out.'

Effie manoeuvred through Paris on a map, her finger directing her steps. As she walked south, the streets became narrower. She sensed that Paris became older. It was less boulevard and more medieval. There were less smart patisseries here – more rag sorters, knife grinders and cobblers. There were antique well heads, street-corner shrines, demolition sites and dirt.

She followed her finger through an arched alley. It was postered with unlikely advertisements, selling the virtues of corsets, bicycles and soapflakes in bright, confident lettering. It smelled of dead ends. The alley opened onto a courtyard that stank of old squalor. It puddled opaquely between the sunken cobbles. This was the arse-end of impolite Paris, which no longer seemed quite so gay.

Effie looked up at four storeys of patched and ragged poverty. She looked down to cobbles that were slimed with spilled straw. It felt like walking across the textures of a different century. She checked the address, wondering how she, with her scrubbed nails and sensible skirt, could be linked to this place. Worse still, how did this link to Laurie? A shabby child sing-songed on a step. Surely it couldn't be?

She found the appropriate staircase. The stairs were irregular and glassy with use. She felt her way, fingertips skirting the greasy walls. The sensation that caused her stomach to convulse was a mixture of revulsion and fear. She wished that Henry, with his striped suggestion of sportiness, was by her side.

Were the floorboards slanting too, or was it her imagination? The boards complained beneath her boots as she walked along the corridor. The wallpaper was peeling at either side and there was a smell of damp and old uncleanliness. Ahead, in the dim light, she counted five doors. A sewing machine was humming behind one of them and somewhere a baby was bawling. Effie stood in front of the door of apartment 13B. She thought of a space called 12M and considered what had brought her from one coordinate to the other.

It isn't quite over yet. There is something else. She heard the hissing sibilance of Laurie's letter-communicated consonants. She knew now that the mysterious something definitely wasn't a present.

Effie put her ear to the door. There was no sound within. Perhaps she could go on without knowing what was behind this door. She had, after all, got this far without knowing. Perhaps she should just not care, should just dance and let striped men slide their arms around her.

Effie knocked. Instantly it felt like a mistake. Suddenly all of her instincts were telling her to run. She heard the scraping of a chair on the other side of the door. She could also hear her own heart beating. Footsteps became bigger as they approached and her heart beat faster. In the doorway there was a face that Effie knew and yet didn't. Her breath failed her. She fell.

She came to looking at a ceiling. At first Effie thought she was back at Everdene. She thought that she saw swagged garlands, but, on focussing harder, it was only rings of damp. For a second, in her confusion, she recalled a fictional ceiling and the spreading ace of hearts that signalled Alec D'Urberville was dead. She sat up and tried to determine what these strange surrounds signalled. She was in a narrow room that seemed to be serving as parlour, bedroom and kitchen. There was a lot of grimed clutter and little light. A man – the man that she knew yet didn't – sat with his back to the window. Effie stared at his silhouette. She tried to remember and recognise his lines.

Suddenly the squalor and the stink didn't matter. Effie stood up from the bed and walked towards him. He angled his face away, but she knew it as the light cut across his turned cheek. The man who was absent and elsewhere, who was last sighted slumped under an ash tree, the man whom Laurie had executed, whom she had been ashamed to be unable to name, was sitting in this room.

'Is it you?' She peered at him, not certain that he wasn't a hallucination or a trick with mirrors. How could it be possible? How could it be so? Was the Parisian mystery a ghost?

Joseph Young turned to face her.

'Why are you here?' His voice creaked, as if he was unaccustomed to using it.

'Why are *you*?' said Effie. '*How* are you here?' She extended her fingers towards him, unsure whether they would pass entirely though. There was something in Joe's expression, however, in the creak of his unaccustomed voice, that pushed her fingers away.

'Did he finally leave you?'

'Who?'

'Your fancy friend.'

'Laurie?'

'Laurie, is it?'

'He's dead,' said Effie. 'And so are you.' Was she dead too? Was that what this was? Was Laurie about to enter stage-left and complete a triangle of ghosts? Was hell a Parisian bed-sit?

'Greene is dead?'

Joe's mouth split into a grin, then. He laughed and Effie didn't like it. This was not Joe's mouth as she remembered it. This was not the smile that she kept in her locket. These were not his steady eyes. This was not Joe who was a breadwinner, who was a safe bet. Effie suddenly didn't like the odds of this bet. There was something hostile in Joe's half-forgotten grin. Had it always been there? Had she somehow skipped over it in his photograph? Or was this what casting away arms did to a man?

'What a tragedy for you,' he said. He smiled. 'Poor good, gallant Laurence, eh? Such a decent chap. Such a man of his word. Perhaps they'll put up a statue to him now.'

'He's dead and you're alive. How can it be so?' He *was* dead. She had felt it. Maybe not heroically dead, as she had thought, but she was sure he wasn't alive.

'Quite.' Joe stared at his hands. 'It appears that I am. It appears that I always was.' He flexed his fingers as if to test it. 'I've been alive for the last ten years, Effie. Why are you here now?'

Joe walked to the table and poured himself a drink. There was something not right about his movements when he walked. His limbs were twisted, as if they had come away and been tacked

212

back on by an enthusiastic but inexpert seamstress. As he moved into the light she saw what time had done to his face. What had happened to the well-scrubbed boy with the prospects and the piano? Joe no longer looked like he had prospects. He looked like hope had left him a long time ago.

There was an image of a soldier glued to the wall behind him. 'It's Charlie.' She pointed. The picture looked as if it had been torn apart and stuck back together. She also noticed a birdcage with a stiff canary at the bottom. The canary looked beyond repair.

'What's that to you?'

He turned and leaned against the table. There was a cigarette burn on his shirt and his lips were stained purple. Effie had a fleeting memory of a boy with whom she'd once gone winberry picking. She had made him stick out his tongue. 'If it stains your tongue it's proof that you're a liar,' she had told him. 'Everybody knows that.' The boy's stained lips had curved into a smile then. She looked at those same stained lips now. Could it really be the same boy?

'But it was in the paper: Dead of Wounds. I went to your memorial service. I cried in the church. Your name is on the war memorial.'

'Do you have many correspondences with dead men?'

She wondered. Laurie wrote to her still.

'I don't understand.'

'Neither did I. But I understand it now that I see you with your face paint and your Park Road pronunciation.' He looked her up and down as if he found this abhorrent. 'He did make you his fancy piece, didn't he?'

'But – '

'Did you have your fun, then? You and darling Laurie. How conveniently it worked out for you both.' He drained the glass and refilled it. He gave off sour waves of alcohol when he

213

moved. 'Here's to Laurence. Here's to dead, darling Laurence. I'm so glad you came. It's made my day that the bastard's dead.'

'How could you? How can you?'

She had once loved him. Was it really the same man? Was this the man that she had waited for, hoped for, would have made excuses and herself a widow for?

'How could I? *How could I?*'

He smoked his cigarette down to a stub and swore at his burnt fingers. She remembered that Joe did that. There were a lot of other things, though, that she didn't remember. She turned her everlasting engagement ring.

'So it's my turn again now, is it? Has the better offer expired? Must be a sorry let down for you, eh?'

'But, I –'

'I've no interest in the second-hand goods that you're selling.'

He spat it at her. He looked at her like he hated her. How could he hate her when he was meant to be dead?

'But I didn't know. How could I have known? I had no idea that you were alive.'

'Who do you think sent you the letter?'

'I don't know what you're talking about.'

'Oh, fuck off with your lies.'

The ring was between her finger ends then.

'Here,' she said. 'If it's over.'

'It was over ten years ago, wasn't it?'

He knocked the ring from her hands and suddenly she was falling. It was shock, more than pain, that she felt as her back hit the wall. The ring spun in a circle on the floor and then was still. The circle closed. It was over.

'Take it. Pawn it. Do what the fuck you will with it. It's nothing to me.'

Had she wasted so much time? Had she given up so much? She looked at the ring that meant nothing. 'How can you be like this?'

'How can you ask that? This is what he made me. This is what you made me. This was your choice.'

'My choice?'

'I didn't necessarily expect you to welcome me back, Effie. I know what I did. I know what I am. But I wanted to explain to you. Do you know how difficult it was to try to begin to explain myself to you?'

She shook her head. 'I don't know what to say. I wanted a letter from you. Of course I did. But there never was one.'

'All I ever had was an envelope full of excuses from him. Nothing from you. I waited a year but still there was nothing. I took that as your answer. I realised, then, what this was. I realised what it was between you and him. So I said 'Yes' to Sophie. I married Sophie and -'

'You married? You waited a year and then you married?'

'Don't look like that. You've no right to look like that.'

'But I waited for you. I loved you.' It felt final in the perfect tense. 'I waited *ten* years for you.'

'Liar.'

'No.' Effie got to her feet. 'No, I'm not a liar. I never was. I am the only one who wasn't a liar.'

'Oh, go,' he said. 'I'm ten years past caring.'

She looked at him and saw that it was true. He walked back to the bottle and she walked to the door.

'We had a gentlemen's agreement, you know. That's what he called it. *Entente*-bloody-*cordiale*, he said. Only he didn't have the balls. Only he was too much of a coward to finish the job off.'

'To finish the job off? I'm not sure that I know what you mean.'

He stared. 'You don't, do you?' He laughed at her. 'They call it the *coup de grâce*. A prettier sounding thing than it is. Anyway, it was his duty as an officer. It was his duty as a gentleman. That was his side of the bargain.'

He leaned towards her as he put the two fingers to his temple. His face was only inches from Effie's then. His mouth twitched into a smile. His eyes widened. Her own frightened face was reflected in his eyes.

'Bang!' he said.

His laughter followed her down the corridor.

Effie didn't notice the squalor as she went back, the rag sorters, or the saints or the shoring up. The streets broadened and turned back to boulevard. She didn't see the patisseries or the milliners, the windows full of fashions, or dolls or Flemish lace. All she saw was Joe's ruined and accusing face.

Chapter Thirty-Nine

Effie took Joe's photograph out of the frame so that she might examine it more closely, so it wasn't distorted by the refraction of glass or weight of silver plate. There was a graininess to it up close. He was all small points of sepia that congregated into eyes, lips and soldierly attire. Holding his nose just below her own, Effie scrutinised Joe's face. She looked for a sign. She looked into his eyes for a hint of something hardening, but they were just steady and grey. She looked at his lips for a signal of a sneer, but his mouth told her nothing. She looked at his uniform, at his khaki smartness, for an indication of something malign that might have seeped upwards, but there was nothing lurking. There were no signs or signals. There were no hints of latent or nascent badness. He wasn't bad. He was just a soldier.

As Effie stared at the boy in the photograph, she saw the prisoner in the chair there, and the man who had told her yesterday that he was ten years past caring. They were all the same person. He had been that same boy all along and, all that long time, he had believed that it was she and Laurie who had done this to him.

'*This is what he made me. This is what you made me. This was your choice.*'

Was there a way back from that? She couldn't presently see that there was.

She placed his photograph back next to Laurie's. They didn't seem to want to look at one another now. They didn't seem to be in the mood for cooking up cordial understandings. Like Laurie's conscience, Effie felt that her consent to their understandings had been somewhat taken for granted. She wasn't sure that she wanted to look at them either. She laid both photographs flat.

The noise of Paris insisted at the window, the car horns and crowds, the jazz and bustle. Was Joe out there? She wasn't sure that she wanted to go out again. Perhaps she could just take a taxi to the station and leave Paris behind. But where to run to? Home was stuffed stoats and twinned chairs. Effie saw it now like a stage setting. They had all just been acting. It was all a script and make-up and false ceilings. Effie was sorry that she'd failed to consult the list of players before making her entrance. She wished that she could be surer of her own role, her backstory and motivations. Somewhere along the lines, she had seemingly lost the plot.

Effie buried her head in the black-and-white bed. Is this what Joe's mother felt, when she had turned on the gas? Is this what had sent her own mother into the special hospital? Did she mean to go there too? She might now have stepped off the ledge. She might now have let go. So was this the end of hope? Effie shut her eyes. She wanted to sleep and not wake up.

Effie dreamed herself onto a train. Her back was to the forward direction and it all pulled past in reverse. She slid out of the suburbs of Paris, through the greenness of fields and past Ypres which was patched from lace. She saw her reflection smile for the soldiers who had graves, who were quietly and decorously and definitely dead. Her glass face slid over waves, over sea, past bathing huts and seaside jollity and the white cliffs of blithe Blighty. She moved through a cathedral spun from smut and ironwork, where chaps tipped their hats, and up, through damp English agriculture. It left her in a slightly frayed armchair.

'Bit of a bugger, eh?' said Laurie from the facing chair. 'Still, there's shrimps for tea.'

'I don't think I like them anymore,' she replied.

'That's because you're stingy with the cayenne. You have to let me help, see.'

She nodded.

'Tess is dead,' he said. He looked, slightly exasperated, at the book in her lap. 'Tess is always dying.'

'I do wish that people would make their minds up.'

'About shrimps?'

'About dying.'

'You don't like much anymore, do you?'

She shook her head. The stuffed stoats sniggered.

'Silly sausage,' said Laurie. His face no longer had the scars from the gas, she noticed. But he no longer had the green glow of halo either. 'Open your eyes,' he smiled.

Chapter Forty

'Effie, let me in.'

Henry was talking through the door. He'd been talking through the door for some time. She hadn't replied, hoping he would decide she wasn't there, or get bored and decide to go and find some lawn sports.

'I do know that you're there.'

Effie rolled her eyes. She was tied in a tangle of sheets and didn't intend to be untied. She wanted only the numb silence, but Henry, seemingly, didn't mean to let her have it.

'Please, Effie. You've lumbered me with rotten Reginald and I don't know what to feed him.'

She sighed. 'Sausages.'

'At last,' said the door.

'Or ham. Diced. Or anything involving sweetened cream.'

'Effie, please let me in,' said Henry. 'I'm worried about you.'

Part of her did want to talk to him, to spill it all out, to share and accept Henry's care. Part of her didn't want to speak to anybody ever again.

'Please. Open the door.'

'I'd frighten you,' she said. She kneeled up on the bed and looked at her reflection in the dressing table mirror.

There is a type of woman who can cry prettily. Indeed, Effie knew, there are women who practise crying. She had read of women who practised with pinches and onions and self-inflicted sorrows in order to finesse the effect of their crying. If it is socially appropriate that tears should be summoned, they will glide in a slow choreographed slide from lowered lashes, down china cheeks, glittering in sympathy-inciting exquisiteness, before they are scooped into swooping gentlemen's pocket handkerchiefs. A small feminine sniffle may be issued, to give depth and drama to the lacrimonious show, but never a snivel or a sob. A lip may tremble minutely, if the tear-summoning matter is of the magnitude of a bereavement or a wayward beau. Flushed cheeks, however, are a faux pas. Streams of mascara are a disaster. A red nose is a total write-off. There are women who, after attentive apprenticeship to the emotional arts, can cry extremely well. Effie, however, was not such a woman.

Her face in the mirror was just a mess. She was a wreck of tears and smeared cosmetics. Effie saw that her painted face wasn't pretty. Perhaps Joe would approve of her more now? But Joe's approval no longer mattered.

'Give me an hour?'

'Of course, Fairy Palace. I'll meet you downstairs, yes?'

She nodded at the door.

'And there's a letter for you.'

'Oh,' said Effie.

She opened the door a couple of inches and put her hand around it. She didn't mean to let Henry see her with her mascara-striped face.

He held her fingers.

'I am on your side, you know,' said the other side of the door.

She knew it from the tone of his voice, more than from the words. She knew it in the feel of his fingers. She smiled at him behind the door. 'Thank you.'

He placed the letter in her hand.

'I'll see you in an hour.'

It was his handwriting. Laurie had written directions on the envelope that it was not to be delivered to her room until after the 12th of June. How had he known? How did he know? She pulled her dressing gown around her. It sometimes felt as if Laurie was still watching. Water banged from the bathroom taps as she read her dead fancy man's words.

Caroline Scott

Where to begin? Where to end?

Now you know. That's why there's no grave.

Joseph has probably told you, but, if you'll hear me out, I'll give you my explanation. I hope that you can bear to hear me out.

It is my fault. I know that. Yes, I was the coward.

I was meant to finish him off, to deliver the coup de grâce. It was my duty. It would have been the right and decent and humane thing to have done. But I failed. I knew that Joseph was still alive, but he was only just alive. I didn't think that he would live. I couldn't find it in myself to end his life, though. Perhaps I'd seen too much death by then? Perhaps I'm making excuses for my own cowardice? They took his body away. I remember the white of the stretcher. I remember Joseph's lips parted and the give-away red staining his teeth. Frank – your brother-in-law – carried the stretcher, you know. He cried. I possibly shouldn't tell you that. They dumped Joseph. He was dead meat. But, you see, he wasn't.

And then, a few months after the war had ended, a letter came. We were already living together, you and I. It was only because you were out that you didn't see his letter. I was glad you were out.

He was alive and in France. He wrote to tell me that he hated me. He hated what I had done to him. Or, rather, what I hadn't done. I had denied him death. I had denied him his right. I owed him the right to die. Joseph didn't want life, but I, and his body, had betrayed him. He wished me dead for that.

There was also a letter for you. To my shame, I burned it. I feared what it contained.

He writes to me on the 5th November each year, the anniversary of the day that he should have died, to remind me that I have given him a living death. I replied at first. I tried to justify my actions, tried to explain the idiot indecision of that moment. I wanted him to know how sorry I was. To my shame, I haven't always replied in recent years, because sorry just seems so utterly inadequate, no matter how many times it's repeated.

Should I have told you? I don't know what was in his letter to you. I looked through the ashes after I had burned it, but it was all just black. Perhaps your life could have been different, but there was a bitterness in his words that I wanted to keep from you. I feared that he would make your life black and bitter too.

I am a coward and I am selfish. I thought that I could give you a better life than he could. But I don't know if that's true. I do hope that it is true, else I've betrayed you too. I meant it well. I meant to protect you. I hope that, at least, you can see that.

So now you know. I don't know if I have done the right thing by telling you. Perhaps this is a further act of selfishness? But you would have received a letter in November. And so, you see, I felt that I had to prepare you.

I wish that I wasn't a coward. I wish that I had had the courage to pull the trigger. I wish that I had killed him then. That is my sin, though it does seem like a back-to-front offence. You too may hate me for that.

You know it all now. I don't know what you will do with the knowledge. 'What use is dishonest experience?' I said to you once, knowing myself dishonest, asking the question of myself. I hope that you can move forward from this experience, Effie. I hope that you can be happy. Go forwards, Effie. Please.

Laurence

The bath ran over.

Chapter Forty-One

'So no souvenir son, then?' Henry looked about the café for comic effect. He looked under the tablecloth.

'The surprise was a little larger than I was expecting.' The waitress brought Effie a coffee. She smiled thanks.

'Twins? Triplets? A tribe of miniature Lauries?'

'Joe.'

Henry's eyes widened. 'Bugger me. Sorry. Really? But how?'

She stirred in rather too much sugar. 'Exactly.'

'But Joe is dead. Wasn't he? Isn't he?'

'It would appear not.' She told him, then, about the trigger that wasn't pulled, the stretcher and the letter.

'Poor sod,' said Henry.

'Who?'

'Both of them.'

She sipped at the coffee. It was too hot.

'So how was he? How is he?'

She put down the cup and stared at her un-ringed finger. Henry followed her eyes.

'Oh.'

'He's angry. He's bitter. I suppose he has a right to be. I gave him the ring back. He doesn't want anything to do with me.'

'More fool him.' Henry smiled encouragingly at her. 'Was he okay with you, though?'

'Can I have a cigarette?'

'Effie?' He handed her the packet. 'Effie, what happened?' Henry's encouraging smile had gone.

'It was only words, really. What was it that we used to say at school? 'Sticks and stones may break my bones, but words will never hurt me'.'

'*Only* words?'

'No broken bones.'

Henry's chair scraped back. 'Where is he? What's the address?'

'Why?'

'Because I'm going to knock his bloody block off.'

'Henry, please.' She held his arm. 'I don't want that.'

'I genuinely thought it was a 'handbag'. Had I, for a second, suspected otherwise, I would have insisted on going with you. Christ, what was Laurence thinking?'

'Henry, sit down. *Please.*'

'Jesus!'

'Laurie thought he was doing the right thing.' That, at least, she hoped was true. 'I don't want any trouble. I've had enough. I just want to leave it behind now. It's over.'

'If he can be like that with you then it has to be over.' Henry looked at her earnestly. He jabbed grains of sugar into the table top as he emphasised the end of his sentence.

'It is. He's married, you know. He was married all of this time.'

'Oh, Effie. I am sorry.' They both stared at the coffee cup. 'Perhaps it's best, though. That he's married to someone else, I mean. He doesn't sound like the sort of man that you ought to be married to.'

Effie shrugged. 'He looks a mess, Henry. Really a mess. He doesn't look at all well. He looks unhinged. He looks like his own ghost.'

'He might be a mess but that doesn't give him the right to take it out on you.'

'No,' she supposed. 'I do feel as if I'm in some way responsible for what happened to him, though. And he clearly feels that way too.'

'You didn't do this.'

Effie shook her head. 'I don't know.'

'I do know: whatever Joe might have become, it isn't your

fault.'

She sighed a non-reply. 'I went back to Laurie's diary. I wanted to know what he felt in the days that followed. But it just stops. I turned the page but there's nothing else.'

She'd turned through all of the remaining pages of his diary – carefully, one by one – hoping to find some extra words hidden away, some moral or concluding remark. But there was nothing. There were just empty pages. A month later, in the December of 1917, she knew he'd been gassed and was on a boat back to England. But what had his thoughts been in those intervening weeks?

'I need there to be something else,' she said to Henry. 'I need to know that he really did regret his part in it. I need to believe that he felt sorry.'

'Do you have any doubt about that at all? Perhaps the fact that the diary stops tells you exactly how he felt?'

'Perhaps.'

Henry polished a red apple on his shirtsleeve. Effie thought of Joe's tell-tale red teeth as Henry's white teeth bit the red apple.

'You've taken your locket off,' he observed.

'Yes.' She wasn't sure how to begin to articulate a rational explanation.

'No engagement ring? No sweetheart nestling into your neck? In fact, not a single nine-carat shackle to be seen about your person. Miss Shaw, you're looking strikingly like a single woman this morning.'

'It would seem so.'

'Tally ho,' said Henry. He offered her a bite of his apple and a wink.

'My fiancé came back from the dead yesterday – and informed me that he's married to someone else. Meanwhile, the man that I've lived with for the past decade has just confessed to being responsible for the death of my fiancé. Only, well, he wasn't. Obviously. Forgive me if I'm looking a bit befuddled. Flattering though your twinkling at me may be, I'm not sure I'm quite ready for tally ho yet.'

'Sorry, I do want slightly for subtlety in the twinkling department. That aside, your quondam fiancé is emphatically alive this morning – and so are you. You have the right to begin again.'

The waitress was chalking up a menu on a blackboard.

'Can I begin by having something to eat?' asked Effie. 'I didn't eat yesterday.' Her stomach grumbled in emphasis.

'I know. I spent most of the day camped outside your door.'

'I am sorry, Henry. I'm a rotten friend.'

'An absolute hound.'

'Egg mayonnaise,' said Effie, following the loops of the waitress' handwriting.

'Indeed. We shall feed you and then we shall see the sights. We are young, free and single in Paris in June and all we have done is have a rotten time. It really isn't on. I understand if you're not ready for tally ho, but it's wrong to entirely waste Paris.'

'I'm not sure that I feel up to sightseeing.'

'But it's over. You said so. That's the past. You have to move forwards, Effie.'

'Everyone keeps saying that to me.'

'Because it's the truth.' He laid his hands flat on the table and looked at her. 'Would you like to go to the top of the Eiffel Tower?'

'I'm not sure that I like heights.'

'Today, Miss Shaw, your future begins. Today you become daring.'

She dabbed out the cigarette and wondered whether, if daring was measured in metres, she hadn't already been to the top of it.

Chapter Forty-Two

Effie wasn't sure she wanted to leave the hotel. She certainly wasn't sure why she put on lipstick to do so. But she did.

They walked through the sunny June streets of Paris looking like young, free and single things. Henry, still in stripes, whistled something cheery. He rattled change in his trouser pockets. Effie gave him a doubtful look.

She surveyed the parade of faces: the holidaymakers with eyes full of sights, the shop girls watching their watches, the trinket pedlars, the between-bar dreamers, the coin-counting housewives and the in-service girls rushing through errands. She looked for eyes that once had been steady. Suddenly she felt Joe's eyes everywhere. And, yet, why would he look for her? A man was dancing on the corner in an African mask. Its white grin loomed toothily towards her. Effie shrank into herself and cast her eyes down. She took Henry's offered arm.

They passed over the bridge and, leaning on the railings, looked down at the river. It glittered pink and grey and blue. A barge passed beneath. Because today had been declared a holiday, they sucked on Laurie's crystallized violets.

'I have to get back to Kate soon.' Henry turned to face her.

'I'm sorry. I'm so selfish,' said Effie. 'I almost forgot, what with everything. Poor Kate. Where did you leave her?'

'She's in Amiens. She's palled up with a buxom widow from Wigan. Mrs Hawes is solid and takes no nonsense. She certainly exhibited little patience for my brand of nonsense. They're enjoying challenging the symmetry of cemeteries together. They're quite safe, Wigan women, aren't they? Only, your side of the Pennines is a wilderness to me. Katie's not in danger in Lancastrian hands, is she?'

Effie flourished her fingers and made an effort to look menacing.

He studied her wiggling digits. 'I'll bet you make a lovely

cake.'

'My Bakewell tart is legendary.' She re-heard Laurie.

'That was almost a smile, then,' Henry observed.

'So when do you have to go?'

'I promised her that I'd be back by Friday.'

She counted it out on her stilled fingers. 'Two days.'

Henry nodded and looked sorry.

'You will come and try my Bakewell tart, won't you?'

'Armies couldn't keep me from it.'

She tried to picture herself creaming frangipane for Henry. She saw the kitchen of Everdene, her well-scrubbed table and newly-blacked range, the jar of flaked almonds and last summer's raspberry jam, but somehow couldn't see herself stirring the bowl. She could no longer see herself in Laurie's home.

'I preferred the almost-smile.'

'I'm sorry, Henry. I'm just worried about what happens next. What happens when I go home?'

'I'm sure it will be all right. I'm certain that your Laurence wouldn't leave you destitute.'

She shrugged. Nothing now seemed certain.

'Chin up, eh? If the worst comes to the worst, I will help you out, you know.'

'But you hardly know me.'

'Well, we'd better do something about that, hadn't we?'

They crossed to the island. The river was now between her and Joe. It felt slightly safer, but Effie kept hold of Henry's arm. It had rained overnight and it doubled dancingly in the puddles. Pigeons pecked about the feet of tourists as they walked through wet, glinting gothic. They stood in front of the cathedral and took in its kings and saints, its apostles and angels, its rampant arches and tooled intricacies. Over the doorway Saint Michael was placing souls on weighing scales. While the pious gazed heavenwards, devils corralled the chained damned. On the right-hand side sinners plunged, writhingly, into lively torments. Effie thought about the men who went bubbling under the mud at Ypres, sighing into the sulky black water. Perhaps Laurie had already been judged? Old prophets in glass glimmered mutely.

'It's all spikes and spires.'

'Another fairy palace?'

'No,' said Effie. 'It's much too deliberate. It's a statement in stone.'

'You should write a book on architecture. You're quite the student of it.'

'Don't be daft. I have a book in which I write about cake.'

'Really?'

'Really.'

Pigeons scattered. The flags were swilled and scrubbed with a stiff brush, out of summer-season propriety. It foamed in the cracks, which Effie didn't stand on, lest she be obliged to marry a rat. They looked up at the Last Judgement.

'I understand cake,' she said.

The shops were smart north of the river. They passed windows full of polished leather goods, the silver shine of canteens of cutlery and patisseries full of bright sugar-spun architecture. Effie lingered in front of a coiffeur, where plaster mannequins pouted beneath various angles of bob, wave and crop.

'Daring,' said Henry.

'Very,' said Effie. 'Louise Brooks or Clara Bow?'

'Miss Brooks.'

She nodded.

They walked into a broad palace courtyard. The afternoon sun picked out earnest men of art and Corinthian columns, gave it shadow and sobriety.

'This is the picture gallery,' he said, unfolding the map.

'It looks like a wedding cake. Do they have Cezanne?'

'I'm not sure. I think that all of your Impressionist chappies might be skulking in the Luxembourg. Do you want to have a look inside?'

She shook her head. 'It's too big. I wouldn't know where to begin. Besides, I like walking.' She felt the lurch in Henry's linked movements. 'It's not a problem to walk?'

'We could dance our way there if you prefer it?'

Motorcars, carts and carriages circled an Egyptian needle. Effie squinted at the strange hieroglyphics and wondered if the circling transport was under some pharaonic spell.

'This is where they had the guillotine,' said Henry. He sliced across his throat, illustrating with his index finger. Sea nymphs and marine gods frolicked in a fountain.

'Paris is over the top,' observed Effie.

They looked along the avenue to the triumphal arch. There were sparkling hotels, chic strollers and a noisy weave of traffic in between. They agreed it was somehow excessive. There was something that was too much about the chicness, the traffic and the triumph.

'Paris is a show off,' she said.

Effie looked up at the tapering height of webbed iron. They had seen the tower from afar but, standing underneath, Effie cowered at the scale of it. It seemed to bend the sky.

'But how do we get up there?'

She discerned a zigzag of stairs.

'1,665 steps.'

'Is that one of your frivolous facts?'

'I read it in a pamphlet this morning. Are you suitably impressed?'

'I'm dizzy.'

'Delightfully so.'

Her eyes dipped to Henry's leg.

'Don't worry. There's also a lift.'

'But do we really want to go up there?'

'Yes, we're daring, remember.'

They took the elevator to the first floor. Effie found herself wanting to stand very close to Henry, which the crowd conveniently allowed. She shut her eyes and listened to multilingual expressions of excitement. She felt the sensation of ascent, the hydraulic push of it. She felt the wheels go round. She opened her eyes to see Henry looking down at her.

'It's only physics and mechanics. There's nothing to be scared of.'

'If you insist.'

The crowd pushed them out. It wasn't quite as bad as she had expected, as long as she stood well back from the edge. He coaxed her and they took a tour, identifying landmarks from the panorama panels. They pointed to where they had been and to where they meant to go. Effie pointed mainly at landmarks on the opposite side of the river from Joe.

'I've never asked you what you do.' She pointed at Henry, then.

'Balls,' he said. He smirked. 'Sorry, I never tire of that.'

'Balls?'

'Ball bearings. My family made ball bearings.'

'What are ball bearings for?'

'It was bicycles and tractors when my old man set it up, all agriculture and innocent leisure, but it became munitions and tanks.' He looked like he was sorry about the transition. 'I sold up a couple of years ago.'

'Laurie's father assembled brass God-knows-whats. It was something to do with fuses. It was only because of the fuses – them giving his father the power to pull strings – that he was able to get his commission. He had bad eyes, you see. They would never have taken him had it not been for his father's fuses.'

'Ruddy fuses, eh? Ruddy fathers. I can't say that I'm glad your Laurence and I had that in common. I can think of happier coincidences. Just think of how life might have been different if our fathers had been proprietors of ice-cream parlours, or picture palaces or manufacturers of ladies' modesty garments.' Henry grinned at the possibility. 'But that's the past, isn't it? It's all change now. I'm training to be a potter, of all things. Centrifugal force: it focuses the mind.' He made demonstrative motions with his hands.

'That's rather a long way from manufacturing ball bearings.'

'A splendidly long way. I'm yet to make a penny from it, the back pain is appalling, I'm up to my elbows in mud and I love it. There's something profoundly direct and honest about it. It's the truest thing that I've ever done. In fact, I'll go so far as to say that it's the next best thing to being a modesty garment manufacturer's son.'

'You look well-scrubbed for someone who plays in mud.'

'I am in possession of a nail brush. And I scrubbed up especially for this excursion.'

'That's nice,' said Effie, who took a professional interest in tableware and liked men to possess grooming accoutrements. She remembered how Laurie had come home from his watercolour excursions with landscape-coloured hands, but he'd always been clean in time for tea. 'Laurie wanted to be a painter, but his father didn't think it a proper thing to do. He said that it was an indulgence and a weakness and was sure to make him depraved. His future was in fuses, his father said. Only, well, it wasn't.' She smiled at Henry. 'I'm glad that you get to play with clay.'

'There's a danger of depravity in artistic endeavours? I never realised that,' Henry laughed. 'Crikey. I'd better be careful.'

'Perhaps you can make me a teapot. That seems like a sober task to focus your mind upon.'

'Steady on. I'm still on wonky bowls. It will be some while before I achieve a teapot, sober or otherwise.'

'I can wait,' she said.

Paris stretched to the skyline. It was grey and gold and geometric in the afternoon sun. Effie remembered standing at the top of another tower. She saw herself in a downwards blur of floral frock. Henry offered her a swig from his hip flask. They looked out together at endless Paris.

'This isn't the first tower I've climbed this week,' she began, and then wondered whether she should have done.

'Oh?'

'Your fairy palace – the Cloth Hall – I climbed to the top of that too.'

'You did what? Why?'

'I'm not really sure why. I was upset and then suddenly I was up there.'

'You didn't really mean to do something silly?' He held her squarely by the shoulders, as if suspecting that, as a serial tower ascender, she might abruptly spring and somersault the edge.

'I'm silly in many respects, but suicide isn't one of them, it seems.'

'But you thought about it?'

'I thought about it,' she affirmed, 'and didn't want it. I'm not ready to let go.'

'I'm very glad of that.' He let her go then, but kept an aside eye on her. 'Hell's bells, Effs.'

They looked, side-by-side and silent, at the view.

'I can't see beyond it,' she said eventually.

'Nor me. But I rather like that.'

They leaned together.

'I found your Edward. I haven't told you.'

She turned and stared at Henry. The last week had all been unfound graves and grave findings. She half wondered if Edward too might be alive and stashed away with a secret history or a Belgian barmaid.

'His grave?'

'Yes.'

'But how did you know where to look?'

'It's not too hard. I had a name. There are means.'

'How is he?' She wondered if she perhaps ought to have gone to look for her brother and left Joe dead.

'Quiet. Tidy. There's a red rose planted next to him.'

She liked that. It seemed appropriate for Edward. And she liked Henry for doing it. 'Thank you.'

They watched people below weave through the tower's lacy shadow.

'Have I told you about my mother?' It suddenly struck her that they knew very little of each other's facts and figures – though her mother, on reflection, possibly wasn't a winning place to start.

'No.'

'She's mad. Quite mad. She had a turn when Edward died and never came back round again. She lives in an insane asylum. She's happy enough, she crochets and takes an interest in tittle-tattle, but she won't believe that Edward's dead. She won't believe that the war's over. She asks me for news of it, as if it's still going on. It's impossible for her to accept that it's finished. She thinks the hospital scissor it out of the newspapers, that it's some great conspiracy. Having confessed my tower antics, you probably think me mad too.'

'Only slightly.'

'I normally tell people that she's a nun, you know. It seems nicer. Only I'm sure that nobody believes me.'

'So what niceness shall we fabricate about your predilection for towers?'

'I'm a student of architecture, remember.'

Caroline Scott

'Of course. What heinous thing did poor old mater do?'
'She assaulted a vicar.'
'A vicar?'
'With an umbrella.'
'An umbrella?'
'Don't smirk. It's not funny.'
'I'm sorry. It is a bit funny.'
'I shan't tell you if you laugh.'
He pressed his lips together. 'I apologise. Do tell me, if you want to.'

She told him about the Reverend Harwood. Her mother's actions might not have had such dire consequences, but it wasn't the first time that the cleric in question had been assaulted by a grieving mother.

'I supposed that she was made an example of too,' said Effie. 'So Grace got the house, I got mother's sewing machine and mother got sectioned.'

'I am sorry,' said Henry. He looked like he wasn't sure what else to say. 'Gosh, that really isn't funny at all.'

'I probably shouldn't have told you.'

He shook his head. 'It's everywhere. It affects us all. I'm glad that you could tell me. I'm glad that you could trust me. It's not something to be ashamed of, and I am truly sorry that I laughed.'

'I sometimes wonder if she's right – if perhaps the war isn't over. There are days when it feels like it isn't. It stretches on and on. Like Paris.'

'I'm not certain that Parisians would be flattered by the comparison, but I do understand. Come on – next storey.'

She watched the metal beams slide past.
'I feel like I am flying.'
'Less of that,' said Henry. 'Remember that I suspect you of

unhealthy predilections.'

It seemed considerably higher at the second floor. Her hands gripped the guardrail and her knees felt slightly unsteady. She definitely didn't feel like letting go.

'Since we're sharing today, there are things that I ought to tell you.' His eyes were suddenly serious.

'I seem to have told you all of my most shocking secrets, but I know hardly anything about you. What terribly bad manners I must have.'

Henry leaned on the railings. She watched his profile. Though she might know hardly anything about him, Effie found it agreeable and steadying to look at him. In the background, schoolboys were spitting experimentally over the edge.

'It all stops and starts at this.' He knocked the cigarette packet on his knee.

'Can you really play spoons on it?'

'Only at Christmas.'

'Tell me. If you want to, that is.'

He turned back to profile. She looked out with him.

'It was the first proper action I saw. Before that it was all just drill and singsongs in estaminets. I had been having rather a jolly time. I liked being a soldier. I liked feeling part of something. But then they sent us south to the Somme. We were in and out of that sector from July through to October.'

He hesitated.

'Go on,' she said, uncertainly.

'I –' He looked down. He seemed to be examining the hand rail. 'Well, if you've read your Laurence's diary, you probably have some idea of what it was like. I'm not certain that I can begin to find the words for what it was like. Suffice to say,' he turned to face her, 'and what I mean to say, is that I can understand why your Joseph walked.'

She nodded. 'And your leg?'

'Bloody great piece of shrapnel. They had to take it off. I was lucky. They tied a ticket to me that had an 'S' on it. 'Ship', you see. I got back and it put me out of it. My war ended in 1916. I framed that ticket. Daft, eh? It's still on the wall over my desk.'

'Were you in hospital for a long time?'

'Months – and then convalescence. The war was over by the time that I was coming home. Katie says that if I take my cod liver oil there's a good chance that I'll grow a new one.'

He brightened and then flagged. He blew a sigh of smoke and looked at her. There was something measuring about that look. Effie wasn't sure what that measuring look meant.

'And?'

'I had a fiancée too. Clarice. She was very pretty. Too pretty, probably. She found all of this too much to cope with – my spare parts, or lack of parts, I mean. And I can understand that. I can. I don't blame her for it.'

'She broke it off?'

'She said that she didn't think she was up to it, that she didn't have the strength for it. It hit me hard. Words can hurt as much as sticks and stones, can't they?' He turned his eyes to Effie, then.

'I had no idea how much hurt there was in the world. I didn't know until now that life was like that.'

'I'd never hurt you. Life doesn't have to be like that.'

'But it is, isn't it? Even Laurie. If there was a moth in the house he'd catch it so carefully between his hands and put it out of the window. I wouldn't have believed that Laurie could have hurt anything or anybody, but suddenly in that diary he's ripping and roaring and slicing. And worse.'

'Ripping and roaring and slicing were somewhat unavoidable in 1916. Alas. I vaguely recall that they used to call it patriotism. Funny old word, eh?'

'I used to think that I understood the rules,' said Effie. 'You know? I thought that I knew what life was like. But suddenly it seems that I have absolutely no idea how the whole thing works. It makes me want to throw my hands in the air. I think I might become a hermit. I'm not sure that I trust or like people anymore. I don't want to feel anything ever again.'

'A hermit? And the world would be denied the wonders of your Bakewell tart?'

'I'm not sure that pastry matters any longer.'

'Well, now you're just talking silly. Any more of this mad talk and I'll have you committed.' His smile changed. 'I honestly believe, after everything I saw, that we aren't really like that – that men aren't really warlike. Not instinctively. I believe that people essentially want a quiet life – and most people are fundamentally decent. What they want is homes and families. I saw bad things back then, but I saw far more small acts of kindness. It's those – the instances of generosity and sympathy, of compassion and patience – that I choose to remember. I don't personally think that you've misunderstood the rules at all.' Something earnest showed itself around Henry's eyes. There was something momentarily intense in his expression. But then he was blinking and apparently embarrassed. 'Sorry. I'm going on, aren't I? Kate says I'm given to the occasional pontification.'

She stared at him. 'You are a nice man, Mr Lyle. Do you know that? A thoroughly nice man. It's a great pity that your Clarice couldn't have tried harder. So what happened after – after the hospital?'

'I moved back up north and Kate took me in. I'm afraid that I went very down. I've given her a lot to cope with.'

'You mustn't leave her to cope in Amiens on her own.'

'I know. I won't. There hasn't been anyone since Clarice. It all rather knocked my confidence.'

She looked at him against the grey-gold geometry of Paris. He watched her as she straightened his tie, and somehow then her hand found itself in his.

'There's something about you,' he said. 'You're a difficult person to lie to.'

'I'd boast of my needle-sharp insightfulness, but other people seem to have had no trouble hoodwinking me.' She tilted her chin to him and smiled. 'And what lie would you tell me, if you could?'

'That I'll make it all right. That it all gets better from here. That I'll never let anyone hoodwink or hurt you again.'

'That's two lies and a tenuous statement of optimism. You can't make it right. I know that you have to go. I would like to believe that it might get better, though.'

They pressed their noses against the window of the souvenir shop, which sold a multiplication of miniature towers, made from brass and wood and plaster and plastic. There were ashtrays and charms and tea towels. There were snow globes, towers with saints, towers with roses and towers that were clocks. It rather surprised her that Ypres' innovative recyclers hadn't yet managed to place a shell-case tower in this window.

'I shall buy you a keepsake,' said Henry, 'something to commemorate our daring. This is the nearest that I've ever got to heaven, you know... apart from once, maybe, in a casualty clearing station.'

She watched him through the window, Henry in his sporting stripes amongst the souvenirs. He gave her an over-the-shoulder grin.

'There.' He handed her a pyramid of brown paper. 'For your mantelpiece.'

She imagined her hand placing it between the cut glass and the cut lilac. She saw her hand hesitate.

'I'm meant to have Crêpes Suzette at the Café Metropole.'

'That sounds jolly. One of Laurence's whims?'

'Yes.'

'I approve of whims,' said Henry. 'And I'm partial to Crêpes

Suzette. Laurence was a man of excellent taste.'

'I think that the two of you would have got on,' she said.

'Do you? I shall choose to take that as a compliment. We must find this Café Metropole and raise a glass to Laurence.'

They took the lift to the top of the tower. Effie shut her eyes again.

'Come on,' he said.

'I think I'm going to be sick.'

'What a criminal waste of egg mayonnaise.'

She gripped the sharp corners of her souvenir tower and looked at the skyline through a squint.

'Look out, not down.'

'I can't look down.'

'Open your eyes.'

She re-heard Laurie and opened her eyes to Henry's face.

'There, see,' he said. 'That's the ticket. That's my brave girl.'

Chapter Forty-Three

The beggar stretched a palm towards him. *'Monsieur?'*

'Aveugle. Ancien combattant. Mutilé,' said the sign around his neck. He placed a coin in the beggar's hand. There were yellow and green ribbons pinned to his chest.

Joe watched the shadows of the crowd move along the pavement. He saw the traffic slide in shop windows. A horse and trap clattered past, with a crate-encased statue on the back. A white stone soldier was thrusting heroically upward from the packing crate. The café talkers took their hats off for the cenotaph soldier. Eyes lowered reverentially. Joe looked away.

He walked back past the dancing mask, the clown and the snake charmer. Men were curled asleep on the benches. Women were laughing in the cafés. A palmist was telling fortunes by the entrance to the cemetery.

It was quieter inside the gates, the city jostled against him less and his steps slowed. He lit a cigarette and looked at the long-ago graves. Sophie had told him that this place was a field once upon a time, a green space in the midst of the city where young people had come to drink and dance polkas. There were *buvettes* she said, streamers and lanterns in the trees. Sometimes Joe imagined the girls in white dresses dancing. He saw them dancing between the graves, with faraway faces.

He walked the avenue between the mausoleums. A woman was feeding the sparrows. They fluttered about her feet. She looked up and looked through Joe. The sparrows scattered as he passed. The avenue tombs had ornate porticoes and stained-glass windows. Their inhabitants frowned in profiles and tilted their chins upward in busts. Marble women wept over them and stiff-winged angels. The leaves were brushed away from the avenue tombs.

Sophie had danced in a white dress once. There had been a fete in her village. It was only a few months after the guns had gone quiet, but grass was starting to grow over it and people were returning. They were still living under corrugated iron then, salvaging and scrimping. The returning people had raised voices and pointed accusing fingers. But, that night, there were strings of paper flowers strung across the square – dipping lines of red and white and blue. Sophie's father had been playing a melodeon. Joe told her that he played the piano and then she had danced around his chair, laughing in a white dress.

There were women in black in the cemetery now. These women didn't dance. They put red, white and blue flowers on graves and stuck photographs of soldiers to them. In November they brought chrysanthemums and, in the drab winter days, the cemetery was full of colours. Families promenaded along the avenues, after lunch, on All Saints and All Souls. They swept their tombs and talked to the neighbours until the attendants blew their whistles for closing time. They left candles burning on the graves.

'Chrysanthemums smell of death,' Sophie had said. Joe recalled the flicker of the little lights.

The grandeur and care diminished along the cemetery's side-streets. Here the windows of the tombs were broken. Doors hung on their hinges. Leaves shifted dryly. Roses crumbled. Joe turned left where the smiling woman slept silently with a small dog at her feet. He knew the residents of this quarter. He nodded to the moss-grown manufacturer and verdigrised man of letters. He touched his hat to the blueing photograph of the grinning boy soldier.

Joe's fingers clawed into soil. He scratched back the grass. His fingers pulled through the sharpness of root and stone. There were yellow marigolds on the neighbouring grave. Joe took the yellow bird from his pocket and placed it in the shallow hollow that he had made. It was Sophie's bird, her caged pet, always beating at the bars. He couldn't stand how its wings beat against

Caroline Scott

the bars. It looked gaudy in its little grave. It looked pitiful. He pulled the earth over it.

'Who killed Cock Robin?' Joe laughed.

He had followed Effie as far as the river, had watched them pass over the bridge. If she had written back, returned his letter, would he be the man walking over bridges with her? Could Sophie, then, be dancing around a different man? Would he prefer it so? Joe took Effie's ring from his pocket and pushed it into the soil with the canary. It seemed better to bury it.

Chapter Forty-Four

Eugene Bernot pulled his fingers through Effie's hair. She watched his face in the mirror. He appeared not to approve of what his fingers found.

She had pointed at the mannequin and said 'Louise Brooks.' He had given her a look, as if deciding whether she was worthy of a Louise Brooks, before nodding not-before-time consent. 'I do propose to pay for it,' she'd added.

Eugene tugged a comb. It caught in the tangles, which he attacked with a long-suffering expression. Eugene Bernot, his name above the door, wore a velvet jacket and waxed whiskers. Effie supposed he wasn't accustomed to English women's tangles.

'I'm sorry. It hasn't been cut in some time.'

Eugene raised his eyebrows to signify that this was no surprise.

'So,' he said. 'We are to attempt an entry into the twentieth century?'

His unanticipated English raised Effie's eyebrows.

'Yes. Definitely.'

He aligned his splayed hands either side of her jaw. She noted that his nails were nicely polished. 'This much?'

Effie's hands pushed Eugene's up an inch. 'This much.'

He nodded approval. 'You are braver than you look.'

'It seems that I am,' said Effie.

Her hair was parted and combed straight. She looked at her reflection and thought that the woman in the mirror didn't look very daring. She looked dowdy and older than she ought. In time for her three o'clock rendezvous at the Café Metropole, Effie intended to look like a girl who only goes up towers for larks and who shimmies to jazz in clubs. She intended to look the cat's pyjamas. Effie no longer meant to be mistaken for a widow.

The scissors snipped. She shivered at the touch of cool steel on her neck and thought of Henry with his guillotine gesture. She also thought about Henry's bloody great piece of shrapnel, about him wanting to be part of something and in the process losing part of himself. It had shocked her that he couldn't find the words. Henry always found the words. Quite often he found too many words. But, then, Laurie had only been able to find the words on paper.

Eugene straightened her head and raised her chin. 'Still,' he said.

As he advanced around her jaw line, she saw her hair fall. Eugene's burgundy slippers trod through discarded lengths of mousy Effie.

'Hmm,' said Eugene, philosophically.

Effie's eye strolled through the glitter of bottles, the sparkle of potions, balms and unguents. Eugene's scissors flashed in the mirror. It was prettily frosted and flowered and reminded her of the Venetian mirror over the fireplace – the one which had been Laurie's mother's. She remembered watching his face in it as she attempted to dust the stuffed stoats and he, in turn, smiling as he watched her swear.

There is a man with red eyes in my shaving mirror. I'm not sure that I know him. She recalled the line Laurie had written in the April of 1917. They were in trenches west of Saint-Quentin and he had just got back from a raid. *He is more reckless than me. He thinks about statistics and odds and chance. He takes risks that I wouldn't take. He is older than me. He is tired. I have always been a careful and a cautious person. I have always taken life timidly. If this is ever over, if the odds come out in my favour, I mean to recklessly embrace life.*

Eugene made a point at Effie's cheekbone with a '*Voila.*'

She tried to remember whether there was a mirror on the wall in Joe's room. She couldn't recollect that there was. There wasn't anything on the walls apart from that stuck-together picture of Charlie. Would Joe recognise his own mirror face? She wasn't altogether certain he would have a reflection.

Eugene bit his lip in concentration as he snipped and combed. He hummed something that a bobbed girl who went to jazz clubs would probably recognise, but which Effie didn't. He stood back, appraised and approved. The hand mirror showed Effie the back of her head. She had never seen the back of her neck before and made note that she must now remember to scrub it.

'Thank you,' she smiled at the girl with the shiny bobbed haircut. She looked rather younger than Effie. She looked like a girl who might swing a bag in carefree circles, who was irresponsible and indulgent and well-informed about hemlines and dance moves. She looked like a girl who might recklessly embrace life.

She smiled less when Eugene presented her with the discreetly folded bill, but it pleased her to shake her head and feel her high-priced hair move. She shook Eugene Bernot's polished hand. He wished her *'Bon courage.'*

The Café Metropole, as it turned out, wasn't far from the hotel. She powdered her nose on the street corner and, in the compact mirror, looked herself in the kohl-ringed eye. She still knew herself. She wasn't doing the wrong thing. The compact snapped closed.

The café was lively and shimmering. There were red banquettes and mirrored walls and a noisy, glossy crowd. She took a deep breath in the doorway.

Henry appeared from behind an English newspaper. The cigarette dropped from his mouth. 'Hell's teeth! You did it. You look the cat's meow.'

'Cat's pyjamas,' corrected Effie. She sat down next to him on the banquette. 'Please don't stare,' she said.

'Effs, you can't flounce in here looking like that and not

expect a chap to stare.'

'Well, stare discreetly, then.'

'I'll try.'

Reginald pawed at her knee.

'Has he been good?'

Henry nodded mutely.

'It's only a haircut,' said Effie.

'It's a smashing haircut.'

She let Reginald up on her lap. 'Come on, then. Crêpes Suzette. You'll have to pay, though, because I'm broke.'

He nodded again.

'I preferred it when you prattled.'

The waiter pushed a trolley alongside.

'Ah, the operating table.'

Various apparatus were aligned either side a silver spirit warmer. Given the way he was staring, Effie wasn't certain that Henry's spirits required warming. She nudged him to watch the waiter. 'Focus,' she directed, with a sharp application of elbow.

Henry nodded consent for the champagne to be poured. 'I must say, you don't look like a girl who makes Bakewell tart.'

'I don't look like a tart?'

'No, you look luscious.'

Effie studied the flamboyant swirling of copper pans, admiring the waiter's show of dexterity with spoon and fork. It seemed an act of well-plotted culinary theatre, designed to make them salivate and duly succeeding.

'I did it once for a dinner for some of Laurie's old school friends. But I was over-generous with the spirits and my flambé got out of control.'

The waiter administered the liqueur more soberly than Effie had done, and, with a small blue gasp, the pan flamed.

'Pretty,' she said.

'Capital,' said Henry. He took a mouthful of wine and looked at her. 'Do you know what the best meal is that I've ever eaten?'

'Tell me.'

'It was July 1916. We were in billets west of Albert. We'd already been up to the front for one dose and were waiting for our second. I spied a line of potatoes in a garden. It was otherwise overgrown and the house all shuttered up. My mucker, Dawson, and I went in with our entrenching tools. We boiled them over a primus and mashed them with a tin of sardines. We'd just come out of the line. It tasted like the food of the gods.'

She watched him smiling at his recollection. 'Stolen spuds and mashed sardines?'

'Mashed sardines.' He shut his eyes as he said it. He lingered through the words as if the very sound of them was delicious. His head rolled back against the banquette and then onto her shoulder. He sighed theatrically. 'Seriously, it was nectar and ambrosia.'

'How silly. I'm sure that we can do better than that.'

'It was the Everest of comestibles.' He leaned forward again with a grin. 'In the spirit of sport, I will permit you to attempt to better it, though. And you have to meet Dawson, as well. He's my potting chum and a bit of a guru. These days he bakes excellent bread.'

After some further demonstration of proficiency with the fork, the waiter placed two plates before them.

'Shall we raise a toast to Laurence?' Henry asked.

She looked at her hand on her glass. She thought about Laurie's red eyes in the shaving glass. 'Yes,' she said. 'To Laurie, luck, the indulgence of whims and recklessly embracing life.'

'Blimey. And there was me just thinking of proposing a toast to mashed sardines.'

They linked their way back to the hotel. It was going dark and the bars and cafés spilled light and music into the streets.

'*Paris pittoresque*,' said Henry. 'Don't you love it? I think I might be a bit in love with it.'

'I'm not sure that I love the idea of being in Paris alone tomorrow, picturesque though it might be.' Effie thought about blundering through Ypres, reeling for the absence of a man who was now in this city, but who didn't want her. It was less than a week ago. She clung tighter to Henry's arm. 'I wish you didn't have to go.'

'So do I.'

'Promise that it's *au revoir* and not goodbye.'

'I promise.'

They left Reginald with a collation of chopped cold meats and walked to the Kitty Kat Club. The band was banging out a raucous *Tiger Rag*. She wanted to get lost in it tonight, to tumble mindlessly in a jazzing, gyrating, glittering void.

They took a table and shouted 'Champagne!'

There were a lot of Americans in, young and loud and brave. They had white smiles and sleek hair and danced like they didn't care.

'I want to be like that,' she shouted in Henry's ear.

'My mother would call it frightfully vulgar behaviour,' he mouthed and laughed.

'Perhaps I want to be frightfully vulgar.' She stuck her tongue out at him.

The number finished and the room applauded. The orchestra struck up the Varsity Drag.

'Come on,' she dragged him up. They laughed and leapt, stamped their feet and swung exaggerated arms. She felt the percussion of the dance floor as the club slammed feet to the beat. They held hands and spun together.

Effie looked up to the spinning daisy ceiling. It blurred to white with the speed of her spin and suddenly she was looking up again at the arch of lost names. Her spin stilled. The music stopped. She watched the room grin and gyrate. All of the faces were painted. It was all a gaudy cabaret and behind the painted faces were the white names. It was all glittering and bright and blithe because this was all a dance to forget, an incantation to conjure the void, to hide and block out loss. They were all pretending. They were all hiding. The odds had come out in their favour, but they had all still lost.

'Mercy,' said Henry in her ear.

She nodded and they went back to the table.

'It feels like the end of something tonight.'

'I don't want it to be.'

'Me neither.'

Would he slide his arm around her again? Having found daring up a tower, been bobbed and rejected, she didn't feel inclined to resist this time. Lifting her glass, she saw the mark where her engagement ring had been. It didn't fade. She sank the glass.

They watched the dancing crowd. There was something slightly feverish in the atmosphere tonight. They clapped for *Crazy Rhythm*. She wanted the glitter and the gaiety. She wanted her head to be full of beats and lights and nothing more.

'*I feel like Emperor Nero when Rome was a very hot town,*' smoothed the crooner. It went into *Ain't She Sweet?* and Henry crooned too. They were back on the dance floor, circling and laughing.

'*Oh me! Oh my! Ain't that perfection?*' sang Henry.

Effie put her arms around him. He smelled clean; not like Joe, who smelled sour. She leaned her head against Henry's chest. It

Caroline Scott

was both safe and dangerous. His close-up lips smiled. She lifted her chin and moved her lips to his.

Now it was Henry's turn to run. Suddenly Effie was alone on the dance floor. *Oh me! Oh my!* circled mockingly around her.

'Henry?'

She saw him pushing through the dancers. The crowd pushed against her as she followed.

'Henry!'

She found him leaning in the doorway. She watched his shadowed profile for a few moments before she approached. There was something different about the way that he was standing. His breathing didn't seem to be quite right.

'Henry, I'm sorry.' She put her fingers through her over-priced hair. What had she been thinking? Was Henry going to carry her off into his world of frivolity and bookishness, this foolish woman who had nothing? She had no role, no home and no right to frivolity. She had nothing but the obligation to chaperone a Yorkshire Terrier and have horrible surprises sprung on her. She put a hand on his arm and felt him flinch. 'Henry, is something the matter?'

'It's me that should be saying sorry, Effie. I am sorry. That was bloody stupid.' At least he smiled then. 'Can we go and get a coffee?'

They sat outside a café. He insisted that she wear his jacket.

'But you're cold. I can hear your teeth chattering.'

'I'm fine.' He sat on his hands. His shirt was damp. She saw him shiver.

'You don't look fine. You don't look at all fine. I'm worried about you.'

'Well, you mustn't. The last thing that you need is another fool to worry about.'

'Don't be silly. You can tell me, you know. You can share it with me.'

252

He looked at her. 'How can I expect you to take on my problems as well?' He looked at her seriously. It was the same look that she had seen as they sailed into Boulogne.

'Is it about Clarice and what happened?'

He laughed like he didn't mean it. 'Something like that. Can you see now why Clarice couldn't cope?'

As he said it, he held out his hands. Effie put her own out towards them. She tried to still his hands but found she couldn't. Her hands were shaking then with his convulsions.

'It's okay. It will stop.' He pulled away and wiped his eyes. 'They call it shock. Some bloody shock. It's ten years back. You'd think that, with a decade, I might have gotten over the shock.'

'Oh, Henry.'

'My wiring sometimes goes a bit on the blink. It's like my nerves are all tangled up and sometimes they short circuit. I get these occasional illogical rushes of panic.' He crossed his arms and hid his trembling hands in his armpits. 'What a blithering idiot.'

'I don't think you're an idiot. You're not an idiot at all.'

'Thank you.' He crouched over his knees as if he wished to compress and force the shaking back in. 'It's not a regular problem. It hasn't happened in a while. I'm mostly well now. I don't jump off towers or attack vicars with umbrellas. I can just be a bit rattly on occasion. That's what the pills and the pottery thing is for. It helps me focus. It's about control. This does happen less often than it did.'

His still-unsteady hands were now curled around a coffee cup. It looked like it took a great effort of concentration. Effie watched the cup lurch as he raised it to his mouth. She wanted to help, to hold it to his lips. She wanted to exchange the cup for a glass and to help Henry drink to the future. But she didn't know what was needed or wanted and she didn't know what the future was.

'I'm sorry,' he said. 'You really don't need this. You've got enough to cope with.'

She uncrossed her legs and leant towards him. 'I do understand, you know. Or, at least, I understand enough.'

'You shouldn't have to understand these things.'

'Laurie liked the gramophone and his paints, his Lakeland poets and his Hardy heroines. That was his pottery, if you will. Those were the things that made it go away. That was his focus, his control. But it didn't always work. He used to dream that he could hear the gas alarms. He'd go back there night after night. I used to have to cover the mirrors because he'd sleepwalk and attack his own reflection in the night. He'd stand there, staring at his feet, his poor feet all covered in glass, and not know where he was and what he'd done. I'm only just starting to understand why those things happened, why he had those nightmares. But I do want to understand.'

'Laurence was very lucky to have you.'

'Perhaps I was lucky to have him.'

Henry's un-laughing eyes looked down and then up at her with sudden force. Suddenly all of his tapping, fidgeting energy was focussed into a look of such intensity, of such fierce earnestness, that Effie could barely hold his gaze. 'I did it too, you know,' he said. 'Oh, only for a couple of days. Can I tell you this? I've never told anybody else this.'

She nodded consent to the confession that it seemed he must give her.

'I'd been on leave and I just couldn't bear the thought of going back. I just couldn't do it. So I hid in a hotel room. I cowered under an eiderdown in Charing Cross. But the noise of the station... I put a pillow over my face and tried to cut it out, but I couldn't. And I don't know which was the greater cowardice, the cowering there or the fear that sent me back. What a bloody fool. It was only for a couple of days. But I was a Captain. Of course, I got a ruddy great dressing down. There but for the grace of God and all of that.'

Effie stared at him. 'You poor man.'

'I've never told that to Kate. I've never told that to anyone before. You seem to draw my secrets from me. It's just a pity my secrets don't shine a more complimentary light.'

'I'm learning that secrets rarely flatter their keeper. I guess that's why they're secrets.' They sat together in silence for a while.

'I'm not very dashing or daring, am I?'

'Me neither,' she replied. 'You'll do.'

'I'm not really very good on the spoons, either. I exaggerated. Oh, yes, I can knock a tune out, but the truth is that I'm no virtuoso.'

'Heavens,' said Effie. 'Now that is a disappointment. And there was me hoping to come and see you in concert. In compensation your jacket smells nice.' She submitted his collar to an olfactory examination. 'You smell of shaving soap and laundering and libraries.'

'That's very precise. You should have been a perfumier.'

He sniffed her hand reciprocally. 'Pears Soap, violets and custard – with a bit of Paris thrown in too.'

'Paris smells of drains.'

'Well, I'm partial to girls who have a suggestion of Parisian plumbing.'

His hands were stilling now. She observed the effort of application with which he lit a cigarette.

'Katie says that I'm frightening when I get the jitters. If you now wish to scarper in the opposite direction, I will understand.'

'Kate is probably frightened for you. No, I think I like you better for being a bit rattly.'

'You do? You are a very odd young woman. Are you real?

Have I dreamt you up? Men are meant to have balls and bottle,' said Henry, putting his eyes to the night sky to find the right words to define men's must-haves.

Effie looked up too. The moon was huge and as shiny as a new shilling. Henry exhaled and she watched the smoke wind from his lips.

'Not that my... Not that I mean to imply... Oh, hell.' He laughed. 'Damn it. I'm making this sound so much worse than it actually is. I can just occasionally be a bit bad with my nerves – that's all.'

'Don't worry,' said Effie and put her hand over his. It had finally stilled. She unwound Henry's fingers from around the cigarette.

'I can still *tango*,' he added meaningfully. 'There's nothing wrong with my tango.'

'I'm quite certain of it,' she said. 'You blush as well. It's rather endearing. I'll add that to the positives column.'

'Can we go home before I feel utterly emasculated?'

Effie's flicked cigarette bounced brightly across the pavement and she took his arm.

'Parisian plumbing? *Really?*'

Chapter Forty-Five

Northern France, 1919

'Everyone is dancing in Berlin,' Sophie had said. Her father had been playing the melodeon in the garden, squeezing out waltzes while the chickens scratched about his feet. 'I read about it. But it is a *danse macabre*. It's the dance of death.'

'A dance of death?'

'Eudore says that they are starving in Berlin. There is nothing left to do but dance.' Joe watched as she painted a lipstick line around her mouth. *'Mon beau gosse,'* said Sophie's red lips in the mirror. *'Mon pauvre gars.'*

He thought about the girls in Berlin, dancing with hollow bellies and dead eyes. He imagined all of the dead rising up and dancing.

'Will you dance with me?' Sophie's reflection asked the question.

'Me? Dance?' He pushed his palms against the arms of the chair. 'How can I dance?' It seemed as implausible as the chorus line of deceased soldiers that he'd been picturing just instants earlier.

'I'll hold you. I won't let you fall. Do you trust me?'

He looked up at Sophie. She was standing over him and smiling now. That smile had been the first thing Joe had seen when he had opened his eyes again. Weeks had disappeared; he'd been between life and death for a long time. When he came round the frost flowers on the windowpane had been replaced by apple blossom and there was a girl next to the bed, smiling and saying, *'C'est fini.'* Those were the first words that he had heard: *'La guerre c'est bien fini pour toi, soldat.'*

'Yes,' he said to her. 'I trust you.'

Joe put his arms around Sophie, as she insisted. Her hair swung against his face. She had just sprayed her neck with a purple bottle of scent and he could almost taste the flowers. It took him back to a wood where they had dug graves among the wild violets.

'Does it hurt?'

'Yes.'

The pain shot down his right leg. His knees shook when he tried to straighten and then he'd pulled her over. She was lying across him and laughing, her head on his chest. Her rippling laughter took away his anger.

'I'm sorry.'

She stepped back, smoothed her hair and handed him the whisky bottle. Her earrings were made from polished bullet cartridges, he noticed. They glimmered grotesquely. He wanted to tell her to take them out.

'*Encore?*' she said. 'Let me take your weight.'

'I can't.'

'You can.'

He clung to her. He could feel the effort in her muscles and hear it in her breath. And, then, suddenly – for the first time in over a year – he'd straightened and was standing.

'*Ça va?*'

'Yes. I think so. I'm not sure that I can let go of you, though.'

'You don't have to.'

She leaned her forehead against his. He could see her white teeth against the red lipstick.

'Your father has stopped playing. There's no music to dance to now.'

'You can kiss me instead,' Sophie said.

He watched the dawn light stretch across the ceiling. The clock in the next room struck nine.

'You're shaking,' she said. '*Tu trembles.*'

Her hands pulled his face towards hers.

'Why do you cry in the night?' she asked.

He turned away and sat on the edge of the bed. He could hear the couple next door arguing. The empty whisky bottle was on the floor – and the envelope. It must have fallen from his pocket. He picked it up and re-read Laurence Greene's words.

I'm sorry, said the letter. *I'm sorry that I broke our bargain. I'm sorry that I didn't do the thing that you meant for me to do. I'm not sorry, though, to know that you're alive. I can't make myself sorry that your life didn't end.*

He found himself checking inside the envelope again. That was it. There was nothing from her. Joe had counted the number of times that Greene had used the word sorry. Effie hadn't sent him so much as one word.

'Who is she?' asked the girl on the bed.

'She?' He looked back towards Sophie. Stuck to the wall behind her bedhead was a flight of jolly bluebirds that she had scissored from greetings cards. Embossed doves delivered *billets doux* and fat cupids angled arrows. A cherub curled at the corners.

'Who is the woman who wrote the letter that you keep re-reading?'

'It's not from a woman.'

'So who is the man?'

'A bad memory.'

'Perhaps you ought to forget him, then?' Her hand reached towards him.

'Yes,' Joe had said. 'Perhaps I should.'

Nine years later, he read that first letter again. There had been nine more letters since that first. It was always him, Greene, saying sorry. Why, after nine years without a word, had Effie been there standing at his door? Joe struck a match. He burned Laurence Greene's apologies one by one.

Chapter Forty-Six

Paris, 1928

Effie went with him in the taxi to the station. Henry was quiet. All of her over-breakfast attempts at conversation had trailed away. Finding herself mid-soliloquy on the subject of the next week's weather forecast, she had resigned herself to watching him move croissant crumbs around his plate. Effie looked out at the speeding-past pavements now, at the traffic and the shops and the too-fast rolling meter.

'I'm leaving the day after tomorrow,' she said.

'I wish that we were on the same boat. I could help you with Reginald.'

'It'll be okay. I have a scheme with brandied cream.'

'You don't need me and my pills, then?'

'Not as much as Kate does.'

His fingers tapped a rhythm on his knee.

'Working on something for Christmas?'

His fingers stilled. 'I'm not feeling very festive,' he said.

Effie looked out at the Seine and the sightseers. 'No, me neither.'

'Will you go out dancing tonight?'

'What, me and Reginald? Don't talk daft. I shall find a cheap and cheerful café and think sober thoughts,' she clarified, so as to underline that Henry wouldn't be missing out on any mischief.

'Not too sober, eh?' said Henry, though his effervescence seemed to have subsided.

'Middlingly sober,' moderated Effie.

Whether it was the confine of the taxi or the confusion of the previous evening's conclusion, a certain caution seemed to have entered the cadence of their conversation. Reginald looked from one to the other, registering the awkward rhythm of their sentences.

'I am sorry about last night, you know,' said Henry, seemingly having decided to go head-on at the awkwardness. 'I can be such an awful idiot.'

'You aren't and you weren't. I'm sorry too.' It was a relief to acknowledge it.

'Now we have both apologised to each other and we are equal.'

'Kate said that.'

'Kate is very sensible.'

Reginald panted on the seat in between them. Perhaps he too was relieved that the awkwardness was acknowledged and over.

'He will miss you.' Effie stroked Reginald in anticipatory compensation, though he didn't yet look inclined to pine. Reginald never really did do much pining.

'And I shall miss him.'

'I shall miss you,' said Effie.

'And I you.'

The taxi pulled in at the front of the station. She looked up at the theatrical statuary and triumphant columns. It seemed a long time since she had arrived here.

Reginald forgot to miss Henry as soon as concourse was in his nostrils. He knotted himself around ankles and collided with suitcases.

'He's a railway enthusiast,' explained Effie, 'or, at least, very keen on the smell of stations.'

'Evidentially,' said Henry.

They found the platform. The train was already in.

She stared at Henry, who ought to prattle, but didn't. The crowd moved around them. He lit a cigarette and gave her the packet. 'Keep them.'

She pocketed them and took the cigarette from his fingers.

'Thief.'

'I like stealing your gaspers.'

'You are quite the fallen woman.'

'Not entirely.' She put the cigarette back in his mouth. 'You'd better get on your train.'

'Are you trying to get rid of me?'

'Yes, I need to pick up another feller to help me smuggle Reginald home.'

'Rotten Reginald.'

They both looked down at the dog. He seemed preoccupied with Henry's brogues.

'Go on. You'd better go.'

'There's something I have to explain to you, something that I ought to tell you.' Henry hesitated. 'There's so much that I ought to tell you.' Effie watched his mouth start to make words and then stop. 'I'll write to you.'

The guard whistled.

She stared at Henry, wondering what the unsayable something could be.

'You will take care, won't you? I worry about you.'

'I will.'

'*Très bon.*'

Effie put her fingers to his mouth. She wasn't sure whether she wanted to keep his words in or whether she meant to take them from his lips. She looked at her fingers on his lips and then suddenly he was gone. Effie watched until the train was out of sight. For a moment she was a girl again, watching a train pulling out of Exchange Station. The formerly loud crowd had stood in silence as that train slipped away. They had looked at each other in wordless surmise. There was just the banner left, hanging across the tracks; *To Berlin (via Morecambe)* it had said. That train (whatever its detours) had failed to bring Joe back. Effie was struck with a sudden horror that she would never see Henry again.

Chapter Forty-Seven

It was the clapping hands that she heard first. A crowd had gathered around. Effie looked between the hats and the hairstyles. The street-corner singer was stretching her fingers out towards the paused strangers. Her voice lisped through the lyrics. She rolled her eyes towards her coconut-shell percussionist. The girl was over-playing the song's sentiments and, despite unsaid somethings and uncertain *au revoirs*, Effie found herself caught up in the melody.

'*Oh, I didn't mean to ever be mean to you-oo-oo-oo.*'

The girl shook her head, the percussionist gestured protest and a ukulele player put a hand over his heart. Effie looked around with a jolt of the crowd. That was the moment that she saw it. A blue flash arrested her eye. A figure spun and pushed away along the pavement.

'*If I didn't care, I wouldn't feel like I do-oo-oo-oo.*'

The girl made emphatic fists, the ukulele player shrugged. Effie glanced back a second time.

('*Did I get it wrong? Right or wrong, I don't blame you.*')

She turned, registering something strangely, fleetingly familiar, and then she was pulling out of the crowd and following the figure that, for some reason, she was certain had been following her. She weaved through students, strollers and sightseers, keeping the blue jacket in her sight. She swerved, side-stepped, apologised and found herself breaking into a run.

('*Why should I pick somebody like you and shame you?*')

The figure stopped and Effie stopped with it. They stood, frozen, while the song and the boulevard split around them. She wondered whether she ought to be running away, rather than running after. The Ypres boy's blue eyes flashed in her mind. She waited for him to turn. She readied herself to run.

('*I know that I made you cry and I'm so sorry, dear.*')

He looked back. He looked directly at her. His look told her everything.

'Joe!'

She ran to the corner, where she had seen him turn, but he was lost into the bustle and back alleys. Effie held herself up against the railings.

(*'But what can I say, dear, after I say I'm sorry?'*)

The singer bowed to the crowd.

Effie stepped into a church. Glass lanterns bled weak electric light. Brown birds plunged through the painted sky above. She remembered how Laurie, en route to the Somme, had prayed fiercely that he might live. She had seen something quite the reverse in Joe's face.

Effie lit two candles – one for a dead man who had meant to recklessly embrace life and another for a man who would rather his life had ended ten years earlier. She prayed, then. She prayed that after death it all stopped, that there was silence and stillness. She prayed that there was no re-wind and no recrimination and she prayed to God to forgive her sin – though she wasn't exactly certain what that sin had been.

She sat amongst the plaster saints and old stones and wished away the lyrics that looped in her head. What could she say? What more could she say than sorry?

Chapter Forty-Eight

Paris, 1920

'Joseph will play.'

Her hands, which had pulled him to the piano, were now on his shoulders. Joe stared at his own hands, palms upward above the piano keys.

'*Allez! Jouez!*' Sophie's arms were now exclaiming.

He turned and watched her walk away. She glanced back at Joe, but Barbier's arm was round her then and they were dancing. They arm-in-armed between the tables. Sophie's crowd clapped along. Joe didn't know why there must be piano music when the gramophone was already blaring out Dixieland. Moreau kept standing up to sing a verse of the *Internationale*. The old men on the benches were betting on dice. Only Sophie wanted the piano.

'*Allez!*' She spun towards Joe and then was screaming. Barbier had lifted her feet off the ground. She arched her back and laughed.

Joe leaned his head against the piano. The smoke was stinging his eyes tonight.

'Play!' said Sophie's spinning voice.

Joe looked at his hands suspended still above the keys. He had no idea where to place them. He had no idea where to begin. It was like he had never sat at a piano before in his life. He lowered his fingers onto the keys and stared at them there. He could feel the sweat creeping down his back. The Dixieland beat from the gramophone seemed to be getting faster.

'Play! Play! Play!' shouted Sophie and then she was clapping her hands.

A tangle of notes came quietly from under Joe's fingers. He stopped. He tried to hear. He wanted to remember. But a clash of sound was coming from his hands. None of the notes were where they ought to be. They seemed to be slipping away under his fingers. A glass smashed behind and he looked up. All the pictures over the piano seemed to be at odd angles. Sophie's hands clapped; a room full of hands clapped. Sound crashed from under Joe's hands.

'Joseph?'

He turned around. The Dixieland Jazz Band were still doing the *Tiger Rag*, but the laughter and the dancing had stopped. They were all standing. They were all staring. Joe was out on the street and running.

The photograph flared as he lit the lamp. He had found that if he fixed his eye upon it for long enough, a ghost of the image loomed there for a moment when his eyes shut. Joe was trying to sear it onto his retina, to fix it into his brain. He tried to conjure it into colour and make the image speak, but it wouldn't. The image wouldn't speak and it wouldn't stick. When he saw Charlie now, what he saw was that sandbag. He was forgetting Charlie's features. He was losing him. He couldn't really remember what Charlie looked like.

'*T'es impoli.*' Sophie leaned in the doorway. 'That was rude. Must you behave like a savage in front of my friends?'

'I'm sorry. I told you: I didn't want to go.'

'You never want to go anywhere. Soon I shall have no friends.'

She walked around behind him, her hands on his shoulders again. The jazz beat was still coming up from the bar below. Sophie's foot tapped along. He shrugged her hands off.

'Joseph, I worry for you. This isn't good for you. You need to go out. You need to think about something else.'

'I want to go and look for him again.'

'But we've tried.'

'I need to find him.'

'Perhaps he's not there to be found.'

'I have to find him.'

They'd gone back the previous summer. She'd pushed his chair through the cemeteries. None of it was the same. It was like it had all been shaken up and fallen down differently. Charlie wasn't where Joe had left him. The wheelchair had got stuck in ruts. Joe shouted and Sophie had cried.

'Joseph?' She moved around and crouched in front of him. 'I know that you want to find him. I understand that, *mon cher*. But must you always look backwards? What about me? What about us? What about our life?'

He looked away.

'Why won't you look at me? Why won't you look me in the eye? Am I not good enough for you? I am jealous of a photograph of a dead man.' She laughed and then frowned.

He turned his back on her and reached for the bottle. But then she was there pulling it away. They struggled over the bottle, stumbling against each other, prising at each other's fingers. She conceded and stepped back.

'T'es bourré?'

He shrugged and sat down on the bed.

'Where are you?' she sat next to him and stared. It felt as if she was trying to look into him. 'You're not here, are you? Where are you, Joseph?'

He put his hands over his ears.

'Joseph?' She pawed at him, sighed soft words at him. 'Tell me. Talk to me. Please.'

'How can I? You wouldn't understand.'

'You don't try to talk to me. How can I ever understand if you won't let me in?'

'You couldn't understand.'

'You think that you are the only person who has ever lost.' She stood up then. Her hand struck his forehead. His chin jerked back. 'I lost my mother, my uncle, my home. You think you are the only person who remembers? You think you are the only person who suffers?'

'Leave me.'

'No! I cared for you. I stitched you back together. I refuse to let you pull yourself apart.'

'I didn't want it.' He walked back to the bottle and heard himself shouting. 'I didn't want to be stitched back together and stitched to you. Why couldn't you have just left me? I didn't want this. I didn't want us. I didn't want this life.'

The canary warbled through its manic scales. He hit the cage. Its wings beat against the swaying bars.

'*Salaud!*'

Her hand struck his cheek.

'Fuck you,' she said.

He laughed. He remembered Fitton saying it to Laurence Greene. His face smarted where she had slapped him. He held her by the wrists and saw her eyes switch to the photograph on the table.

'It's true, isn't it? You care for him more than you do me – for this soldier, for this dead man.'

'Of course I do.'

She was too quick. She pulled away from him and had the photograph between her fingers then. Her eyes slid to the side and goaded him.

'You'll never find him,' she said. 'You'll never have him back. *Il n'est plus là. Il est fini. Il n'est rien que de la poussière.* He is all just dust.'

He watched as she tore Charlie apart.

Joe looked beyond his reflection into the black night. He watched Sophie's tearing hands in the glass behind him and leaned his head against the window. It was just the ghost of an action. It was eight years ago. But eight years had re-wound when Effie entered this room. What was left, after all of that time had reeled back, was the immensity of Charlie's absence. That was the thing that had stayed in the room when Effie walked out of it. He felt it physically, pushing at the walls. He stared at the pieced-together photograph. As Joe's fingers gripped against the window frame he knew it with absolute certainty: what still mattered – what had to matter – was getting Charlie back.

Chapter Forty-Nine

Paris, 1928

Effie said goodbye to Paris. She suspected that it was goodbye and not *au revoir*. She was sorry not to have seen the little boats in the Luxembourg Gardens or the barrel organ that played *The Blue Danube*; but she had seen enough. The train pulled out. Squalid courts, graffitied sidings and smart villas slipped past. Would she ever see Joe again? Effie supposed not. She had dressed in black today. She wasn't sure that that was logical. It just somehow seemed right.

The train accelerated. Picardie was a bright patchwork. Square-cornered cornfields were glossy in the sun. It glimmered through trees, yellow-lit antique villages and picked the texture of rooftops and kind folds of fields. The train passed ox carts, bell towers and innocent lanes. Green agriculture stretched in verdant, vibrant peace. Nobody would have known.

She was directed to the same room that she had stayed in a fortnight earlier. Could it be that it was only a fortnight? She leant out of the window but still couldn't see the sea. The taste of it was on the wind, though, and the bell of an ice-cream cart. She remembered Laurie being here too and turned back so that she might see the sea through his eyes.

One day I shall come back here, Laurie had written in February 1916, *when it is all different, when there is no sound of artillery to spoil it, when the only sound is the sea. I shall write my name in the sand and, knowing it is over, I shall thank God for every grain of sand and every instant that comes after.*

There were no longer any guns or khaki camping. It was a sunny, June Sunday and the front was busy with promenaders, taking the brisk air. The men were in flannels and blazers, with trilbies and cloth-caps and straw boaters. There were games with bats and balls and skittles and kites. Children paddled in rolled-up trousers. The cafés spilled out. They took tables and chairs down onto the sand, to be nearer the sea. There were dominoes and cards, weighted with pebbles against the wind. Pastel-striped bathing huts backed on to the casino. There were sandcastles, songs and a donkey. Waves broke whitely as seagulls cawed above and mademoiselles strolled with parasols.

Effie put her face into the saline wind. The sea made her gasp as it tickled coldly around her toes. Reginald barked at its back and forth. She felt alive – sharply, vigorously alive. The wind and the tide took the rest of it away. She breathed iodine sharpness. She shut her eyes to the glittering light. There was just her and the sea.

A child splashed seawater and unintelligible French. It broke into her reverie. She looked down to see her skirt washing around her knees and retreated with wet hems. Reginald lay just back from the water's edge. Effie smiled at him as she began to pull a finger through the sand.

There was a woman gathering seashells where Effie wished to form her last letter, plucking cockles and mussels in the waves' retreat and collecting them in the damp fold of her skirt.

'*Lauri-e*,' read the woman in black, turning as Effie diverted the final 'e' around her.

'Alive, alive oh!' said Effie.

'Your husband?'

'A friend.'

'Nathalie,' the woman offered a sandy hand.

'Effie.' The two black figures shook.

Nathalie was dark-skinned and pale-eyed. The angle of her cheekbones made her handsome rather than beautiful. There was something serene, Effie thought, about the line of her smile. She squinted into the sun.

'It's a fine day to be alive. I'm of a mind to celebrate with a bowl of cockles, only the continentals are reticent with vinegar.'

'I can't abide chips without vinegar,' said the handsome woman called Nathalie. 'It's just not the same.'

'It's just not right,' replied Effie.

They nodded in unison.

'But I shall give them their due with pastry,' Effie conceded.

'Bakery products in general,' expanded Nathalie. 'Though I am craving proper pie and gravy.'

Their conversation lengthened from culinary critique (on which Effie and her interlocutor generally agreed) to correctness in the convention of soup spoons, bed linen and public hygiene. Nathalie was a seamstress from Sunderland. She had small white teeth, a hat full of black feathers and sensible opinions on domestic matters.

'I take it that you're not on your jolly holidays?' said Nathalie, nodding at Effie's attire.

'It's not been very jolly at all.'

They talked of errant other halves, of lists, regulations and resurrections. Nathalie had not heard from her Reuben, a tailor who wrote poetry, since the November of 1918. She showed Effie the letter. She held it still against the wind, but she needn't have bothered. It was the same class of calligraphy as Joe's. Nathalie pored over its lurches, attempting to give them meaning. But it had neither rhyme nor reason. Nathalie had spent the last ten years looking for Reuben.

'I even saw a clairvoyant,' she said, as they queued for the ice-cream booth. 'She told me that Reuben was wounded, but wasn't dead. I suppose that she wanted to give me hope, but instead she gave me a decade of searching.'

'My treat.'

As Effie ordered ice-cream wafers she considered whether she should have spent the last ten years searching too. She had read

272

about spiritualist meetings and spirit photography, about widows (those who *knew* they were widows) and mothers communing with the souls of their lost ones, finding metaphors and meaning. These women saw signs. Could she have seen signs if she had tried harder to look? Could she possibly have found him, had she put more effort in? But, then, did Joe really want to be found? She recalled that night in the barn when Laurie had suggested he write. She recalled the not insignificant matter of a wife.

'I've been around all of the military hospitals,' Nathalie went on. 'There are thousands of amnesiacs. The French newspapers are still full of faces with no names, waiting to be claimed. I had to look through colour cards and pick out Reuben's eyes and his hair, had to pick out his nose and mouth. They're photographing them, cataloguing them. Can you imagine that? Like butterflies.'

Effie thought of Joe's eyes and hair, his nose and mouth which had suddenly regained their focus, three dimensions and colour. Joe's recalled features rearranged themselves into the look he had given her on the Parisian pavement. She shook her head. They sat on the sand.

'I've picked through lost property, through penknives and combs, rings and razors, cigarette cases and picture postcards, all of which are the property of dead men who are waiting to be given names.'

'And there's been nothing? No hint? No sighting? No clue?'

How could she have been expected to look for Joe, Effie considered, when his lost property had been returned, when there was no clue that he was anywhere other than in that cemetery? Why should she be obliged to feel guilt when there had never been any hint to suggest that he was anything other than heroically dead?

'I've had a few false alarms – and really that's the worst. I've gone to hospital bedsides and psychiatric wards and boxes of personal effects and I've not known whether it's disappointment or relief that I've felt when they've turned out not to be Reuben.'

'I am sorry,' said Effie. Nathalie wore a rabbit's foot brooch on her blouse, she noticed. It had gone rather shiny on the knuckles where she must have rubbed it for luck. Effie supposed that Nathalie needed all of the luck she could muster.

'They're carving out the names of the missing now.' Nathalie shrugged and licked her ice-cream. 'It's as if it is over, as if those that would be found have been found, as if it is done. It's as if it's accepted that the missing will now remain missing. And perhaps they will.'

'Perhaps,' said Effie. 'Possibly.' She thought about the arch of names in Ypres. There must be thousands of corresponding never-knowing Nathalies. For a couple of days she had believed that she might be one of them. Couldn't Joe have tried harder to let her know? Was one letter all their relationship had been worth? 'And now? What next?'

'Well, that's just it.' Nathalie seemed to be examining her ice-cream rather intently. 'I'm not sure that there is a 'what next', I made a decision today. I can't keep coming back. I sound hard, don't I? I don't like hearing myself saying it. But I can't keep on looking and hoping forever. I'm no longer sure that I am going to find him.' Her eyes lifted to Effie's, then. 'I've decided to let go.'

Effie looked at Nathalie's face. But there wasn't the sadness there that she expected to see. Should Nathalie be sad? Should *she* be sad? Should they (could they?) keep on carrying the weight of this sadness?

'It's not wrong,' Effie said. She wasn't sure that it was right either, but she knew, as she looked at Nathalie, that the only way to go on was by letting go.

Chapter Fifty

'I've been here before,' said Henry. Suddenly he saw it. 'Good God. Isn't that odd? I've only just realised.' He accosted the waiter's elbow and ordered an aperitif. 'It was called something different back then. The Grand? The Globe? How strange that I've only just recognised it.'

'Are you seeing ghosts?' Kate smiled.

He looked at her across the table. A piano was playing dining-room Debussy. Now and again the notes plunged into the foreground before retreating once more behind the conversations and cutlery. Kate's finger tapped a rhythm on the rim of her glass. She was dressed in black tonight. He always looked at her a little more closely when she chose to dress in black, anxious to understand the meaning of her choice. But she also had a string of red beads around her neck tonight – and she was talking. He liked it when Kate was in a mood to talk. More so when she talked and smiled. Sometimes Kate herself could look like a ghost, but not when she was in red beads and smiling.

'It was different. It's all been re-done. I think that's why I didn't immediately see it. There were mirrors all around the walls then.' There was now wooden panelling where there had once been reflections. 'There were economically-attired ladies painted on the ceiling and cracks. The ceiling was flaking. It was drifting down like icing sugar.'

"Economically attired?"

'We kept having to fish bits of naked lady out of our drinks.' There was only the flicker of candlelight across the ceiling now. Henry wondered if the painted ladies were still there, being immodest underneath the new plaster.

'It gives the impression that it's looked like this for centuries. It looks like its clock stopped long ago.' Kate's fingers twisted through the beads as she critiqued the décor. 'What was in the mirrors? Tell me. You so rarely tell me anything from back then.

What would I see if I could look in those mirrors?'

'You really want to know?' He shut his eyes and tried to rewind the clock twelve years. 'I remember that the food tasted wonderful, but then anything decent did after rations. I can't recall exactly what it was that I ate. Something in a cream sauce, I think. The waitresses were very lovely. Perhaps that was on account of rationing too? Their graciousness was all the more remarkable because the crowd was rather raucous. I remember that Dawson picked up his plate and licked it. If you could look in the mirror you'd have seen quite a lot of hijinks. Perhaps it's best that you don't look in the mirror. It might make you blush. It might make *me* blush.' He opened his eyes. 'This room seems to have shrunk, you know. It seems much smaller. Or perhaps I am in the wrong restaurant?'

'The walls have probably closed in with the mirrors having gone.'

'Hell!' Henry sat back in his chair.

'What is it?'

'I remember: we were all writing on the mirror. There was a girl with a diamond engagement ring. She was attached to one of Dawson's lot. We passed the ring around and we all signed our names on the mirror. The maître d' kept shouting at us. He shouted at us in broken English and then began to swear at us in French. But we were moving up to the front the next day, you see. We didn't care how red his face got or how blue his language. He was distinctly less charming than his waitresses. I do hope that he isn't still here.' Henry slid down in his seat.

'I never had you down as a vandal.'

He pulled the tablecloth up to his shoulders. 'I didn't make a habit of it.'

'I think you're more conspicuous under the tablecloth.'

The waiter brought his drink. Henry sat up and offered copious compensatory thanks. 'I'll leave a good tip. Heck.' He made an alarmed face at Kate.

'Did I tell you that Mrs Hawes and I had a picnic on Vimy Ridge?' The red beads swung round in a circle. 'We took one of those motor tours, all piled into a charabanc with a party of Canadians. They all had perfect manners. We went in a trench.'

'Good Lord.'

'Don't worry. It was all concreted and clean. Not a rat in sight. Actually, I was quite disappointed not to see a rat.'

'I –'

He heard the crump of the detonation, then. For a second he struggled to separate actuality from memory. But the chandeliers rattled and the piano player's notes seemed to scatter. A chair banged to the floor as a woman stood up suddenly.

'What the – '

'It's all right, dear.' Kate's hand stretched across the cutlery. 'It's only Russians.'

'You didn't even flinch.'

'They're detonating duds. They've been at it all week. Mrs Hawes and I have just about stopped jumping every time one goes off.'

'Battle hardened, eh?' Henry took a mouthful of vermouth. *Clair de Lune* resumed. Kate hadn't even looked up from the menu.

'Veritable veterans. They're blowing up the pillboxes too. I took Mrs Hawes' photograph in a tin hat. Have I already told you this? I'm not quite sure why she wanted to pose for a photograph in a tin hat. Do you think she'll show it to her children? I can't imagine wanting to pose in a tin hat. It was a curious composition; she was wearing a fox fur stole that day. It had nasty dangly little legs and its horrid head was poking over her shoulder in the shot, as if it had crept up on her from behind.'

Henry laughed. 'In her no-nonsense overcoat and her sensible brown shoes? Your composition sounds quite surreal.'

'It was. It was all a bit surreal this time, actually. It's like it's all suddenly become a stage version of itself. Do you know what I mean? It's as if suddenly it's all for show. There are tourist groups everywhere and souvenir stalls and parties out picking over the ground. We kept seeing them by the roadside with it all laid out on lengths of hessian – bits of pipes, buttons, penknives, rings and razors. Then there are horrible flaking rusting things. It's like they're Roman relics. Only they're not, are they? Mrs Hawes saw a cigarette case that she thought could be her Leonard's. I don't think it's nice.'

'I suppose that people have come back and have lost their homes and have to scratch a living. They have to go on as best they can.'

'Oh, you're right. But who wants to buy these things? Am I odd that I find it ghoulish?'

'You take soil home. That probably qualifies you as odd.'

'I suppose.' Kate dabbled with the olive in her drink. 'I wouldn't let her buy the cigarette case.'

'She probably sneaked back and bought it anyway. I'll bet you. It's probably under her pillow now.'

Kate's nose wrinkled. 'It could be anyone's. I think she just wanted it to be his.'

'If it helps her sleep, why shouldn't she have it? Why shouldn't she be allowed to believe it?'

'At what stage did my little brother become so bloody reasonable?'

'Don't swear, Katie. Mother would smack your hands.'

She kicked him under the table.

They ordered *steak-frites*. 'Mrs Hawes says that it's usually horse.'

'I doubt it. Not now. You have to pay a supplement for neddy now.'

'I could eat it, I think. If I had to. I wouldn't be silly about it.'

'I imagine that you could do most things, darling.'

The waiter poured the wine. Henry raised a glass towards his sister. The young couple on the next table were entwining their finger ends. Kate raised an eyebrow.

'Home tomorrow. Are you going to call in on Patrick again before we go?'

'You don't mind?'

'Of course not.'

'It has been different this time, you know.'

'Having your playmate? Dressing up in tin hats and hoping to spot rats?'

'No, not just that. It was different in the cemetery, now that it's nearly finished. For five minutes it was quiet – perfectly quiet – and, just briefly, there was something profoundly still about that place then. It was calmer. I felt calmer, less raw. It was peaceful – in every sense – in the fullest sense. I don't know whether I'll bring a plum tree over again. I started to understand, this time, why they want it to be like that – why it needs to be all uniform and aligned.'

'No more smuggling, then?'

She smiled and shook her head.

'That's a pity. I've always rather enjoyed the subterfuge.'

'I know. You particularly seemed to enjoy it this time. I'm sure that if you ask nicely you'll be permitted to traffic a Yorkshire Terrier again.'

'Poor old Reginald. Good chap, though he does smell a bit off.'

'But his companion smells agreeable.'

'Can't say as I noticed.' He tried to make an oblivious face and failed.

'You're a vandal *and* a liar, Henry Lyle.'

He helped her into her coat in the foyer.

'Darling, this isn't your mirror, is it?'

It was hardly recognisable as a mirror any longer. Kate's reflection blurred in the glass, her face all fractures. The surface of the glass was covered over now, all etched away with cramped and interwoven script. There were signatures, insignia, initials, cyphers, cartoons and rhymes. There was something about this crammed-in, scratched script that made Henry think about the walls of a cell – there was something claustrophobic and frenzied about this mark making. The dates all said 1916.

'Good God.'

'Perhaps you started something.'

'It must have given the maître d' paroxysms. Poor man.'

'I wonder how many of them are still alive.' Kate curled her arm through his. Their joined reflection had no definition. He was reminded of a quote he had read somewhere, a writer saying that the war had used up and worn out all of the words in the world. As Henry looked into the mirror he understood what that writer might have meant. He could think of nothing to say. There were no words left.

For a second he looked through the web of script and saw a room full of cigarette smoke and khaki camaraderie. Just for a second he saw the drinks rise, the eyes glint and the mouths stretching into youthful loudness – into mouths that had everything to say. It came at him, just for an instant. It roared out of the mirror and then was gone. It might as well have been a hammer through the glass.

'We are,' he turned to his sister's steady eyes. 'We're alive, Katie. And we should celebrate it with a nightcap.'

'Was Patrick with you that night?'

'No, he… Egads.' He suddenly realised whose face he'd seen in the mirror. 'I've just remembered who else was here that night.'

'Henry?'

His eye scanned along the glass, looking to locate their signatures.

Kate followed his finger. 'Is it a guessing game?'

'Here. Here we are. Do you see?'

'That's *him*?'

Henry nodded.

'Did you tell her?' Kate asked.

'The time never seemed quite right.'

'Will you tell her?'

'Do you think that I should?'

'That's a matter for your conscience – and it depends on whether you mean to see her again.'

'I will tell her,' he said. 'I will.' Kate's reflection put a hand to his shoulder. 'There's still such a lot that I have to tell her, isn't there?'

Chapter Fifty-One

Everdene was empty and entirely still. Effie crept through its rooms behind closed curtains. There wasn't even the ticking of the ormolu clock, which, in the absence of Laurie's weekly winding, had frozen, making it forever just about time for tea. She crept through the shadows and silence, feeling like an outsider prying on a stopped-clock domesticity. She crept past stuffed stoats and earthenware allegories, moving noiselessly between cross-stitched mottoes and moorland landscapes and Mr and Mrs Greene, respectively in India and ocelot. She thought of the house near Cabaret Camp, with its forgotten ornaments and fossilised violence. Laurie's ornaments might be more Anglican, but the atmosphere was the same. '*God is Love*,' said Mrs Greene's embroidery silks. Effie was no longer sure quite what God was.

She saw herself reflected in mirrors, within picture frames and fragmented in the facets of cut glass. She saw the movement and the muted colours of herself. She saw her shadowed features against the patterns of wallpaper that had once signified home. It no longer looked like home. Though the scenery remained unchanged, a fundamental something had shifted since she had last seen herself in this setting. Her fingertips stretched to feel the texture of the mantelpiece. She was almost surprised to find it solid. She leaned her forehead against the cool, smooth, surprisingly-solid stone and looked down at the grate where Joe's long-ago letter had apparently turned to ashes. She must herself have brushed away its soft, hushed revelations. Effie decided to light the lamps, turn on the radiogram and wind the clock.

She heard the familiar tread of her boots on the linoleum of the kitchen stairs. Some things, at least, were unaltered, like Reginald who was reliably scrounging in the kitchen. Effie surveyed her shelf of long-life comestibles and decided to indulge him with a tin of ox tongue.

She put the kettle on the gas ring and lit one of Henry's cigarettes on the flame. In the absence of courteous company, she smoked over the kitchen sink. The ivy tapped against the window. She watched her reflection smoking; her mother would have called it slatternly. The woman reflected in the window didn't look like she was deriving much glee from her descent into slatternly habits.

Smoke stung in her eyes. She turned her back on her reflection. Her stung eyes looked at his kitchen. There was copper and china, bright against the burnished dark of the dresser, cruet sets and coronation jugs. It was all from Laurie's family, the flotsam of a family history with which Effie had only an employee's connection. It was suddenly like looking at objects in a museum, objects of which she no longer entirely understood the meaning. The silver punch bowl caught the light and Laurie next to it in a daguerreotype. Effie let her hand trail along the shelf touching the objects, connecting physically if she could not connect with their history. She picked the photograph up. It blurred to black at the edges, as if Laurie was coming out of the dark. He was a boy in a sailor suit eating an iced bun. She had smiled, as they'd flicked together through his family photograph album, and asked if she could have it in a frame in the kitchen. He had conceded to her whim with a blush. Laurie's eyes didn't quite connect with the camera. She tried to remember: had he ever entirely looked her in the eye? The kettle hissed and spat.

She sat at the kitchen table and leafed through the post. It was just condolence cards, circulars and the evening paper. There were no further letters. It seemed that her trail of enveloped shocks had come to an end. Effie wasn't sure whether she was glad of that or not. She opened the paper at Situations Vacant and vaguely wished that she could trade the rosy teacup in her hand for a champagne coupe. She thought about Laurie's drinks cabinet, but sensibleness ruled that her employment prospects would not be enhanced by addiction to strong drink. In the absence of alcoholic amusement, Effie decided to spend the evening polishing her pastry skills. She would rehearse her much-bragged-about Bakewell.

She carried her suitcase upstairs and changed into an everyday dress. Did the woman in the bedroom mirror look any different than she had a fortnight earlier? Did she look like experience had made her stronger? Effie peered at the glass. The silvering was flaking from the reverse and regions of her mirror face blurred. Was it worldliness or just fatigue that was showing around her eyes? Opting for the former, she raised her chin slightly higher, practising the pose of a woman who meant to make a future for herself.

A dance band on the B.B.C. crooned *Among My Souvenirs* and Effie creamed to the accompaniment of the radiogram. It was cheering to again see her wooden spoon circle. '*Some letters tied in blue, a photograph or two, I see a rose from you among my souvenirs,*' sang Effie and licked frangipane from her fingers. She wished that she still had the accompaniment of Laurie's footfalls on the floor above.

With the Bakewell in the oven, Effie decided to make absolutely sure that Laurie too wasn't back from the dead and being furtive in his bedroom. As she pushed the door, she was braced to see him there, turning at the desk with an empty teacup and a smile for her. But all there was was a room full of early-evening shadows and a smell of something faintly medicinal.

Effie sat in Laurie's desk chair and looked at the room from his angle. Had they really spent a decade sitting across the same table? If so, how had he kept his secrets so silently? How had she known so little about who he was? Effie looked at the young man in the khaki portrait, with the polished buttons, pastoral backdrop and his seated, solemn-faced mother. There was a limp arrangement of allied flags behind him, and an aspidistra on a velvet-draped stand. Was this the man she had lived with? Was this the man that had done that to Joe?

On Laurie's walls there were Japanese woodblock prints and French lithographs, William Blake's sinuous angels and Rossetti's angular stunners. She smiled in recollection of Henry's definition of ascetic. There were also picture postcards (Whitby, York and Bridlington) and a selection of Laurie's own better efforts on paper: West Pennine landmarks multiply in watercolour, a lot of moor, mill, bruised skies and square civic architecture. Her finger traced where he had let the colour run. Indistinct industry ran into foreground town.

Her hands moved over the surface of his all-too-tidy desk. It was here that he had sat to paint. She remembered it as a chaos of papers, the jam jar of brushes and wet colours. She remembered him sorting tubes as they had talked. The grey tubes in Laurie's hands had leaked colour. His fingers, creased in the colours of moor and mill, had flexed and flicked through the sketchpad, through nature notes, ecstatic stars and factory chimneys. She'd watched over his shoulder and attempted inexpert critique. He had left a progression of fingerprints. 'Messy,' Effie had chastised and handed him a cup of tea. As he'd turned the cup round in his hands it too had become fingerprinted in paint. His eyes had lifted to hers and creased kindly at the corners. 'You're a merciless critic,' he had said.

A month on, her fingers found the cool brass of the handle of the desk drawer. She knew it was prying, but perhaps she ought to have pried rather more.

In the drawer was his old tin watercolour box. She thought of his hand feeling for it in his pocket as he watched the barn burn, before Joe's heroics and fall. She put her own hand to its pitted surface. Curiosity opened the box. These cubes of bright chemistry seemed to Effie to be a work of art in themselves.

Besides the paint box her prying fingers found a purse that contained brown coins and small treasures: a desiccated cornflower in a fold of paper, a round pebble, a pencil whittled to a stub and a hairpin. Effie measured their thin gravity in her hand; attempted to divine their meaning. She felt the enchantment of these souvenirs, these small, mute objects that he had seen fit to preserve, even if she could not understand their significance.

She turned through stacked sketchpads and instructional books on watercolour technique. And then, in a photograph, she saw him. Laurie was swaggering by a Belgian henhouse and laughing. She looked up close at the caught moment, at him with his hilarity and his walking stick and Solange Roland's gardening hat in his hands. She thought about Joe, sitting for his portrait, with eyes that were not quite right. It was that week, in October 1917, that it had gone wrong. It was that week that it all turned and changed. She wished it had not been so, that Laurie had been able to go on making comic poses. She wished that that moment could indeed have been put in aspic, could have been fixed and forever more. It was Laurie as she would have wanted him to be. Effie wiped a tear away. She would place the image alongside her bun-eating boy.

Inquisitiveness pulled her onwards to the bottom of the drawer, which produced a manila folder marked *1915-1917*. She pulled it out onto the desk and reverently opened the cover. It began in Morecambe, with beach watercolours and waltzes. She laughed at them, boys then, pirouetting in front of a shop window. It was a long time ago, but somehow Effie felt that she was looking at scenes she had seen but recently. The edges of these early papers were yellow and damp-warped, but the pigments were still bright and the waltzes still spun. She sailed to

Boulogne, where the colours disappointed, and marched with Laurie south. Some days were just a detail. Other days filled pages. He drew the humdrum of soldierly domestication, he drew boredom and frustration and violence. Effie understood, then, why this was hidden. These bottom-of-the-drawer drawings became a confession. The drawings said more than his words could communicate. The drawings said too much.

She turned through 1916. She recognized Joe everywhere. She saw his features in laughter and concentration, in sleep, in anger, in mirth and fear. More faces, unknown; all male, unshaven, heavy-eyed. These were hooded, like condemned men, bug-eyed against the phosgene. These lay in summer ditches, chewing on grass and idling, like a pastoral fancy. Then came the grotesques. She turned through smashed faces and open chests, ownerless limbs and exposed muscles. These were un-whole, were fragments, mementoes of men. She pictured Laurie crouched over it, striving for precision, searching as a scalpel. Some were watermarked and warped, but worked graphite glinted off the spilled limbs and the broken faces. She wondered how Laurie's blithe smile, his amiable eyes, could have recorded and hidden such images.

It is astonishing what one can grow accustomed to, Laurie had written in the November of 1916, *the violent, the grotesque, even fear itself. I see it marking the men, though. I wonder if one day, when this is over, whether it will all catch up with us.*

She wasn't certain whether she wanted to progress through 1917. She wasn't sure that she wanted to see it catch up. She wanted to look away. Perhaps that was what she had done. She tried to remember whether they had talked about it. She remembered talking Wessex, but not about the war. Laurie then had liked to talk about Effie's day, to plan outings and deconstruct recipes. They had always looked forwards. They had never deconstructed what had come before. Had she not asked?

Should she have asked? A breeze through the slightly-ajar window stirred the papers.

She stood to close the window. Black was creeping back across the leading and so she made mental note to scrub it with soda. There were flowers in the nets, she saw anew, and shields. In the window frame, with Laurie's family photographs, were several fragments of broken glass and a shard of tile. They were arranged like objects of veneration. The evening light cut greenly through them. 'See,' he had once said, and shown her. He had called them relics of his adventures. She suddenly remembered a shell-hit house and a hot triangle of tile held out in her brother's hand.

Effie wondered how such sights, seen first-hand, could ever be forgotten, could ever be purged? How could gentleness remain and the material things (the angularity of irises, the taste of almond paste, the glow of light through glass) hold any pleasure? But perhaps, then, that was the key, and the core and the cure.

A crude clay deity stood amongst the circle of relics. Effie turned it in her hands. Laurie had shaped it with his own. She could see the imprints of his fingertips. He had explained to her that it was Mithras, who looks out for soldiers. The number of these amulets had multiplied as she had worked her way through the diary. He had told her how they had wished on flames and trinkets, on turns of coins and cards. He had told her how they had traded ghost stories in the trenches to pass the time. He said that they had seen inanimate things vivify, the mud and the stones, the petrified tree stumps and the powerful roots that bound it all down. The dead and the living lolled together, Laurie said, only Effie hadn't realised quite how closely they entangled. She replaced the idol in the window frame. Effie wasn't sure that Mithras had done much in the way of looking out for Laurie.

She braced herself for 1917. Her hand hesitated over the page. Her fairy palace, in ruin, was the first image that she saw. She barely recognised the town around it. The same was true of Joe's face. Laurie had drawn that day – the 5th November – scene by scene. She saw Bladen and the barn, the lane, the tree, the chair, the pocket handkerchief and then the volley and the slump. Effie saw Joe die. Joe died over and over again.

A smell of burning recalled her to 1928. She cursed as she took the blackened cake from the oven. Her pretty scattering of flaked almonds smoked. She sat on the kitchen floor and cried. Effie cried for her burnt cake and the fact that it was too late.

Chapter Fifty-Two

Somme, 1916

A flare went up. It soared and then seemed to hang in the sky. The stretcher bearers froze as the light wavered. Joe crouched lower and looked up. The sky was like Christmas. The stars seemed to be closer to the earth than they ever had been before. He wondered if the planet had spun off its axis. Were they all now spiralling through the heavens? He waited for the flare to fall.

He slid over the top on his stomach. It was the second time he'd been out. He'd got Greene back first. They'd sat together in a shell hole for a while. Greene kept passing out. When he came round he had given Joe some sort of clay figure. It seemed to be important to him that Joe have this thing.

'For luck,' he had said.

'I don't know if I believe in luck.'

'Shall we test it?'

He'd pushed the figure back into Greene's hand as they put him on a stretcher. His face was blue. Joe had had to drag him back in the end and he figured Greene's need for luck was presently greater than his own.

A bullet fizzed past. Joe felt the air streak across his face. It seemed to leave a line of phosphorescence arcing away, hanging there in the dark. He imagined the trajectory of the bullet, linking him to a finger on a trigger. He dropped down amongst the mud and wire and looked out into the malign blackness beyond. Mist clung in the low places ahead. It twisted into shapes that one minute were wraiths and the next an enemy patrol. He held his breath for a moment as he watched the shapes resolve themselves. Was an eye observing him from the opposite side of the thinning mist? His fingers pushed lower into the mud. The stars were bright and silent.

He was out beyond the wire now and it had started again. They had passed a commentary on the pyrotechnics from the trench. Coloured lights had been rising from the opposite line, calling in the artillery. Pollard had said that there was going to be a real show now. Joe was crawling forward on his elbows when the first blast hit. And then it was coming in from all around. He ducked his head as mud rained down. He felt like he was clinging on to the earth, as if he would fly off it if he didn't hold on, as if gravity had gone awry. The ground shook. He could smell sulphur. Hot fragments hissed as they fell.

There were a lot of men to be brought back. Some cried out, some reached out, some were full of holes and some were a long way off whole. They churned in the earth. It heaved all around them. The dead convulsed and shook their limbs as if they meant to rise up again. Joe looked at the faces. He had to look at the faces. He pulled their features toward him. There was something diabolical about these faces, with the fires leaping out of the ground all around, the sky tearing above and their hands stretching out towards him.

'Charlie?'

He knew him by the cap comforter that Florrie had knitted him. They'd ridiculed his aunt's knitting experiments when it had arrived, but Joe was glad of it now. He put his fingers to Charlie's wrist, as he'd seen the medical officer do. Was it Charlie's pulse that he could feel or his own heartbeat? A blast struck just ahead. The ground felt to be falling away. Red light pitched in the sky.

'Stretcher bearer!'

He shouted but his mouth made no sound. The bombardment took away his voice. It also seemed to have taken the stretcher bearers away. He looked around but there was just the mist and the smoke and the quivering darkness. Suddenly Joe seemed to be alone in the middle of it.

He grabbed Charlie by the arms and, crouching, began to drag him. He was heavy, heavier than Joe had ever remembered him. His hands kept slipping through Joe's. His tunic caught on wire.

'Charlie! For fuck's sake, help me, man!'

The fabric didn't want to come free. Joe yanked at it and the wire gashed across the palm of his hand. He was staring at it as another shell hit. The ground roared up behind, throwing him forward and taking him completely off his feet. For a moment there was nothing but whiteness, a fierce, bright, blinding whiteness, but then night closed around him again. He blinked reality back in: he saw stakes, the twisting line of wire, a crater where there hadn't been one moments before and Charlie's legs covered over in earth. Joe clawed the earth away. His hand ached.

There was nothing for it but to try to carry him. Joe stooped and tried to pull Charlie's weight onto his shoulders. With his knees bent, the weight of Charlie made him pitch forward. He tried to straighten until he stood upright in the middle of No Man's Land. For an instant he saw himself from afar. He looked like the last man left, like the only survivor in the middle of a shipwreck. His focus pulled out and he saw the cataclysm all about. But then the ground was quaking, a machine gun rattled and he was running, as best he could, towards the line.

He stumbled, his ankle went over and he was down again with Charlie sliding forward on top of him.

'Stretcher bearer!'

His shout was more in hope than expectation. He heard his voice crack. It was frustration that made Joe cry. He sat with his head in his hands, feeling more tired than he could ever remember feeling. He felt ready to crawl down into the earth with the dead. He reached his hand out towards Charlie's.

A sudden force of determination filled him then. He had to get back. He had to take his chance. He thought of the good luck charm in Laurence Greene's hand and for a brief moment wished he hadn't returned it. Joe screamed as he heaved Charlie up onto his back. He staggered forward. It roared and erupted all around him. All that mattered was to get Charlie back.

'Frank!' He made it to the edge of the trench.

'I've got him.' Horrocks was there too. They took Charlie from him and together they lowered him down.

'Come on, Joey.' Pollard extended his arm. Joe fell into the trench.

'You mad sod,' said Carver.

'I had to bring him in.'

Frank handed him a water bottle. 'Here, lad.'

The whisky hit the back of Joe's throat. 'Jesus! I wasn't expecting that.' He spluttered. He laughed without knowing why.

'Figured you might need it. Bloody hell, Joe.'

Charlie was being lifted onto the firestep, Joe saw from over Frank's shoulder. Horrocks was bending over him. He seemed to be putting a sandbag over Charlie's head.

'What the fuck are you doing?'

Frank's hand was on Joe's arm. 'He's been dead for hours, son. You know that. You do know that, don't you?'

'No! He was alive. He was alive five minutes ago. I felt him breathe.'

'He's stone cold, Joe. He's stiff. It killed him straight away. No way back from that.'

He pulled Frank's hand away and shouldered past Horrocks.

'No, Joey. Best not look. Don't remember him this way, eh?'

Pollard stood in front of him. Joe pushed him aside. A flare screeched into the sky.

'Charlie?'

Joe had seen it then. They had to hold him down.

Caroline Scott

It was the same each time. It had been for twelve years. When he woke up the faceless soldier was standing at the end of his bed. Joe turned to the wall. He curled in the damp sheets. His hand stretched towards the glued-back-together boy. Joe could still feel the weight of him. It was there every night. He was still carrying Charlie and knew he would be until he could see him in his grave.

Chapter Fifty-Three

Lancashire, 1928

'Is this whisky?' Effie sniffed at the flask.

'It's medicinal.'

'And that's why it's disguising itself in a thermos flask?' Effie handed her mother the tin of jam tarts. 'I take it that Grace came in, then?'

'Aye, she did – for all of five minutes and me with not a word in edgeways. She's dangling babies, brass blonde and blathering on about how she's broke. I'd told her that I was out of sweets, but she forgot.'

Margaret Shaw enjoyed cataloguing her daughters' shortcomings. There was a tacit sisterly understanding that they countered with mutual defence.

'If she smuggles whisky in, I'm surprised that you don't want me to go away more often.'

'She made the child sit on my knee, as if that ought to be compensation.'

'Wasn't it nice?' said Effie, who wasn't averse to dandling other people's offspring.

'It wasn't recompense for a quarter of Pontefract cakes. And it snotted on my cardigan. I told Mrs Hargreaves, what with one daughter married badly and the other an old maid and gallivanting around the Continent, it's happen a good job that I'm in here.'

'I was hardly gallivanting, mother.'

She wondered whether to tell her mother about Henry, with whom she had almost gallivanted, with whom she hadn't behaved like an old maid. She'd had a letter from him that morning. *There's so much that I need to tell you*, his letter had said – and then gone on to tell her nothing. His handwriting seemed less sprightly than it had. It seemed like he'd got stuck.

'What were you doing, then?'

'I told you. I'd gone to see Joe.'

'And he's a waste of space. Still idling?'

Since her mother had never believed Joe dead, Effie decided not to attempt to explain his unexpected resurrection. She watched her mother's crochet hook weaving.

'Something like that.'

Margaret Shaw's fingers abruptly stilled and pointed at the absence of her daughter's engagement ring. Her eyes widened. Her expression looked something like excitement. 'Did he break it off?'

'Joe has been married to someone else for almost a decade,' Effie disclosed.

'Well, the dirty beggar. That's hardly idling. Still, his mother always struck me as unstable, so happen it's for the best.'

'His mother has been dead since 1919.'

Margaret nodded, as if this confirmed the matter, which, on later reflection, Effie supposed that it perhaps did.

'I always held that you could do better. Why settle for a back yard when you could have had a garden?'

'I've got a garden.'

Margaret raised an eyebrow.

'And I shall be sad to say goodbye to it.'

Effie thought of her blowsy borders and blackcurrant bushes. She thought of sitting on the lawn, shelling peas in a late afternoon of last summer, and then Laurie arriving with an apology and a shirt lap full of runner beans. She thought of looking up to see him – back-lit, sun-lit, bright-edged in silhouette and, in the shadow, the shape of a smile forming.

'Sadder than to say goodbye to Joseph?'

'It's different,' replied Effie.

'Well, it doesn't sound like much of a holiday to me. Did you not have chance of any outings?' asked Margaret, who, in her time, had liked a charabanc and a singsong. 'Did you not even sit on a donkey?'

'No. Nor a tram, nor a merry-go-round.'

'Well, I never,' replied Margaret, clearly considering this a great squandering of opportunity for sitting on holiday surfaces.

'I did paddle and eat pastries and visited some of Laurie's old haunts in Paris.'

'Paris is it, eh?' Margaret laughed.

'Yes,' said Effie quizzically. 'What's so funny about Paris?'

'Oh, it's just a pretty way to put it.'

Effie frowned, measuring her mother's come-and-go sanity.

'A pretty way to put it?'

'Oh, Euphemia.'

'Mother, I don't understand.'

'Don't you see? It's dressing up. It's just pretend. Laurence Greene wasn't in Paris after the war. I don't know that he was ever in Paris.' She took her daughter's hand. 'Don't you get it? Haven't you guessed yet? Laurence was in here.'

Effie looked around the room, with its crochet-encrusted surfaces and lack of sharp edges. It didn't look much like Paris.

'In here?'

'Well, not in this room, silly. But he was in this asylum.'

'He was in the special hospital?'

'Special? Is that what they're calling it now? I think I prefer Paris.' Margaret patted her daughter's hand and returned her own to the crochet hook.

'Laurie was in *here*?'

'Do you need your ears syringing?' The crochet hook stopped. 'That's why we worried when you first went to work for him.' She shrugged at the walls into which she had been committed since 1916 and then the looping and hooking began again. 'It wasn't so strange. This place was full of young men then. There *were* special wards back then.'

'Yes. I remember, mother. I remember that it was horrible. But why was Laurie on the horrible ward?'

'Why are any of us? He had some sort of breakdown. It was his nerves. I remember that he drew a lot. He had nice manners and nice dressing gowns. He was quite the gentleman. I think he'd tried to do away with himself. That's why I didn't object when you went to work for him – because he had nice manners.'

Effie saw Laurie's across-the-table smile. She'd never seen any hint of suicide. It suddenly occurred to Effie that, with hindsight, she hadn't seen much at all. She stood up and, realising that she didn't know where to move next, sat down again.

'Why did nobody tell me? Did nobody think to tell me?'

'Would it have made a difference?'

'I might have taken better care of him. I might have held on to him longer.'

Her mother's fingers nimbly clicked and knotted. Effie thought of Ypres, of looking down on the lacy gothic of its rooftops. She had never imagined that Laurie might have let go.

'Would you? Could you have? It wasn't nerves that finally got him. It was gas. No amount of baking and laundering and care taking could reverse that.'

Effie sat with her head in her hands and listened to the rhythm of her mother's fingers. It was a final secret that Laurie hadn't meant to share. He had asked for neither her pardon nor pity. Effie felt overwhelmed with both.

'Why does nobody ever tell me anything?'

'Kindness? You tell people that I'm in a nunnery.'

'Well, that's…'

'Paris.'

The nurse rattled in with the refreshment trolley. They switched to well-mannered small talk over the teapot.

'It's a lovely day,' said the nurse to the window. 'Will you not take Euphemia out for a walk in the gardens?'

Margaret, who held that her daughter warranted a garden, but who had no desire to walk her through one, declined. 'There are flies,' she replied.

The nurse looked disappointed for Effie's sake. But, having just learned about Laurie, Effie didn't feel much like walking through gardens either. She stared at her teacup and tried to think of something polite and light and sensible to say. In the absence of appropriate conversation, Effie put on a pleasant face and flicked through a ladies' magazine. In a far wing of the hospital someone was playing a piano. She tried to focus on the recipes and letters and household hints. There were five ways to spruce up leftover lamb and wondrous cleaning properties of white vinegar. But, then, the turning pages stopped. In the society section, a blond smiled palely in plus fours. Mrs Clarice Lyle was winning a charity golfing tournament. *Mrs Lyle, wife of Mr Henry Lyle (formerly of the Bright Spark Ball Bearing Company), proved to be a bright spark on the golf links*, Effie read. She suddenly realised that she hadn't been a bright spark. She suddenly realised what the something was that Henry couldn't say. Tea slopped in her saucer.

'Nosy cow,' said Margaret to the closing door.

'Don't be mean, mother.'

'Don't be soft. She'd be rummaging in my baked goods, if you weren't here. They get you out and then they're in. Mind you...' Margaret made a critical face at a jam tart.

'I'm sorry. I baked you a cake, but I burnt it.'

'Is it really that bad?'

'It's worse.' It seemed suddenly doubly worse.

'Maybe I shouldn't have told you about Laurence,' considered Margaret, removing raspberry seeds from between her teeth. 'Only I figured that you'd perhaps already worked it out.'

'Perhaps I'm no good at guessing games after all,' conceded Effie, and helped herself to a compensatory jam tart. 'I liked to think of him being in Paris. I might keep it that way.'

'For me your father is forever in Whitby. He was very dashing once in Whitby.'

She smiled at her mother.

'Whether you prefer him in Paris or not, Laurence won't be paying your wages for much longer, will he?'

'No.' Effie looked at the crumbs in her lap. 'I've applied for a position with a Mr Warburton – a semi-detached, a wheelchair and cockatoo to clean out. He was mentioned in despatches for gallantry.'

'Well, let's trust that he brought his gallantry home with him.'

'I do hope that he isn't finicky. Laurie was never finicky. He was always so appreciative. He was such a pleasure to cook for.' As she shaped the words she weighed their precision. She wasn't certain, on measuring it, that she had appreciated Laurie enough.

'Aye, well, don't get carried away hoping for another Laurence. You got lucky there. It might not happen again.'

'I wish it would.' Though she was reluctant to admit it to herself, there was part of her that had wished that it might happen with Henry.

'I wish for a millionaire, a motor car and a mink.' Margaret shrugged. 'I am sorry, though, you know. He was a nice young man.'

'Yes,' said Effie, 'he was.'

She wished for just one more letter from Laurie. It wasn't that she wanted to hear another revelation; it was just that it seemed awfully quiet now that their conversation had ended. She missed him. The only communication regarding Laurie was the stonemason's notification that his headstone had been erected – and now the news that it could have been erected ten years earlier. Suddenly, with the headstone and the lovely golfing wife, Effie missed Laurie very much.

'I shall expect something iced next week.' Her mother's expectations broke into Effie's contemplation. 'Or, at the very least, choux pastry. Show some confidence. Show some skill. You may practise on me. Pretend that I'm this Mr Warburton and that I'm gallant but fussy,' she instructed and made a fussy face. 'Not coconut, mind. It makes me cough. Mr Warburton can't abide coconut.'

Duly admonished and dismissed with a directive for icing, Effie left her mother to her crochet cocoon and decided to go and inspect Laurie's headstone.

As she turned onto Church Road, she thought about the prize-winning wife. Was the emotion that she felt jealousy? Was this what Laurie had felt, then? Suddenly she was aware of the intensity with which Laurie could feel.

She stood by the cemetery gates. She recalled the pretty wicket gate of *Deux Arbres*, where Joe should have been and wasn't. Would she, if she could, re-wind, and have him in his grave? It might have been tidier and, after all, he wished it upon himself. She found that she couldn't, however, wish it on him.

She walked along the avenue, glancing at the lean of the ancient headstones where Laurie had liked to peer. They had often enjoyed a Sunday stroll through the churchyard, him identifying antiquities and she passing comment on the flowers. She heard herself telling him to be careful of his ankles in the brambles and saw the dismissive wave of his stick as he disappeared into the overgrown edges. After they would sit on a bench and he would peel a pear with his penknife. She had once asked him, as they sat there together, what it was like to be dead, aware that, after he had been gassed, he had briefly been there.

'It smarts,' he had said, and smiled as he licked pear juice from his wrists.

Effie hoped that it didn't smart but, if it did, why had he voluntarily revisited it? Back then though, back at the start, he still believed that he had done away with Joe and perhaps that was enough? Perhaps he meant for it to smart?

There were no co-ordinates to find Laurie. She knew where he was. She knew that he was under the yew tree, next to his parents (she with her nice line of Keats and him with letters after his name). Though, given that everyone else was seemingly playing at graveyard hide-and-seek, perhaps he too was now idling elsewhere or had shacked up with a farmer's daughter. Effie imagined a girl called Rosie or Bessie, with apple cheeks and guileless Wessex ways, who would bake Laurie pies and ruffle his hair. For his sake she hoped that he might be tumbling in a farm girl's arms.

Effie stood in front of Laurie's grave and knew – absolutely – that he was in it. She had stood here a month earlier, so sure of her facts and figures and so entirely wrong. But there was no doubt now.

The headstone had been completed to Laurie's specifications – not the soldier-white stone that he could have claimed, but a simple marker of local sandstone. There was no rank or regiment, just the too-close years of his entrance and exit and Tess's last line incised.

This happiness could not have lasted.

Effie knew that it would be here, but to see it cut in stone, and to understand finally the in-between of Laurie's dates, made her sink to her knees.

The flowers of his wreathes had withered and begun to rot. She wondered if Laurie was likewise in his box below. She curled on the new grass of his grave. There were bumble bees and the stop-and-start scales of choir practice. The grass was sharp but sweet against her cheek. She put her ear to the ground; there was no down-below sound, but there was the sweetness and the scales and the lulling hum of bumble bees and Laurie sleeping silently beneath. Effie too wanted to go to sleep.

'I miss you,' she said to the incline of the earth.

Chapter Fifty-Four

Henry fell back onto the floor and played dead for the amusement of the dogs. They pounced about him excitedly.

'Don't eat Lyle,' Dawson instructed. 'You don't know where he's been.'

'Paris,' said Henry.

'Quite.'

'No Lucy today?' Henry leaned up on an elbow.

'She's visiting her father.'

'Is that why your kitchen is full of wet wool?' A line of khaki-coloured socks was dripping limply from the ceiling.

'My sister, Esther, still knits them. I've surely told you, haven't I? It's like she can't stop. She must have clicked her way through miles of khaki wool. I don't think she knows what else to do with herself – apart from sip cherry brandy all day. Lucy says that I ought to have a talk with her.' Dawson shrugged. 'I launder them when she goes to her father's.'

'But doesn't she realise that you're wearing them?'

'One khaki sock looks much like another.'

'You should buy her some blue wool.'

Henry tickled dog ears while Dawson adjusted his washing line.

'What's with the get-up, anyway? You look like the ghost of 1916.'

Dawson was wearing an army greatcoat. Henry had stepped back in surprise when the greatcoat opened the door, but it had enveloped him in a friendly smother before he'd had opportunity to do more than point a finger at it. It was a curious ensemble when twinned with carpet slippers.

'Good. That's the intention.'

'And there's clay all over the back of it, you know.'

'Authenticity in everything, *mon cher ami*. I've been posing for Bainbridge. You've just missed him. He's got a commission to paint a mural, so he's collecting sketches of glum soldiers. I'm trying to look careworn.'

'Is that why there are holes in your coat?'

'There are holes in my coat because there are moths in my wardrobe.' Dawson lifted the kettle and an eyebrow.

'Yes, please. Whose is the coat, anyway? Did you thieve it from a bantam?'

'No, it's mine. Can you believe this?' Dawson attempted to pull the buttons together. He grinned downwards. 'It's a good three inches off fastening now. How on earth did I used to get a tunic under this? Lucy gasped when she saw, but I told her that it's her fault for feeding me so well.'

'It doesn't really say glum and careworn,' said Henry, taking a chair at the table. 'More contented and cosseted.'

'Perhaps if I suck my cheeks in?'

'Not a chance.'

Dawson poured the tea and they clinked their mugs together.

'I was about to offer you a biscuit, but as you've been frightfully rude I shan't now.'

A tray of gingerbread was cooling on top of the range, surrounded by lines of drying pots. Henry looked at the stacked bowls. There was something melodic and vital in the shapes that Dawson made. Watching him work made Henry think of poetry; each action was precise and fluid and true. Copying Dawson's actions, feeling and following those rhythms, had stilled Henry's hands and made the nightmares stop. The kitchen smelled of clay, spice and wet wool. It was an agreeable combination.

Dawson took off the overcoat and moved the gingerbread to the table. 'Anyway, how was France? You're looking conspicuously well on it. You look all sparkly-eyed and eager.'

'Complicated. Peculiar. Delightful.'

'Delightful? That's a new one.'

'I went to Paris.'

'You did? Really?' Dawson shook gingerbread crumbs from his beard. 'But I thought that you were on pilgrimage to Patrick?'

'I was. I got waylaid.'

'Can I interpret, from the look on your face, that you were waylaid in the lady way?'

'Yes. Shockingly.'

'Good God. I'd love to see Clarice's face. Bugger tea. Shall we have a snifter?'

Dawson stood on a chair to reach the top of the kitchen dresser. The walls of the kitchen were lined with framed family photographs. Henry had a strange second-hand affection for these sepia aunts and outings and grouped wedding outfits. He glimpsed a hint of Dawson in his mother's bridal smile.

'I do wish you'd put a shirt on,' he said. 'It's quite off-putting having to look at your vest.'

A jar of garnet-coloured liquid was placed on the table. 'You won't care what I'm wearing by the time that we've had a couple of these. Last year's damson gin,' Dawson explained. 'I've got to finish it off before I start the new batch. It's not optional. It's cellar management.'

'Funny place to keep a cellar.'

'I have to keep it where Lucy can't reach it. Tchin-tchin.' Dawson grinned across the glasses. 'Well, I never. A mademoiselle in the Lyle net, eh? I feel like I ought to ring a bell or something. You should get waylaid more often. It's clearly good for your constitution.'

'I'd be quite happy to stay waylaid – to keep the aforesaid female, if I can. Actually, you might be able to help me with that.'

'You want to build a cage? A pit? A mantrap? Is there such a thing as a ladytrap? Perhaps one baits it with kittens?'

'I want to make a teapot,' said Henry.

'You mean to keep her in a teapot?' Dawson looked at his glass. 'Has this stuff re-fermented?'

They went through to the sitting room while Henry explained about Bakewell tarts, towers and teapots. More gin and ridicule were administered.

'Are you badly afflicted?' asked Dawson, moving aside a sleeping cat.

'I may well be,' confessed Henry.

'Well, I'm glad to know that you've still got it in you.' Dawson held the sagging cat at arm's length. He looked like he was about to present it to Henry as a prize.

'Did you have doubts?'

'Yes. Best not tell Lucy yet, mind.'

'Why?'

'Because I now owe her a guinea.'

'Sod.'

'So how imminently do we launch Operation Teapot? Have you any thoughts on design?'

'Before I think about timing or design I really need to figure out whether I even have the right to consider making a teapot.' Henry looked across at his friend who was offering the cat a *dégustation* of gin-dipped gingerbread. The cat seemed to be more of a cherry brandy girl. 'Only, it's complicated, isn't it?'

'I'm guessing that by complicated you're alluding to Clarice?'

'I sent her a letter. I've asked if I can see her this weekend.'

'You're permitted to request a visit? Can it work like that? I thought you had to wait to be summoned? What's she got you pretending to be this time?'

'Oh, I'm still selling printing presses in Scotland. It keeps me nicely distant. I've just been reading a book about typesetting, actually. I know it's absurd, but I do like to get my terminology right.'

'Absurd is the word. Couldn't she have let you pretend to be something more fun?'

'Yes, just think, I could have sold cocktail shakers or speed boats or sequins to circus folk.'

'The printing presses are sour grapes. That woman enjoys putting you through the ringer – or should I say the press?' Dawson took a mouthful of drink. 'Adjectival woman. She makes me get all flustered in my metaphors.'

'She probably has a right to sour grapes.'

'Does she hell as like! I'd bluster at you but you already know my opinion of La Lyle.'

'I've got to talk to her, haven't I?'

'Yes,' said Dawson, putting down his glass. The grandfather clock softly struck the hour. 'And, if I can be permitted to say so, it's about bloody time. When you sold the factory you told me that life's too precious to spend it doing something that your heart isn't in. You were quite evangelical on the matter. You were having one of your speech-making days. It's about time you took another measure of your own medicine, old man. Unless, of course, you wish to be a pretend printing press salesman for the rest of your life.'

'I want to make a teapot.'

'Well, then. You'd better start working on your speech for Clarice. I found my old tin hat when I was looking for the coat. Perhaps you'd like to borrow it?'

'Pity that full plate armour went out, isn't it?'

Chapter Fifty-Five

I didn't know, Effie wrote.

Her hands moved across the surface of the desk as she searched for words – the desk of the man that did know.

I can't think how I can say that more emphatically. What can I say to make you believe me? I swear to you, Joe, that it is the truth.

A month earlier, as she re-read his letters, she had wanted to take back all of the words that she had sent him then. She had wanted to re-write her half of their history. She wanted to be more empathetic, more adequate in her response, to work arrangements of words that would gently encourage him on. She wanted to find the note that she had failed to find before. She wanted to make it right. Her pen faltered now, though. She felt herself failing again. She still didn't seem quite able to find the words that she wanted.

On the 5th November 1917 you died. There was a telegram. There was a notice in the paper. There was a memorial service. And then, after all of that, there was your name on the war memorial. It says 'In grateful memory' over your name. Your name is under Charlie's. It says 'Gave their lives for their country' underneath. There was nothing to make me think otherwise. I never had any suspicion that it might be otherwise. I certainly never had any letter.

What words had he put in his letter? Did it tell her about the day he had run and about what Laurie had done? Did he still want to be with her? Did he consider that their arrangement still held? Had she, at that point in 1919, still been his fiancée?

Laurence kept it from me. I know that now – and the reason why he chose to do so. He didn't do it in order to keep you and me apart (at least not expressly so). He believed that he was doing the right thing for me. Perhaps that was too great an assumption. Perhaps it was a decision that he had no right to make. Perhaps he was meddling where he had no place to.

She looked around his room. Had Laurie struggled with that decision? Had he regretted not giving her the letter? Did he regret not letting her make her own mind up? Was that why he sometimes gave her those long looks? Even at the end he still seemed to be measuring whether he had done the right thing.

I do know that his motive wasn't to hurt or harm you, though. He meant to give, not to take away. He meant to give me a future. He didn't mean to take yours away. He never wanted to take yours away.

Effie looked at Laurie's photograph smile. She thought about him at this desk, smiling as he turned towards her. She thought about them - him and Joe - together in the stone circle on Salisbury Plain and knew it was true – that he had never meant to hurt Joe.

You got it wrong about Laurie and me, Joe. You've misunderstood that part. There was no conspiracy, or set-up or deceit. It was never the way that you seem to assume it was. I did wait for you. I never drew a line through you. I need you to know that.

Would it have been different had she received his letter? Would she have gone to him, had he asked? She thought about how she couldn't make herself say his name to Alan Welch. On reflection, she wasn't sure that she could have gone to Joe. And anyway, twelve months later Joe was married to someone else, so perhaps his letter hadn't asked. Could she, if she had known that then, have stopped waiting? Would it have been different with Laurie?

I know nothing about the woman that you chose to be with, but I hope that you have found some happiness there. I am glad that you found someone. I say that in all sincerity. I want to believe that there has been some happiness in your life.

She tried to imagine the woman that he might be with, to

imagine them together, but couldn't picture it. The man she had met in Paris didn't look like he remembered how to be happy. She wished it otherwise.

I went to Ypres to visit your grave. I had no reason to believe that you were anywhere other than in that cemetery. Though you might be sorry not to be there, I can't feel the same. I re-read your letters recently. I read about Edward. It felt as if he had died all over again. Edward is in Guillemont Road Cemetery. I know that. I know that won't change. Edward won't one day reappear in Paris. He can't have that chance. I am glad that you have this chance. I am glad that you are alive.

The light cut across Laurie's circle of relics – the triangle of tile that had passed from her brother's hand to his, the shards of smoked glass salvaged from the ruins of Ypres and Mithras, still doing his bit for old soldiers.

You wrote to me once: 'It seems but luck to be alive.'

She stared at the arrangement of charms. Did Laurie keep these things here to remind himself? Or to punish himself? Effie decided that perhaps Laurie had done enough penance. She reached out towards the clay deity that Laurie had put his hope in. Had this thing ever had any power? Was there any luck left in it? She took one of Laurie's handkerchiefs from the desk drawer and wrapped the figure up. Laurie didn't need luck any longer.

She looked down at the letter.

'Can't you see how lucky you are?' she said.

Chapter Fifty-Six

Paris, 1922

Marius Godin had wound the gramophone again and the bar was full of *Saint Louis Blues*. Joe watched the surface of his drink vibrating to the beat.

'Is she having a child or a calf?' asked Boisnard, as the clarinet solo ended and Sophie's cries resumed.

'Don't cows bellow when they take the calf away?'

Boisnard shrugged.

'It is the saddest sound,' said Valentin Roux, 'when you take the calf away.' He nodded solemnly. Sophie had told Joe that Roux had been a farmer in Normandy before the war. 'I have known that sound all of my life and it never becomes any less wretched. It made me sob as a boy.'

'You ought to go back to your cows,' said Druet.

Joe could still hear Sophie's screams above the bovine debate. The crowd at the bar turned towards him each time that Sophie screamed.

He looked down at his glass. He had been looking into a glass when she told him. He'd looked up to see Sophie smiling, her hand on her stomach. *'Maintenant tout va changer,'* she had said. It was the note of absolute certainty in her voice that had made him look up. 'This is our chance. This is our future. Our luck will change. This child will turn a light on in your life.'

A bottle of brandy suddenly appeared on the table in front of him and a hand was on his shoulder now. *'Courage,'* said Marnot. 'My wife was in labour for thirty-six hours with the first.'

Godin changed the record over and the bar filled with Debussy. Joe placed his fingers on the table top, trying to find a sequence of notes he had once known.

The bar talkers drank silently. They turned their backs to Joe now as Sophie screamed. He shut his eyes and tried to follow the flow of piano. The notes buoyed him out on a current, pulling him away. There was nothing, for a minute, but the drift of the notes. Then Sophie was screaming again.

'Wasn't her father a butcher?' asked Druet.

Debussy tapered away and Sophie's pain pushed into the room. Her scream took him back to a hundred screams, to Charlie roaring out of the burning barn, to their collective howl the first time that they'd gone over the top, to the wood full of dead and shrapnel and shouting, and to that sound that had come from his own mouth when he had first seen Charlie's face. His head was full of screams. He put his hands over his ears. Could she be right? Could their luck really change? Could this new life make the screaming stop?

'It's finished.' Boisnard was mouthing the words.

'Joseph.' Marnot's hand was pulling at him.

'*Ecoutez!*' Godin's finger pointed upward.

'*Rien*,' said Valentin Roux.

Druet put his hand to the gramophone needle. Debussy screeched aside and then there was no noise. All of their eyes asked a question of the ceiling and lowered then to ask the question of Joe.

'I have to wait,' he said. 'I'm not allowed to go up. Madame Ducos told me to wait.'

'Your wait is over.' Marnot nodded towards the opening door.

Odile Ducos was standing in the doorway. She was wiping her hands on a cloth. Her hands were red in the creases. She looked at Joe and shook her head.

Joe stood in the cemetery in front of Sophie's grave. She and her son had been in it for the past six years. The child had changed everything. In that moment it had felt like the world had stopped turning. He had felt it jolt. He had felt the last of his hope finish. That had been the end of his future.

When he'd come round on the first day, the day in 1918 when he had first opened his eyes again, he could hear Sophie laughing in the next room. He couldn't hear her laughing any longer. Sophie never danced among the graves in a white dress. When he thought of her he could smell the chrysanthemums. In his nightmares now Sophie screamed too.

Chapter Fifty-Seven

They took the bicycles up beyond the reservoir. There was a drift of dandelion clocks in the sun-bright ditches, turning to cotton grass and then the stretching purple curves of the tops.

Effie's skirt caught in the chain. 'Gracie, wait for me!' She back-pedalled. 'That bloody settles it. I am taking up my hemlines.'

Grace bit on her fingernails as she glanced back over her shoulder. She looked thin, Effie thought, in her summer frock. Before she took up her hems she should take in Grace's seams.

'You're not in Paris now, you know. If mother sees your knees she'll have a seizure.'

'Bloody Paris. Bloody mother.'

'Like that, is it?'

'It is.'

The road became older as the skyline came closer. Yellow grass pushed through the setts, splitting and reclaiming the Roman road.

'It rattles my bones,' Effie said.

'Everything rattles you today.'

They gave in to the gradient and pushed their bicycles towards the summit. There were cartwheel tracks worn into the flagstones. Effie thought of the tread of legionaries, heard the tramp of ghost soldiers.

'Where does the road go, beyond the standing stone?' she had once asked Laurie, as they walked here together. The ditches were a froth of cow parsley back then, weighted and bright with rain. He had been furnishing her with facts about centurions, concrete, turnpikes and trans-Pennine packhorse routes.

'O'er the hills and far away,' he had sung and twirled the black umbrella that they shared.

'Do all roads lead to Rome?' she had asked.

'Some roads just go to Rochdale,' he had replied.

Magpies and memories scattered. 'Two for joy,' said Grace. They left their bicycles by the kissing gate.

Effie followed along the path. Church bells were pealing down below, sounding like a summons. There had been a service of remembrance in the memorial garden that morning. Effie saw their names, tidy in white, the stone-cut roll call making it ordered and honourable and right. She had stared at Joe's name filing alphabetically and falsely in line.

They walked out onto the rocks. There was the remains of a camp fire amongst the boulders. Effie remembered a scene lit with Chinese lanterns, the smell of autumn and the faraway sentiments of a pre-war Bonfire Night. The light had wavered against the rocks and made grotesque silhouettes. Charlie had been singing a coarse song about an inn-keeper's daughter, while the chorus stamped a rhythm. The Guy, an arm around Effie and Grace, had the Kaiser's curling moustaches. That night Joe had told Effie that he was going away.

'I'm going to go and be a soldier,' he had said.

And she had said, 'You'll look handsome in a uniform.'

Three years to the day later, Joe was sitting in a barn, waiting to be shot.

'I've written to him.' She told Grace.

'You've done what? Why? What can you hope to achieve?'

'I need him to know that I didn't deceive him. I need to defend myself – and Laurie. I can't stand him thinking that we in some way conspired against him.'

'Be careful, Effie. Some things are best left well alone. There are some things that it's best just to forget.'

'But I can't forget.' There was a sharp edge to the breeze. Snagged wool shifted innocently on the barbed-wire fence.

'Maybe you need to try harder.'

'I have nightmares about him, you know. It's like I've brought his ghost home with me. His unhappiness now feels like a heavy thing that I have to carry around.'

'But you didn't do anything to cause him to be unhappy. None of that was your fault.'

'Perhaps. I don't know. I needed to say my side of the story.'

They sat side-by-side on the rocks and dangled their legs over the edge. Effie shut her eyes into the wind. The sun felt warm on the back of her hands.

'You really didn't know?' she asked.

'Of course I didn't know. You can't believe I'd keep a thing like that from you?'

'Only I wasn't sure whether mother perhaps had it figured.'

'Don't talk daft. Mother thinks that Edward is still over there and we'll all be eating sauerkraut by Christmas.'

Effie kicked her heels against the rocks. 'I feel like the world has tipped off its axis. This is my life, but a few degrees out. Everything is the same and yet it's all changed. This woman wears my clothes and talks in my voice, but this isn't what my life is like.'

'She's got a better haircut than you,' observed Grace.

'Mother told me about Laurie, that he was in the asylum. I suppose you knew that? I suppose that you saw fit to keep that from me?'

Grace shrugged. 'Would it have made any difference?'

'That's what she said.'

'He went through a bad patch. He got over it. If he didn't want to tell you about it, and you were settled enough with him, well, you didn't need that fly in your ointment.'

'Some things are best forgotten?' echoed Effie.

'Happen more things ought to have been left forgotten.'

It was Effie's turn to shrug then. She squinted at the view, assessing the angle. The shadow of a cloud was moving across the contours of the crag. A lapwing's call took her back to Laurie's moorland ramble as he had lain unconscious in the casualty clearing station. 'He used to come up here to draw, you know.'

'Laurence?'

Effie nodded. The view was there, over and over again, in his sketchpads. She'd known the shape of stones, recognised the twist of a tree, had felt the sharpness of the grass whipped by the wind and seen the same nest full of bird bones. Then she'd started to find the other sketches; a girl's image appeared over and over again. Sitting at Laurie's desk, turning through the pages, Effie had, at first, not connected the dislocated elements of female face. Then, with a shock of recognition, she had remembered the girl, her elements rearranged, from a mirror long ago. Effie assessed herself in graphite and in his eyes. She put her fingers to her face as if to test the truth of it. He had drawn her over and over again. Effie had seen herself at every angle and occupation. He repeated her features like verse rote-learned.

'It's good for a man to have a hobby. I do wish that Frank would get a hobby.' Grace picked a blade of grass and whistled a fanfare between her thumbs.

'How many children are you up to now? I'd assumed that Frank had a hobby.'

Grace flopped back onto the grass and groaned. 'I was thinking of something with stamps or matchsticks.'

Effie retrieved the paper parcel from her bag. 'Marble cake with candied peel,' she said. 'I'm practising. It's fancy.'

'Who says that you need to practise?'

'Mother.'

'Bloody mother,' said Grace, with a mouth full of fancy marbling. 'Was it yesterday that you saw your Mr Warburton? You haven't said how you got on.'

'He was rather busy with his fingers. He patted my backside

twice. I think he might be after something more than housekeeping services.'

'I take it that wasn't in the advertisement?'

Effie raised her eyebrows in reply. 'He was just the right ruddy height in that wheelchair.'

'Well, was he nice looking?'

'Not nice enough. He does have fish knives, though.'

'Now, that is a dilemma.' Grace smiled. 'He offered you the job?'

'Commencing with a week in Matlock Bath. He always takes the waters in the autumn.'

'Are you sure that that's all he wants to take? Effie, you mustn't. Wait. Find something else. Find something new. Take a chance. More than candied peel, I mean.'

'I think that candied peel is about as far as my courage extends at present.'

'Don't talk rot. I've seen you free-wheeling that bicycle down Campania Street.'

'Some days I think that I might fly.'

'One day you'll fly over the handlebars.' Grace buffed her bitten-down nails. 'What happened to your amputee, anyway?'

'Nothing. And nothing will happen there. It was just a bit of a fling.'

'So did you...?' Grace's grin curled the unsaid end of the aside into a question.

'Don't be so bleeding nosy.'

'Well, I think it would be a damn shame if you didn't. Oh, write to the bloke, for Christ's sake. What did I just say about being brave?'

'Not to go over the handlebars.'

'I start to think that you and Laurence were as bad as each other. You'll leave it too late.'

'It's already too late,' said Effie. 'It always was. Henry's married. I didn't know. He didn't tell me. I saw his wife in a magazine.'

'Are you sure?'

'I'm sure. She has Marcel waves and an excellent drive. That's what the paper said.'

Grace blew cigarette smoke at this reply. 'Why, the lying toad.'

'Anyway, we don't all need to troop in two-by-two.' Effie heard herself using her most sensible voice. She didn't mean to linger upon the subject of Henry as it somewhat strained her sensibleness. 'And I've more pressing matters to fret about,' she informed Grace. 'I've got to see bloody Allerton tomorrow. I've got to meet him in the café. I'm not sure that it's proper to be meeting him in the café.'

'Mr Allerton? Laurence's solicitor?'

'I don't want to leave Everdene, Grace. I don't want to lose Reginald. I don't want to let go of Laurie.'

'Look on the bright side: at least you won't have to dust stuffed rats any longer.' Grace elbowed her encouragingly. 'If the worst comes to the worst, you can come home, you know. Frank's all bluster. He wouldn't see you on the streets.'

'If the worst comes to the worst...' She had watched Henry say it, as they'd stood on the bridge, the Seine barges sliding by below. She saw him smiling. How could she have so entirely misinterpreted that smile?

'No,' she said to Grace. 'I'm grateful, and all. And I do know that I owe Frank an apology. But I don't mean to let it come to that. I'd choose Mr Warburton's fish knives over Frank's bluster.'

'But Matlock Bath!'

'Apparently Lord Byron found it very romantic. Apparently taking the waters is very invigorating.'

'That's precisely what I'm frightened of,' said Grace.

Chapter Fifty-Eight

Effie hovered in the doorway of the Café Monika. She tried to think about how Alexander Allerton had trembled in a trench, with a juvenile moustache and a foolish monocle. The shop bell announced her entrance. The clientele was mercifully sparse and predominantly female, at single tables or in pairs. A gramophone-conjured string quartet filled the gaps in conversations. Allerton appeared to be conducting the quartet with a cake fork.

Mrs Harwood helped her with her coat. 'Are you well, love?' she asked.

'I'm not sure,' answered Effie.

'Dear Miss Shaw,' said the conductor, rising from his seat. 'Splendid to see you again.'

Effie took Allerton's proffered hand and reminded herself that he was scared of ponies.

'How very well you look after your travels,' observed he, his eyes sliding over everything but her face. He pulled a chair out for her. 'Veritably blooming. Was Paris suitably gay?'

'Travel is most enlightening,' offered Effie, who felt more inclined to wilt than bloom.

'Excellent,' said Allerton. 'Excellent.'

Effie considered the inscrutable 'excellents'. Did Allerton know why she had been sent to Paris and the matter to which she had been enlightened? She decided, as he nodded approbation, that perhaps he didn't know what he was nodding at after all.

'I was in Paris after the war,' he went on, smiling. 'We had a rather wild time. Oh, you know, parties, dancing, youthful exuberance, etcetera.'

Effie watched him wistfully recall the wildness and concluded that Allerton's being in Paris was probably beyond doubt.

'Etcetera. Indeed.'

Mrs Harwood's hand appeared on Effie's shoulder. Her

fingers gave a sympathetic squeeze. 'Sir?'

'Crumpet,' said Allerton, after some moments of contemplation. He looked across at Effie. 'Couldn't you relish a crumpet? I do sink in an afternoon.'

At her companion's pressing Effie conceded to a slice of tea loaf. She pulled the napkin over her lap and wished that she could disappear entirely under it.

'And so to this sad business,' Allerton began, and knocked a knuckle on a file that bore Laurie's name. He looked as though he meant to awaken the sad business from slumber.

'Oh dear,' said Effie, who by now had decided it was perhaps best to let sad business sleep.

'I am awfully sorry, by the way. Have I said that yet? I am awfully sorry for your loss – for our loss. I'm very sorry to be having to administer this. It seems dreadfully premature, doesn't it? I shall – I do – miss Laurence. He was a better soldier and a better man than I. I'm certain that you must miss him a great deal.'

'That's a nice obituary. That's a generous thing to say, Mr Allerton.' She liked him better for the admission, though she still feared what he was about to administer.

'I say it in all sincerity.'

Allerton slewed cutlery aside with the file, displaying great indifference for the symmetry of silver plate. Was there, despite the nice obituary, also a want of reverence for Laurie's wishes? Effie wasn't sure it was appropriate that Laurie's last wishes should be executed in a tea shop. But, then, given Laurie's partiality for teatime comestibles, for macaroons and meringues and a well-brewed Assam, perhaps it was, after all, apt. Allerton steepled his fingers over the file.

'As you know,' he commenced the formalities, his chin now supported by the steeple, 'Laurence's parents are deceased and there is little in the way of immediate family.'

'There's an uncle in Ripon, an aunt in Richmond and a smattering of cousins in the south,' interrupted Effie, hoping that Allerton might have unearthed a kindly Swaledale spinster, who would want to keep Everdene in aspic, or perhaps some bright young cousins, requiring party catering and knowledge of Continental cuisines. It might, after all, be fun to have the house full of bright young voices and the option was certainly preferable to Grace's back bedroom or Mr Warburton's reinvigoration in Matlock Bath.

'Actually, I have had some fun with the family tree,' diverted Allerton, pushing the file aside and brightening. 'Did you know that Laurence's uncle is a bigamist? He has one wife in Ripon and one in Scarborough.'

'Goodness,' said Effie, whose scenarios hadn't included keeping house(s) for a bigamist. 'Is that Uncle Herbert with the gout?'

'For a man with gout, he gets about.'

Effie contemplated the practicalities of triangulation and what the catering requirements of a bigamist might be. 'I suppose it's preferable to a vegetarian,' she concluded after some consideration.

'I'm not entirely convinced the wives would concur.'

Effie watched Allerton's fingers flex on the folder. Did he understand that it contained her fate? Was he having fun making her wait? She regretted that her interruption seemed to have derailed the formalities.

Mrs Harwood arrived with the tray. Effie pondered Allerton's tactics as she straightened cutlery. Perhaps he was in need of a housekeeper? His whites certainly needed some work. But could she abide his foxy looks and fondness for dirty foreign women? She decided to make him aware of her culinary accomplishments, just in case. Allerton was, at least, less direct than Mr Warburton.

'Tea, tea, tea. Always tea,' said he. 'Laurence and I composed a poem about it once, you know. We versified the virtues of tea.'

'I know,' replied Effie. 'I read it. I was impressed that you succeeded in rhyming quite so many swearwords.'

She watched him smilingly remember rhymes as he set about his crumpets.

'I started work in here, you know,' Effie began, seeing as Allerton didn't seem inclined to. 'On Victoria sandwich and coconut rocks.'

'Ah, yes. I recall Laurence expounding on the subject of your coconut rocks.' He put a cigarette between his lips and offered her the packet.

Effie shook her head. She recalled Laurie expounding on the subject of Allerton's lewd mouth and how that mouth had mocked Laurie for lusting after shop girls. She felt suddenly defensive.

'It was a friendly place to work, a nice place to work. It felt like part of being a family – a *respectable* family,' she weighted for Allerton's benefit, 'with a sense of pride and particularity and decent opinions on how far to go with butter cream.'

'Butter cream can be the devil's work.' He shook out the match and looked at her earnestly.

'But it can,' said Effie. 'People go too far. There's no finesse, no measure. Have you seen how they slap it on in the Café Apollo? I aspire to patisserie, not plastering.'

Allerton laughed. Effie wished he would stop laughing and get on with the executing. He seemed to be primarily interested in applying butter to crumpets and somehow her own voice was becoming the solo accompaniment to the buttering.

'Anyway, what I mean to say is, what I'm trying to say is, I have no shame at having been a shop girl. Being a shop girl can be very nice.' She put her teacup down for emphasis.

'Perfectly,' he agreed and patted her hand.

Effie took her hand away and stashed it under her napkin. It was a mercy that the Café was quiet on a Monday afternoon. She took a steadying mouthful of tea and watched the cigarette smoulder in Allerton's saucer. She noticed that he did indeed seem to enjoy his crumpets well buttered. Perhaps that accounted for his levity with butter cream and his failure to focus on the important matter in the folder.

Effie polished a fingerprint from her knife. Somehow she found herself compelled to continue her lopsided conversation. 'It's not what it was, though, I'm afraid. Not since Mr Schumann's day. There's not the attention to detail that there once was,' she observed. 'It was very important once – detail and polish.' She looked at Mr Allerton's cuffs and wondered whether he could fully appreciate the slippage of standards.

'Well, you ought to take that up with the management, Miss Shaw.'

'Mrs Harwood does her best. I do know that. But she's getting on and what with it being up for sale, and all, there isn't the commitment any longer.'

Allerton grinned his Big-Bad-Wolf grin. Melted butter glistened in his moustache. Effie noticed that his topiary could have done with some trimming and concluded that his standards had probably slipped some time ago. She decided that being the case, she couldn't abide being his housekeeper after all. He put the cigarette out in his saucer.

'Are you by any chance in possession of a vanity mirror – those snappy things that ladies have about their persons?'

Effie duly fished in her handbag and produced the compact that had been a long-ago gift from Laurie.

'Do you have something in your eye, Mr Allerton?'

'My eyes are full of pleasant things, Miss Shaw.'

He opened the compact, making buttery fingerprints on the

blue enamel, and showed Effie her own powder-misted reflection. She wondered if this was perhaps some form of flirtation.

'So, go on.' He laughed.

'I'm sorry?' Effie's reflection looked less than amused. She suspected that Allerton had partaken of a lunchtime libation. Perhaps, she thought, a lunchtime libation was something to which he was accustomed and thus his inclination to afternoon sinkage.

'The management,' encouraged Allerton. 'Go on. Chastise them. Berate them. Rebuke them. Scold them for their sloppy standards.'

'I'm afraid I really don't understand.'

'Sweet lady, may I shake your hand?'

She conceded dubiously and they shook on the mysterious matter. Effie once again felt excluded from the rules of the game.

'Mr Allerton, will you please tell me why you're holding my hand?'

'Dear Miss Shaw. It's an awfully pretty hand. Can you blame a fellow for finding occasion to hold it? But, you see, I'm holding it because I mean to offer you my congratulations. I believe that the silver is overdue your attention.'

The penny – and the compact – dropped.

'Me? Here? But how? Has Laurie secured a position for me?'

'It's somewhat more than a position, Miss Shaw.'

'Indeed. Of course. A respectable position. A happy position. A respectable position that I'd be happy to accept.'

'I'm so glad that you're happy to accept,' Allerton's moustache curled upwards at the corners. 'But it is rather more than that. Don't you see, dear girl? Laurence made provision in his will for the Café Monika to be purchased. Your name is on the deeds. Laurence bought the Café for you.'

Effie looked around the room. She looked at Allerton. His hand reached over the table, lifted her chin and closed her gaping mouth.

'Goodness, I enjoyed that.' He sat back in his chair and grinned into his teacup. 'If every client reacted that way, I could re-find the relish for this lawyering lark.'

'But how? But why?'

'Because he wanted to. It seems that you were somewhat more than a passing fancy.' Allerton looked up to the ceiling mouldings. 'I do hope that he's watching.'

'Laurie bought me the Café?' Effie's eyes took in the wood panelling, the counter and the potted palm and the seating for forty-five. All of which was now suddenly hers it seemed.

'Don't milk it now, dear. Yes, it's all yours. And Everdene as well. And an annuity that will keep you sitting pretty. There's a somewhat whimsical proviso regarding the dog, a stipulation for the provision of sugar mice and some such nonsense, but nothing overly onerous.'

'Reginald? I have to keep Reginald?'

'I am sorry, my dear. It would seem that you have little choice.'

'That perhaps makes me happiest of all,' said Effie and began to cry.

Allerton patted his pockets and produced a hip flask (kept expressly for the purpose of calming fretful lady clients, he assured her). Effie was encouraged to a restorative swig of brandy. She thought of how she had passed a flask with Alan Welch in the cemetery where Joe might have been. She wondered if Joe would mind that she now had her name on the deeds of ceiling mouldings and seating for forty-five – and then realised that Joe's minding really shouldn't matter anymore. Joe had a wife and Effie had a café. She also suddenly found that she had pride and purpose and a lot to thank Laurie for.

'We danced in here, you know,' she told Allerton. 'Years ago. Back in the early months of the war. My sister, Grace, and I, that is. She dragged me up. She's like that. The gramophone was playing, like today. It was a tenor singing about losing his sweetheart, I remember. I didn't want to dance and everybody stared. Because, well, it isn't proper dancing in a café, is it? Not this sort of café, at least. But, when we stopped, they all clapped. And I felt brave, then. At that point, at that instant, I felt that I was the bravest that I had ever been. I thought that it was the bravest that I ever would be. But we had no idea then, did we?'

'Absolutely no idea,' he replied, with straight-faced sincerity.

They parted in the doorway of the Café.

'I must have a word with Mrs Harwood,' said Effie. 'She'll be wondering at the commotion.'

'Do you mean to get the old dear buffing the silver already? I had you down as a benevolent dictator.'

'I plan to be the most civilised of despots,' she replied. 'I shall indulge old dears, respect the whims of dogs and be liberal in the buttering of crumpets. You will find that I'm a stickler for the silver, though.'

Allerton leaned on the door frame and grinned. 'I've had a jolly time,' he said. 'You wouldn't fancy doing this again, would you? Not the bequest bit, of course, but perhaps we might go for dinner somewhere? You like dancing, don't you? You know, you're really rather pleasant company, old thing.'

'That would be my – what was it now? – winsome proletarian politeness and titillating smell of small change,' Effie quoted and winked. 'Thank you, Alexander. You'll find that we're open nine while seven.'

It was starting to go dark by the time that she walked home along the park. The lights were just coming on in Manor Road.

She looked through the draped window dressings. Electric chandeliers lit families at respectable firesides. These were the homes of manufacturers, mill owners and merchants, of men who had means and meetings and days that required a diary. Effie turned the corner into Park Road and told herself that she was a local businesswoman. A solicitor, after all, had said so. Her chin lifted a little higher. She felt removed from the pavement along which she walked.

She leaned on the garden gate and looked along the iris path. Everdene was in darkness but the evening sky glinted in its windows. She wished for a glimpse of interior movement in those windows, a flash of a familiar profile or the beat of an upstairs dance band.

'I do still wish that *you* had asked me to dance,' she said. 'I'd still swap it all for a dance.'

Chapter Fifty-Nine

He had cursed the chrysanthemum on the train. He'd had to sit with it between his feet. People had stumbled over it and tripped around it and looked at it like it wasn't a proper thing to have on a train. Joe was repeatedly obliged to apologise. Standing with the pot in his arms in a connecting station, he thought that the weight of it was increasing with the distance that he carried it. It began to feel like the sort of task that might be given as a lesson in a fable.

In between the cursing and the apologising he had re-read her letter. He had torn it up when it arrived three days earlier and then pieced it back together again. Amidst her torn-apart denials and appeals, she had mentioned Edward's grave. Effie had said the name of the cemetery where Edward was. Could Charlie still be there with him? The possibility had nagged at Joe until he found himself queuing in a florist's shop and consulting a railway timetable.

Standing by Charlie's grave, the first time, Joe had felt resentful of the rushed words and not-quite-convincing sentiments. He'd been very conscious of the not-quite-true angle of the cross and the fact that Charlie must share his pit like a workhouse pauper. The flies had bitten at their hands. The noise of the guns had broken up the hymn. He'd needed to go to an estaminet afterwards.

He placed the chrysanthemum in front of the grave. The bronze petals glowed against the stone. Sophie had pushed him through this same cemetery eight years ago, he'd realised, when it was all still earthworks and a confusion of crosses. Had he passed him then, all that time ago? Could they have passed that closely and not known? On his gravestone Charlie was still nineteen years old. It suddenly seemed to be an awfully long time ago.

They had seen the first of the white stones in 1920. He had

thought them too uniform, too tidy, too clean. There was something false in their cleanness and order, something fraudulent in it, because that wasn't how it was. He remembered feeling angry. Nasturtiums scrambled around the bottom of Charlie's white stone. Joe moved them aside to read the inscription. *Sleep peacefully, beloved sons*, it said. He stared at the last letter, aghast at the implications of that plural. He felt the weight of that simple, final acknowledgment. It was twelve years since he had last heard his mother's voice. Twelve years of anger seemed to rush at him and from him. It left him feeling strangely still inside. He leant his head against the gravestone.

A tourist party came in the afternoon. They strolled between the graves and commented on the flowers. Joe walked along the row. Edward Shaw was at the end of it, with a red rose planted by his side. Joe wondered, remembering them side-by-side in the shared grave, how Charlie and Edward could have moved so far apart. What great eruptions had come between them? Perhaps it was best not to know and just to be contented with the clean stones and the quiet. A laurel wreath had been leant against Edward's grave. Had she been here? Had she really been to look for *his* grave?

Believe me, Effie's pen had implored. He touched the letter in his pocket. *Please believe me, Joe. I honestly didn't know.* His mind kept going back to her torn-apart appeals. *He simply didn't have the heart to kill you*, her letter had concluded. *Is that such an unforgivable crime? Please forgive him and let it go.*

He took the idol from his pocket and unwrapped it. He had recognised it straight away; it was the same clay figure that Laurence Greene had put in his hand when he had gone out to get Charlie back. 'For luck,' he had said. Joe remembered returning it, folding it into Greene's stiff fingers. And now Effie had passed it back once again. Was this amulet intent on following him? Seemingly, it didn't mean to let him go. He also recognised the handkerchief in which it had been wrapped; the initials were the same ones that had once been pinned to his chest. Joe wondered quite what luck was.

With a movement at his side, he looked to his left. A woman was on her knees by a grave further along the line. Her lips formed a chain of silent words; her fingers stretched towards the name on the stone. Joe looked away quickly, suddenly feeling like an intruder. He stepped back from Edward Shaw's grave. The woman glanced over her shoulder, as if abruptly woken from a dream. He saw that she had been crying.

He walked back to Charlie. Had Effie really cried at his memorial service? Had she really never known? A church bell rang out some distance away and a blackbird was singing. Could he let go?

He knelt in front of Charlie and lit a cigarette. He felt a peculiar urge to offer one to the gravestone. 'I'd ask you if you want one, only...'

'If it's going spare, I wouldn't say 'No'.' The woman's shoes halted at his side.

Joe offered the packet as she sat down on the grass next to him.

'An old comrade?'

'My brother.'

'You poor man. How terribly sad.'

'Your husband?'

She nodded. Joe lit her cigarette and shifted his feet so as not to show the holes in his socks.

'Twelve years,' said the woman. 'Can it really be twelve years?'

'All of a sudden, today, it does seem like a very long time ago.'

'Funny thing, time, isn't it? It trundles by so slowly and then, for an instant, you look away and suddenly it's all zipped past.'

The woman took out a compact mirror, licked a handkerchief and wiped the smears from around her eyes. 'What a fright. Suddenly an awful lot of it seems to have zipped past.'

Joe was reminded of an image of Effie, then. He'd watched her painting on a smile on the street corner, before she'd stepped into the Café Metropole. Joe had seen the mirror flash a circle of light across her face. He thought he'd understood what Effie's reflected expression said. Could he have misunderstood? Could he have got it wrong for so long?

The woman's compact snapped shut. Joe realised she was staring at his hands. 'You ought to play the piano with those hands,' she pronounced.

For some reason the remark made him laugh. The woman's face disappeared into her own hands and then emerged also laughing. It was like an electric light flicking on when she laughed.

'Good God! I'm sorry. What a thing to say to a man sat by his brother's grave. Does it make it any better if I explain that I'm a piano teacher? I'm clearly an over-zealous one. I sound like a recruiting party. What a perfectly stupid thing to say.'

'What's the proper thing to say in a cemetery? I did once – the piano, that is. A long time ago, though. Then, when I tried again, after the war, I'd completely forgotten how. I just couldn't do it. I didn't know where to begin. It's like the notes have all fallen out of my head.'

'They're probably still in there. It's probably just blocked. I've read about things like that. Stopped clocks restart and tell the time perfectly well, don't they? You might sit down at the keyboard one day and Beethoven come thundering out through your fingers.' The piano teacher thundered her fingers illustratively. She raised her chin and gave him a lopsided grin. 'Do a favour for a stranger and promise me that you'll try again?'

Caroline Scott

Effie's letter had said: *You wrote to me once: 'It seems but luck to be alive.' Isn't it still, perhaps?*

'Yes,' said Joe to the stranger. He watched as she turned the chrysanthemum, removed a fading flower head and smiled back towards him. 'Yes,' he said. 'Perhaps I might.'

Chapter Sixty

'Sometimes you just have to let go,' said Clarice.

'Are you still talking about painting the flat or have we now moved on to psychiatric advice?'

'Both,' she said. 'Perhaps.'

They sat on a bench. Henry looked at the ducks and Clarice splayed her gloved fingers in front of her face. She appeared to be appraising the stitching. The hands sprang shut and she turned towards him. 'I was glad to get your letter. I wanted to see you.'

'To discuss painting schemes?'

'God, no. It's already done. It was never up for debate.'

'Of course.' Clarice was wearing her efficient face; she had painted on her abstemious mouth. 'So are you going to tell me why we're meeting like spies in the park?'

'Don't you like it? I thought you liked the ducks?'

'Well, I do,' he said 'but…'

'Gilbert is at the flat.' She bit her fraudulently abstemious lip. He would swear afterwards that he could actually see her pupils dilating in this instant. She clearly expected the Gilbert information to provoke a conflagration.

'Gilbert is always at the flat. I know exactly where Gilbert has been because he leaves a trail of brilliantine imprints. Like a centre-parted slug.'

'That makes you sound like a horrid sneak.'

'It's difficult not to notice another chap's brilliantine on one's bedhead.'

'Don't make it sound like something that it's not. It hasn't been your bedhead for the best part of a decade. You should have locked me in a nunnery if you feel like that.'

'You'd have made the most awful nun.'

'No, I wouldn't. I could have put my mind to it. I know how to do cross-stitch and I like singing hymns.'

'What rot.'

'Anyway, we're not here to discuss my candidacy for the sisters of charity.'

'So, go on. Why did you want to see me? You've clearly got an agenda.'

'Actually, it is Gilbert that I want to talk about.'

'Really? What a treat.'

Clarice stuck out her bottom lip. She had a wide thin-lipped mouth. When he was younger Henry had thought that there was something alluring about the curve of Clarice's mouth, but these days her lips just looked manipulative. 'Don't be like that,' the mouth said now.

'I'm sorry. Please continue.'

'Gilbert wants to marry me.'

'To marry you?' In the flicker of an instant the pout had turned into a grin. Clarice's emotions had always moved at high speed. Henry wondered if Gilbert was better able to navigate them than he had been. 'But I'm married to you. Well, notionally, at least.'

'Precisely. Bit of a pickle.'

'I suppose you want to ask me to un-marry you?'

'Oh Henry, you always were a bright boy.'

'Not always. I occasionally lapse into outright idiocy.'

'You're not going to be Victorian about it, are you?'

'No, darling. I shall be positively *à la mode*. My modishness may well stagger you. Would it be terribly vulgar if I were to throw a party?'

'Appallingly.'

'But I thought that divorce was a no-no? I thought your mother would never stand for it? You said it would make your father spin in his grave. Isn't that why we've played out this pretence for the last ten years?'

Clarice shrugged. 'It was a no-no. Now it's a yes-yes.' She leaned towards him. 'You might look a bit more surprised, though. You could pretend to be devastated for five minutes.'

'Would you like me to beat my fists on the path and chew on the bench?'

'You could try to look slightly disappointed. You actually look relieved.'

'I'm suppressing, dear heart. It's a struggle, but I'm a stoic sort. If you find me hanged in the morning headlines, know that it's all your fault.'

'Gil locked the door after I left. He was worried that you might want to hit him. Clearly he needn't have worried.'

'I might glower at him a bit, but I certainly shan't hit him.' A loud hiss took his attention to the pond. A swan was flapping its wings at a schoolboy who had been attempting to skim stones on the water. 'Quite so,' said Henry.

'That's the letting-go amply ticked-off, then? Good. I'm glad. Thank you.' Clarice swivelled on the seat and stared at him. 'I am glad you're sane again.'

Henry felt as if, with Clarice's up-close scrutiny, his sanity was being assessed. 'I was never not sane!'

'Oh, you know what I mean. You look stable now, solid again. I can tell that you're better because you've stopped wearing cardigans.'

'Is that the definition, then? Is that the tell-tale signifier of instability?'

Clarice raised an eloquent eyebrow.

'I thought the low point was poetry, anyway?'

'God, the poems! I'd forgotten about the poems. It wouldn't have been quite so excruciating had you not insisted on reading them aloud to me. There's only so much mud and blood that a girl can take. Your rhymes didn't even rhyme.' She smiled at him. It was the steely smile, the one that always made him think of the Traitor's Gate. 'Was I an awful wife?'

'Atrocious. Was I a hopeless husband?'

'Pathetic.' She showed her teeth again. 'No, I'm being mean. I shouldn't be mean. You were quite acceptable until the mud and blood bit.' She peeled off her gloves and examined her nails. 'Gil's already bought a ring.'

Henry laughed. 'I was with Dawson this week. He says that you're a harpy.'

'Well, of course he does. Dawson adores you. I was never ever going to be good enough for you. I hope he at least has the courtesy to think me a pretty harpy.'

'He's helping me make a teapot.'

'You're still doing that, then? You really have a notion of being a potter? How utterly preposterous.'

'No, it's not.'

'The war made it impossible for women, you know. You men that served together, you're all closer than wives. It's like a club that's impossible to gain entrance to. We women have no chance now.'

'I'm sorry if you felt shut out.'

'I'm not sure that I was ever in in the first place.'

He could hear a Foxtrot from the direction of the bandstand. Women had been waltzing around it in pairs as he passed. They seemed entranced by the dance, as if nothing existed beyond it. There had been something profoundly melancholy about the scene.

'I wasn't ever horrid to you, was I?' he asked her.

'Those cardigans were pretty horrid.'

'I might give Gilbert one as a wedding present.' He felt one of Clarice's gloves make contact with the back of his head.

'Will you come back? Gil is going to make cocktails.'

'How jolly. Perhaps I could give him some tips.'

'About cocktails?'

'About harpies.'

'On second thoughts, maybe you ought not.'

338

'I've got a train to catch, anyway.' He put on his hat to emphasise that he had no intention of partaking of Gilbert's Gin Fizz.

'Where are you going?'

'I've got a printing press to sell.'

'Aren't you going to tell me her name?'

'I'm sorry?'

'Henry, it's written all over your face.'

'Is it?'

'You're smirking. I'm not certain that I've ever seen you smirk before. I bet she lets you drone on and on and on about the war, doesn't she? Do you do re-enactments in the drawing room? Do you sit cheek-to-cheek at the piano and sing grim soldierly songs? Does she let you recite poetry at her? Does she keep your home fire burning?' Clarice's eyes widened with the multiplication of possibilities. Her head rolled back against the bench as she laughed.

'You actually cackled, then. Does Gilbert know that you can cackle?'

'Oh, tell me about your khaki love nest!' She clawed at his thigh. Her nails were filed to polished points.

'It's not like that. And, no, I shan't.' He removed her hand. 'All you need to know is that she's very lovely.'

'Not like me, you mean? Poor girl. How hideously happy you must be together.' Clarice cocked her head to one side and smiled. The attitude made her look like a waggish parrot. 'I didn't mean to cackle at you, darling. I do hope it works out for you. I shall always be sorry, you know, that we went so badly wrong. I am sorry that I wasn't kinder.'

'And I'm sorry too – especially about the cardigans.' He squeezed her hand. 'Will you give Gilbert my congratulations – and commiserations?'

'Thank you for being nice about it.'

'I'm damnably nice. I'm through-and-through nice. Did you never notice before?'

'It will be your downfall.'

'Not for a while yet, I hope.' Henry looked at his watch. 'I'd better scoot for that train.' He kissed her cheek. 'Goodbye and good luck, Mrs Lyle.'

'You do look well, you know. You look happy. Are you happy, Henry?'

'Yes,' he said. 'I think I am.'

Chapter Sixty-One

'Can I help you?'

Effie was just starting to become accustomed to the shrill overhead hysteria of the shop bell, but the face at the door made her take a step back.

'Effie,' said Frank.

'Frank,' said Effie.

'I thought that I might be able to help *you*.' The door swung closed behind him. Frank Fitton looked somehow incongruous, Effie thought, framed in the doorway of a café – even one that was half-painted and draped in dust sheets. 'I was on an early shift,' he explained, with a manner that seemed almost like embarrassment, 'so Grace sent me with a paintbrush. And I thought that perhaps we might have a word.'

'You're a bit late. I'm on the second coat.'

'Aye, well, happen an extra set of hands will get that second coat finished.'

Effie eyed her brother-in-law, assessing motivation. 'Can't say as I expected your approval, never mind you volunteering your services.'

'I'm here, aren't I? Must we have an inquest into it?'

'Are you expecting me to pay you?'

'I'm trying to be civil.'

'Is our Grace paying you?'

'You're not making it easy for me to be civil.'

Effie gestured for Frank to enter. There was something different about his movements, something awkward in the curve of his shoulders. Was this what the proximity of paper doilies could do to a man? Frank looked entirely uncomfortable.

'Well, get on with it, then.'

'If you'll show me the paint can.'

'I meant the speech.'

'For Christ's sake, Effie. I'm trying to be nice.'

Caroline Scott

'Nice? Have you been drinking?'

'No, but I have been thinking.'

He passed the paintbrush from one hand to the other. His eyes cast down. Effie wondered what thought could have so transformed Frank.

'Well, spit it out, man.'

'You are a difficult woman.' He turned, seemingly preferring to address his words to the wall. 'My mother always told me, 'Don't put off until tomorrow what you ought to say today. Because tomorrow might never come.' Wasn't known for her sunny disposition, my mother. The thing is, I was going back over it, and, you see, it's not that it changes what your feller did, that he was the one that said 'Fire,' and all, but the fact that he maybe gave Joe a chance, well, perhaps he wasn't all bad.'

'He wasn't bad at all. He did what he had to do. He didn't have any choice, did he? If he'd refused, he'd have had the same fate as Joe. And the guilt, well, that was enough to make him try to take his own life, wasn't it? He couldn't live with the thought that he had done the wrong thing. He was a man who always tried to do the right thing. Laurence Greene was a good man.'

She stared at Frank's back. Had it occurred to Laurie that he might be giving Joe a chance? Did he consider that? Could it have been a conscious act of kindness? Joe himself had called it an act of cowardice. She decided, with Frank, to give Laurie a chance.

'And, maybe,' Frank carried on making faces at the wall, 'what he did – or didn't do – wasn't your fault.'

'I never even knew,' said Effie. 'Nobody told me. So how could I have known if I was doing wrong – or not?'

'He was a good officer. We had far worse. There were plenty that were all shout and swank. But Greene was decent and we respected him. When it came to it, he had balls, he led from the front. We liked him until that point.'

Frank turned around and looked at her directly, then. Effie realised it was probably the first time that Frank had ever looked her in the eye.

'We gave him a hard time afterwards,' he went on. 'We weren't very decent with him. Sometimes it's easier to go on giving someone a hard time than it is to stop and admit that you perhaps got it wrong. I left it too late to admit that to him. I figured that I probably ought to say it to you, though.'

'You did get it wrong,' said Effie. 'But, then, I got it wrong too.'

'I tried to stop Joe, you know, when he ran, but it was too late.' He looked down at his hands and then back at her. He looked at her as if it mattered that she must know this. 'I didn't shoot him. I couldn't have done. I deliberately aimed away.'

'Most of you did, apparently. Most of you missed. If any of you were actually aiming, well, it's no wonder that it dragged on for four years.'

A smile briefly twitched across Frank's face. 'I'll hear none of your aspersions. Tin ducks quake when I step onto a fairground. I was once banned from the Buffalo Bill stall.'

'You helped him.' She thought of them sitting in the shell hole together, their fingers fleetingly touching in the water. 'I didn't realise how much. I'm the one who ought to say sorry.' She offered him her hand. '*Entente cordiale?*'

'Eh?'

'Shall we share a pot of tea and agree to try to get along? There's a scone in it if you get that wall done before dark.'

'You bargain like a bastard,' he said, but they shook on it.

Effie pulled out a chair and nodded for her brother-in-law to sit. She wasn't sure whether she was keen on taking tea with Frank Fitton, but, then, it seemed that he wasn't quite the person she'd supposed him to be. Perhaps, after all, they might exchange civilities and favours. His neck was still terribly grubby, though, she noticed. She wondered how her sister could abide to make babies with a man with a grubby neck. Would their new shook-on civility extend far enough that Effie might be able to recommend a flannel?

She sat down opposite him, clattering cups. He stared at the table top, as if he too wasn't quite sure how to commence the civilities.

'That scone,' he ventured. 'Don't suppose you'd consider a down payment?'

Frank fell about the food with a sense of urgency.

'Blimey, Frank. Does she not feed you?'

'Have you tasted your Grace's cooking?'

'There's some meat pie left over if it's that bad.'

'Grace says that her hands are too hot for pastry. She's passionate, see. Hot blooded. Her character compromises her shortcrust,' concluded Frank, taking unaccustomed care over his elocution.

'Is that what it is?'

'It's an affliction,' said Frank gravely.

'I can think of others,' said Effie.

She supposed that Frank considered her to be a cold fish, but he seemed keen enough on the products of her cool fingers.

As she cut pie in the kitchen, she wondered at how Laurie's death and Joe's resurrection had brought her to a juncture where she felt sorry for Frank Fitton. She gave him extra gravy in the spirit of new beginnings.

'Who'd have thought it?' she asked Reginald.

But Reginald seemed only to have thoughts for meat pie.

'It's decent of you to give your Grace a job.' Frank tipped cigarette ash amongst the pastry crusts. 'I'm grateful for that.'

'Well, I don't like her taking in washing. There are nicer

ways to earn a living. It's better than laundering strangers' smalls. And, besides, she takes no nonsense and I trust her on the till.'

'She's very fetching in her uniform.'

'Have you ever thought about collecting stamps or keeping pigeons?'

'I don't like their feet,' said Frank.

'Are ferrets' feet any more agreeable? Or perhaps rambling, or angling or dominoes?'

'I'll take that apology back.'

'I never thought I'd see the day!' said Grace as she entered. 'Are you two having a cosy catch-up?' She pulled up a chair and looked from her husband to her sister.

'Very cosy, thank you,' answered Effie. 'We were just planning to run away together and set up in sin in Scarborough.'

Frank spluttered Ceylon.

'It's very green,' said Grace, her attention turning to the walls.

'Oh, don't you start.'

'No, I like it. It's modern. It's different.'

'The colour is called Jade Pagoda and it's a new beginning. It's meant to make you think of palm courts and genteel colonial gatherings, of cool, fragrant functions with ceiling fans and string quartets and elegant refreshments. It'll be better when the second coat is done.'

'Genteel colonial gatherings?' repeated Frank, who wasn't at all attired for a *thé dansant*. 'Palm flaming courts?' He stood, with an inelegant scrape of chair, and continued to issue impolitenesses as he ascended a ladder.

Reginald pawed at Effie's knee. 'He can't abide profanity,' she advised her sister and gave him a compensatory sugar mouse.

'Doesn't put him off his food, does it? That dog is fat. Has he got any teeth left? I'm not sure that Laurence meant for you to feed him exclusively on sugar mice.'

'He doesn't just eat mice, Grace. He developed a taste for brandied cream in Belgium. He likes his niceties. It comforts him for the loss of Laurie.'

'He's clearly been doing a lot of comforting. He'll be lucky if he lasts the year out.'

'Don't say that. Now I feel mean.'

'A bit of meanness wouldn't do him any harm. And you look different,' said Grace, circling a finger in Effie's direction. 'There's something about your face. There's something going on in your eyes. What is it that you're not telling me?'

'I heard back from Joe yesterday.'

'Please don't say that you're off to Paris. I'd rather have you being scandalous in Scarborough.'

'She's dead,' said Effie. She shook her head. 'Joe's wife died. She had a miscarriage. He lost both her and the child. I think he probably did love her. I think he loved her as much as he could.'

Grace stared at her hands in her lap. 'Poor lad,' she said at last.

'Quite.'

'Is he okay? Will he be okay?'

'He's better now than he has been. He's just found Charlie's grave. That seems to be important to him.'

'And you've made your peace?'

'I think he's forgiven me.'

'I still don't know what you needed to be forgiven for.'

'He told me to go forward with my life and not to look back.'

I have spent the last ten years looking back, Joe had gone on. *Something snapped. I got stuck. I kept having to go back to places in my past and I couldn't make it stop and I couldn't make it right. But then, finding Charlie again, it feels like something has changed. There are places that I don't need to keep going back to any longer. And that made me realise, there are other things that I can – and ought to – let go. Perhaps there are some things that I can put right. The enclosed is yours,* he had concluded, *and I now consider the transaction closed.*

'He sent me this.' Effie passed the folded paper across the table and watched as Grace opened it. It had yellowed crisply in the creases. A ridge of trees glinted in long-ago graphite. Across the kind fold of fields slanted Laurie's writing.

'*I.O.U. 1 life,*' Grace read. She looked up. 'Is this what I think it is?'

Effie sank into Laurie's chair. Though it might need reupholstering, it had lately become her own. She liked to look at Everdene from his angle.

She had lit the fire when she got home and a log smouldered white in the grate. Her mother's Staffordshire spaniels had joined Laurie's ornaments on the mantelpiece and, in between, Effie's Eiffel Tower. She had wondered, after the golfing wife revelation, whether the tower ought to come down. But, while she might not like to be reminded of Henry's not-quite honesty, she considered that a daily reminder of his incitement to daring was not such a bad thing.

She stretched her hands towards the fire and the post slid in her lap. She hadn't recognised the writing; condolence continued to arrive from soldierly quarters and she was accustomed to not recognising writing. But, as her eye shifted from Eiffel Tower to envelope, Effie knew whose writing this was.

She wasn't sure whether she should open it with delight or dread, or whether it ought to go straight in the grate. Either way, she opened it at speed.

What-ho, Fairy Palace, began Henry Lyle.
This is a bit overdue, isn't it? My excuse is that I've written

and re-written this letter a dozen times. I could probably re-write it a dozen more, but you won't remember who I am by then. There is a proper reason for the rewriting. It's not that I'm a pedant for a polished turn of phrase. My proper reason is that I needed to send you a confession. (No, don't yawn.) I know that you're a stickler for the truth, and, while I didn't lie, I didn't quite tell you all of the truth. It's about time that I filled that gap. I'm afraid that the thing that fills the gap is a wife. The truth, you see, is that I'm married. Well, sort of. Will you allow me to explain?

'Too late, but go on,' said Effie to the letter.

Clarice and I were married before the war. Her father played bridge with my old man and it was all rather wrapped up for us. It was jolly enough at first. We went to a lot of parties and she mixes a good Martini. But the war rather changed all of that. Clarice said that I came back morose. She still wanted to go to parties, but I no longer cared to mix – or for a mixer in my drink. Clarice also had issues with the spoons. She liked me when I played rugby; she liked me less when I was reduced to spoons. In fact, Clarice found the spoons so disagreeable that for the past eight years we've lived apart. We pull further apart.

I should have told you all of this when we first met. I certainly should have told you when we were exchanging facts and figures. But I was ashamed, you see. I'm ashamed that I wasn't a better husband, a better soldier, a better man. I did intend to tell you, but then, that last night in Paris, well, I figured that you didn't need an extra complication in your life. I didn't mean to burden you with my complications. I meant, for your sake, not to see you again. But I'm afraid, Fairy Palace, that I'm struggling with that last bit. I'm afraid, darling girl, that you've rather gotten into my head.

There. Now you have my confession. I'm in West Riding at the moment. My window looks out towards Haworth Moor. That would normally be a pleasing thing, but the Pennines have recently started to remind me of No Man's Land (less wire, more sheep). I can't go forwards until I've made this confession. But, then, putting this down on paper makes me question whether I should think of advancing at all. I could understand, with the omission and its attendant complications, if you didn't want to see me again. Am I a fool to harbour a hope? I miss you, Miss Shaw.

There being no champagne in the house, Effie was obliged to drink the last of Laurie's sherry. She thought about standing on the platform in Paris, fearing then that she might never see Henry again. Could it, after all, be possible? Could she get past the omission and attendant complications? The souvenir tower glittered in the mirror. Was she daring enough?

Chapter Sixty-Two

Its eyes connected with his as he came out onto the roof. Joe saw the hook of beak, the curve of claws and the red feathers. It blinked. There was something slow and cold and ancient in the shutter of its eye.

He ducked as the wings rushed at him. The hawk screamed as it plunged and the wings stretched away. He spun around on the rooftop and the city twisted to a blur; Paris bent under the hawk's wing. The still, cold eye circled him before it turned and was gone. It dropped him. His knees gave way. Joe clung to the roof as the revolving skyline lurched around him.

It was some time before he looked up again. When he did, it was all as it ever was: smoke drifted, zinc roofs shimmered and rain dripped from the railings. The sky was empty. The skyline was still. The hawk might never have been there, it might have been a fantasy, but for the feathers.

A bird was thrashing against the wire of the loft. It flickered through the open door, as Joe approached, as if to show him his culpability. Glimmering over the rooftops, it could have been a ghost. Joe watched as it arced between chimney stacks and ventilation shafts and away.

He crawled inside the loft and crouched amongst the feathers and the mess. The bird that he held in his hands was limp, its chest gashed, the muscle raggedly pulled away. The eyes were blind and dull. Joe thought of the frenzy of the predator in this place, that confined panic. He pulled his knees to him and curled among the dead pigeons. There were no birds to come back. Had his hope been misplaced? Had his luck not changed after all? Clocks were striking across the city. He wanted the hawk to gouge him out then, to leave him dull and numb.

The rain-slicked roofs beyond were grey and green and reflected the last light of the sky. He stood on the ledge and looked down on the glint of windows and red chimney pots. A zigzag of electric lights flashed up and down the Eiffel Tower like an exclamation. He heard glasses smash and voices raised in the alley below. His fingers were sticky. He pulled them down his face and shut his eyes.

Joe extended his arms. Swaying with the wind, he felt the momentum in his legs. He imagined himself diving into the skyline of Paris: he saw the window-framed gasps of servant girls as he hurtled past attics. Railings and gutterings were accelerating and he was plunging down through the crisscross lines of washing. Cobbles and kerb stones rushed up and he sighed into the slam of the street. Joe saw himself from above, saw himself in the alley with his limbs all wrong. He wanted to dive at it, to dive into that image of himself, to feel the rush and the slam and the silence. But his feet refused to step forward; they stuck stubbornly to the ledge. Much as he might want to let go, he, once again, found that he couldn't.

He thought about falling out of the apple tree, when he hadn't wanted to fall but couldn't help himself, when his hands had flailed and grasped. He hadn't thought about that day in years. An image of Charlie's red hand flashed. And suddenly, then, he could see Charlie's face. He could see him in such sharp detail: the up-close texture of his skin, the fragile blue of the veins at his temples, his quick, intent, amused eyes and the mist of breath around his mouth. Joe's shut eyes stared at Charlie. He breathed out in a shudder.

With the nearby noise of wings Joe opened his eyes. The white bird rose from amongst the roofs. It soared skyward in front of him, circled, swooped and settled flutteringly on the top of the loft. It had always been an inexplicable miracle that the birds came back. The white bird glowed in the thickening darkness. He felt a sudden rush of affection for it. The feeling surged through him like the hawk tearing into the loft. For a brief, but all-altering moment, Paris was beautiful below.

Chapter Sixty-Three

'Is it like Paris?'

Effie shrugged. 'Not really. It's not excessive enough to be like Paris.'

'Not excessive enough? It's verging on obscene,' said Grace.

They stood back to admire the bountiful counter.

'It's like a painting,' offered Mrs Harwood.

'A painting of an obscene quantity of cake?'

'And I could cry over your curd tart,' Mrs Harwood persisted. 'Is it the allspice? Have I told you how proud of you I am?'

'Yes, it is – and you have.' Effie squeezed Mrs. Harwood's hand. 'At least a dozen times.'

'Are *you* quite well, though? You look peaky. Is it first day nerves? Did you not sleep last night?' Grace tucked Effie's hair behind her ears and addressed her apparently peaky eyes. Her fingers smelled of silver polish.

'I'm fine,' Effie lied. She meant for it to be so. She meant it to be fine and positive and light. It wasn't the time to dwell on Parisian excesses or to contemplate the motivations of printing press salesmen. 'I'm just worried whether he's going to get that finished before we open.' She nodded to the ladder and the signwriter's legs.

'Unless there's a pronounced stutter to his painting, I'm quite confident that he can manage two letters in the next hour.'

'Happen if you hadn't kept distracting him with cups of tea and fluttering lashes.'

'He's got a nice smile,' said Grace.

'Am I paying him to smile?'

The noise of the bell occasioned a wagging of Reginald's rear. Effie, crouched to stack cutlery, watched him waddle to the front of the counter.

'Have you finished, Mr Clegg?' she said, over loudly, from

behind a small hillock of teacakes.

'I don't know about Mr Clegg, but it looks like you've finished the catering arrangements for the regiment.'

'I'm sorry, sir. I thought that you were the signwriter,' said Effie, emerging from glazed buns.

The chap across the counter tipped his hat.

'Henry?' A cake knife slid from Effie's hands and clattered to the floor.

Grace dragged Mrs Harwood out, suddenly keen to assess the progress of the painting.

'Fairy Palace,' Henry Lyle smiled under his tipped hat. 'Do you object awfully that I'm here?'

'I don't know,' Effie considered.

She came out from behind the counter. Henry's eyes creased kindly at the corners. She stared at him – Henry Lyle, who she had conspired with, laughed with, danced with and confessed to, who had an awfully nice smile and an awful undisclosed marriage, was standing there in her café.

'But your letter… You only just wrote. I haven't decided yet what I mean to reply.'

'Oh,' said Henry, his smile suddenly losing wattage. 'Well, I wrote it and then thought that it's not the type of thing that one really ought to write, is it? As soon as it was in the post box and irretrievable, I realised that it's not the sort of thing that one ought to politely put in a letter. I ought to say it to your face. So, you see, I got on a train. And now I'm standing here, gazing at your face and I'm not quite sure what to say to it.'

'I've had worse in letters,' said Effie.

'Of course.' Henry's hat turned between his hands. He looked like he had no idea what to say next. Effie felt a little sorry for him.

'That was impetuous of you. To get on a train, I mean.'

'Wasn't it? I even shocked myself. Are you glad of it,

though?' He asked. 'Only, I can't tell.'

'I really don't know,' she replied.

'So it's the Café de Paris, eh?' he said awkwardly and gestured at the signwriter's legs. 'Well, Café de Par at present, but I got the point. Or perhaps you're pining for Cornwall? Have I missed the point?'

'Laurie was there after the war, wasn't he? Paris, not Cornwall,' clarified Effie. She continued, keen that Henry should not misconstrue the point: 'Paris is of significance for Laurie. I shall always think of Laurie as being there.'

'I hoped, when I saw it, that it might be of significance for you too. It is for me.'

'The significance to me? Gosh, where do I start?'

'I can see that you're angry at me,' he observed.

'Are you surprised? You lied to me… or, at least, you encouraged me to believe something that wasn't true. I trusted you. I wanted you to write. I wanted there to be more to it than just Paris. But, I was a fool, wasn't I?'

'You weren't a fool, Effie. I was the fool. I should have been straight with you right from the off.'

'Yes, you should,' she said. 'Because you weren't, it's spoilt. I don't know that I could ever trust you.'

'You can, Effie. Please. Darling girl, I promise you that you can. I can prove it to you. I didn't drag you through the history of Clarice and me because it was already just that: history. It was already over. Please, Effie. I'll tell you every ugly detail if you want to hear it and I will never again tell you an untruth, a half-truth or even a miniscule fib. I swear to you.'

'I don't have time for this today.'

'I'm sorry. I shouldn't have forced this upon you. That was selfish and I didn't realise that the timing was so rotten.' Henry gestured around the café. The jolly just-about-to-open bunting looked suddenly mistaken in the background of Henry's shrug.

'So, I'm at the Red Lion. When you want to talk – if you want to talk – you'll find me there.'

With that, and a tip of a hat, Henry Lyle left. Effie stared at the door, around which, with a too cheery clatter of the bell, her sister's head quickly appeared.

'Didn't slap him, did you?'

'It's over between them,' said Effie, still staring after Henry.

'Why you scarlet woman! I never had you down as a home breaker.'

'Don't, Grace. Please.'

'All done, Miss Shaw.' Mr Clegg stood in the doorway, exhibiting his admirable smile.

'All done,' said Effie, who didn't feel at all like smiling.

The day advanced with a crowd and congratulations, with noisy sociability, a happy percussion of cutlery and a whistling accompaniment of kettles. It was right and bright and busy. Effie was rather too occupied receiving orders and compliments to dwell on Henry and what he might have to say in the Red Lion. The counter emptied, the cash till filled and the shop bell rang out in celebration. Effie thought that Laurie would look down with satisfaction.

A bunch of yellow roses arrived at the end of the afternoon. *I'm sorry. Please believe me. This is an agony. You can trust me. I can prove it*, appealed the accompanying card.

Effie remembered a flutter of yellowed petals that had fallen from *Jude* as she had returned the book to Laurie's shelf. It was the rose that Alan Welch had given her back in Ypres, where he had winked and left her standing in the square. 'You can't hold your breath forever,' he had said. Was she still? She looked up at the loud and lively café and considered that she was getting along quite well without roses and respiratory challenges. Effie returned to buttering teacakes and told Grace to take the redundant roses into the back.

'Oh, go!' said Grace, returning from the kitchen with a tray of clean crockery. 'It's calming down now. I'd far rather mind the fort than watch you moping. If you become dreary, I shall rethink my employment options.'

'Frank likes you in that uniform.'

'Exactly. Don't give me another reason to dislike it.'

'But how do I know if I can trust him?'

'Sometimes you just have to take a chance,' said Grace. She helped herself to a broken gingerbread man as she mused on the moral question. 'Don't be like Laurence. Don't regret not finding the courage. Besides, the poor bloke is clearly mad about you. It was written all over his face. I couldn't help but feel sorry when you sent him out with his tail between his wooden legs.'

'Was that terribly mean of me?'

'Downright wicked. Now let me mind the shop and go. At least hear what the sorry sod has to say for himself.'

'But what about plans and ambitions and independence? What about my feminine self-assertion?'

'Have you been reading pamphlets again? You've got plans now. You've got your ambitions and your independence. Who's saying that you have to give that away?' Grace flourished the now multiply-amputated gingerbread man around the café. 'There's no rule that says you can't have some pleasure too. Besides, I'm fed up of you standing on my toes when we dance. Go and assert yourself in the Red Lion.'

Chapter Sixty-Four

Henry sat on a bench in the churchyard and leaned his head back. There were swallows above and a smell of privet hedging. He measured his breaths; if he concentrated, if he focussed on his breathing and the details of the immediate, he could stop it from happening. He watched a woman breaking bread for the sparrows. A man took his hat off in front of a grave. There was a yellowing pot of chrysanthemums on a cross. Henry lit a cigarette and then threw it away.

His mind kept going back to her face. He had looked at her as he closed the door. Her face in the doorframe said all of the things that he wanted her to say – and all of the things that he had feared she might say. Did she despise him? Was it irretrievable?

The lines of old graves leaned. Ivy climbed up through copperplate lettering, through the In Memoriams and Loving Memories. Lichen bloomed on the loved and the lost. The shadows rotated around the graves. He looked down at the wreath in his hands.

'Hello again, old man,' said Henry to the headstone.

He took off his hat. Fragments of long-ago conversations returned to him, as he stood over the grave. Half-forgotten faces flickered and, again, the face that had glimmered out of the Amiens mirror.

'It really is pretty bloody appalling to see you like this. It's inexcusable, you know. Couldn't you have made more of an effort?'

There were irises planted around the grave. The blades reminded him of a line of bayonets that he'd once seen protruding from a blown-in trench. He blinked away the memory and thought of her kneeling by his grave. He imagined her fingers clawing into the earth, covering him over with flowers.

'I'm glad that you finally told her how you felt,' he said. 'It was about time, wasn't it?'

He read the line again, running his finger through the new-cut lettering. He saw a young man in a college garden reading the last chapters of *Tess of the D'Urbervilles* aloud.

'This happiness could not have lasted. It was too much. I have had enough; and now I shall not live for you to despise me.'

The reader was using his theatrical voice and they had all howled in the appropriate places. Henry knelt by that same young man's gravestone.

'Why could it not have lasted, Laurence? Can it never last? Can't we try?'

He looked at the lines of irises. Somewhere a blackbird was singing.

'Would you object awfully if I were to try?'

Henry placed the wreath and put his hand to the headstone.

'God bless. Sleep well, old chum,' he said.

Chapter Sixty-Five

At seven-thirty they turned the sign to *Closed* and the volume on the gramophone higher.

'My feet,' said Grace.

'My God!' said Effie, as she surveyed the awaiting washing-up. They agreed that they needed to advertise for a girl.

'So do you really mean to snub him?'

'Who?' enquired Effie.

'Charlie chuffing Chaplin, of course.'

'I haven't got time for such things. I've a business to run.' Effie made a soapy splash with a stack of plates in order to show it.

'Gosh, you're dull,' said Grace. 'I preferred it when you were a scarlet woman. Must we have it framed and on the wall behind the counter?'

'What?'

'That ruddy I.O.U.'

The sky was still light and full of the sound of blackbirds. Effie cut across by the church. There were boy scouts playing hide-and-seek in the graveyard, boisterous laughter and the smell of privet. She detoured via Laurie and saw that a wreath of glossy laurel had been put on his grave. She supposed that one of his regimental old muckers had passed by; it pleased her that they still did, that they still judged Laurie to be deserving of laurels.

'I wish I could talk to you,' she told him. 'I wish that you could tell me what to do.'

But all there was, in reply, was blackbirds.

She found Henry drinking tea in the lounge bar of the Red Lion.

'Well, I say. That's not much of a show of loyalty.'

'I'd far rather be partaking of your orange pekoe, but wasn't at all sure I would be welcome. Will you?' He proffered a teacup.

'I'd prefer something stronger.'

She observed Henry at the bar. His movements seemed more awkward than she remembered. He moved like his hinges needed oiling.

Effie leaned against the table by the fire and stretched her fingers towards the flames. There were pot cowherds and coy milkmaids on the mantelpiece and, in between, a jug of late dahlias. She saw her movement distort in the yellow gleam of brasses.

Henry smiled as he turned with the drinks. 'Here, let me.' He rushed to pull out a chair for her. 'At least permit a feller an act of chivalry,' he insisted.

She would rather he didn't draw attention with his insistent chivalry.

'So, you're well? You look well.' He sat down opposite.

'Do I?' she asked.

'You do.'

They touched glasses. The clinking of glasses with Henry didn't ring out quite so cheerfully as it had before she knew about his clandestine wife.

'I am well,' she said. 'It was our opening day today.'

'I guessed that from the smell of polish, the bluster and the large banner that said *Grand Re-opening*.'

'It's mine,' said Effie, 'the café. Laurie left it to me in his will. I mean to make a go of it.'

'I'm quite certain that you'll succeed.'

'I mean to get it right. I mean to make him proud.' She took a steadying mouthful of her drink and tried to think about polish and pride. 'I mean to make myself proud.'

'Laurence meant for you to be happy.'

Did Henry have any right to make assumptions about what

Laurie wanted for her? She supposed she couldn't deny that he had meant her happiness.

'And Reginald? My old pal is in fine fettle?'

Effie nodded, turning her glass. Must he complicate with courtesies? Did he mean to trip her up again with his gallantries? Had Henry returned with a display of degraded manners it would have made the situation so much simpler. 'Reginald is in glad spirits,' she replied. 'I left my sister secreting him cake. And she reckons that *I'm* making him fat.'

'I missed your smile,' Henry said, dipping his face to engage with her eyes. 'But I'm wondering now where it's gone. Did I imagine it? Did you lose it somewhere on the return trip? Is it languishing in a railway lost property office?'

'I'm sorry,' said Effie.

'Not as sorry as I am. I can't begin to tell you how sorry I am.'

He put his hand out to touch hers across the table top and she consented to look at him then. She remembered looking at him at the top of the tower, opening her eyes to his face and there being nothing, not fear, not loss, not shame, not altitude or the panorama of Paris, that mattered other than that. He had filled her focus. There was just Henry's face and it had, somehow, seemed right. In that instant she had trusted him entirely - but to trust him again demanded more daring than Effie presently possessed. She took her hand away and stashed it under the table.

'And how is Clarice?' The diversion wasn't subtle and it wasn't meant to be.

'Oh, blithe. Clarice works hard at being blithe.' He put a cigarette between his lips and offered her the packet.

'She surely can't be happy at separating?' Effie shook her head.

'On the contrary; she made a speech at me about letting go.'

Effie wasn't sure where to look, so she sipped at her sherry.

'You both enjoy making speeches, then?'

He laughed briefly before his face disappeared into his hands. 'Are you firmly encamped in the moral high ground?'

'It's not morality. It's just that it's all far too complicated.'

'It's not complicated for Clarice. She got engaged again last week.'

'Really?' The surface of Effie's drink seemed suddenly to have become somewhat choppy. 'Isn't that rather putting the cart before the horse?'

'It's putting the whole damned carriageworks ahead of the horse.'

Effie made her initials on the table in spilled sherry. She remembered her mist-carved initials slicing through France and wondering how differently she would have felt had the last letter been Joe's. She didn't want to feel widowed again, or to feel that she was taking away another woman's husband. Clarice, however, with her unconventional horse-and-cart conjugation, seemed set on un-complicating matters.

'Will you tell me about her?' she asked. 'I would like to know.'

She watched Henry's face as he talked, as he précised a pre-war summer of young marriage and a subsequent ten-year decline. He smiled as he talked about Clarice, but there was something terribly sad in his smile. He put out the cigarette.

'I don't blame her at all for not wanting me. She lost her father in the war. She just wants to forget it all now, to look forwards, turn the music louder and move on. But I'm a lumbering great *aide memoire*. I'm a sorry souvenir of something that she'd far rather disregard.'

'But you still love her?'

His mouth opened to make an answer but then closed. He sat back and seemed, for some moments, to be making a study of his beer glass. 'No, I'm not sure that I do. In fact I can't remember whether I ever did. It was fun once, but that seems like a lifetime ago. It seems like somebody else's lifetime.' He pulled a hand through his hair. 'Goodness, you don't need this, do you? It's really not right of me to inflict this on you. This is exactly what I didn't mean to do.'

'It matters that you trust me,' she said.

'I do.' He paused, as if he expected her to reciprocate. Effie wished that she could. 'Will you wait here?' he asked. 'If I dash away for five minutes will you still be here?'

'If you'll get me another drink, I will.'

'That's my girl,' said Henry. 'Five minutes, I promise. I've a present for you.'

Henry returned with a cardboard box. He carried it at arm's length, as if he were nervous of its contents.

'You don't look very daring today,' Effie observed.

'I think that my train-boarding impetuousness might have depleted my supplies.'

'Perhaps you need to ration your impetuousness.'

'I wasn't feeling impetuous when I made this.' He handed her the box. 'In fact it took me a fortnight of entirely un-impetuous hard graft.'

'It's a teapot,' she said, peeling away its wrappings.

'It's the first one I've ever made.'

'Does it pour?'

'Yes, everywhere. I painted your name on it, though.'

'You spelled it correctly. I suppose that that's something at least.'

'I'm sorry that it's not splattered with roses or anything, but, when it comes to these matters, my instincts are somewhat rustic. The extent of my talent is possibly rustic too. It's a vernacular teapot,' he expounded, warming to his theme, 'full of wholesome integrity and truth. You can tell that because it's

Caroline Scott

brown. The poem isn't mine, I'm afraid, but the sentiments are.'

'*Strange fits of passion have I known,*' Effie read.

'It's Wordsworth: '*Strange fits of passion have I known, And I will dare to tell, But in the lover's ear alone, What once to me befell.*''

'I remember it,' said Effie. She remembered Laurie handing her his book of poems opened on this page. She remembered reading it on the day that he had died.

'There's something else that I ought to show you.'

Henry sat down again. Effie watched his hands beat a rhythm on his knees. With the look on his face, she half-expected him to break into his jitters again.

'Are you quite well?'

'I think so. I'm trying to decide where to start. I'm trying to put my cards on the table, as plainly as I can.'

Effie watched while Henry mentally shuffled his cards.

'You see the thing is,' he began, not looking entirely confident as to where this beginning was proceeding. He looked down at his shoes. 'Well, it's just that…'

She remembered him starting and then stopping in the station in Paris. 'Please, Henry, just blurt it out.'

He took a mouthful of beer and then laid his hands flat on the table. 'I didn't want to have to do this, but it seems I must. In the interests of honesty I have to tell you this. You can trust me. I can prove to you that you can trust me.'

'Go on.'

Henry reached into his jacket pocket and produced an envelope. He placed it on the table between them. Effie, even upside down, recognised Laurie's letters.

'But how? That's *his* handwriting.'

'The truth is that Laurence and I weren't strangers. I actually knew your Laurie very well. We were chums at university, you see. So, of course, I knew about you too. I've actually known about you since 1913 – since he came back at Michaelmas term full of talk of finding a fallen angel amongst the fairy cakes. We did tease him, I'm afraid. You became Titania Queen of the Fairy Cakes, the Venus of the Viennoiseries, the Madonna of the Coconut Rocks, the…'

'That's quite enough, now,' cut in Effie. 'I'll never bake another ruddy coconut rock.'

'And I've been here before,' he went on. 'I came up to visit him in that horrible hospital.'

'You knew about 'Paris'?'

Henry nodded. 'And Laurence knew that I went to France every year. It's the anniversary of Patrick's death. I always go back with Kate. So, when you happened to be going over, when Laurence planned it, he wrote to me. It wasn't accident that we were on the same boat. He told me to look out for a 'glimmering girl with an excellent fellow of a canine companion'.' Henry framed the phrase with his fingers and smiled as if he was fond of it. 'You didn't take much tracking down. Though I hardly expected you to drag me into a lavatory conspiracy.'

'It was arranged?'

'I was to discreetly chaperone and intervene in the event of emergency. Should I have needed to expose my cover, Laurence gave me this.'

He pushed the envelope across the table to Effie. She saw her name formed in Laurie's script. She opened the envelope; the card enclosed read:

I, Laurence Greene, testify that the bearer of this bond – one Henry Gabriel Lyle, identifiable by leg (insufficiency) and spiel (surfeit) – isn't a rotter. He may blather on a bit and have frightful notions about poetry, but he is not a cad, a cardsharp, a cattle rustler, or any other form of nasty or n'er do well. I vouchsafe that he is safe.

'And, well, there was an emergency.'

'There was?'

'Yes, I'm in the middle of it right now.'

'You are?'

'I was to see you across the Channel and to be a contactable acquaintance should you find yourself requiring one. But the trouble is, I found myself requiring you rather more than you required me.'

She looked at the man who somehow required her. 'And did you know about Joe? Did you know that was why Laurie was sending me to Paris?'

'I didn't. I promise you that I didn't.' Effie felt the table shift as his palms made emphatic contact with its surface. 'Laurence told me that I had to play the part of your guardian angel, only he failed to brief me on everything that the role involved. He omitted to tell me the part about Joe being alive. A rather fundamental part that too, isn't it? I honestly believed that the surprise was a hat or a handbag. Perhaps he thought that I wouldn't approve of him forcing the pair of you face-to-face? Do you think that he did the right thing in telling you?'

'He wanted to be honest in the end,' said Effie. 'Yes, he did the right thing.'

'I liked the idea of being your guardian angel. It's a role I rather enjoyed. I probably enjoyed it too much. I'm afraid that I had hoped to reprise it. I want to help you, Effie. I want to be with you. If I'm being honest now I have to tell you that.'

'Laurie never mentioned you,' she resisted. 'There was never mention of a Henry. Had you really been friends, I'm sure he would have mentioned you.'

'Laurence knew me as 'Gabby'. My middle name is Gabriel, see. Mother suffered an attack of Catholicism in her twenties. It's a mercy that I'm not an Emmanuel or a Moses. I was pejorative Gabby at school and it stuck. Gammy Gabby in recent years. Self-sacrifice for the sake of alliteration, eh? Talk about suffering for art. I am a martyr to art.'

'You're Gabby? Gabby who sends Laurie auction catalogues and mouldy books? You're, well, not brown enough to be Gabby. I always imagined Gabby to be dusty, a little shabby and certainly more short-sighted.'

She remembered Laurie writing to Gabby in the spring. 'He's a good old stick,' Laurie had said. 'You should meet him.' And so Laurie had arranged that she should.

'Steady on,' said Henry. 'Less of the mould and myopia, if you please.'

Effie stared at the man that Laurie arranged for her to meet, who wasn't at all mouldy or myopic. She wondered what Laurie meant for her to do next.

Effie switched on the electric lights and watched her windowed reflection showing Henry her café, her ceiling mouldings and wood panelling and seating for forty-five. Her reflection seemed to be doing rather a lot of smiling. She told it to moderate the teeth.

'We have three-tier cake stands, a trolley and a selection of ten premium teas,' she informed him. 'I'm going to make it work. I have ambitions for it. I mean to go places with my afternoon teas and innovative savouries.'

'If I didn't know that the proprietress has a penchant for rolling around in Parisian gutters, I might think that I'd inadvertently stumbled into the Ritz.'

She turned towards him with a slice of Bakewell tart. 'You once said that armies couldn't keep you from it. But a blonde with a pitching wedge nearly did.'

'You should see what she can do with that pitching wedge.' He took the cake fork from Effie. 'Is this like a suitor's quest, then? A test of my suitorly suitability? Will I be obliged to string a bow or slay a dragon next? If I say it needs more jam am I out?'

'Entirely.'

They sat at the table in the kitchen. Effie surveyed the room with him as he ate, its clean, orderly clutter, its businesslike stacks of bakery accoutrements, its ingenious appliances and the gleam of its handed-down copper. It was still strange that this was all now hers – and still stranger was the sight of Henry Lyle eating Bakewell tart against this backdrop.

'I had an odd experience, you know, a few weeks ago.' Henry wafted with the fork. 'I don't think I've told you this. Kate and I were having dinner in a restaurant in Amiens and I suddenly remembered that I'd been there before. I'd been there with Laurence. We'd written our names together on a mirror and it was still there. It was like falling through a hole in time, for an instant he was young and alive and by my side.'

Effie watched him lick raspberry jam from his fingers. 'Will you dance with me?' she asked.

She rifled through records as he wound the gramophone. They drank a toast to the tango.

Josephine Baker sang about bluebirds as they danced through the empty café. They danced around tables and the serving trolley, skirting the counter and the columns and the potted palms. Effie remembered dancing here with Grace and the shock of her own act of boldness back then. At what point, she wondered, had she become brave? Effie smiled at the man who dared her to be daring and to dance, who had been sent and sanctioned by Laurie and who somehow required her.

She saw her fingers wind through his. She saw his laughing mouth a locket's length from her own. The orchestra ended. They faced each other suddenly unsmiling.

Acknowledgements

I am indebted to Laura Hirst, at Pen & Sword, for giving a first-timer a chance, for her generous encouragement and confidence in this project (ever there when my confidence wobbled), and to Karyn Burnham, for her intelligent, thoughtful and patient editing. Thank you both. Sincerely.